FALLING DARKNESS

Also available from *New York Times* bestselling author Karen Harper

South Shores

DROWNING TIDES
CHASING SHADOWS

Cold Creek

BROKEN BONDS
FORBIDDEN GROUND
SHATTERED SECRETS

Home Valley Amish

UPON A WINTER'S NIGHT
DARK CROSSINGS (featuring "The Covered Bridge")
FINDING MERCY
RETURN TO GRACE
FALL FROM PRIDE

Novels

DOWN RIVER
DEEP DOWN
THE HIDING PLACE
BELOW THE SURFACE
INFERNO
HURRICANE
DARK ANGEL
DARK HARVEST
DARK ROAD HOME

Visit karenharperauthor.com for more titles.

**Look for Karen Harper's next South Shores novel
coming soon from MIRA Books.**

KAREN HARPER

FALLING DARKNESS

MIRA®

ISBN-13: 978-0-7783-3060-8

Falling Darkness

Copyright © 2017 by Karen Harper

For questions and comments about the quality of this book, please contact us at CustomerService@Harlequin.com.

www.MIRABooks.com

Printed in U.S.A.

I would like to thank Mary Ann and Dr. Roy Manning and Lee Ann and Jim Parsons for their friendship to us and for helpful background information for this novel.

FALLING DARKNESS

CHAPTER ONE

2014

After their airplane skidded over the water and sank, their two life rafts tied together seemed so small in the vast, dark sea. Claire held her four-year-old daughter, Lexi, close to keep her warm and calm, though she was neither of those things herself. The child had gone silent, no more screams or sobs. Claire's husband Nick's arm around them felt like a band of iron, a moving one, since he too was shaking from the cold and shock.

Her ex-husband, Jace—Lexi's father—was the third person in their raft. He'd been the pilot of the borrowed private plane that had nearly plunged all seven of them beneath the surface to drown. So far, only Lexi's nanny, Nita, in the next raft had been seasick, though they were all sick at heart and scared to death. Nita was praying aloud and, no doubt, the others were doing so silently.

"Where are we, really?" Lexi asked. "Near a beach at home?"

Her teeth chattering, Claire told her, "Not quite, but off the coast of Florida." She didn't add they were in the wide Straits of Florida but much closer to dangerous, forbidden Cuba.

The sea, so rough at first that their little rubber islands had slid from trough to trough, seemed to be calming now. Breaks in the clouds revealed a scattering of stars that looked like they were dancing and a crooked sliver of moon like a sharp, tilted smile.

"Nobody's gonna find us til mornin'." Bronco, their family bodyguard, spoke up from the other raft. The big, bold man was trying to be strong, but his voice quavered too.

Nita, who had been moaning, began to cry again, though she was sheltered in the other raft between her cousin Hector, called Heck, Nick's tech genius, and Bronco, who had his arms around her.

Heck said, "Yeah, well, we're valuable to the FBI, so they'll have their net out for us. Just hope someone else doesn't, and they tampered with the plane. You-know-who has a long arm—and an army of spies."

"That can't be," Nick said. "Before we took off, Jace checked the plane and Bronco guarded it. It had to be a malfunction, not sabotage."

Bronco said, "But you know, boss, the plane was parked by that dark Key West field. I didn't tell you, but some guy came up and asked me how much it cost. Took my eyes off the plane to get rid of him, head him back to the terminal."

"I did all the checkups," Jace told them, "but that was before I hit the john when all of you were still in the terminal. I still can't believe it. And since the FBI arranged for that plane, who knows if we can trust them? Maybe you-know-who got to them too, or at least to that contact guy Patterson. I don't trust anyone anymore—except you, Lexi," he added and rubbed the child's back.

"And you trust Mommy and Nick too!" she insisted.

"Listen up, all of you." Nick took over the conversation again, like them, raising his voice to be heard over the wind and waves. "So far our adversary's dealt in torment, not total annihilation."

Lexi stirred against Claire. "What's nilation?"

"Don't worry about that, or anything," Claire whispered to her. Nick was evidently using big words so Lexi wouldn't catch on to the deadly mess they were in whether they were rescued from the water or were onshore.

They had fled Florida with the help of the Federal Witness Protection Program, WITSEC, to stay safe until the US government could locate and extradite Nick's nemesis, a powerful international businessman with a long reach. The FBI wanted their hands on Clayton Ames as badly as Nick did, but Ames made a habit of living abroad and moving around. When it came to catching, extraditing and prosecuting the man who was now among the US government's most wanted, Claire knew Nick wished he was a vigilante or hit man instead of a criminal lawyer who could only accuse and testify.

"Okay, enough about all that for now," Nick said. "Whoever rescues us, the new identification papers I have for all of us in this waterproof pouch are what we will have to go by. Lexi, we are going to have new, pretend names for a while, but it's a secret only the seven of us can share. I was telling you on the plane that we are going to live in a new place for a while, and we need to learn these names and the story of where we came from."

"Is it like a game?"

"Yes, but a very serious, important game."

"Like life," Jace muttered. Then he said louder, "That box I had strapped to my wrist has some drinking water, some medical supplies and a few rations. *Semper paratus, semper fi.* Listen up, everybody. You're with a former navy pilot who has never crashed before but has training for it. We're going to be rescued, but meanwhile, we need to keep our heads up and work together. Like Claire said when we first made it into the rafts, we'll be okay."

Tears stung Claire's eyes and not just from the saltwater spray. The only two men she'd ever loved were with her: Jace, her ex, who had claimed he still loved her when he'd helped her out of the sinking plane and into the raft; and Nick, who had taken her life and love by storm. They had been forced by his nemesis, Clayton Ames, to marry, but she had come to not only desire but love Nick. Thank God the three of them were getting along in this desperate flight. But to live all together as the WITSEC program had planned? That scared her almost as much as this shifting, sliding, endless sea.

As dawn broke, raising their hopes they would be spotted, Jace passed around the water canteen again so they could each take a drink as a chaser after a tasteless biscuit. Nick saw that Jace had put the dry jacket he had loaned him around Lexi. Jace looked like a Viking at sea, ruddy and blond compared to Nick's dark hair dusted with silver.

The two men's gazes met. They'd been at loggerheads over Claire, so Nick hoped they could work together to be rescued. But their hideout plans for that had been for Northern Michigan, not on a rubber raft in the middle of the Straits of Florida.

Nick looked away and hit his fist hard on his knee. He'd left his prosperous Naples, Florida, law firm of Markwood, Benton and Chase in the hands of the other partners. He'd used the cover story he was leaving immediately for Belgium to assist an important government figure with legal advice. He'd told them he was taking his family and a small support staff with him and asked them to cover his cases.

True, they were used to his going off to work on his private South Shores project, for which he advised and sometimes defended people shattered by suicides that could be murders. But his lies haunted him, since he wasn't allowed to trust anyone but this group with the knowledge of his part in the Witness Protection Program, which was run under the aegis of the FBI.

Hell, he thought, forget the desertion of his friends and his law firm being the worst that could happen. Not only had their plane crashed, but he'd just seen a fin—more than one—slice through a wave near them. Sharks! Who knew how long they'd been so close in the dark. And Jace had fallen into the water getting them off the plane.

A shark—that was the way he'd always thought of the man he was certain had not only ruined his father financially, but had murdered him too and made it look like a cowardly suicide. Clayton Ames, a deadly, devouring shark.

"Jace!" Nick hissed, and the man's eyes flew open.

What? Jace mouthed. Nick pointed at the circling fins and read Jace's lips as he cursed silently. There were at least three sharks near them.

Nick noted Heck had seen them too. His right-hand man had mentioned these waters were full of them, a threat to Cubans fleeing the island, though it hadn't stopped the influx to the States. The refugees included Heck's and Nita's Cuban parents years ago, looking for a better life for their families. It was what he wanted for his new family. Maybe he should have stuck it out in Naples, though Ames knew they were all there. He had to be stopped, and the US government's help was the best way.

"Time for the name game," Jace whispered. "Let's not focus on new dangers."

"Hard not to," Claire put in, as she'd seen them too.

Nick wondered how she had stayed so calm. Despite her disease of narcolepsy, the woman had guts and stamina. He'd seen that up close and personal in the two murder/suicide cases they'd worked together. He also saw now that, though her eyes were wide on the fins, she quickly shifted Lexi lower between her spread legs rather than on her lap so that the girl could not see the sharks. Now, if only everyone else would keep their mouths shut...

"Let's not talk at all about things we see here," Claire called out, "but instead learn our new names and identities. That way, when we get ashore, we can just get some help before we all

head to Michigan—to Mackinac Island, with all the horses, remember, Lexi?"

"I'm going to find one I like to ride."

"Right," Nick said, opening the seal on the plastic pouch he
wore under his shirt like a wide belt. He'd kept their newly created passports, credit cards and quite a lot of cash in mostly big
bills dry. He pulled out what he'd thought of as his cheat sheet
with the names he and Rob Patterson, their FBI contact, had
come up with for everyone.

"Okay," he said, giving his stepdaughter a one-armed hug,
"we will start with Lexi. Our family's new last name—you, Lexi,
your mom and me—is Randal. Oh, yeah, Jace's too." He spelled
Randal and let her repeat it. He tried to ignore Jace's scowl. As
supportive as he was being, since he was on Ames's hit list too,
Nick knew Jace was thoroughly teed off that he had to act the
part of Nick's brother and Lexi's uncle.

"And your first name, Miss Randal," Nick went on to Lexi,
"is Megan, but you can be called Meggie if you want. It's up
to you."

For a moment he figured she was going to say she wanted to
keep her own name or take her best friend and cousin's name
Jilly, but she said, "Meggie is more like me."

"Good!" he said. "Did everybody hear that? This is Meg-
gie Randal. Her mother's name is Jenna Randal, mine is
Jack Randal, and Jace is Seth Randal, my brother and Le—
Meggie's uncle."

They all went around and said their new names: Heck was
now Roberto, called Berto, Ochoa; Nita was his cousin, Lorena
Ochoa; and Bronco Gates was Cody Carson.

Bronco piped up. "Suits me. Nothin' much suits me but glad
I'm here to help all you and 'specially Lorena Ochoa, here,"
he said, giving Nita's shoulders a squeeze. "Glad to make your
'quaintance, Senorita Lorena."

Heck rolled his eyes and shook his head over that. He knew

Bronco had eyes for Nita, and that obviously annoyed him. No, he must be looking at the sharks again, staring off a ways at the horizon.

But was Jace nuts? He was getting to his knees in the raft, rocking it more than the waves did.

"Seth," Nick said. "What?"

"To the south. Is that a boat?" he asked, pointing.

Everyone sat up and craned to look. It was, even though the silhouette was small. It was slow moving but seemed to be coming straight for them.

"We need to make a flag, a banner that shows up against the sea and sky."

"I'm wearing something bright," Nita said. "My skirt." Without a moment's hesitation, she wriggled out of it as Heck twisted around to look at the boat again and Bronco stripped off his jacket to cover her panties and bare legs.

"Everyone sit tight!" Jace ordered. "I'm the only one who stands."

Nick tried to brace Jace's legs as he got up and stood shakily. Using his arm as a flagpole, he waved the bright pink skirt until they were certain the small vessel turned even more their way. Unfortunately, the sharks were still circling, and the ramshackle craft looked like it was coming from the direction of Cuba, where it was rumored Ames might be living all cozy with the Castro brothers. So, Nick thought, as desperate as they were, with all the deceit and treachery they'd faced already, would the boat bring friend or foe?

CHAPTER TWO

Claire prayed silently that the boat would be American, but, as it came closer from the south, she knew better. It was all wood, with peeling green-and-white paint, draped with fishing nets, old and battered, maybe twenty-five feet long, so unlike the solid, sleeker fishing boats she'd seen going out of Naples or Miami. Held up by four poles, a makeshift canvas canopy flapped over the back half of the boat. The hand-painted name on the prow read *Alfredito*, and the flag that flapped above the stern had blue and white stripes and a single white star in a red triangle.

"Cuban," Nick said over the loud but uneven sound of the motor. "But not an official boat and with only one man. I think we're safe, but can we get him to take us north, not south? I have some cash. Heck, you do the talking. Maybe he doesn't even speak English."

Claire knew some Spanish but only caught a quick word or two in the shouted, rapid-fire exchange between the fisherman—if that was what he was—and Heck. She'd learned not to trust anyone but those closest to her since she'd worked two cases with Nick and had seen Clayton Ames up close and personal.

Finally, using broad gestures, just as the boatman had, Heck turned back to them to translate. Claire knew the fact that Nita had taken it all in and was crying was not a good sign.

Heck told them, "He is Hernando Hermez, called Nando, out of Cuba, but not Havana. He say—he says—no way his boat can reach Los Estados Unidos. That not allowed, against the law. He is from a small fishing village called Costa Blanca about forty miles west of Havana. He comes here to this spot, pretty far out, once a year on the date he lose—I mean, he lost— his son Alfredito. He fell in where sharks eating their catch in a net, but Nando not start fishing yet today. He like to kill them all, maybe same ones as these."

"Mommy, are there sharks in the water? That kind with the really big, sharp teeth?"

Claire hugged Lexi harder. "Shh, it's all right. They can't get us." But that reminded Claire that Lexi had seen too much killing. She prayed this Nando would take them aboard. Even that rattletrap of a boat and a small, Spanish-speaking fishing village or a prison cell—even facing Ames again if he did live in Cuba now—had to be better than this. She tried never to hate anyone, but she hated Ames and silently vowed again, despite their desperation, that she would help Nick and Jace bring him to justice someday.

Heck's voice interrupted her frenzied fears. "These sharks are killers, Nando keeps saying, so he says we be careful if we come on board."

"No kidding," Jace muttered, then spoke in a louder voice just as Nick was about to say something. "Tell Nando I'll try to get aboard first to help the others—Lexi first and the women after her."

Claire wished that didn't remind her of that old cry of "women and children first" when a ship was sinking. But surely that boat could hold them all, get them off the water, and then they could find a way not to go home but to hide out. But how to contact the FBI in Castro-controlled Cuba? Fidel was supposedly retired, but his brother Raul was in charge now. There were rumors that the US and Cuba might make peace someday soon, but it hadn't happened yet. President Obama had even shaken hands with Raul at a foreign conference, but Cuba was still a hostile Communist nation.

Heck and Nando talked more in Spanish. "He say, maybe Jesu Christo and the Virgin Mary, they give to him your lives in place of his lost son, his only son, Alfredito. He will take us to his house, give us food, place to sleep. Then we go to Havana, pay someone to take us home, not get seen or caught, he says."

"Not be seen? Fat chance of that," Nick muttered. "We'll have to do everything undercover—somehow." He said louder, "Tell him we are grateful to him and to the Lord for bringing us together on this great sea. Everyone, tell him *gracias*."

A little chorus followed with Lexi chiming in. "Nita," the child called out to her nanny, "I remembered what you taught me, but I can't tell his other words. *Nada*."

"You will, my Lex—my Meggie," Nita called to her. "You will."

The boat gently bumped against the nearest life raft, the one holding Heck, Bronco and Nita. But Jace was determined to be the first aboard, in case there was a problem climbing up the side where Nando was now dangling a rope he'd tied to one of the posts of the canopy.

Jace put one leg over, then rolled into the other raft and secured both of them to the side of the boat near the stern. Oh, Claire thought, so that was what the single rope was for. She had been scared they must climb that to get on board the fishing boat.

Nando secured the heavy, hand-knotted rope net on the side of the boat. Jace, of course, went up it easily, shook Nando's hand, then leaned over the side. Nick was on the move, coaxing Lexi from Claire's arms and handing her into the other raft to Bronco. Both rafts tilted and rocked.

"Close your eyes, sweetheart," Nick whispered to Lexi and shot a quick "trust me" look back at Claire. Her arms felt not only stiff and sore but so empty now. "Claire," Nick said, when she made a move toward the other raft too, "stay put. As they say, don't rock the boat. I'll be back for you."

Lexi wrapped her arms so tightly around Nick's neck that his face went red, but he didn't tell her to let go. Claire gripped her hands together, praying, trusting. When Nick passed Lexi to Bronco, who stood with Heck's help and passed her up to Jace, Claire slid across the slippery inside of the raft to be closer.

"Let go of me, honey," Bronco told Lexi as he lifted her up. "Your daddy—Uncle Seth, I mean—he got you."

And he did. Claire burst into silent tears of relief as the men handed Nita up to Jace and then, thank God, it was her turn. Not only did she want to be with Lexi, but it had suddenly seemed she was so terrifyingly small in the raft by herself, as if it was just her and the vast sea and sky.

Dragging her big purse with her essential narcolepsy meds, she rolled into the other raft. Nick helped her to her knees over to the rope ladder. Slinging her purse over her shoulder, she stood, rocking a bit on legs that were cramping, and he gave her a boost up. When Jace grabbed her wrists, Nick let go. It was, she thought, just the opposite of what had happened in her life with these men. Jace had left her; Nick had grabbed for her.

Her stomach scraped hard against the side and top of the boat as Jace hauled her in. If she was newly pregnant, she thought, that could do her in. She wasn't sure but had missed her period. Still, with all the upheaval in her life, that didn't mean a baby, and she hadn't mentioned anything to Nick yet.

"Got you," Jace said as Lexi left Nita's embrace to hurl herself against Claire. Lexi hugged her hard before Nando urged them away to sit on the deck, leaning against what must be a bait box because it smelled bad.

Quickly, the three men followed up over the side, Nick last.

Nick told Heck, "Ask him if he's going to cut the rafts loose or drag them. They might give our presence away when he puts in."

"Forgot to tell you, boss," Heck said. "He asked if he can have the rafts. If we don't need them again, he can sell them on the black market for Cubans who want to escape. He say with rumors of a deal between US and Cuba, more people are leaving since they think the dry-foot-on-land-you-can-stay in US policy might end. You know, if a Cuban refugee makes it to dry land in the US, he gets to stay, but not if he's caught at sea. He says—"

Nick cut in, "Tell him he can have the rafts but never to say where he got them. Why isn't he heading toward shore?"

"He want to curse the sharks one more time. Even if El Senor—the Lord God—made them killers, he curses them for killing his son. He has a daughter but he has to fish alone now since his father died last month."

"Tell him I am sorry his father died and his son too. I understand."

Heck spoke at length to Nando, who nodded as he opened the box next to the seated women and took out a plastic pail of bait that now smelled even more horrible. Nita, looking green in the gills again, almost gagged, and Lexi buried her nose against Claire's shoulder.

Nick asked Heck, "He's not going to fish for these sharks, is he?"

"No, boss. He says he's going to poison them."

On the way toward the northern coastline of Cuba, Nando shared the bread and black beans with anyone who wanted some, which, Nick saw, only Heck and Bronco did. His own stomach was twisted so tight he would have heaved them up, and they were rocking again on the way in. Bronco was still tending to the seasick Nita. The big bruiser had fallen hard for her, and—when she wasn't hacking over the side—she seemed to return the feeling. Heck had been upset at first, wanting to protect the young widow who was his cousin. But since he'd lost his laptop and cell phone in the plane crash, he seemed to be mourning the loss of all that. They all had bigger things to protect now, Nick thought, namely their lives.

With Heck translating, Nick had convinced Nando to let them off the boat at a more private location than his village fishing dock. They had directions of where to find the Hermez home, which sounded like it was a little ways out of the village. Unlike in Havana and other Cuban cities, Nando claimed, government men and informants were scarce in the area of fishing villages and farms with vast tobacco and sugarcane fields that used to be owned by rich Cubans before *la revolucion*.

Heck had whispered to Nick, "Everything was different before the revolution. Maybe if we go to Havana I can see my grandfather's hotel and hacienda. I always dreamed I could see it someday, even if I never get any of it back."

Nick had only nodded. Jace had overheard that and told Nick, "We'd better make it clear this is not some damned sightseeing vacation. One wrong move, and we're staring at bare walls and bars. Same for you with your vendetta against Ames. If he's here, no way you—or we—can go after him or let him know we're here. Most we could do is tip off our contact where their number one most wanted is—when and if we get back to the US."

"I know. First things first. We're off the plane, off the rafts. Now, all we've got to do is get all of us out of Cuba and to an island in Northern Michigan, damn it."

"Look—shoreline. I've flown over this big island more than once but never wanted to put down like some of my pilot buddies have. I know a guy claimed engine trouble so he could make an emergency landing in Havana just to say he'd seen the place."

"Yeah, well, you had real engine trouble, and we still need to find out why."

"It could have been mechanical. Then too, I've known pilots

who have crashed their own planes for their own reasons. Don't look at me like that."

"I wasn't looking at you like that. I just want you to swear you can live with the idea of Claire being married to me and you passing as my brother and Lexi's uncle."

"I have to live with it, don't I? One wrong move here or even in WITSEC protection, if we get that far, and I—we—won't be living at all, not if Ames and who knows who else has his way."

Nick nodded, and they shook hands. He could only trust and pray that Jace would continue to be helpful and protective, because, on top of everything else, he feared Jace wanted Claire and Lexi back.

The shoreline, Jace noted, as he looked through Nando's beat-up pair of binoculars, was hardly how he'd pictured Cuba. On the one narrow, rutted road he could see two horse-drawn wagons instead of the 1950s vintage American cars he'd seen in photos. No palms but pines clinging to the hills and shadowing the short cliff hovering over pristine, deserted beaches. And red soil with rows and rows of tobacco plants waving in the breeze as far as the eye could see.

"Bonita, no?" Nando asked him with a proud grin, as if he owned every acre of the scenery. "Costa Blanca!" he said, pointing at the shoreline with a distant dock and cluster of small, tile-roofed houses on a gentle slope of hill. He pointed higher up, more to the west. *"Mi casa,"* he said and Jace nodded.

"Berto!" Jace called out, using Heck's WITSEC name. "Be sure he's going to let us out away from the dock and village."

"Oh, yeah, he knows," Heck said and rattled off more Spanish to Nando, who kept nodding. "He says, with us, his house will be crowded, some must sleep on the floor. His daughter, Gina, she comes home this weekend from university in Havana where she studies to be a doctor, very smart."

"Then they will be a wealthy family someday," Jace said.

Heck translated, then answered. "No, that's why he wants to sell the rafts, even though he have to hide them for now. Doctors in Cuba, they only make as much money as someone lays bricks or sells T-shirts on the street."

Claire's voice came from behind him where she had stood up to stretch and flex the cramps in her legs. Lexi was sleeping on the deck with her head on Claire's purse for a pillow, covered with a coat. His ex-wife, whom he'd discovered too damn late he still loved and wanted—much of the divorce was his stupid fault—was frowning at the nearing shoreline.

"Communist country, Jace," she said. "We're about to see what that really means."

"If Ames is here, it doesn't mean he makes as much as a bricklayer or street vendor. He may be helping to fund the Castro kingdom and somehow making big bucks here, I know it."

Heck spit over the side of the boat and said, "The Castros ruined everything. Took my grandfather's lands, his house, his money—my family, my heritage. Took a lot of lives, firing squads their favorite way. But we're not gonna get caught. He's not gonna take nothing else from us—maybe the other way 'round."

Jace turned to him. "Just don't do anything to screw this up— this secret mission we didn't ask for but have to handle. Getting in and getting out of here, together, everyone in one piece."

"'Course not. I'm gonna want out of here, fast as you. 'Specially 'cause I hear this place is locked up tight for social media, email, online research, all that I need to do my work. And what's out there is monitored and controlled. Coupla dry-foot escapees told me that not long ago."

"Great, just great," Nick groused as he came to stand beside them. "With the internet off-limits or monitored, we're going to have to use something like passenger pigeons to contact the FBI so they don't think we're dead, so they can help us get out of here."

"We're as good as back in the Dark Ages here," Jace said. "Outnumbered and outranked, but we won't be outthought or outfought. We got this far and we'll make it in and out."

"Just remember what Lincoln said during our own country's terrible war," Nick said, bouncing a fist off both Jace's and Heck's shoulders. "We have to hang together, or we'll hang separately."

As if they'd made a vow, both men nodded solemnly. Claire did too as she moved to stand between Jace and Nick. Suddenly, Nando spewed out behind them what sounded like an order.

"He says," Heck told them, "he sees the place where he can drop us off and where we can hide the rafts for him. But we'll have to wade a ways and wait for a couple of hours before we walk to his house."

"Dry land sounds good—wading for it, dragging rafts or not," Claire said.

"Piece of cake," Jace added with a sarcastic snort. "All of this."

"You can say that because you've been in combat," Claire told him.

Nick said, "Nothing may be what it seems here, just like other things we've been through. To quote another wise man, 'All for one and one for all,' so let's remember that—live by that until we all get out of here."

CHAPTER THREE

In a small, lovely inlet edged by a narrow band of blinding white sand, the rescued party sloshed ashore in the late afternoon. Since the crystal clear water where Nando let them out was waist deep, Jace carried Lexi. Nick and Bronco tugged the two orange rafts in to shore, hoping they could find a spot in the lush greenery to deflate and hide them until Nando could find buyers.

It was the least that they could do for him, Nick thought. He didn't want to tip off the man or his family that he had a lot of cash on him. It was obvious that money was tight on the island, at least for average people. He'd heard things had been tough after Castro's 1950s revolution and got worse when the old USSR then Venezuela and China abandoned supporting Cuba. Evidently, Raul Castro had finally eased up restrictions on some small, private businesses. And, of course, if international billionaires like Clayton Ames were here, all cozy with the Castros while most Cubans had it hard, well, that was obscene.

"Strange, but this scary place seems like paradise," Claire said to him, her voice shaky. "It's so beautiful and serene, but evil lurked in Eden and led people astray."

"We'll be careful," he assured her, but he was on edge too. Surely, if Ames was in Cuba, he would not have hired that rickety boat to come out to bring them into his latest realm, using Nando so they wouldn't suspect a trap. But he put nothing past his father's murderer, a master manipulator with long arms.

Nick flinched as a brown pelican dived so close it splashed them when it scooped up the unsuspecting fish in its bill, swallowed it whole and wagged its tail in delight. Yeah, even this Eden had its dangers.

Waiting for dusk, when they would head for Nando's house, they hunkered down in a patch of sun as their clothes dried stiff and salty against their skin. At least they weren't cold now. When Lexi kept asking to play in the sand, things almost seemed normal. They didn't want to be spotted, but finally they let her, over on the side of the little inlet, partly hidden by the cliff. Claire was with her. Would Lexi's light hair and Claire's red tresses draw attention? Obviously, some non-Cubans lived here, surely redheads, but his wife was a striking woman. Thank God, they had Heck and Nita to act as translators and buffers.

As if he'd read his mind, Heck said, "'Cording to what Nando said, we're going to have to go into Havana to get to the internet. How else we gonna tell Patterson we're not lost? Surprise! We are here, come get us—somehow."

"I know," Nick said. "We could try the British Embassy, where I read there's a so-called American desk upon request. But some of us would stand out like sore thumbs there, and we need to stick together. The Brits might not believe us, and we'd have to go through red tape, declare who we really are to get American help. Then there's Gitmo."

"Guantanamo? The US prison for terrorist enemies here?"

"Everything's up in the air right now, a long shot. At least there would be Americans there, officers and soldiers who go back and forth to the States. Let's just take this one step—one very careful step—at a time."

★ ★ ★

When the shadows grew long, Nick and Jace decided it was time to hike to the road above the beach and head for Nando's house. Claire and Nita walked with Lexi between them up the curving path since they couldn't get around the cliff to the thin stretch of shore under Nando's home.

"Look at that red soil with all this tobacco," Heck said.

Lexi piped up. "I thought tobacco was bad for people, Mommy."

"Cuban cigars are famous, and a lot of people like them," Claire said only. She was exhausted. She'd taken one of her earlier meds with a gulp of water from Nando's canteen. She hoped she'd warded off the chance of a narcoleptic nightmare, but she feared falling asleep in the middle of a step or word. All she needed was a psychotic bad dream now when reality was so awful.

"Hate to admit it, but this is real pretty land," Jace said. "I see patches of tomatoes and what might be coffee besides the tobacco. I could use a good cup of java right now."

"It's the Castros and their cronies who are bad," Heck put in, "not Cuba or its people—most of them, I mean."

They found Nando's house just where he'd said they would. It looked like a kind of stucco with a slightly slanted, orange tile roof, but many of the tiles were cracked or broken. Nando stood in the door watching for them. Beside him stood a short woman, her long white hair in the setting sun such a contrast to Nando's salt-and-pepper look. His skin was much bronzer than hers.

"Maybe his mother live here too," Heck said. "Generations, the old ones, at least, stick together, even if he said his daughter lives in Havana, goes to university."

Though no other houses or people on the road were in sight on this western edge of the village, Nando quickly herded them inside. Despite the warm breeze and fingers of red setting sunlight stretching through the glassless windows and door before Nando closed it behind them, Claire shivered.

Inside, standing in the small, central room with its table and few chairs, Nando introduced them—with Heck's help—to Carlita, his wife, not his mother. Nando whispered something to Heck, who in turn told them in a hushed voice, "Her hair go white real fast when the sharks take their only son."

Claire bit her lower lip and blinked back tears. Lexi had been abducted once and that had been a near-death experience for her. As different as she was from this woman, Claire immediately sympathized with her. Their names even seemed an echo of each other. Yet they were so far from home—wherever that was now—and so far from safety.

Sleeping on a tile floor with only a piece of canvas under him didn't bother Jace. In Iraq, he'd been through worse, even though pilots were usually housed in the best of the worst places. His stomach was full of fish, black beans and rice, though he sure could have used a beer or something stronger than some sugary drink called *guarapo*, made from sugarcane juice. The coffee, though, had been home-ground, hot and strong.

With the other men, he'd sat outside after dark on the small back patio, hearing the sound of the sea. The patio was eroding from sea salt air and age, but just a few steps away served as a urinal for the men while the women used a chamber pot inside. Nita, who didn't speak much but to Claire, Lexi and Carlita, had told them that it was Carlita's dream to have a toilet with running water and a drinking spigot someday soon, just like the ones in the village that had better pipes. At least they had running water from a cistern in the small kitchen. But the stunning view out the back of the little place—wasn't that worth something?

Jace shifted onto his side. Bronco, lying next to him, looked like he slept the sleep of the dead. Except he snored. Nick had insisted on taking the first watch. He was sitting up with his back against the wall near the front door, which had no real lock on it, just a double-hooked latch. Hell, in a way, they all had their backs against the wall.

Claire and Lexi slept in the second small room off this main one in the Hermez daughter's single bed. Nita was in a sort of sagging cot in that same crowded room. Clarita had fussed over Lexi, washing her hair and combing it out. Then Claire and Nita had washed their hair in rainwater from a barrel out back. All that by lantern light, though they said the village had electricity between blackouts. No wonder Nando had considered two rafts to sell on the black market a gift from God.

Jace just hoped when the urban daughter, Regina, called Gina, showed up for a weekend visit tomorrow she wouldn't be a flaming commie or want to turn them in. How much were people brainwashed on this island, especially in Havana? In a wood-framed photo, Gina stood before a mural of Fidel and Che Guevara with the words *Viva La Revolucion!*

Jace had noticed that Heck spent a lot of time staring at the picture as if he knew her. She was easy to look at. Glossy long dark hair and flashing brown eyes. Lithe, young, sexy in trendy clothes that would have done her well on Miami Beach. Her tight T-shirt read in English *I'm gaga for Lady Gaga!!!* She looked like she came from another planet compared to this fisherman's house where she'd grown up. He'd seen no photo of the lost son Alfredito or of the family together.

The wind had picked up outside, and Jace saw Nick stand and look out the front window through the open wooden shutters. It was pitch-black outside. Keeping quiet, Jace got up and stepped over the sleeping Bronco, who would be taking the early-morning watch after him and Heck.

Jace whispered to Nick, "I'm awake. I'll start now."

Nick nodded and fist-bumped Jace's shoulder. He moved to take his spot on the floor. Jace thought that they could almost be friends, especially since Nick, WITSEC alias his brother Jack, wasn't sleeping with Claire tonight.

When Nick lay down with a deep sigh, Jace did some stretching to get his blood moving and his muscles awake. How did things keep spiraling down, getting worse? It was as if they were under some curse.

With his back to the wall, he sat on the floor and became one with the night shadows.

On Saturday—Claire thought she was losing track of time and her sanity—Nando went fishing since he'd lost his catch when he'd brought them home the day before. Carlita walked to the village to meet the 11:00 a.m. bus their daughter was supposed to be on. See, Claire told herself, time did not stand still, even here where it seemed it should.

"Let's have a powwow before Carlita gets back with their daughter," Nick said to their group, and except for Nita, who stayed inside with Lexi, they all went out on the patio. The village of Costa Blanca circled around the fishing dock about half a mile to the east, and they could see some of it from here.

"This girl Gina is obviously way different from her parents," Nick began. Considering how intent and edgy everyone looked, he felt like he was making a plea in a courtroom. "Who knows what they indoctrinate students with at the university? Nando told Heck that Gina is studying to be a doctor, so she's probably bright and as modern as it gets around here, maybe a dedicated Communist. No doubt ambitious, though Nando said doctors earn minimal wages."

Claire put in, "But wanting to go through all it takes to be a doctor for little money makes me think she could also want to help people. She sounds altruistic or at least a people person."

"Good point, forensic psychologist," Nick said with a nod and a smile. "I'm remembering why I hired you to figure people out for me, even ones who are gone from this earth. I need—

and value—all of your opinions, because we're still flying blind here."

"Flying's my gig," Jace said. "Like you guys said, we've got to get to the internet somehow, so we can send out an SOS for help. And fast, before someone figures out we don't belong and calls in the—whatever they call them here. Man, I'm starting to feel we're on an alien planet, like in that old TV show *Star Trek*."

"Just hope it doesn't turn into *Star Wars*," Nick said.

Claire thought it seemed not only a breath of fresh air but a whirlwind that came through the front door with quiet Carlita. Gina Hermez was gesturing with both hands and talking rapid-fire Spanish, until she suddenly switched to English.

"Who says nothing happens outside Havana?" the pretty girl exploded as her big dark eyes jumped from one of them to the other. She propped her hands on her shapely hips before flinging gestures again. "Well, that's just another government lie, because you are really, really here!"

She wore cutoff jeans and a pink crewneck sweater that might have come from Abercrombie & Fitch. Her glossy raven hair hit below her shoulder blades, and her clear plastic backpack was crammed with books. She spoke strangely accented English, Claire thought—most forensic psychologists were good at placing accents—with a Slavic or Russian tang to her voice, not the usual Hispanic lilt.

"It's kismet our papa found you," Gina went on before anyone else could speak. "And where we lost Alfredito. Please, let us sit at the table and talk. And, oh, a *bonita* little girl..."

Everyone talked at once then, cross-counter introductions, greetings. Nick made some explanation of their plight, using the cover story they had been flying to a vacation when their plane went down, and that the man who owned it was going to be very angry if he caught up with them, so they needed to call a lawyer friend of Nick's in the States.

"You are a lawyer?" Gina asked. "You know what Shake-speare said—'First, let's kill all the lawyers.' Now, you know, we Cubans are well educated, yes? Free education, free health care here, so not all bad, but the joke now is if we could only find breakfast, lunch and dinner, yes, Mama?"

Carlita, who seemed to have next to no English, said nothing but beamed and nodded. It was obvious she adored her daughter but probably didn't understand her much lately, whether she spoke English or Spanish. What a contrast in the two women, Claire thought, hoping she and Lexi never got that different. The new Cuba versus the old, that was for sure. And, however Gina had got the money, Claire had seen Carlita quickly put some paper bills in a jar. Claire decided she'd tell Nick. When they left here, he could leave some American money for them as well.

"Of course, I can help you find assistance in Havana," Gina promised, without taking a breath, "but since you are illegal *Norte Americanos*, sometimes called *Yanquis* here, and since you not come by legal means, we have to be careful. Oh, it's my dream to go to your country. Doctors are special there, have more money and respect, yes?"

The one thing Gina said, Claire noted, that didn't jibe with her good English vocabulary and slight Slavic lilt was that she said *jes* instead of *yes*, just the way Heck did.

"That's true about doctors in the US," Nick said. "As for Havana, we have friends who can come for us if we can just get them word, then settle things at home about the lost airplane later. We don't want to draw attention to ourselves in any way."

"Well, they cannot come here to get you, 'specially in Havana, or Raul's security arrest you," Gina explained. "Once you contact your friends, you need a rural meeting spot, probably for a boat, not a plane, maybe around where Papa dropped you off. Cuba security can find illegal planes in our airspace."

"Good advice, because, of course, we don't want to take the

chance of being detained or being publicized or even recognized."

"Right. I love that you use big words. I need to learn more and more, but I *comprendo*—understand—what you say. Lucky you have two good *Espanol* speakers here," she said with a blinding smile that took in Heck but not Nita.

Claire had been studying Gina intently, trying to psych out her true character and intent. But she also noticed that Heck—who had been introduced to Gina as Berto Ochoa—was all eyes for the *senorita*. He practically had his tongue hanging out.

"Oh, for sure," he said, sounding as breathless as if he'd run miles. "Anything I can do to help, work with you, I will."

Oh, boy, Claire thought. You might know hormones were roiling here. She hoped it could work to their advantage, but what if it didn't? Matters were already complicated enough considering her own problems with Jace and Nick, not to mention Heck keeping an eye on Nita since she and Bronco were lovey-dovey.

While Carlita, with Nita's help, put quesadillas on each plate and poured homemade papaya wine, Gina suggested something they hadn't thought of, something that made Claire hope they could believe and trust her.

"I got to explain something to Berto here—" another smile at Heck "—since he say he is a—what was that?—a computer trekky?"

"A techie," Nick corrected her.

"Oh, yes. But I think I know a way getting to the internet that is safer than going near the embassy. We have what you call internet cafés, only the lines long and most Cubans believe what they write is watched by—you know—the government," she added, whispering. "I have a laptop, but it only connects with university areas that been approved and what we call SNet, the Street Net. If you have any money, you should check into a real nice hotel, then rent an hour of worldwide net online, maybe between eight to fifteen dollars, so pretty expensive."

If this woman thought that was expensive, Claire thought, things were indeed bad here.

Lowering her voice again, Gina went on, "They say others—well, you know, the government—watches that internet for problems, so the hotel, bigger the better, might work best."

Her voice returned to normal range and she began to gesture again. "See, I was dating a musician, played at the Nacional, best hotel in Havana. Foreign tourists, European, Canadian stay there, not so many *Americanos* anymore, not for years, since the horrible dictator Batista and his gangsters ruled here, but that might work for you. If there's any rooms available, if you have some cash. Cash is king here, American dollars, even."

Nick told her, "We might be able to arrange that. When you head back to Havana tomorrow on the bus, can we all go along, maybe the last bus in the evening?"

"First of all, no streetlights there. Dark for you to be getting around at night. Besides, I have to take a bus at dawn, but I know where I keep you hidden until afternoon. Then you go to the hotel about the time a plane would land and you would arrive. We take another taxi to the airport first, since you got some money."

This girl was proving herself as bright as she looked, Claire thought, even thinking of little details, but was she after their money or did she really want to help? At least there was just one more night's sleep here in crowded conditions with the breeze whispering through the old wooden shutters and bad dreams to make her think someone was coming after them.

Claire hated to dwell on dangers, but they'd been through so much. When she first became a Certified Fraud Examiner and Forensic Psychologist, she'd never imagined it would lead to more than interviews of Americans who might have broken the law, even though she'd realized she could be dealing with criminals. And Nick as a criminal defense attorney certainly never planned to be defending his own life.

Later, over a dessert of amazingly little bananas that had been soaked in rum, though Claire made sure Lexi's was without the liquor, Gina was still talking. "I know where to get some clothes to loan—or is it lend?—you all, except little Meggie, but we will manage. And you won't have suitcases, but I know where to borrow one or two. Still, once we leave this *casa*, 'specially when we be in Havana," she said, looking intently at each of them in turn, "until you get a place to stay, think of it as hiding in the shadows so you not get caught."

CHAPTER FOUR

After several more rural stops, the bus to Havana became crowded, though they all had seats since Costa Blanca was near the beginning of this line. Nick noted there weren't many cars on the road until they neared Havana.

"No es facil," Gina whispered to him and Claire from the seat behind and patted them both on their shoulders as if to buck them up. Lexi was on Claire's lap, nodding in sleep, and Gina was sitting with Heck. "That's my motto," Gina said. "Nothing is easy, even getting around in the city. We'll get out near where I live."

Nick had noticed, despite the buzz of voices on the bus, that Heck and Gina had sometimes switched to Spanish, though she'd said she wanted to practice her English. Claire had clued Nick in like he was some idiot about Gina and Heck. At least Heck was smitten, because you couldn't really tell about her. They needed her to help them, but Nick agreed with his personal forensic psychologist that Gina needed watching. Everyone in Cuba did. *No es facil*, indeed.

At first the city seemed to him a sprawl of huge, block-like apartment buildings with an occasional blast from the past like

an aging Spanish hacienda, some with wash on the line and people watching out the window. Many were smoking. Kids played
in the potholed streets, and old men sat on barrels over games
of checkers. They passed a series of buildings painted Pepto-
Bismol pink. Nick's stomach was roiling and not from being
rattled on this bus. He could use some of that stuff right now,
but what couldn't they use? He'd quietly left one of his smallest
bills, fifty dollars, in Carlita's money jar. He was nervous about
flashing big bills—would stores even have change?—to get un-
derwear and a change of clothes for everyone.

Claire poked him in the ribs. At least she had the brains not
to say anything. Their Spanish might be sketchy, but they could
both translate the words on the huge mural with Fidel Castro's
bearded profile they were passing: *Solcialismo o muerta*. In other
words, *Socialism or death*. Somehow, that threat was the least of
their worries right now.

But when they looked out the other side of the bus, it was
pure beauty. They were driving along what Gina called the
Malecon, a gorgeous avenue with a seawall and the glittering
water just below. People were strolling or just hanging out. He
spotted some who must be tourists.

"*Caramba!* There, there!" Gina said, bending low to look
ahead of them. She pointed at a huge, turreted building, blinding white in the sun on an elevated area overlooking the city
and the green-and-violet sea beyond. "The Hotel Nacional de
Cuba," she told them, then repeated it to Bronco and Nita, who
were sitting behind her. Jace was across the aisle, sitting next
to a man who was bringing sunglasses into the city to hawk on
the streets. "Later," she told Nick. "We will go there later, not
looking like this, yes?"

"Yes, okay," Nick threw over his shoulder. He, Jace and Claire
had decided that they would go with her tourists-to-the-hotel
plan. But first they were going into the heart of the city to the
university area.

"Next stop," she said. "Here, we get out here." She shouted *"Chofe!"* to the bus driver over the noise and got up to lead them to the exit. Nick hefted Lexi, and they straggled out into an area where ficus trees lined the avenues and some lovely old buildings cast sharp shadows.

"This way," Gina said, starting out with Heck at her side. Nick reminded himself he had to tell him not to answer every question Gina asked, despite her charms. They'd been talking about life in the US most of the way here.

His legs were stiff after sitting tense for so long. Gina turned away from the vista ahead with large homes and the huge main university building beyond, leading them toward a run-down-looking place that must have once been beautiful.

Heck turned back to tell them, "Gina says she can take me later to see the small hotel and hacienda my grandfather owned. She said not to get my hopes up that they look like my family said."

Which, Nick saw, was the name of the game in this area where Gina lived, in what he would call student housing—cheap student housing. Her building must have once been grand but it was falling apart. The broken back gate they went in took them past a long-empty swimming pool with a broken diving board. They had to duck around tropical plants, no doubt once tended, now run rampant like a jungle. They walked in on the ground floor and followed her up three flights of dusty, partly crumbling stairs.

Jace carried Lexi now. She was always clinging to one of them, and Nick could see why. If he was nerved up and Claire looked it too, what must this child be thinking?

"This the old servants' stairs," Gina told them. "Wider ones in front, but we not need to see people if they not on canvas."

"Campus," Heck corrected her. "You said to tell you if you use a wrong word."

"Campus, campus," Gina recited. "I was even thinking for one *momentito* it might be circus."

Claire said, "But your English is quite good."

"I learn most of it from my Russian professor of anatomy couple years ago. English from a Russian, a good joke, yes?"

Nick saw Claire nod. He knew she was relieved to hear the explanation for the girl's unusual accent. Like him, Claire's brain had been running wild with suspicions about Russian spies and Cubans following them. That was ridiculous, of course, at least so far, but she had good instincts and she'd whispered to him more than once on the bus that the back of her neck was prickling with her woman's intuition that they were being watched. He'd just forced a smile and shook his head at her. Of course they were being watched, but just because they stood out on the rural bus.

"No one should be here in my apartment, so no worry," Gina assured them again as she had when she'd laid out her plan last night at her parents' house. "My two girlfriends busy with their—their admirers, and Eduardo, he is away until late tomorrow, so you be gone by then, be taken care of."

Claire's stare collided with Nick's. There were two ways to interpret what Gina had just said. But, right now, they had no choice but to trust her.

Claire nearly collapsed onto the sunken settee in the main room of the apartment Gina shared with two other women and one man. The antique piece was covered with faded and worn red velvet, probably a survivor of the good old days. A few other dark wood furniture pieces looked patched together from somewhere grand, a ball-footed table and five mismatched chairs, a cubbyhole desk that boasted a laptop. Heck hovered over that as if it was a magnet.

"Berto," Gina said, "I tell you, it only go to university sites unless Eduardo connects to the wires we have to string outside, along rooftops. Under that pillowcase, our *telemundo*." She pointed. "But unless he left the packet for the week here, sorry, but little Meggie can't watch old TV shows today."

"The packet?" Heck said.

"We pool some money, he take our hard drive to a secret location and get it loaded with mostly American TV. We see game shows, watch things like *Homeland*, about spies and secret agents, so don't think we don't know American things. I told you, I love America.

"Okay, now," she went on, shrugging off her backpack and disappearing into one of the three doors that must lead to sleeping quarters—and, hopefully, a bathroom. "Here some suitcases you can use, look like you flew into Havana."

She dragged out three, two of which looked presentable, despite their scuffed surface and small size. "You have to pretend they are heavy—tourists always come and go with heavy ones—but you won't have much in them. How about I take Lorena and Berto, and we try buy a change of clothes for all of you, then you try look like European or Canadian or something."

"Or something is right," Bronco spoke up, though he hadn't been saying much.

"Berto," Nick said with a stare at Heck, "we'll all go out later to see your family's places, so keep to business now, okay?"

"Oh, sure, boss. I waited my whole life to see those places, wishing I could get them back, so I can stand it a little longer."

Nick gave Heck two fifty-dollar bills he'd taken out from his plastic money belt this morning and had stuck in the front pocket of his pants. Gina's eyes widened when she saw them. "Oh, I hope they have money give us back. Maybe we best go into a real shop, not somewhere on the street. We'll bring back food too, not be gone long. You want nap, is okay to use my friends' beds. Jenna looking like she can sleep right there," she said with a nod at Claire. "So—you not answer the door. This plan, it will work. If it does, you think your friends who come get you in a boat will mind one more person? It would kill my parents if I go, but I got to look ahead—just kidding, I think. All of us got to keep our eyes ahead, even if it is a dark road at times."

Jace thought things were looking up when their Spanish-speaking trio were back in an hour with a change of clothes for everyone and hot tamales. Gina hauled out cans of a soft drink called TuKola from a tiny refrigerator in the corner. The girl had a good eye for clothing sizes. His jeans fit pretty well, though they were beige. Ironically, they'd got Nick the same outfit, which made them look more like the brothers they were pretending to be. Lexi liked her yellow-and-white-striped dress and kept saying Lily would like it, so she must be remembering some friend of hers from home he hadn't met. Claire's outfit was white tennis shoes with a turquoise three-piece slacks outfit, though the blue kind of clashed with her red hair.

With Bronco bringing up the rear and Gina leading, they set out in separate groups, walking a few yards apart to see Heck's Cuban family's past property. All wore sunglasses Gina had bought from the man on the bus. Nick carried a map of this area called El Vedado that Heck had bought. "*El Vedado*, that means 'the forbidden,'" Heck whispered to Jace, "but don't know why."

"Let's just hope we don't find out and don't like the answer," Jace told him.

As tired and wary as she was, Claire thought the Vedado was lovely. Some of the mansions dated back to the 1860s, but most were from the 1920s. Many were still kept up, though some were in total disrepair. It was hilly and windy up here, a lovely day that partly lifted her spirits.

Heck, though, she noted, was a mess. He was finally so close to his heritage, one he shared with the now-deceased grandfather he still cherished. Gina was as good as a tour guide—that was, until she led them to a break in an iron fence behind a bougainvillea bush and said, "We cut through here. Good shortcut and beautiful inside. We never stop to pay at the gate—too much."

Heck said, "But it's a cemetery. What if we get caught without a ticket? We don't need to be reported."

"Is okay," Gina said with a quick downward slice of her hand. "We cut through here all the time, to university. Berto, it closer to your family house too. The guards at the gate know my friend Francesca, ignore us even if they see us. Come on, everyone through."

Maybe it was her narcolepsy meds speaking, but once inside, Claire felt she had actually stepped into a city of the dead. She was stunned to see so many life-size stone statues of long-gone people. Several had their arms outspread as if to welcome them. Again, she felt that strange, shivery sense that they were being watched or followed, but it was surely just the marble eyes on them and the blank darkness peering through the grates of elaborate crypts. Even in the warm afternoon sun, she shuddered again. Shadows seemed to reach out, trying to touch them or snag their steps. She took Lexi's hand and ignored what the child was whispering about someone named Lily.

"Famous Cubans, big monuments here," Gina told them, pointing this way and that. "Over that way, old-time independence leader General Gomez and Eduardo Chibas's tomb back there. To protest the cruel government, he killed himself during a radio broadcast before the revolution, so bold and brave!"

Claire saw Nick's head snap around. Any mention of suicide shook him up.

"When he was buried here," Gina went on, "a young university student, Fidel Castro, did jump on his grave and make a big speech, started the revolt against the old ways. But we going by the one I want you to see, 'specially you, Jenna, since you have little Meggie," she said, turning to look closely at Claire.

And maybe not only little Meggie, Claire thought. She was still obsessing over her missed period but tried to tell herself that all this upheaval could have made her body skip it. She still hadn't told Nick, since he didn't need another distraction right now.

"Was it someone famous who had a daughter?" Claire asked as they skirted around the site Gina must be referring to. Again, the raised tombs were crowded so close together it felt oppressive, as if all that stonework was leaning in. They seemed to be pretty much in the center of the massive cemetery. Ahead of them loomed the marble figure of a woman clinging to a tall cross with one arm and a baby in her other. Claire gasped. But for a slightly rounder face, the statue looked like her. Nick and Jace both gaped at it, then her.

"Look, Mommy," Lexi said, tugging on her arm. "It's you! But you don't have a baby. And the statue of the little girl with her head bowed standing over by the flowers—that could be me!"

"That's really somethin'!" Bronco said when the others seemed suddenly voiceless. Nita kept crossing herself. The flowers strewed or carefully placed around the statue reminded Claire of the photos of the floral excess when Princess Diana died. It was almost as if this woman had just died yesterday.

Jace cleared his throat and put in, "They say there are doubles for everyone somewhere. But this lady lived and died a long time ago. Look, Jenna, she was your age now."

Gina pointed out the woman's burial vault nearby, one with four huge iron rings.

"This my favorite place in all this Necropolis Cristobal Colon," Gina said, her voice so solemn. They all stopped, gathered around her. "This the tomb of Senora Amelia Goryi, called *La Milagrosa*, the miraculous one. She died giving a birth in 1901. Her husband so sad, he devious."

"Devastated?" Nick prompted, his deep voice shaky.

"That's it. He have a broken heart and visit the grave many times a day. Always, he knocked with one of those iron rings to wake her up and backing away to keep her grave and statue in sight longest he can. But here's the thing," she added, turning to Claire. "When her body exhumed years later, it not one bit decayed. And the dead baby which was buried at her feet was in her arms! So she was holy, not a saint yet, but a special help, a miracle. Many people come here, knock on the tomb and back away, like her husband did, praying she solve their problems."

Nick put his arm around Claire's shoulders as if he had to protect her, and Jace stepped closer. She couldn't help it but still stared into the stone face of the statue. The slant of sun made it look as if her lips were moving. One of Claire's professors had always made his students memorize that being a forensic psychologist meant "The dead still talk if you know how to listen."

Claire prayed this statue would not haunt her, not talk to her in dreams. She'd had narcoleptic nightmares in which the dead clutched at her in the night. Her doctor had said that was typical of the disease—and maybe her chosen career—and she'd managed to deal with it. But now, with all this...

Nick's voice cut through her agonizing. "So, Gina, are you thinking we could rely on this long-dead woman's favor to get us safely out of here?"

"I hope and pray so. If not, we, the living, we must find the way."

CHAPTER FIVE

Nick had never seen Heck cry. The guy was usually all business, rational and unemotional, his no-nonsense tech adviser, and for five years he'd relied on him for that. But seeing the small, once-elegant hotel his grandfather had owned and that had been taken away from him in the Cuban revolution moved Nick's friend to tears. Luckily, it was still named La Rosa, so that and the street name had been enough for Gina to locate it without giving out his family's real last name.

"It's a mess," Heck choked out, glaring across the avenue at the splotchy exterior of the building where blue paint had peeled away like huge scabbed sores. The intricate metal balconies overhanging the Quinta Avenida were rusted and looked dangerous, although laundry hung from some like mismatched flags, and a few had people leaning on the railing and smoking, just watching life go by—and watching them.

Gina put her arm around his waist, and Heck leaned into her. "Many once-grand places like this now," she told him, her voice soothing. "Lots of families live there, so that helps that they have shelter, yes? Place like this, so many of them, called *ciudadelas*, like a little city to many people. Best we not go in, yes, Berto?"

"Right, right," he said as Nick put his hand on Heck's shoulder. "But to be so close and yet so far."

"Also," Gina said, "we not want to stand here staring. Most neighborhoods still have what we call CDRs, you know, a kind of neighborhood watch to report strangers or bad talk. We should move on now."

"Right," he repeated. "I dread seeing what's left of the family home, but I'd still like to walk down to the old hacienda."

They started off again. Nick hoped Gina didn't pick up on the fact that Heck was going by the last name Ochoa, and he hoped he hadn't told her it was his maternal grandfather who once owned these buildings, not his father's father, in case she checked on that.

Nick was trying to keep an eye on Claire, who had obviously been shaken by the statue in the cemetery, and he kept glancing back to be sure they weren't being followed. He could tell Jace was really on edge too, but this was the least they could do for Heck. Best he see all this, then put it behind him. If they hadn't come with him, Nick was afraid he might have gone off with Gina alone, and he didn't want anyone to be out of his sight here. They had to escape soon. The entire place oppressed him, especially because the odds were good Ames was here somewhere, lurking.

They trekked down what was turning into a lovely avenue, one with fewer cracks and potholes, and little traffic. Suddenly, Lexi said, "I'm tired of walking and Lily is too," and yanked her hand from Claire's.

Nick's gaze slammed into Claire's. She said, "I guess all this has given our Meggie an imaginary friend."

"She's not 'maginary," Lexi insisted, her voice sassy, "just because you can't see her, because I can. She has her own talk only I know. Not Spanish. Ours."

Lexi—holding no one's hand but pretending to—turned and skipped back to walk with Jace, who was bringing up the rear.

"I can understand her being distraught," Nick whispered. "She ever do this before?"

"Never. But she's missing her best friend and cousin Jilly."

"Jilly, not Lily?"

"Yes. Maybe she's put that together with her own name, I don't know. And with all this fear and upheaval, I hope we can keep her under control—keep her being Meggie."

"Yeah. We could all use an imaginary friend, but as soon as we check into that big hotel, I'm going to try to get us a real friend, namely Rob Patterson. Let's let Le—Meggie have this friend but try to comfort her and keep her grounded."

"But grounded in reality?" Claire challenged. "Reality is pretty awful right now. I'm so shaky. I just hope I can help her, calm her."

"You're taking your meds?"

"Thank God, I brought extra. Nick, if I run out, I—"

Gina called back from ahead of them, "There it is! And, look, Berto, it looks fine, maybe like the old days, yes?"

Nick saw his friend wipe his eyes again. Ahead of them where Gina pointed, Nick recognized the big hacienda from a photo Heck used to have as a screen saver on his laptop. This large, two-story white building could have stepped intact from the past. Its wood-and-glass windows were thrown wide open on the top floor. The well-kept place sported a filigree of black iron balconies, an orange tiled roof, white curtains fluttering at an upper window, an ornate, gated entry with painted tiles and the musical sound and spray of a fountain within all framed by blooming pink-and-white bougainvillea.

They all stood and stared. Finally, Heck spoke. "Just like it was before my family had it taken away with the hotel and our country house—had our lives taken away. Look, some sort of sign by the gate, there on the wall."

He walked across the street. Nick could not name the make of the squat black car that sat in the entry on the other side of the closed gate. They all waited nervously as Heck studied the sign and the car. Gina went over and stood next to him. When they came back, Heck said, "A Russian name, a Russian company, a Russian-made car, a Lada. No way we can ask to look inside."

Gina said, "Some fine old places in this area are being bought by foreign investors who cozy up to—to you-know-who. I think these places once government offices, so it saved them. My roommate Francesca has a special friend like that. He's rich, from Hong Kong, investing here and other places in the Caribbean. I think most of these people paying the Castros." Again, though no one but them was visible on the street, she lowered her voice when she said anything about the Castros.

But when her words sank in, Nick jerked alert. "Her special friend is from Hong Kong? Not American?"

"Oh, there a few of those here too, but not legal unless they make good deals with—with you-know-who. There are getting to be more foreign fish in the sea here, like my father says."

Lexi piped up. "Are we 'lowed to talk about that bad man that took me? He had a house like this with a fountain. And lots of fish swimming inside tanks that ate other fish, but Lily wasn't afraid of them."

Claire tugged Lexi away and leaned down to whisper something to her. It hit Nick hard that this could well be the area where Ames would put down roots in Havana. If he could just find out if and where he was in this El Vedado area, he could somehow let Patterson know where to find the bastard, not that the FBI or the marines guarding Guantanamo could swoop in to arrest and deport him.

Nick whispered to Heck, "There has to be a way to learn who is here and where, and I don't mean Castro." When Gina came closer again, Nick went on, "Berto, someday, maybe if the US relaxes the embargo and relationships get better, you can come back, visit the place. But we don't need to be dealing with the Russians that run that business right now."

"And meanwhile," Heck said, "we got more important things to do. We shouldn't be concentrating on getting into someplace, but getting out."

Though Claire felt exhausted, she talked Gina out of taking the shortcut through the cemetery again to get back to her student housing. Claire knew she needed to have a firm, private talk with Lexi soon. If it was some comfort to her to have an imaginary friend for a while, perhaps there was nothing wrong with that. But the child seemed not only disturbed but defiant, and that wasn't like her. Claire had psyched out her own daughter before when times were tough, but not under such daunting circumstances.

She let Nita take Lexi up into Gina's building with her and Bronco, while she, Nick and Jace hung back by the ruined swimming pool for a quick conference.

Jace, with a pointed look at Claire, said, "I understand longing for old times and people loved and lost. But I hope Heck has his anger about wanting his family's property back out of his system."

Claire was grateful Nick decided to ignore that. Or had Jace not meant anything personal by it? Was she the one seeing trouble behind every tree, every house, every tomb?

Nick said only, "Let's clear out of here, get a taxi to the airport, then one to the hotel. I'm going to follow Patterson's emergency plan for covert contact. Too bad it has to come from a Havana hotel and not Heck's laptop in Northern Michigan."

"We have no choice but to trust Patterson," Jace agreed. "But the thing is, WITSEC deals in deception, so how do we know he's really working for Uncle Sam and not your phony 'uncle' Clayton Ames?"

Claire put in, "And how do we even know we can trust Gina? I'm reading her that we can, but how ambitious is she? And did she mean it when she said that she'd like to go to the States, except for the fact it would kill her parents? Well, she didn't mean it like that. I'm even worrying about Lexi. She has to be my first concern, despite the way you men handle things."

They stopped talking when a strikingly beautiful girl, a bleached blonde, no less, overly made up, more or less slithered down the back stairs and sashayed past them. She ignored Claire but batted her long lashes and smiled at Jace, then Nick. Her skirt was short and looked painted on her ripe body. How she managed such high heels on the broken terrazzo walk was amazing, Claire thought.

She found her voice as the woman disappeared onto the street. "That's a student living here?"

They'd evidently stayed behind too long, because Gina came down the stairs looking for them with Heck right behind her as if he were her bodyguard now.

"Did you see my former friend Francesca?" Gina asked them, propping her hands on her hips. "Oh, yes, I see by the look on the men's faces you did. She said she's moving out for good, right now, didn't want any of her things. I can sell some, but that means more money for rent every month from the rest of us, and none of us can afford it."

"She's not a student, then, is she?" Claire asked, trying to keep the edge from her voice. Why did she always feel she was conducting a forensic psychology interview on this woman for some sort of crime? She hated not being able to trust the person who probably held their safety in her hands.

"Well—she started out that way," Gina admitted with a shrug. "Before she met her so-called special friend at a *paladore*—a private restaurant—where she was working at night. Now she good as spitting on her former friends. Truth is, she what is called a *jinetera*. You see them up where the foreigners go, even on the streets. She did not start out that way, but took her chance."

Heck said, "But *jinetera* means a female jockey. She rides horses? That woman?"

Gina frowned and shook her head. "Called that because the foreign men with money—well, you see, she ride them, in more ways than one."

"A prostitute?" Heck demanded.

"Yes, but not like—not like a whore. *Jineteras*, they choose real careful, stick with only one man. It's different here, Berto," Gina insisted, her voice rising too. "She stay faithful, he buy her nice presents, visit her family. If he's a rich foreigner, he might take her to his country, like Francesca says she going. That's why she doesn't want her stuff. I know one got married."

Heck swore under his breath and grabbed her arm to spin her slightly toward him. "You never did that, did you? You said you want to go with me. I'm not rich. You don't think that—"

"*Caramba!*" she spit out, breaking his hold on her. "You think that, you never speak to me again. I want to be a doctor, help people, trying to help you, all of you. I do not trade myself for anything, even going with you out of here, so—"

Breaking into a sob, she rushed inside with Heck right behind her.

"Oh, great. Just great," Jace muttered. "This whole gamble could be screwed up by a woman, but it wouldn't be the first time." He gave Claire a pointed look.

"I suppose," Claire put in with a sharp voice, "you never realized that Eve only ate the apple and listened to the serpent in the garden because Adam was too busy somewhere else."

"Meaning I was gone for my pilot career a lot? You were the one keeping secrets about your narcolepsy."

"If you had paid more attention, then—"

"Stop it," Nick demanded. "Both of you, stop it. If we don't get our act together, you'll have plenty of time to be mad at each other and me while we rot in a Cuban prison. Now let's get inside and calm things down. We need to get to the Hotel Nacional in Old Havana, and I need to get on what we can pray is a secure internet connection. We're all strung out, including Lexi, so let's shape up here."

"Yes," Claire said. "Sorry I came with baggage, Nick," she said with a glare at Jace. "Speaking of which, let's get up there and practice pretending those small, scuffed-up suitcases are full of clothes for a lovely Havana vacation."

"Right," Jace said. "Honest, I was trained better than losing it under pressure in the service and in the pilot's seat. I—we— just snapped."

"Then let's go in," Nick said. "Onward and upward—or else."

CHAPTER SIX

Jace thought the main building of the International Airport nine miles south of Havana looked like a winged bird of prey waiting to take flight. He wished they could take flight themselves, that he could be at the controls to get them out of here. Despite the fact their plane crash had not been his fault, he had been in the pilot's seat. Guilt sat heavy on his heart while he and Heck went inside to check the arrival boards in case they were asked about their flight times at the hotel. As he watched planes take off and land, he yearned for the bustle of an airport. Trouble was, he yearned for Claire too when she wasn't his anymore.

For a while, he'd convinced himself that he'd moved on. Moved on in his career, moved on to Singapore, where he'd spent some downtime at the other end of his Pacific flights. Seeing that knockout woman back at Gina's student housing had reminded him of the brief affair he'd had there—and made him feel guilty all over again.

But now, being with Claire, seeing her with Nick but wanting to protect her—to have her again—really hit him hard. He had to keep his head in all this, help to get them the hell out of here, but he kept thinking about him and Claire, how fast they'd fallen for each other, how intense it had been, how—

"Okay, everybody, listen up." Nick's voice sliced through his agonizing when they rejoined everyone outside the airport between taxi rides. "Remember, we're Americans, but we've flown in from Toronto, Canada. I have our passports if we need them. We'll have to hire two taxis again, but we'll be sure the drivers know to keep us together. Hotel Nacional, here we come, and, hopefully, not for a long stay. Meggie, Gina says they have a big swimming pool there."

"That's right," Gina put in, evidently wanting to boost Lexi's pouty attitude. "And lots of nice music right there at the pool too. Guitars, bongo drums, maracas—a happy salsa beat."

"Lily likes songs with bad words," Lexi insisted, crossing her arms over her chest.

Claire said, "Gina doesn't need to hear about Lily, so can you just keep her a secret?"

"Well, she's going swimming with us!" Lexi said so vehemently that even passing strangers looked at her. Jace saw Nick bite his lip, but what did he know about handling Lexi? Claire looked like she was going to cry, but she was a psychologist, so she'd better figure this out with her—their—kid. If it was up to him, he'd just tell Lexi enough of that nonsense right now or else. But around here in what might as well be a galaxy far away, what did "or else" mean?

"What a place!" Bronco said, looking up at the massive hotel when he'd seldom said much since their plane crash. Nick had seen that Nita kind of herded the big guy around, explaining things to him when she could, translating quietly now and then. He only hoped Bronco's protective instincts were on alert since he was obviously overwhelmed by culture shock. Well, weren't they all? Nick was really worried about Lexi, but he had to take care of business first.

The Hotel Nacional, they learned at the desk when Nick checked them in using their new passports, had nearly five hundred rooms. Gina had told them it used to be "the place" for Americans before the revolution, but it was now also a major foreign business center in Havana. That not only comforted Nick, since he wanted to get online fast, but it scared him. Who knew if Clayton Ames or his lackeys might be here on business and spot them?

Gina had also told them that the hotel had once become a ghost town, but had been rebuilt in the 1990s with billions of dollars of foreign money. No wonder the cost of a top-floor suite had been outrageous, but they needed room for the seven of them. Gina wasn't staying but would be back for dinner tonight, and Heck looked forlorn already. Bronco, Jace and Heck would sleep in the living area; Nita and Lexi in one bedroom; and Claire and Nick in the other. But again, Nick thought, *please, Lord, don't let us be here long before we get out of here somehow.*

Claire had taken Lexi off to their bedroom to talk to her, so he left Jace guarding them and went downstairs to the lobby with Bronco, alias Cody Carson. They walked toward the bank of laptops guests could pay to use. Ten dollars an hour here, and Gina thought that was expensive.

He'd already paid for the online time, so he just handed the guy in charge his receipt and sat down at a vacant laptop station. His hands were shaking. He should have Heck here, but he'd walked Gina downstairs to say goodbye until later.

In case someone tried to stop him, Nick had not brought the paper Rob Patterson had given him about covert contact. He'd type in the message first, then address it so it couldn't go out by mistake before he had it just the way he wanted it:

My stock market investments have crashed, but we'll get through it with your advice. We want to return to your firm. Any thoughts on how to get back in the market? I'd hate losing everything. I'll keep a low investment profile until I hear from you. Hotel Nacional in Havana is excellent. Jack Randal

He typed in the email address he'd been given by Patterson. It sounded like an investment firm in Chicago. Then he hit Send.

Claire bought Lexi a bathing suit in one of the first-floor shops, then let her go to the pool with Nita and Bronco. Lexi had promised that, if she could go swimming, she would only whisper to Lily and not repeat anything her friend said. Jace had gone down to the pool too, just to keep an eye on things from the shade, he'd said. Claire took a fast shower, and then Nick took his turn.

When Nick came out of the bathroom, Claire almost hurled herself in his arms. With just a wet towel tied around his waist, he sat on the bed and lifted her onto his lap. "Hang in there, sweetheart," he tried to calm her, but she knew he was on edge too.

"I know we don't have time for this, but I—I just needed your arms around me," she stammered. "I put mine around Lexi to try to comfort her, but she was kind of not there. Stiff. Angry. I mean, I understand but I just couldn't seem to talk her out of Lily—to help her."

He rocked her a bit. She clamped him to her. "We'll get out, get back to normal—whatever that is living under WITSEC protection—until they get their hands on Ames."

"What if these rooms are bugged?"

"I don't think so. They'd lose their business if anyone found out and word spread. This is a hub of savvy, greedy foreigners with money the Cubans want, so they have to be careful. At least we won't stand out here, except for our lousy wardrobes. Want to go down to the pool, get a bite to eat there, keep an eye on Lexi until we hear from Patterson?"

He shifted her closer. Claire could tell he was wavering about making love to her. She wanted that, but the world spun whenever Nick touched her that way, and they needed to be aware and wary. She almost told him she thought she might be pregnant, but there had to be a better time than this for such momentous news.

Clearing his throat, he said, "So Heck should be back by now, and I need to talk to him about our next step online—waiting for my so-called investment banker to contact us with instructions. But if we go down, I can check to see if there's a reply yet. I'm hoping—praying—he responds fast."

She lifted her head from his shoulder. "Heck didn't come upstairs with you?"

"He wasn't with me. He walked Gina out, said he'd only go as far as the Malecon and be right back. He'd better not be hanging with her longer than that. Go look in the suite for him, and I'll get dressed."

She went out but soon came back in. Her slacks around her hips were darker blue where his towel had spread its dampness. "Nick, he's not here."

"Let's go down to the pool to see if he's there," he said, not bothering to tuck in his shirttail. "Right now."

But Heck wasn't at the pool. The others hadn't seen him.

"I really don't think he'd just go off with her," Claire said.

Jace, who was with them now, said only, "Guys in love have done stranger things. But—once again—can we trust her? He would be easy to interrogate with his Spanish—and his ties to the old regime."

"Don't even think that," Nick muttered. "Let's look in the café bar. Maybe he or both of them ducked in there, couldn't say goodbye to each other even for a few hours. I should have done a better job reading him the riot act about her, but he's always been so loyal and levelheaded."

Claire watched the lobby from the door while the two men

walked around inside. She overheard a woman with a British accent say, "I heard this bar used to be terribly chic years ago. Look at the pictures on the wall of Sinatra, Errol Flynn, Clark Gable and—oh, what's her name, over there, she married Sinatra. Oh, that's right, Ava Gardner. And I heard it was here Sinatra was spotted with gangsters and that shot his reputation."

"Indeed," her male companion said. "At least it was only his rep that was shot, since some of the blokes who had monetary interest in this place got shot by Fidel and Che's firing squads."

Despite the warmth in here and the strangely comforting smells of cigars, coffee and coconut pastries on a tray near her, Claire shuddered. The statue of Venus in the corner past the bar reminded her of that statue—and her own face—in the cemetery staring at her. She felt slightly nauseous. And where was Heck?

Since Claire felt a little queasy, Nick walked her up to the room. Jace was sitting in the lobby, waiting for Heck, and Nick planned to go down to join him. "It's terrible not to have cell phones on us," Claire said as she lay down.

"Yeah. I've seen people with them but they use them like pagers, and Gina said you can't risk any sort of questionable conversation on them anyway. You just lie here, and I'll go down and tell Nita to bring Lexi—and Lily—back up here."

"Don't even kid about Lily. Nick, I'm worried about Lexi. She's deeply disturbed. Aren't we all, but she doesn't have the resources to handle it."

"Kids are resilient. Once we get out of here she—all of us— will be fine."

He kissed her cheek and went out. She heard him lock the hall door. So here she was in a top-floor luxury suite in the best hotel in Havana and all she wanted was to be in some nice little house, safe in Naples with Nick and Lexi. But there were sharks between here and there—sharks here too.

She put her hands gently on her flat, upset stomach. Could

there be a child growing there? She could never love another one as much as she loved Lexi—but, of course, she could, especially Nick's baby. Besides, this might still just be upheaval and nerves and her powerful meds and...

Exhausted, she drifted on the sea for a while, but she sat straight up when she heard the woman's distraught voice.

"Mrs. Claire? Mr. Nick said you're here. Where are you?"

Nita! Nita must be back with Lexi.

"Here! In here!"

Claire got to her feet, feeling slightly dizzy. There was something wrong. Nita sounded panicked, and she never raised her voice. Was Lexi hurt in the pool?

She rushed into the living room. She saw only Nita with tears streaming down her face.

"Where is she? Where is she?"

"She being naughty. When we step out of the elevator, she run back in and press the button, saying Lily did it. I try to stop the door, but it close. I hit the button, but the elevator leaving. I watch the numbers. She go down, maybe to second floor, maybe lobby. I wait for that same elevator to come back, and she not there, she not there!"

CHAPTER SEVEN

"We're a pair," Nick told Jace as they watched for Heck by scanning the faces of people coming toward the hotel. "Two guys whose past careers and current lives depend on keeping cool, calm and collected, and we're both a wreck. Getting out of Cuba's starting to vie for first priority with getting rid of just one man, one bastard wreaking havoc on all our lives, and I don't mean you-know-who, as Gina always says. Not Castro but Ames."

"And Gina's you-know-who might be harboring Ames, because he's probably in cahoots with the Castro brothers for something. At least he's wanted by the FBI now, a little fact that might save us all and nail him. Man, I hope you're contacted soon by Patterson. But you don't think your friend Heck could have run off with a woman he just met, do you? I mean, I gotta admit I practically eloped with our-lady-in-common, but—"

"Claire is not 'in common,'" Nick interrupted, which really annoyed Jace since he was trying to be supportive. Even though he'd been flying the plane that went down, all of this major mess went back to Nick Markwood. And here Nick was running—

ruining—Claire's and Lexi's lives too. Jace tried to control his anger, but he had to say something.

"Look, Nick, you and Claire got together pretty fast too. But back to the latest problem. The way Heck stared at that ruined hotel and that private Russian firm sitting there in his family's beautiful hacienda, who knows, he might want to stay here. And cozying up to Ames—turning on us—could make that come true."

"I know him, trust him. Something's wrong. I'm going to the computer room to see if a reply came back yet. Then I'm—not sure what. We can hardly go to the Havana police to report him missing. Be right back. And if you change positions, let our bodyguard Bronco know. He's still over by the line of taxis, watching for Heck from there."

Jace checked that Bronco was still there and gave him the high sign to stay put. Taxis here meant mostly cars that looked like they drove out of a 1940s or 1950s movie, so it was a real vintage auto parade in front of the hotel. Jace saw a lavender Ford with huge back fins, big Chevrolets, even some Cadillacs, all shined up, some with parts that didn't belong to them, that somebody had probably bought in a back alley shop. He noted an occasional square, black Lada, the Russian-made car they'd seen at Heck's family's hacienda. And cars that Gina had pointed out, government-owned ones with the distinctive blue license plates, some cruising by, some parked.

Jace edged around the corner of the building where he could see the Nacional's outdoor hotel patio overlooking the sea. Businessmen and a few couples were having lunch, silhouetted by the harbor and the sparkling water. So deceptively beautiful, so luring, this seemingly benign place. He watched some daredevil boys cannonballing off the seawall of the Malecon, barely missing the jagged rocks to splash into the water. That was more like the daredevil mess they were in, he thought. To get back over the water they had a lot of dangerous snags to avoid.

He heard someone call, "Seth!" and turned. He wasn't yet used to hearing that instead of "Jace." It was Lexi's nanny they were now calling Lorena, looking terrified, in tears.

"Where's Mr. Jack?" she demanded. Before he could answer, she went on. "Meggie is missing. She trick me, went down somewhere in an elevator. We have to look for her!"

Suddenly, he felt like he'd jumped and hit the rocks.

Nick was disappointed there was no answer to his email yet. Wasn't the FBI more efficient than that? It had been—he checked his watch—nearly an hour, but maybe Patterson had to lay plans before sending them instructions. If word came they should go somewhere and Heck wasn't back, what then?

He decided he'd go up to be with Claire, see how she was feeling since Jace and Bronco were still on watch at the front entry. If only they had a way to contact Gina. She had to be with Heck, hopefully helping with whatever he'd got into. This was so not like him. If he couldn't trust Heck anymore, what could he do with him when they got to Michigan—if they got to Michigan?

Nick was waiting by the bank of main elevators when one opened and Claire ran out. She gasped to see him, seized his arm in a tight grip and pulled him away into a dead end of the hall behind a cluster of potted palms.

"What's wrong?"

"Lexi ditched Nita by ducking back into an elevator. I've been riding them while Nita looks outside."

"Damn! Heck's still MIA too."

"Maybe she found him and he— No, he'd bring her right back to us. I'm going crazy. What if someone bad sees her, takes her? Why haven't the hotel people found her? I had to risk telling them she'd gone off on her own. I keep checking in the room."

"Have you looked out by the pool?" he asked.

"Yes. Nita did too. Where are Jace and Bronco?"

"Out watching the crowd for Heck and/or Gina. Where

haven't you looked? Is there someplace here she'd go to, wanting to feel safe? Lily may do bad things, but not your girl."

"I—I don't know. I feel like I've lost her in more ways than one, and that terrifies me. Maybe—maybe the store where we bought the bathing suit for her. She liked those stuffed animals in there, and I wouldn't let her have one to lug around and I knew she'd never leave it when we leave here."

"Let's go check that out. Did you tell the lifeguards at the pool in case she goes back there?"

"Yes," Claire said, her voice breaking, her hands gripped together as if in prayer. "That's when I really lost it, started to cry—when he said he keeps a watch on the kids, because they found one last month drowned at the bottom of that big pool."

Claire spotted Lexi the moment she and Nick walked into the beachwear and gift shop. She was so grateful, so relieved, she burst into tears again. Her knees went so weak she almost fell. Standing in the corner, the child had a bright green stuffed toy whale clutched in her arms. But she looked like she wasn't embracing it but strangling it.

"Meggie," Claire cried and knelt beside her. She threw her arms around the child and the whale. Nick squatted beside them and propped Claire up.

"Whales are bigger than sharks," Lexi whispered. "Big enough to kill those sharks we saw, big enough to ride out of here. I want to go home."

"We will," Nick promised. "We will. Sorry," he said when a saleswoman hurried up to them. "She wanted that, and we told her no, but we'll take it."

"I thought she with other people here. You want put it on your room bill?"

"Ah, yes, that would be fine. No, on second thought I'll just pay cash for it."

Claire lifted Lexi and the whale and headed out into the hall.

She overheard the saleswoman telling Nick the price and saw him take what must be his last small American bill out of his pants pocket.

"Lexi," Claire told her as she carried her over to a wicker bench and sat down beside her, "don't you ever do that to Nita or me again! And don't tell me Lily did it. Everyone's been looking for you!"

"But, Mommy, I didn't even know where I was. Where are we? Why can't we be home?"

"Oh, my sweetheart, I'm so sorry about everything. But we're together. We love you, all of us. We're a little family now, but—I guess I'll have to explain things better."

When Nick came out of the shop, Claire stood and hiked Lexi up as if she was a much younger child with her legs around Claire's waist and Claire's arms under the girl's bottom. That stupid stuffed animal was still in the way, but nothing else mattered now that Lexi was safe, but—actually, it did. Everything mattered to get them out of here.

Nick looked both relieved and desperate. "I'll tell them at the desk she's been found," he said, "but I've got to check my email too." He took Claire's elbow and steered her farther away from the shop. "Sit in the lobby. Don't budge. I want to be able to see both of you."

Claire sat with Lexi on her lap on a leather sofa and kept an eye on Nick too as he went into the adjacent room where she could see little cubicles sheltering laptops. Jace must be frantic over Lexi too, all of them. She needed to tell Nita and him their daughter had been found. She needed a tissue to wipe her eyes and blow her nose. She needed Nick to hold her. Most of all, maybe more like her daughter than she cared to admit, she needed her sense of safety and sanity back.

Nick's stomach was in free fall when he gave his card to the guy in charge, then sat at a different laptop from the one he'd used a little bit ago. He typed in his code, and an email appeared on the screen. Bingo! It was from the fake Chicago firm!

Jack Randal: sorry your investment gamble went in the tank, but we can reinvest. I promise we can "git mo," to use an old saying around here about getting you more money with interest. Can you handle that ASAP? Let me know if you're on board with my advice. Investment adviser Robert Patmore.

Gitmo. Guantanamo! That had to be what he meant. Get to Gitmo and the officers there could spirit them out, help them get home—that was, to their WITSEC hideout in Michigan. But the thing was, Guantanamo Bay with its naval detention camp was way on the southeastern end of the island, a long trip away. And Patterson had signed the note with a fake name, but one that echoed his own.

Nick typed a message back: Sounds like good financial advice. ASAP, will do, with all my investments. I realize this could take some time.

He sent the message, then erased Rob's, wishing he could erase the dangers between here and Gitmo—and without Heck, if he didn't get back here soon.

Lexi's little family reunion in their hotel room wasn't pretty, Nick thought. Lexi insisted it was all Lily's fault and that the stuffed whale was named Shark-Killer. Nita kept saying it was her fault, and Bronco kept saying it wasn't, when a loud knock sounded on the hall door.

Everyone quieted and froze. Nick went over to the door and, pressed to the wall on either side of him, Bronco and Jace waited. "Who's there?"

"It's us," Heck cried. "Open up, boss."

Still, Nick looked through the spyhole on the door. "He's with Gina."

Nick swung the door wide and yanked Heck, then Gina, into the room. He stuck his head out to look up and down the hall, then closed the door and locked it.

Jace began, "Berto, where the hell have you b—"

"I know it took me longer than I planned, but I know where your father's former friend that cheated him out of some money is here in Havana." Heck raised his hands as if to ward off an attack. "We got his address, me and Gina, and we walked there, not far from my family's old hacienda. A guard told us to get away, so we did. It was my idea, but she helped. I had to tell her a few things about him. How he hurt your father—financially, I mean."

"You found him—how?" Nick demanded. "Are you sure it wasn't a trap—a setup?"

"It was something Meggie said, how he had those rare fish. Gina and I passed a tropical fish store on the edge of El Vedado. So I said let's go in, and we made like we wanted to buy some of their pricey stuff. Asked who cleaned tanks in a home visit if we wanted it, all of that. Then I left, and Gina turned it on with the guy, one that cleans the tanks, and he boasted about some American bigwig has an office here in a hacienda. So we walked where he said, looked at the place. It's offices but Ames must live there. Big. Fancy. Not far from my family's old place."

Astounded, taking that all in, Nick said nothing at first. Ames was here. And Heck knew where. He'd used a partial cover story with Gina so she evidently wouldn't panic at all the gory details. Finally, he asked Heck, "And are you sure no one followed you back?"

Heck and Gina exchanged quick glances. "No one," he said, "but we spotted a drone. Maybe it was filming the hotel, but maybe not. Couldn't see who was running it, but someone down on the Malecon, I bet. Funny, but it's still hovering outside over the front entrance. If we were on the other side of the building, you could see it. We—"

Nick interrupted. "I don't like the sound of that. Maybe he was looking for us just like we were for him or maybe that guard that ordered you away had you followed. Gina, I see Berto hasn't clued you in on everything, but we needed to keep secret that we—I—have an enemy here who was my father's enemy years ago and maybe caused his death. That guy Seth mentioned at the Key West airport who could have tampered with the plane could have been working for that man. Somehow he learned we survived the crash, landed here—I don't know. Over the years, I've learned to put nothing past him. We've got to go—now."

Claire said, "Jack's right. He's spied on us with a drone before. But we can't just run out the front, then."

"Down the back inside fire-escape stairs and out the back service entry," Nick ordered. "Grab things fast. We have to go now!"

Nita started to cry again, but Nick was amazed at how solid Claire suddenly seemed. She handed Lexi and the whale to Jace and seized her purse with her meds. They had so little, it didn't take long to get ready. They streamed out the door, and Nick practically shoved them down the hall toward a sign that read SALIDA/EXIT. Because Jace had Lexi, he pushed him ahead, let them all pass, then locked and closed their hotel door and raced after them. They didn't get even one night in this place with the inviting beds, he thought.

"And don't make noise on the stairs! Wait for me at the bottom!" he called after Bronco, and the big man nodded as they headed through the emergency exit.

Nick was barely to the stairs where Heck was holding the heavy door for him. "Sorry, boss. Wanted to help. The drone—I didn't know he'd be looking for us here too."

"You did help if we can tell our friends where Ames is. We needed to run anyway. I've been given a plan. Go, go!"

Nick saw he had been right. As the heavy door started to close slowly behind him, he saw two men dressed in suits and ties down the hall burst from the elevator and draw guns. They must have inquired at the desk. What else did they know? Nick watched them for one split second through the hazy glass window in the door. Heck tugged at his arm and hissed, "Boss, come on!"

And then Nick saw what scared him as much as Ames's men. One man produced something from his pocket that opened the door just as the other elevator door slid open to reveal four men who looked like Cuban police.

CHAPTER EIGHT

Heck and Nick rushed down the stairs as quietly as they could. The others were below them, whispering, but it echoed in the stairwell.

"I'd like to fire you for being followed back here, but you've just made a promotion," Nick told Heck. "Keep going. We've got to get out a back door somehow. Heck, I have to know. You sure you trust Gina?"

"With my life."

"Well, maybe," Nick whispered as they heard a door above them in the stairwell slam open with a bang, "you've risked exactly that. Run."

Claire heard a bang, then heavy, fast footsteps above as Heck and Nick joined the rest of them in the ground-floor stairwell.

"Out. Out!" Nick told them. "Not the lobby. We need to get out back."

Here! Jace mouthed. Despite the fact he held Lexi in an iron grip, he shoved one of two doors inward. It opened on a plain back hall with a concrete floor. Claire glimpsed mops leaning against the wall, a barrel, a ladder. Jace thrust Lexi into

Claire's arms and pointed. He whispered, "Go!" and, clutching her daughter to her, she ran.

She saw Jace drop behind the others to jam a ladder against the door, but it wouldn't last long. Would any of them?

They emerged through a back entrance with a delivery bay but no trucks in it now. Looking up for the drone, they darted under a line of trees and ran the only way they could. Nick took Lexi from her, thank heavens. Claire felt dizzy, nauseous. She needed a pill, but not now...

"Palm trees—not much cover," Gina said, panting as hard as the rest of them.

Nick said, "Stick close to the building. Nothing overhead so far, but we have to get out of this alley before those goons with guns find us."

"Gina," Heck said, "I didn't mean to get you in all this. You want to go, go, in case they catch us."

"I'm with you. No going back."

As they sprinted around the corner and then slowed so they wouldn't draw attention, those last words echoed in Claire's mind. *No going back.* "We need to mingle with the crowds on the Malecon, get lost," Jace said. "Split up into small groups but keep in sight of each other. Stroll, not run. Maybe we can get a couple taxis."

"How about we go back to my parents?" Gina asked. "I would want to say goodbye if I can escape with you. Please, let me go too. My father could help with his boat, but we cannot put them in danger."

"We have another contact that may help us," Nick said. "Someone on our side."

Claire thought he still didn't trust Gina. But could they trust anyone on this island, except Gina's parents? Well, surely the marines at distant Guantanamo miles and hours away. And Gina's home was in the opposite direction.

★ ★ ★

Jace tried not to keep looking back. Anyway, once they blended in with the strolling crowd, he felt calmer. As they slowed their pace, he tried to catch his breath. But his heartbeat kicked up again when three police cars screamed past, heading for the hotel. At least the guys dressed in business suits with guns Nick said he'd spotted were nowhere to be seen.

They stopped under a thick fica tree with the seawall and crashing water on the rocks behind them.

Jace said, "Don't we need to cross the street to get taxis heading east?"

"East?" Gina said. "Costa Blanca is west."

"We're going to trust Gina to keep our secret and her father to help us," Nick announced. He was holding Lexi and her green whale again. Claire had seen Jace reach for the girl, but Nick had hung on to her.

Jace asked, "You mean hire him to get us where we want to go?"

"That's what I'm thinking. But, Gina, will he balk taking us to a rendezvous spot, if it means maybe losing you?"

"Rendezvous with who? Another boat? I can ask him, beg him, tell him it's my chance, but my mother… After losing Alfredito… I will not tell my mother and will only tell him at the last minute. We could take the bus again."

"No," Nick said, "we could be trapped in a net that way, if they set up a roadblock or come on board. Let's move on down farther into the crowd, line up for two taxis. Change I got for Meggie's whale, even if it's in *pesetas*, should get us a good ride. Let's go before they search the crowd."

Jace got them one taxi—a two-tone Ford Fairlane Skyliner, it was called. How he wished it was a flying skyliner and he was at the controls, getting them all out of here. The one Heck hailed was an old Cadillac Fleetwood.

Nick, Claire, Jace and Lexi piled in the Ford with Nita to translate while Bronco, Heck and Gina took the Cadillac. Heck had the money for their taxi. "He say he can go only far as Costa Blanca, so he gets back near dark," Nita translated what the cabbie said to her.

"Tell him that will do," Nick said.

But as they pulled away, and the engine seemed to cough, Jace wasn't so sure. And he really got shook when he saw two Cuban policemen emerge from the crowd they'd just left and point after them.

"We'd better change taxis," he told Nick. "The boys back there may have spotted us."

"Let's get a ways out, off the main drag. Lorena, ask him if he can pull off in a block or two and signal so the taxi behind us does too."

She asked, then translated back. "He have to charge you more, half of what you promise him."

"Tell him to do it. And I'm giving him a tip with a tip. If he's stopped, not to say where he heard we were going."

"Tell him," Lexi spoke up, though Jace had been grateful she'd kept quiet so far, "this is a whale, but sharks are after us, ever since the water."

"Meggie, not now," Claire said to their girl and hugged her, but it wasn't enough to shut the child up.

"If he doesn't listen to me, Lily will do something really scary."

Claire put two fingers over Lexi's lips as their cab blinked its lights and pulled off into a side street with the other right behind it.

Nick knew this plan changing taxis he'd hatched so suddenly was a big gamble, but he was afraid to flee straight for Guantanamo. Basically, there was just one main road along the coast that went both east and west. It was possible that the Cuban government had intercepted and decoded the emails and knew they'd be headed toward Gitmo. Or had Ames's people followed Heck and Gina because they looked suspicious outside Ames's Havana hacienda—and they'd called the police? Those guys in business suits with guns loose in a huge hotel—pure amoral Ames.

But could they make it to Gina's house in these two different taxis? His neck was about to break from craning around to watch behind them all the time, and he saw Heck doing the same in the taxi following. If the police located their original taxis, what would the drivers tell them?

But they had no choice, he agonized silently, trying to keep calm. Hitchhiking like they'd seen people do here was ridiculous. Risking the bus? Walking forty miles to Costa Blanca— impossible. The thing was, even if they got back to Nando and Carlita's house, would that old fishing boat get them clear to the other end of the island? Was it his imagination or were those dark clouds ahead and not just the sharp shadows of sunset?

By the time they reached Costa Blanca and got out of their taxis to walk the rest of the way to Gina's house, Claire saw the sun had disappeared in a blinding burst of crimson and gold that was soon devoured by storm clouds on the horizon. Since Gina had decided not to tell her mother she was leaving and to only tell her father just before he got them as far east as he could, she'd been scribbling them a note to explain, to promise she'd be back, that she'd send them money and love them always.

The distraught woman had used her backpack for a make-shift desk on her knees. Jace sat in front beside the driver, and Gina was wedged in next to Claire in the backseat with Lexi in the middle asleep and Nick on the far side. More than once, in tears, though she was writing in Spanish, Gina had whispered to Claire what she was telling her parents.

Strange, but Claire was coming to trust her now like Heck did and Nick still didn't. So far, Gina didn't know their destination was the place her country hated, American-held Guantanamo. And Gina wasn't the only one in tears. Claire was too, and her well-honed forensic psychologist instincts—and her woman's intuition—told her they could trust Gina.

Since they apparently had not been followed, they thought they were momentarily safe in Costa Blanca. Yet rather than burst in on Gina's parents and risk getting caught there, they hiked to Gina's house outside town and sent Gina and Heck in while they waited outside in the windy darkness. Claire carried the whale now while Nick and Jace took turns holding the sleeping Lexi. If only, Claire thought, as she took her narcolepsy pill in the dark with a swig from Nita's water bottle, Lexi's dad and stepdad could learn to share the child like that.

They heard footsteps in the darkness. Then Gina, Heck and Nando rounded the corner where they waited, huddled like the refugees they were.

"He will help you," Gina told them, "but it have to be at dawn he picks you up in *Alfredito* because of the rocks. Berto and I take you to the spot you waited before. *Mamacita*, she say you already pay for much gasoline, a fortune she found in her little jar."

Claire blinked back more tears. Fifty dollars was a fortune? She knew Nick would insist on paying more, and he only had big bills left.

Nick said, "Berto and Gina, does Nando understand we need to go clear to the other end of the island?"

Heck translated for the old man, then explained, "He swear on his son's soul he get you close as he can. He say there nice little beaches along there to put in. I think he guess where you going but did not say so. He does it for Gina since I told him I come back for her someday."

Nando nodded through all that, so Claire wondered if he knew what was being said. He might have guessed where they were going, but he'd hardly figured out that his last remaining child intended to go with them.

Claire wiped her tears on the stuffed whale, remembering the last time she'd seen her mother, her father too, though they'd lost him far earlier. She was so exhausted she was losing control. What if she regressed, had a narcoleptic nightmare or, worse, had her muscles lock so she couldn't move, couldn't keep up? Would they carry her too?

"Come on," Gina said, patting Lexi's lolling head as she slept, then pecking a kiss on her father's cheek. "I have a lantern, and I'll lead the way, stay with you the night while Papa goes back in. The breeze is picking up, but we will pray it doesn't rain on us, yes? Berto has a piece of plastic we can get under, extra one from the fishing boat. Come on, then, and we all get away. Berto says he cannot tell me where we meet that other ship, but we will find it tomorrow."

Claire thought Gina must know too, unless she thought that some boat or pontoon plane would meet them offshore. After all, they were headed for an American navy base in hostile territory, crawling with marines. Worse, Gina had no clue she was leaving her homeland with people who were not who they said they were. She'd be stuck on a snowbound island in Northern Michigan for much of a brutal winter. But Gina had cast her lot with them, with Heck, and they owed her for her help. Together, they were safe so far.

As they started off down the dark road, following Gina, Claire held hard to the stuffed whale as if it was her lifeline instead of Lexi's. Jace carried the child, and Nick steadied Claire with a strong hand on her upper arm. She knew she'd messed up the timing on her meds, which needed to be taken regularly. Was any of this even real? How she wished it was all some dreadful nightmare and she'd wake up next to Nick in Naples. But dangers had lurked there too, thanks to their other murder/suicide investigations—and thanks to that monster, Clayton Ames, who still haunted them here.

She fought to keep her balance as they went single file down the twisting path toward the now-familiar stretch of beach. Along the shore, the waves were whispering a warning, hissing at her. Dizzy, light-headed and scared, she thought for a moment she was plunging into the ocean again, bouncing, as their plane belly-landed and sank. She was in the rocking lifeboat. She was being followed by men with guns and by a stone woman who held a dead baby in her arms and stared at her—and that woman was her!

Was she looking in a marble mirror? She saw a woman there who loved two men. And most frightening of all, as her feet slipped in the shoreside sand, she knew she had not only her child with her but was growing one inside her too.

CHAPTER NINE

Claire and Nita huddled next to Lexi under the plastic tarp while the four men took turns keeping watch. The wind had picked up, and Claire prayed it wouldn't keep Nando and that old fishing boat from reaching them. But in the windy, drizzling dawn, the *Alfredito* appeared, and they waded out.

He'd brought them bread, rice and beans and guava juice, but it was pretty rocky to eat. Lexi nibbled at the bread, and Claire forced herself to drink the guava juice and chew on some of the crusty loaf. She felt she was eating for two now but still wondered when to tell Nick. Did they even have good prenatal care on Mackinac Island, if they ever got there?

She could not fathom having a baby here in Cuba, especially not if they were caught or imprisoned. Gina had mentioned to Nick that government critics used to get prison terms of thirty years. Rob Patterson had told him that, even if they were exposed in Michigan, he'd have to deny he knew them, to say that they had run and hidden on their own. So if they were captured here, whatever would become of them?

At least they were traveling with the wind, not against it. Claire saw Gina hung tight with her father. Maybe these were her last hours with him. Like them, she'd brought next to nothing with her, only a backpack full of medical textbooks, probably dated ones and in Spanish. Claire not only trusted Gina now, but admired her too.

Nando kept up a running commentary on towns ashore as well as spots to catch certain types of fish. They passed Havana Harbor midmorning, when he offered everyone food again. Lexi took nothing this time and stayed under the plastic on the deck in a fetal position curled around the wet stuffed whale. Claire tried to comfort her, but at least Lily wasn't making an appearance now. She vowed silently to work on counseling her to put Lily permanently to rest.

Late afternoon, Nando pointed at the horizon. They looked and saw black smoke rising. Gina said, "Burning the sugarcane fields to harvest it faster. It doesn't hurt the crop and helps the workers get rid of all the extra trash and just leaves the canes."

Claire could see Gina was increasingly nervous. It wasn't just the hovering storm clouds, nor the fact her father had said he'd brought an anchor and would spend the night in a shallow bay before heading home at dawn again. The time was coming for Gina to tell him she wasn't going back. Would he let the rest of them out safely then?

Nita chatted with Nando while Heck took Gina aft and explained where they were really headed. Nick had also given Heck permission to explain their real story and the need for their false names. Claire saw that Gina nodded, though she frowned through it all and looked distraught. So would she still want to go with them?

Claire's stomach knotted even tighter. Heck was steadying Gina with his arm around her shaking shoulders. Claire got to her feet on the rocking boat and walked unsteadily toward them.

"Gina," she said, taking her hands in her own, "I just want you to know we owe you our lives. I've had to make some desperate decisions too, take a step into a storm when I wasn't sure what was coming. I had to decide to cast my lot with the man I loved. Can I or anyone, besides Heck here, who obviously loved you at first sight, do anything to help? Can we help you tell your father? I know you're worried about Carlita, but I promise you, whether Cuba opens up to America in the future or not, my husband and I will be your friends as well as this man whom you first knew as Berto."

To Claire's surprise, Gina hugged her. She sniffed back her tears and squared her shoulders. She nodded and stepped away to speak to her father, gesturing broadly, pointing, giving him the note from her backpack. Heck waited next to Claire, while everyone else watched furtively and silently. Nando shook his head and sounded angry but he turned *Alfredito* toward a small cove, just as—a good omen?—the sun came out.

With tears streaming down his brown, weathered cheeks, Nando idled the engine in the cove. Too much pain and loss lately, Claire thought. But what bravery, and she had to show that too.

Each of them hugged Nando as Jace and Bronco climbed over the side first to test the depth of the water, then helped the others down, all but Gina. Nick had left two hundred-dollar bills in the plastic carrier with the food. Heck finally climbed down but stayed where he was in the chest-deep water by the prow, holding Gina's backpack above his head, while the rest of them slogged to shore. Nita lifted Lexi's whale, and Claire held her purse above her head, to keep her meds dry.

On the narrow strip of white sand, they held their breath to see what Nando and Gina would do.

Still in the boat, she gestured, talked, cried. Nando shook his head and yelled. They thought he might keep her on board, just put out, but Gina hugged him, holding hard. For one moment again, it looked as if Nando would turn the boat away, but they saw him kiss her forehead, cross himself and shout something over the side to Heck as Gina ran to the rail and scrambled down the netting.

Nando was still yelling at Heck, who yelled back as he and Gina waded toward shore. Nick went out to help them, taking the backpack from Heck, trying to steady Gina with a hand on her arm while Heck had his arm around her waist.

"He's not going to just stay there or report us, is he?" Nick asked. "What did he say?"

"He said he have my head and haunt me forever if I not take good care of her, marry her. And if Cuba and the US make a deal in the future, I swear to him by the Holy Virgin I bring her back to visit."

Claire broke into tears again as Nando finally gunned his feeble motor and moved slowly away, not looking back. Yet they all stood there waving as if he'd just dropped them off at the safest, sweetest vacation spot in the world.

"Let's see if we can get there," Nick said. "According to Gina, Guantanamo can't be but a few miles beyond this point."

"You knew?" Jace asked her.

She nodded. "I think my father—he knew too where you are going." She shoved her wild hair back from her face and asked, "But aren't we waiting for a boat or a helicopter to come and look for us?"

"We've got a little hike ahead," Nick said, speaking to all of them now.

His arms crossed over his chest, Bronco frowned at the area where they stood as if the Cuban police or Ames's men would appear again. Nita reached for his hand, and Lexi finally spoke. "Lily is really hungry and tired, and she still wants to go home."

"So let's do that. Listen up, everyone," Nick said, jamming onto his face the sunglasses Gina had bargained for on the bus, which now seemed to Claire like an eternity ago. "We are going to the US but we have to get to the American base at Guantanamo Bay first. As far as Jace and I can tell, we have maybe an hour or so walk to freedom. And we need to do it before the sun sets."

"Sounds good to me," Bronco said with a shrug and the first

smile Claire had seen from him here. "I lost one of my shoes in the water, but I don't care. Let's go 'fore it gets dark or rains again or someone spots us. We get close to the town, we can blend in til we reach the base."

"A man after my own heart," Jace put in. "Let's just hope there's a path swimmers have cut up to the road, because the brush looks pretty thick right here. Onward and upward, right, bro?" he added, addressing his supposed brother, Jack Randal.

Claire gave Gina a quick hug, but the young woman was trembling and clung to her, getting her wetter than she was. Nita patted Gina's back and said in English, "And we be like sisters to you."

Single file, their ragtag group, now increased by one, headed for the upward path.

They could see the low-level sprawl of Guantanamo City in the distance, but the road they took toward it was lined on its landward side with a massive sugarcane field. Claire marveled that some of the cane was ten feet tall, green and waving in the breeze, ripe to harvest. More than once, they saw workers with machetes along the way and horse-drawn wagons loaded with newly cut stalks. The storm had cleared, but they smelled smoke from the cane fires, all in the distance, but nearly blocking out the sinking sun.

They were hopeful as they trekked westward toward Guantanamo City, which surrounded the navy base, on one side of the beautiful bay. Claire sensed Jace got really excited when a big-bellied US naval plane flew over. But their high hopes came to a screaming stop when they saw a problem about a half mile up ahead.

"Is that what I think it is?" Claire asked. "Wish we had binoculars. And isn't there a second roadblock beyond that? That farthest one looks like it might be near the base—I mean, isn't that one of those tall watchtowers? If that first blockade's for us, we're doomed. Despite drifting smoke, I can make out blue license plates on those cars."

"What does *doomed* mean, Mommy?"

Everyone ignored her. Gina said, "Looks like police officers' cars to me."

They edged over farther toward the sugarcane field. Shading his eyes and squinting, Jace said, "It looks like police—and isn't one of those guys up there in a suit?"

They heard a shrill whistle and some of the men in the cluster started toward them.

"We're going to have to duck and run," Nick said. "We can cut into the field, around that first roadblock to the one near the base. Once in, turn right. And don't get lost in there. Stay close together, but go way back in!"

Jace grabbed Lexi and ran with her clasped in front of him. Claire came next, holding the whale. She could feel and hear things in her purse bouncing. Nick followed her. The others were several rows to the west, running abreast through the rows of cane. Claire had once gone through a north Florida corn maze with friends, but this was different, a dark, tall, endless tunnel. And the soil was spongy from recent rain, slowing them down. The shifting, dry stalks and sharp-bladed leaves snatched at them, and their tops of waving tassels whipped back and forth in the wind. At least these rows were wider set than in a cornfield, so they could run without bouncing into stalks to give away their position.

But she could hear their pursuers behind them, running, calling to each other, shouting for them in accented English to "Stop! Stop or else!" More bad news. They must know they were chasing Americans. When Lexi's feet dragged into the canes, the clacking sound made Claire think of distant machine gun fire.

Then it seemed that the voices were muting. "Maybe they're dropping back," Nick said, out of breath. "We're far enough in to cut toward the base. Keep close, everybody. Go!"

He took Lexi from Jace, and they started off again. "Miles,

acres of this stuff!" Claire muttered. Like all of them, she was sweating and out of breath. Only Lexi seemed calm, but she was grateful for that. All they needed was for Lily to be yelling out something to give away their position.

But the running was harder now, and not only from wet soil. The cane grew thicker in this direction, making it almost impossible as they tried to cut through the cane sideways, not down the rows. "It hurts!" she heard Lexi say. "Can't we shoot the bad guys or just hide?"

"Let's go deeper in," Nick said. "Bronco and Heck, you hear me?" he got out.

"Lily doesn't like to run!" Lexi put in.

Claire told her, "Hush. If those men find us they will take away Shark-Killer, so you have to be quiet."

"But others are talking!"

They went deeper into the massive field again. It was like being lost in a forest, plunging through the cavernous rows of trees. They heard a shout behind them. Someone close? Had someone spotted them?

"Over here, officers!" a very American voice shouted. "We got them now! The man will have our heads if we don't get them! They have to be stopped this time!"

For sure that meant Ames's men were here. Claire saw Nick looked livid.

Lexi said, "They are bad men. And, Mommy, what's that smell, like those icky cigars?"

Claire gasped, and she heard Bronco swear under his breath in the next row of cane. The breeze had not been in their faces, but they heard a crackling like popcorn. The sun wasn't out, but the heat got more intense as the wind changed direction.

Gina whispered, "They are burning this field ahead of us, from near the base. *Madre de Dios*, we're trapped between those men and the flames!"

CHAPTER TEN

Not only the crackle and roar of the flames grew louder but some other noise did too. Claire craned her neck to look up. A drone with a camera buzzed overhead and turned back to hover above them, coming lower, lower. No wonder their pursuers had located them in this thick maze.

She ripped her shoulder bag off her arm, grabbed her meds and wallet out in case she lost the purse. She slung it like a boomerang at the low-flying drone. The leather shoulder handle snagged the drone's rotors, and it went down several yards away into the cane.

"Way to go!" Jace blurted. "But we got to go. No time to find the purse."

"It's okay," she said, torn between pride and panic. "I've got my ID and meds, so—"

But as she bent to gather her pill case and wallet, she saw the case had come open. Her pills were strewed on and in the damp soil. She'd stepped on most of them. Without them, she'd be in such trouble.

She went to her knees and started to dig the pills out of the ground, but many had dissolved to wet powder. She clawed at two, three of them, her nails raking the damp soil until Nick hauled her to her feet.

"They're still coming," he whispered, looking more desperate than she'd ever seen him. He grabbed her wallet and jammed it in his front pocket. "Let's go!"

Jace took Lexi again. Nick, who'd been calming the others, snagged the green whale, smeared with mud. He dragged Claire so fast through the cane away from the devouring flames that her feet almost left the ground.

Men's voices, shouts. Suddenly, a towering wall of orange flames roared close behind them. Choking smoke. No choice, she thought. No choice but to die in the fire or run for the road and be taken, maybe shot, maybe kept here forever.

Before they even saw the opening ahead, they exploded from the far edge of the cane field. It was a strip of land with no plants and barbed wire and watchtowers just ahead. It was hilly ahead and blue-gray mountains huddled in the distance.

Their pursuers ran out just behind them, guns drawn. "Stop! Halt! *Alto! Alto!*" different men shouted. Shots rang out, exploding little dust balls near their feet while the flames reached the edge of the cane field, so the men came farther toward them.

Every instinct in Claire's body said to keep running, but there was that fence and barbed wire to keep them from the safety of the base. So close yet so far.

Her brain threw pictures at her of the day she was shot leaving the Collier County Courthouse, the day Nick helped her. In that instant, she felt the fear, the searing pain again. Cloaked in smoke, she stopped running with her back to the intense heat.

Bronco also stopped and turned. Gina skidded to a halt and put her hands atop her head. Jace stopped but didn't turn, no doubt to protect Lexi, cradled in his arms.

Nick turned to face their pursuers, yet he called out loudly enough to be heard in the watchtower behind them, "We're

Americans. We're here seeking asylum from the officers at this base so—"

Claire screamed as someone shot. Nick went down, clutching his left leg. Gunfire erupted over them from two directions as they hit the ground. Shots from the guard tower spit back at their pursuers.

Next to her in the damp dirt, Jace's body covered Lexi. They were not hit but Nick was.

"The marines in the tower are covering us!" Jace shouted at her. "Crawl up to the fence."

He had to be crazy, she thought. There was nowhere to go through the fence, and they'd be trapped against it. Coils of barbed wire topped it. But when he rolled Lexi over to her and belly-crawled backward, she did as he said, on her knees, covering and dragging Lexi.

Lexi was screaming, but Claire ignored that. She darted a glance back. Nita crawled close to help her with Lexi. Bronco rolled toward Nick too; Heck held Gina. Now Jace was dragging Nick, whose leg was leaving a trail of blood behind them.

Suddenly the fence made sense: at least ten marines ran out from somewhere on the other side of it, pointing rifles and handguns through it at their pursuers. When she looked back again, Jace had a belt around Nick's leg, and a green, camouflaged Humvee was roaring madly toward them on this side of the fence. Their pursuers had run along the burning edge of the field toward the road just outside the wire fence, dragging two of their injured with them. The marines didn't pursue them, but helped Nick.

At last, what had seemed an eternity of gunfire stopped, though the smoke and roar of heat and flames from the field was worse, an inferno.

Claire left Lexi in Nita's and Gina's care and bent over Nick.

"Just a leg wound," he told her through gritted teeth. His handsome face was distorted in pain. "We'll be all right now. The marines—and Jace—saved me."

Strong hands helped all of them up, then put Nick first in the big, boxy vehicle. "First stop, the hospital," someone said. Claire saw the others were covered with mud and smudges of smoke, so she must be too. But all of them—even Nick—were safe. And in American hands.

"Those weren't Cuban police, Sarge," she heard one marine say behind her when she climbed in behind Lexi. They had to watch their feet; the marines had put Nick flat on the floor. "Kind of looked like it, but fake outfits. And the guy giving orders was in civvies."

Jace, already in the Humvee, was still holding the belt tight around Nick's leg. "Thank you," she told Jace and gripped his shoulder, then leaned down to take Nick's hands in hers. He was trembling, and his eyes looked dilated.

Lexi squirmed out of Nita's arms and crowded in between Claire and Jace as if they were a family again.

Between clenched teeth, his eyes shut tight in pain, Nick told Jace, "Thanks, man."

Narrowing his eyes in a laser look at Claire, Jace mouthed to her, *I did it for you too.*

"Hey," Bronco said from the seat behind them, the big man's voice as shaky as a child's, "we're in US hands! We're going home—even if it's not quite home."

Claire looked out the vehicle's dusty big square window as they passed through the checkpoint to enter the base. It was getting dark. The marines were lowering the flag from the pole. How good it felt to see the Stars and Stripes instead of Cuba's single star. One palm tree and some scrub pine seemed to guard the entry to Gitmo. Still holding Nick's hands, leaning against Jace, she noted they passed a sign that read:

WELCOME TO US NAVAL STATION
GUANTANAMO BAY

★ ★ ★

That evening was a blur. Nick's leg was tended to at the base hospital, and he walked with crutches, but the bullet had passed through, so they didn't have to dig it out. He'd kidded Claire that he was now on narco meds too. And everyone, even the marines, had told Claire she did a helluva "who-ya!" job knocking that drone out of the sky.

They'd all had showers and been given clothes. Claire's jeans felt tight on her, which was weird since she thought she'd lost weight since the plane went down. Surely, if she was pregnant, she wouldn't be showing already.

Someone had given Nick a bobblehead doll of Fidel Castro, taped to one of his crutches. Gina kept covering the bearded figure with tissues so she didn't have to look at it. They were staying for the night in two apartments for married couples who would be arriving soon. The places were Spartan and smelled of paint. Despite the aura of tradition and tragedy that hung over the area, they were greatly relieved and thankful. And, though they were so exhausted they didn't feel like celebrating, they thought it would be good to take Lexi to the McDonald's on the base. Anything to get her back to feeling safe—and to get rid of her alter ego, Lily.

Lexi had been so thrilled to hear that that Claire wondered for one moment if heading to "Mickey D's" for a Happy Meal could solve the child's trauma. But they'd all been through hell. Their rescuers were nervous about Gina since she had no passport, until Rob Patterson, who had flown in to debrief them the next morning, said she could stay. Jace told Claire he imagined Patterson would give her a very thorough debriefing. What strings he pulled so fast in Washington to get her an entry visa for here and to the US they might never learn and didn't want to ask. He'd even promised her a green card.

Rob Patterson had turned down their offer to join them. Of course, Claire thought, they should have known better than to even ask. He didn't want to be seen in public with them even here, and the marines had snagged one of the bogus Cuban police they were questioning. Patterson had told Nick the guy had done it for money and knew nothing about who was behind it. Now Patterson was consulting with the base commander.

Claire breathed a sigh of relief and free air for the first time in days. They were in good hands and heading back to the US tomorrow, and Heck had Gina leaning against his shoulder. Bronco and Nita smiled at each other, and Lexi, hugging her war-torn plush whale that had been bathed and tended to with a blow-dryer, seemed content. Still, Jace looked—well, restless, staring at her.

Suddenly, although she'd dreaded it before, Claire was glad they'd hide out this winter in the snowy depths of another island far away. Patterson, who now knew Clayton Ames's Havana address, said he'd get his hands on him somehow, get him extradited and on trial so Nick could testify and they could return to their normal lives—whatever normal was since she'd met and married Nick Markwood.

Yes, she thought, as she dipped another french fry in the ketchup, that was the way it would be, calm and quiet in Northern Michigan where Ames could not find them, but he would be found and arrested here. Surely, nothing else could go wrong now.

CHAPTER ELEVEN

Two days later

The noise from the ferry engine heading for Mackinac Island was loud, but Nick would still hear every word Julia Collister, their WITSEC handler, said. Go figure, Nick thought, that the city they'd just left was spelled Mackinaw and the island was spelled Mackinac, but they were pronounced the same, without a final *c* sound. Maybe it was a foreign language, because their destination seemed foreign to him.

But he had trusted Julia instantly, partly because she'd taken care of so many things for them before they'd even met. The ferry was loaded with supplies she'd ordered to get them through the winter: clothing, food, even two snowmobiles. And a laptop in a box at Heck's feet that he seemed to be guarding with his life, though he was upset at the WITSEC restrictions about using it and the cell phones they would try to do without. Too many witnesses had contacted or called home only to be traced and killed.

It didn't bother Nick that the sea was rough today. Now that they'd escaped a plane crash and dangers in Cuba, he hoped it would be smooth sailing from here on. Again, at least for now, they had escaped Clayton Ames and told the FBI where they thought he was hiding.

Claire, alias Jenna on the next island too, whispered, "Isn't it nice not to have to worry about hidden listening devices and cameras? And, either because it's so late in the season or because it's the last ferry on a rough day, no passengers on here but us."

"Love it. Love you," Nick replied. "Julia seems to have taken care of all our needs so far."

"So far," Jace echoed in a low, singsong voice, which annoyed Nick. So, even when they whispered, someone was eavesdropping.

"*She*, at least, really seems in control," Claire added, obviously trying to head off more words between him and Jace. With her great forensic psychology radar, she'd no doubt picked up on Jace's body language, Nick thought. Jace had been riveted on Julia, all smiles when introduced to her or when she spoke to him.

Nick had tried to ignore that at first to keep peace and because he probably owed Jace his life. Ordinarily, he'd be glad to see him look longingly at someone besides Claire, but Julia was business not pleasure. It was kind of sad Jace was odd man out among the rest of them who had someone to care for, but WIT-SEC rules were rules. The stakes of a slipup were incredibly high.

Jace had turned back to watching Julia. Nick squeezed Claire's knee. Despite her asserting herself, she didn't look like she felt better than she had in Cuba, but he could hardly blame her for looking queasy on this rocking boat. The gray spray of waves hitting the surrounding bank of windows on this lower deck didn't help, but, even standing, ahead of where they sat on the wooden-backed benches, Julia looked sure-footed.

"Are we there yet?" Lexi asked the eternal kid's question from behind them where she sat on Nita's lap next to Bronco. That kind of broke the ice. Everyone laughed or smiled, especially when they saw Bronco holding the ragged stuffed animal.

Claire twisted around in her seat and whispered, "Let's hear what Julia wants to say. She has some important and interesting things to tell us."

"Okay, listen up, team," Julia told them with a serious look, as if to back Claire up. "I hope the rocking boat doesn't bother you."

"It's nothing after what we've been through lately," Jace assured her.

"Let me give you a little background about the island," Julia went on.

If she'd picked up on Jace's special interest, it hadn't seemed to faze her. She was probably in her late forties or early fifties, Nick figured, but she was in great shape and looked younger. Only worry lines on her forehead and around her mouth dated her at all. She was athletic-looking and really toned. Tanned too, like maybe she used a sunlamp. Her short, sleek hair was silver but even that didn't seem to age her. Rob Patterson had said she'd been an FBI agent stationed in Washington, DC, but she'd come back to her home last year to care for her ailing father so her daughter here wouldn't have that burden. It was a great setup too for Julia to help them, because her father, Hunter Logan, was their landlord.

"If you could see the outline of the island from here through these patches of fog, you'd see it's in the shape of a huge turtle," Julia explained, gesturing at the bank of windows.

Lexi piped up again. "I used to have a stuffed turtle, but it got lost. Now I just have Shark-Killer, and he's a whale."

"I see he's a whale," Julia said with a smile at Lexi. "Hopefully, no sharks or whales around here. Anyway, the Indian tribes long ago like the Hurons, Chippewas and Ottawas believed their high god they called Gitche Manitou lived on the island, so they used to bury their dead there. Our tourists we call 'fudgies,' because they buy our great fudge, don't realize this island was once a huge cemetery of hidden graves."

"Cheery, isn't she, boss?" Heck said from behind. "Once FBI, always FBI."

"What's FBI?" Lexi asked.

"Later, shh!" Nita said.

"But after the Indians, the French came next," Julia said in a confident voice that would have made her an excellent court-room expert witness, "then the British, then the Americans—and you know how that goes. War. There's a War of 1812–era fort you can visit with a statue of Father Marquette, who had earlier Christianized the Indians."

Lexi again, this time leaning forward and making an attempt to whisper in Claire's ear, "I like that statue that looked like you, Mommy, and that baby in your arms."

"Honey, please listen," Claire whispered. She didn't want to admit it, but the memory of that statue in the Havana cemetery of the woman who looked like her and the story of that dead baby haunted her. She'd even had a nightmare about it.

Julia went on, "I mention the history of the island because, in a way, we're still living it. No motor vehicles on the island, though we do have a fire engine and ambulance for emergencies. Mackinac is only a four-mile-by-two-mile-sized island, so we walk, ride bikes or horses—and even your supplies will be delivered to your house in a horse-drawn dray or wagon."

"Horses! I love horses," Lexi cried, and Claire gave up on shushing her. "Lily and I would love to see all of them."

Julia came closer and smiled at Lexi. "Well, I don't know who Lily is. The thing is, Meggie, of the about five hundred horses which work on the island in season, most of them are taken on ferries like this to the mainland because their food is hard to get here in the winter when the water ices over. But I have eight horses in my stable, and two of them are ponies. Maybe we can arrange to give you riding lessons."

"Oh, Mommy, can I?"

"We'll see. We have some things to settle first, get into our house and all, but we'll see."

"You've made a friend for life," Jace told Julia with a smile.

"Daddy, can I do it?" Lexi blurted out to him.

It was Julia who answered, her voice almost stern now. "Meggie, remember that we all need to pretend that this is a place where Jack Randal, your father, is coming to spend the winter to write a book and this man is his brother, your uncle, named Seth Randal. You need to remember that story and everyone's new names in case anyone asks—and then we can talk about riding lessons."

"Oh. Right. I won't forget." She ran around the bench, careful of Nick's wounded leg propped up. "If I say everything right, can I learn to ride, Daddy?" she asked Nick.

"Like your mother said, we'll see. I think it will work out."

"Yay!" she cried, but Nick saw Jace was furious again. It must be tough for him to see his daughter call another man "Daddy."

"Okay, we're turning into the harbor, and it will be a bit calmer now," Julia announced and went back to peer out the front windows. "Look to the right as we go in, and you'll see two lighthouses. Then when we get nearer to the pier, look up and you'll see the row of buildings on Main Street where your house is. It's a lovely old Victorian—there—that one with the green shingle roof and that fancy cupola. All our houses have names here and that one is Widow's Watch because, they say, a captain's wife used to walk on that railed path around the cupola to watch for her husband coming back from the Great Lakes."

With her hand on Nick's shoulder, Claire stood to look out. He appreciated that she didn't leave him. Several others went to the windows, Jace so close to Julia that he was peering over her shoulder.

Julia ducked around him and went to Claire. "I hope you'll be happy here," she told her. "Rest up. I want to show all of you our famous Grand Hotel in the next few days, maybe when I come to visit so we can all go over possible temporary employ-ments, financial issues, dos and don'ts."

"We're grateful for all the help and support," Nick told her. "But I know, when the time comes, you'll expect the same from all of us."

Claire loved the house Julia's father owned. It was a large, square two-story with a small attached carriage house, all built in the 1880s—evidently not unusual around here—with plenty of room and sleeping space for the eight of them. They entered through a front porch that had two doors, one to a formal par-lor with antique furniture and one to a modern living area with a big-screen TV on the wall, overhead recessed lighting and wraparound leather couches. Exhausted, Lexi planted herself and Shark-Killer in front of the TV and found a rerun of *Dora the Explorer.*

There was a formal dining room with eight chairs, though they didn't match, so Julia must have scouted for those. Still, Claire couldn't quite envision all of them sitting down for meals like one happy family. The kitchen was blessedly modern with a dishwasher and microwave, but what had she expected, a pump over the sink and a wood-burning stove? It did have an antique-looking chest freezer.

The house boasted two staircases, a wide, carpeted one with a banister at the front and a narrow wooden one, once servants' stairs, at the back that led to a separate entrance with its own key. Julia passed out front door keys to everyone. But, mum-bling something about losing a key, she gave Nick the only one for the back stair entrance.

Upstairs a long hall led to four high-ceilinged, same-size bed-rooms. A full bath sat partway back on one side of the hall with a shower and tub and a half bath across from that. All eight of them would share a shower and a tub?

Standing in the hall after peeking in all the rooms, they decided that Claire and Nick would take the back bedroom with the four-poster bed; Nita and Gina would stay with Lexi right across from them with a single bed and bunk beds; Heck and Bronco would take one front room with twin beds; and Jace the other overlooking Main Street.

They didn't go up in the attic, which Julia said stretched the length of the house and could be reached from the servants' stairs. She explained it was just for storage and was the place to access the circular walkway around the cupola, called a "widow's watch" or a "widow's walk."

Claire touched Julia's arm to pull her back a bit from the others who were heading downstairs again. "You said the woman watched for her seafaring husband from up there," she said to Julia. "So if she was a widow, he never came back?"

Julia sighed and frowned. She looked away, so unlike her usual directness, and said, "Lydia Wharton's captain husband did not come back the last time. Lost at sea with his ship in a huge storm. Yet they say she used to walk up there until the day she died, still looking for him, thinking he'd just been marooned someplace and would return."

Tears filled Julia's bright blue eyes. Her sudden shift in mood made Claire wonder what had happened to Julia's husband. Earlier, she'd said she had a daughter who lived here, in her early twenties. Julia had returned here so the girl didn't have to care for her grandfather who had dementia. That way, she could not only oversee his concerns but his rental property on the island.

"I'm sure you'll meet Liz," Julia had told them en route here in a carriage from the pier. "She runs a shop just beyond the fort on Market Street. Like me once, she's an islander who was anxious to leave, strike out on her own. I hoped to give her that chance, but now I don't know. Children—maybe—especially daughters..." she'd said, looking at Claire. "We worry for them at any age, don't we?"

Strange, Claire thought. Then and just now, Julia had suddenly seemed unsure and shaken. Something with her daughter, no doubt, fear of her moving away? But Claire had also had the feeling that the woman was going to say more about the long-dead widow Lydia Wharton, watching for her lost husband, so perhaps Julia had lost hers tragically. Claire wondered where to draw the line between seeing Julia as just their WITSEC handler—a well-trained former FBI agent, for heaven's sake—or a woman and possible friend in this alien place. Well, since Claire knew Jace shouldn't cross a too-familiar line with Julia, perhaps she shouldn't either.

Downstairs again, while Julia oversaw the unloading of their goods when they arrived by horse-drawn dray from the ferry, Claire and Nick huddled in the formal parlor.

"You should lie down," he said. "Are you sure you're all right?"

"Of course," she said. He may be wondering if she was suffering from her narcolepsy, but thank goodness she'd got replacement meds in New Orleans on their way to Michigan, after losing hers in that sugarcane field. "It's just we've been through so much, and I'm still nervous about everything working out. Later, when we're alone, we can unwind a bit. Right now, we—"

"Pizza's here, everybody!" they heard Julia call. Claire heard bedroom doors upstairs open. Lexi had left the TV after Dora "solved her mystery" and now appeared with Jace, the two of them laughing.

Great that someone could laugh, Claire thought. She had to tell Nick tonight what was unsettling her. Terrible timing for a pregnancy, unless she had something else wrong with her. What if her powerful narcolepsy meds had messed with her periods, or she had some dreadful disease? Nick didn't even have a clue what she'd been hinting at when she'd told him she was glad they had a medical center on the island.

"What is it?" he'd demanded on the flight earlier today from the New Orleans naval base where they had caught a flight to

Cheboygan, Michigan, so they could be driven in a van to catch the ferry. "Claire, are you okay?"

"Only lovesick over you." She'd tried to pass that off. But then she'd added a bit of a lie so he wouldn't make a scene on the small plane. "Your bullet wound may take more care, that's all. I have worrying in my blood lately."

"And I have you in my blood," Nick had whispered.

Finally, they would be alone together tonight. Truth time, she'd thought, and they were waiting for pizza now, so her big revelation would still have to wait.

They started across the hall to join the others in the dining room. A lanky teenage boy stood in the doorway balancing four big boxes of pizza that Heck stepped forward to take from him.

"Everyone," Julia said, obviously back to her handler-hostess self again, "this is Jeremy Archer, whose father is our police chief. Jeremy, these are our new renters, the Randals and their staff. The police here ride bikes, too, don't they, Jeremy?"

"Unless it snows. Can't wait til it does because I can have my own snowmobile this winter, not share with my sister. Well, got other deliveries to make, and I have to make sure the pizzas stay hot. Welcome to our island!" he said and beat a fast retreat.

"Don't we pay him?" Jace asked Julia.

"All covered, including the tip, as a welcome." She grabbed her jacket from the china umbrella stand near the door. "I've got to run but I'll be back tomorrow to continue orientation. Meggie, that means plans where we all cooperate, okay? See you all tomorrow," she said and headed out.

"'Bye," Lexi called after her. "And thanks for the pizza. I don't want to hurt Gina's feelings, but it's lots better than rice and beans and fish."

Even Gina laughed. Claire stepped out on the porch alone and called to Julia, who was at the bottom of the house sidewalk.

"I agree that we can't thank you enough. I'd love to meet your father and daughter."

"I love them, can't lose them," Julia said, half to herself with a little wave and a shake of her head. Hands thrust in her coat pockets, she strode off into the darkening, windy night.

CHAPTER TWELVE

"With all eight of us, it's kind of like living in a frat house or a dorm again, isn't it?" Nick asked Claire as he toweled his hair dry after coming back from his turn in the shower. He sat on the edge of the bed, removing the plastic he'd had taped on his wounded leg to keep it dry. Claire thought they'd shared a bed so little in their forced, short marriage that they had never really declared a his-side or her-side.

Despite how nervous she was, she smiled at the dorm comment. Though she really liked her new "sorority sisters" Nita and Gina, she still missed her own sister and her family desperately. Yes, when she started to comfort and counsel Lexi tomorrow, she'd talk to her some about how they would never lose their first family and how—someday soon perhaps—they'd all be back together. That made her think of Julia again. In a way, she had already lost her father. And, as a single mother, if her daughter moved away, how sad.

Claire had already bathed Lexi and sat with her until she fell asleep while Nita spent some time with Bronco downstairs. After Claire had taken her own shower, she'd been unpacking clothes for herself, Nick and Lexi and putting hers and Nick's in a tall chest of drawers that smelled of cedar. Strange to be looking at and wearing clothes someone else had picked out. This was like living someone else's life, and she desperately wanted her own back. What she planned now to tell Nick—that seemed so unreal too. Everything had happened so fast in their lives together.

Nick leaned back against the pile of pillows and pulled the covers up over his legs, ever careful of the bandaged one that could shoot pain at him if he hit it wrong.

"There's just one thing I want more than sleep—and safety," he told her as she turned from the dresser and walked slowly toward the four-poster bed.

"Me, I hope," she said, gripping the post because her legs were trembling.

"Exactly. Peace, quiet and you. By the way, I locked our door with that old skeleton key. We don't need Shark-Killer and its owner coming in here right now. What is it? Come here and let me hold you, or at least you hold me."

He leaned forward before she could answer and went on, "What is it? Claire-Jenna, my sweetheart, whatever your name, what's the matter? It's more than just the turns our lives have taken, isn't it? You've been so strong and brave. Do you still feel ill? Dizzy?"

She walked to his side of the bed and sat, careful to avoid his hurt leg. "Dizzy in love with you," she said, her voice breaking. "But there is something—another complication—I have to tell you about. I know it hasn't been long and things are a big blur, but you know that night on the yacht where you, Jace and I made a deal to trust WITSEC?"

"Sure. And don't you now? I don't believe the plane crash had anything to do with Rob Patterson, even though he arranged the plane. I think it was Ames's lackeys again. And I think we lucked out with Julia Collister. She'll ease us into island life and, hopefully, give us a horse bargaining chip with Lexi, our Meggie."

She had to tell him. She had to tell him now. How could a

man be so dense when she was obsessed with this? She wanted to fall into his arms, but once she did that, she always lost control. So, like some coward, she sat where she was and merely nodded.

Frowning, he asked—in his lawyer voice, as if grilling a hostile witness, "Did Jace say something to upset you, more than his behavior toward Julia?"

"No. I mean, he does upset me because he's so unhappy and trapped, but aren't we all? And now, it's plain that he sees Julia as some sort of diversion, and that's all we need to mess things up even more."

She burst into tears. "Oh, Nick, I'm sorry. I'm just strung out, so—"

He scooted closer and did just what she was afraid of, because she had to be rational about this. He pulled her close and held her against his strong body, his good leg and hip. Just then the wind outside began again, whining, moaning overhead like there really was some woman on the widow's walk, keening while she waited for her husband to come home.

"Nick," she got out, seizing control of herself again, "I'm not sure but kind of sure. That night we didn't use anything and made love—I think I may be pregnant. I swear that only happens on soap operas, one night, then a baby, and—I know it hasn't been long though it seems like ages with all we've been through but—Nick?" she said and lifted her head from his shoulder, uncertain what she'd see or hear.

He looked shocked. Then dazed. Then, thank heavens, happy.

"I—I should have known, my love. I'm paid big bucks to put cases together. But that's why I hired you in the first place to psych out people for me. But—that statue with the baby in her arms that upset you, your wondering about a hospital here, your extra exhaustion and stomach upset… I should have guessed."

He looked down at her midriff as if she would be showing after such a short time. She burst into hysterical laughter with her tears.

"And my missed period, and what an emotional mess I am," she added as he hugged her hard to him again. "Nick, with all we've been through—not to mention my heavy meds I've been on and off—I can't be sure, but a pregnancy is a big possibility. I wish I could have gone to a doctor first, planned us a private, lovely dinner for two and told you then for sure yay or nay but—"

"But just the idea of it," he said, expelling a big breath and rocking her against him as if she was a frightened child. "I know we're in a mess here still, but just the thought of a child of our own is amazing. Lexi would love it too, I'm sure, as soon as she gets through her hard times. And, my love," he added, setting her back a bit and smiling with a devilish gleam in his dark, teary eyes, "we will get to a doctor, and if he says it's true, we'll celebrate both with a romantic dinner and in this bed. But it will be our secret until we know for sure, maybe until you show."

Until you show. The words echoed in her head as she reached over to snap out the light. *Until you show that you can survive all this, can conquer the bad guys, can help Lexi, can love Nick and not Jace for ever and ever...*

"Claire. Feel better now?"

"Yes, of course. Thank heavens you're not upset. But then, I must admit our courtship and marriage was hardly normal, so why should starting our family be?"

In the dark, he kissed her soundly, salty tears and all. He turned her back to him, and they lay together spoon fashion under the covers with his lips in her tousled hair.

"Claire," he whispered, "we'll make up for these tough times. We will make it, all of us, including our new son or daughter if that's what we find out. Just think, maybe floating inside you like a little island in a sea, just like us now here on Mackinac."

His arms tightened around her. He put his hand under her nightgown on her flat belly. "I love you, Claire, and no matter what happens, always will."

"Then I will treasure this moment and have it always in my heart."

She heard Jace's voice boom a laugh from the first floor. She cuddled close to Nick, warm and weary, and finally was swept away, swimming into sleep.

Claire woke still in Nick's embrace, but were they swimming in the sea? No, she stood on a marble pedestal with a baby in her arms. People were leaving flowers at her feet and taking photographs. But was her baby stone-cold dead? And the other child standing so stiff below…that little girl. Where was she? Was she missing? Had someone taken her?

She managed to pull herself from her fears. No, she'd found her daughter, but she wanted to leave the island. She had to get off the island!

Had she remembered to take her medicine, that terrible drink that made her sleep and gave her strange dreams? But was she having a dream now, or was this real?

In some far-off cemetery, she walked and walked in a circle, dragging her heavy stone feet. Where was her husband? Where was her daughter and her baby? Someone said they had buried the baby at her feet but now it was in her arms, a miracle.

"Claire! Claire, you're having a nightmare."

Nick. It was Nick. She was safe here, somewhere, lying in his arms. Oh, right. On the island, in the widow's house, in bed, safe from Clayton Ames and his other house surrounded by poison plants with vicious fish swimming past. He'd taken Lexi, and he'd made Nick marry her, so he could watch them, hurt them all.

"Are you all right, sweetheart?"

Nick's voice again. That was real, even though they had to have fake names and pretend not to be themselves.

"Yes," she whispered. "Just a bad dream."

"No more of those. Sleep. We need our sleep. Lexi's safe

with Nita and Gina. We'll make it, get to go back home when this is over."

She nodded and sighed, fighting now to slip away again. Nick knew how powerful her night meds were, in contrast to the stimulants for narcolepsy she sometimes took during the day. He understood. But then, she'd made the terrible mistake—really a sin—of not sharing her disease with Jace when they were married, and then when he'd found out and felt betrayed...

She tried to relax. Jace had been away so much, flying international routes. It was partly his fault too. But Jace loved planes. She'd seen that hungry, hurt look on his face when he'd seen the naval planes on the tarmac at the airfield across the harbor from Guantanamo, and then at the air base in New Orleans. And the same expression when he'd looked at Julia...

She suddenly remembered where she'd seen the Grand Hotel on this island before, the place Julia wanted them to see. Funny how things came to her clearly when she woke up for her second dose at night or even in dreams. Years ago, she and Darcy had loved that old movie with Jane Seymour and Christopher Reeve they'd seen in reruns on TV, the one filmed at that hotel on this very island. What was the movie's name? Her mind was clearing now. Oh, yes, *Somewhere in Time*, where he fell in love with a woman who had lived years before and managed to slip back in time and into her life. But then he lost her, like the woman who once lived here lost her beloved, like the man in Havana lost his wife and baby in the statue, like maybe Julia lost her husband...

She sucked in a big breath and became even more alert, but this time Nick did not wake up. He breathed steadily, on his back but still pressed against her. Claire shifted slightly away, propped herself up on one elbow and pushed her hair back from her damp face. She looked at the clock and reached for the midnight dose of liquid medication and vowed that, somewhere in time, they were going to help convict and imprison Clayton Ames before they were all lost forever.

CHAPTER THIRTEEN

The Grand Hotel was grand indeed. Claire couldn't believe the size of it as it curved around a hill over the water, with a lower level graced by bright yellow awnings. Above that, a pillared colonnade sheltered a long porch with clusters of white rocking chairs and American flags flapping in the crisp October breeze. Above that were rows of rooms with fabulous views. Below the vast expanse of the building were the famous flower gardens, though the frosts had turned them all to dead plants now, and gardeners were working to take them out and pile them in sad heaps on carts.

"The building is beautiful," she told Julia as they took turns climbing down from the large wagon she had hired to bring them in. "Like a palace from the past."

"Which indeed it is," Julia told them while Bronco steadied Nick as he got down slowly with his cane. When they were all out, the young man who held the reins drove the two-horse team of big Clydesdales off to a resting spot. In her best tour-guide voice, Julia went on, "Grand Hotel—correctly said without the word *the*—was built in the 1880s in the Victorian Age but what they call the Gilded Age here in North America. It was built for the elite but is now open to all—for a fee. Let me give you a tour. Then we'll have that lunch I promised and talk about plans for your employment while you're on the island. We'll be in a private dining room I've arranged."

"You sure know the ins and outs of this place," Jace said, walking ahead with her. "I'm sure you'd be an excellent companion anywhere on the island."

If that was an innuendo, Claire thought, she admired Julia for ignoring it. "I know this hotel too well," she told them. "When I first returned here to be with my father and daughter, jobs were scarce in the winter, so I was one of the night guards here. It's a ghostly place once they close it until the season starts again, but it needs watching, of course." She lowered her voice, perhaps so Lexi wouldn't hear. "Pretty spooky, all closed up at night with the lights off and everything shrouded."

Jace opened and held the door for all of them to enter. Indeed, there was a charge to just view the interior, but Julia whipped out some sort of pass to give to the woman at the table. For the first time, Claire noted she wore what appeared to be a wedding band, but on her right hand. An heirloom? Or was she widowed, or even divorced, and still wanted to wear the ring? Claire scolded herself for slipping. She'd been curious about Julia, but, for once, hadn't looked at something as obvious as a wedding ring to help psych her out.

Suddenly nervous, she began to twist her own rings around her finger. Maybe it was the poster ahead that did it: the two doomed lovers from the movie *Somewhere in Time* she'd remembered last night. The poster was advertising a yearly convention here next weekend for fans of the movie.

Julia must have seen her looking at it. "You were probably a bit young in 1980 when that came out," she told Claire. "TV reruns?"

"Exactly. My sister and I loved that movie."

"Aunt Darcy?" Lexi asked, though she'd seemed too tired to

chatter today. And, miraculously, they'd talked her into leaving Shark-Killer back at the house to keep an eye on it. "Or does she have another name now too?"

"No," Claire said, stooping to whisper as they went farther down a carpeted hall, "but she's a secret here. People named Meggie and Jenna have to keep secrets. Real soon you and I will have a talk about all that again."

"Guess what, Meggie?" Julia asked. "There was another movie made here too called *This Time for Keeps*, and there were a lot of swimming-pool scenes in it. My father has a copy of that with his cowboy movies, so I'll borrow it for you, and you can all watch it."

As Julia gave them a tour of the main, massive dining room and several side rooms, Claire was entranced. The carpets were all flowered and so dramatic, as if to bring the gardens inside even in the colder months. The carpets would have overwhelmed most places but not these vast hallways and public rooms. Polished antique furniture, framed art and chandeliers overhead kept everything in balance.

"It's not a palace. It's a castle, like in *Sleeping Beauty* or *Cinderella*," Lexi said, and even the men seemed in awe. Gina and Nita were all eyes.

"The dining room seats seven hundred and fifty, but we'll be all cozy in our smaller room. Down this hall—this way," Julia said, though Claire saw all of them were hanging back for one last look.

"I'm paying for our meal," Nick told her as they went into a private dining room with a round white linen–covered table elegantly set. The wallpaper flaunted bright green tropical leaves and the floor was beige and green.

Julia countered, "You've paid enough already, in more ways than one." Once they were inside with the door closed, she told him, "One time here, Jack—it's all part of the account. But after this, you're on a budget, and I know you've worked out support with Agent Patterson.

"Meggie," she went on, "I've ordered really the best dessert here for all of us, called the Grand Pecan Ball—that is, if you like nuts, and I know my little girl didn't when she was young."

"Pecans are Southern nuts," Lexi told her. "So they are okay."

"Southern nuts," Bronco said. "Aren't we all? And here we are up North, and I've never seen snow."

"Me neither, have I, Mommy—or have I, Uncle Seth?"

"Nope, so that will be a lot of fun," Jace said. "I'm thinking there will be some real good things to do on the island this winter."

Claire rolled her eyes, but he wasn't looking at her. At least he wasn't ogling Julia, but he'd managed to take a seat beside her. Could he be trying to make his ex-wife jealous? No, Claire scolded herself, that was too conceited a thought, but sometimes she was sure that—

"All right," Julia was saying. With everyone seated, Claire noticed there was one extra place at the table. Maybe, in an old building like this, they had a ghost who ate here. She shivered and scolded herself for such a silly idea, but she could imagine what all this looked like when deserted, as Julia had described it—shrouded.

When everyone quieted and turned toward her, Julia said, "Let me toss out possibilities for employment this winter to help defray costs and so you all won't get cabin fever once the snow starts, which will be sooner than usual, they say. Seth, one of the men who goes out on the tarmac at the airport and brings the planes in to the gates is ill, and you certainly know the territory. It's a small airport with minimal traffic and seldom even a small private jet this time of year, but that's a possibility. Orders are, though, you would not identify yourself as a pilot, just as someone who has worked at an airport. Frankly, it would give you a good way to be aware of any strangers coming here in the winter."

"And are there some?" he asked. Claire noted he'd looked excited at first, but what a letdown. To be near flying but not to fly, not to even let on he knew how, but they were all knee-deep in lies to survive here.

"Strangers coming in who aren't just tourists this time of year?" Julia asked. "Rare, but it happens. For instance, rich guy flew in recently from Las Vegas, who is harassing my father to sell his Gene Autry memorabilia collection for a Wild West Museum on the Strip there. He came on a rental plane and complained about having to leave his own jet off island because it was too large for our runway."

"And you wish he'd skidded off that little runway," Jace put in. "As for the airport job, thanks for realizing how much planes and flying mean to me. That sounds fine. I'll go nuts at Widow's Watch."

Julia finally smiled back at him, then went on, as she quickly turned to the others, "Jenna has said she wants to homeschool Meggie, and Lorena can certainly help as her nanny. Gina, since you've been a medical student, there's a doctor at the Mackinac Island Medical Center on Market Street who can use your help as an assistant."

"I want to go to school somewhere in the US, but I'll need money to do that, so, yes. Very good."

"That will be an excellent cover story while you are here," Julia said. "Our friend Mr. Patterson has also suggested that, if asked, you say you are Lorena's sister, Gina, and you came along with her for the winter. Lorena, is that all right with you?"

"Oh, yes. I am happy to help and perhaps we even look at bit alike, yes?"

"And Gina?"

"I would be blessed to have a sister as kind as Lorena—or Jenna."

"Then that's settled. And once the snow hits and a bicycle won't get you to the med center, I know a very nice doctor who can pick you up on his snowmobile, but we'll get to all these details later."

Speaking of details, Claire was impressed, but she saw Heck wasn't. She was hoping he and Gina would not take her father's parting words to heart about getting married soon. Still, she didn't doubt that Julia or Rob Patterson could come up with legal papers for Gina and then a wedding license. She was starting to think of Julia as their fairy godmother.

"Jack," Julia said, turning to Nick, "we have a cover story that you're a writer, working on a novel, so in case locals ask, you'll need a general description of it. You've read the dossier about your supposed successful business background in Orlando, and we've covered for you there, in case anyone checks, but I bet they won't. However, instead of writing a novel, you'll be consulting, through me, with our agent friend to prepare a case against Ames High, et cetera. Writing affidavits, taking information from Jenna and others—from Seth too, who has also dealt with him."

Jace just grunted and mumbled something under his breath. Claire knew he felt he had a score to settle with Ames, though maybe not one as deeply felt as Nick's.

Claire studied Lexi to see if she was getting any of this, but she was unfolding her elaborately arranged linen napkin and seemed oblivious for once.

Nick asked, "Since you speak of the devil, any word on arresting and extraditing him from Cuba for prosecution?"

"Not yet," Julia said. "Red tape. Delicate international ties. And we're not even sure he's still in Havana, though our man spotted him there just as Berto and Gina did."

"Meaning he is tight with the Castros, yes?" Gina blurted, throwing her hands up. "I tell you, even though we are being careful in a private room miles away, it feels so good to just say things about and against them out loud!"

Everyone applauded, and Heck put his arm around Gina's shoulders. How Claire wished they could all feel free and safe here, but she was starting to relax for the first time in months—really, since she'd first met Nick.

"And, Berto," Julia said, turning to Heck, "your tech skills make you invaluable for working with Jack, and I hope, with me. Everything will have to be encrypted before it's sent, so we must be careful. Meanwhile, we can let it be known that you can do basic computer repairs, because islanders could use that here. I know I can. And my daughter runs a business here and has an online sales site she could use some help with.

"And last, but not least, Cody," she said, turning to Bronco. "Jack has said you're invaluable to him as a guard and assistant. Two things. Do not think you are a glorified errand boy, but you will be our go-between so we do not use phones or internet for passing key information back and forth. And, if you are willing, it would be invaluable to me too if you could spend some time with my father. He'll latch on to you with a name like Cody Carson, and in a week you'll know everything there ever was to know about the old Wild West."

"Suits me," Bronco said with a nod. "Sorry I can't tell him my other name, 'cause he'd like that too."

Lexi surprised Claire by putting in, "We're all sorry about our other names, but you have to use the pretend one."

"That's right," Claire said and everyone else chimed in.

"So," Julia said, "that takes care of everyone's temporary occupations, and we'll see how things go."

Nick said, "You've done a lot of preliminary work, and we can't thank you enough for the hospitality and the house."

"I never placed and hosted this many clients before, such a big—well, family. I really want to get you out to see the rural, more hidden parts of the island before the first snow hits. They say what they call the polar vortex will be harsh this year, and here we are almost in Canada."

She'd mentioned hidden parts of the island. Claire wondered again if there were other WITSEC witnesses—clients—secreted here. Rob Patterson had been right. This location was a great setup for privacy and lack of access, especially with winter coming.

"And now I have a surprise," Julia said. "That is, another one. I've asked my daughter, Liz, who, yes, does know what I do here besides running a riding stable, to join us. She should be outside in the hall, and just wait until you hear what she designs and makes for a living, a very good one at that. Excuse me for a minute, as I asked her to wait until I brought her in. Meggie, you've been so good, and I'll bet you're hungry."

"Well, I had four pancakes, but Lily didn't like them because she wants to go home to Florida."

Darn, Claire thought. That talk with Lexi had to happen soon. Julia had been right about trouble with daughters no matter their age, and she couldn't wait to meet her girl Liz.

But as Julia went out into the hall, before the door closed, Claire overheard her say, "Wade, why are you here? I asked you to stay away from her."

A woman's voice said, "I don't know how he got in, but I really don't think it's a problem if we're careful, so—"

The door to the hall closed behind Julia, but Claire was sitting close to it. She could still hear their voices raised until the others started talking. So she got up and pretended to stretch, standing near the door. Nick knew what she was doing and frowned, but everyone else seemed oblivious.

Julia said, "Wade, shouldn't you be at work? That's a good job in the jewelry store."

"I am at work. I only saw Liz coming in here after I delivered a silver and Petoskey stone ring to that guy Liz says has been bugging your father. Kirkpatrick's staying here. Want me to give him a hint to keep away, to fly back out of this Northern paradise?"

"And tip your tough-man hand? You—and Liz too—both know the rules, and they don't include romantic fraternization, to put it nicely. Please, or you'll have to be transferred, Wade."

"Or if Liz leaves like she wants, that will solve the problem here, so maybe I can get transferred back to Manhattan if you finally let her go."

"Don't try being clever. I have guests, the new renters for my father's property on Main Street, so I have to go back in. Liz, let's go."

Claire just managed to sit down when Julia came back in with a beautiful, blonde, blue-eyed young woman. She might be in her early twenties but looked younger. And the way she was dressed: when she took her floor-length cloak off, Claire saw she wore a long black skirt and loose-sleeved white blouse laced up the front, but it was her embroidered, beaded, lavender, wasp-waisted velvet corset worn over those garments that made Claire gasp and Jace clear his throat.

Everyone stopped talking except Lexi, who cried, "Mommy, I told you this is a castle, because that's the princess!"

CHAPTER FOURTEEN

Sometimes Jace thought he was dreaming and wished he'd wake up. But no, he'd actually ridden a bicycle to his first day working in a small airport owned by a state park and surrounded by a forest in the boondocks of Michigan!

And his new job: not sitting in his officer's uniform in the copilot seat of a huge, international jet but wearing jeans and a lime-green vest, stuck on the ground holding up two orange batons to bring in a small prop plane. They'd even called him a *signalman* when they'd given him the protocols and training this morning, not an *aircraft marshaller*. It sounded to him like he was working at some old train depot.

Still, he told himself, as he brought his first plane in solo to a gate, it got him out of the house where he had to watch Lexi and Claire with Nick. And, yeah, he supposed this gig would help him keep an eye on strangers coming in, especially when the lakes iced over and most of the supplies and visitors were brought in by air. He'd been told that once the ice was strong enough, islanders and visitors on snowmobiles went back and forth to the Upper Peninsula's closest city, St. Ignace, on what they called an ice bridge.

He brought the Beechcraft Baron in with the universal hand signals he'd seen so many times from the elevated cockpit. It was a piece of cake without the busy gates, ground tugs, baggage trains, food trucks and airstairs he'd had to deal with for years.

After the two passengers deplaned with their suitcases and the pilot taxied off to a parking area, Jace paced, waiting for the next plane. At least his earphones weren't just useful to mute noise but for info from the tower. And all this for a little less than thirty dollars per hour salary when he was used to big bucks. The September through May hours were 7:30 to 5:30, and there were only two single-engine planes based here, but he'd love to take one of them up to see the island from the air, to just soar and escape all this.

He needed a diversion and, evidently, Julia Collister wasn't willing to fill the bill. He'd asked her about her family and she'd said no husband, just her father and daughter. Still, he loved a challenge and she was that, so he didn't plan to give up on her. Besides, he could tell it annoyed Claire and Nick.

He looked around the tarmac again. Yeah, what a place, with no fuel available and Great Lakes Air the only regularly scheduled planes.

He was glad to get word of another aircraft approaching to stop his thoughts. This one was a Cessna Mustang, an aircraft he'd flown briefly, years ago. He brought the plane in and started back inside for his lunch break, walking behind the man who'd emerged from the plane. The guy was well dressed in a black overcoat and gray slacks, totally out of place around here, and he wore fancy, tooled Western boots. Silver-haired and muscular, he strode with a purpose, almost strutted. When Jace got info through his headphones he was to lead the Cessna to a parking place in the hangar, he went into action again, walking backward most of the way while moving the orange batons.

When he headed back toward the terminal, he saw the passenger from the plane standing and smoking at the edge of the tarmac by the terminal. Yeah, he sniffed it before he saw it. The guy was smoking a strong-smelling cigar.

"You spend a lot of time near the planes even when they're not coming or going?" the man asked, expelling a plume of heavy smoke. He had a broad face, dark bushy eyebrows and a narrow mouth.

"Guilty as charged."

"I was hoping to fly my Hawker biz jet in from Cheboygan, but they said short runway here, so I had to lease this smaller one. I came on the regular flight a few days earlier but just went back to check on my plane and rented this one with the pilot to wait here for me. I'll make it worth your while if you'd keep an eye on this prop plane and give me an idea of a reasonable place for the rent-a-pilot to stay in town. I'm at the Grand, but he doesn't need all that. An econo place will do."

"We're not allowed to recommend lodgings," Jace said, to cover the fact he had no clue about a place to stay but the Grand. "Inside, though, they could help you."

Another plume of smoke went skyward. "Well, then, when you're here, just keep an eye on the plane for me. Call my cell if there's any problem with or question about it."

Jace could tell the guy was used to giving orders. He extended a card to Jace, which he glanced at but didn't pocket.

"Sure," Jace said. "So—Las Vegas, and you're here?"

"Business. And if you'd like to make some extra money, tell me how to reach you. I may well be buying a lot of things here in the near future and will need someone to help me transport and load them."

"Against the rules again, so—"

"The rules are for those who need them. The rest of us rise above. Forget it, then," he said, grabbing the card back from Jace. He stooped and rubbed the lit end of the cigar carefully on the tarmac between them. Then, with Jace still glaring at him, he took a flat cigar case—made of tooled leather that matched his boots—out of his inner coat pocket and put the unsmoked half of the cigar carefully in it. The inside of the box had one word, *COHIBA*.

"Big bucks a pop," he said, "even if I have a source. Didn't get where I am wasting money or time."

As the man went inside, Jace didn't budge. He didn't care if the guy complained about him even on his first day at work. He guessed someone like that would rub most people the wrong way around here. The guy reminded him of Clayton Ames, not in looks but in manner, and that bastard could have his tentacles out anywhere.

So he'd just remember what he'd scanned on the card in case the guy was obnoxious again. He didn't catch the cell phone or fax number, but he'd sure remember the name VERN KIRK-PATRICK, LAS VEGAS WILD WEST MUSEUM AND SHOW.

Claire was aching to go up into the attic to access the widow's walk and see the view from there, but Nick didn't need to climb all those steps yet. Nor did she want to do it without him or go alone. And she didn't want Lexi to know how to get up there, because who knew what her imaginary friend, Lily, might do. So she'd spent much of the morning talking to Lexi in an attempt to comfort and assure her and to insist on a plan to get rid of Lily.

They sat on the sofa in the parlor because the TV on the wall in what they were calling the family room seemed to distract Lexi, even when it wasn't on, almost as if she was seeing a show on the blank screen there.

"Good behavior like we talked about is worth some rewards," Claire said when the child was getting antsy after about a quarter of an hour. But she wanted to summarize things they'd gone over, to comfort her more and give her hope. And she was yet to actually deal with Lily.

"Mommy, I already let Shark-Killer stay here to guard the house instead of go to lunch at the grand castle."

"And I appreciated your cooperation on that. I know we have had a hard time these last months, but this will be a great vacation for us here, and there is nothing to be afraid of anymore."

"I hear some lady crying at night. At first I was scared it was you."

Claire sucked in a quick breath. Her heartbeat kicked up.

"No, no, sweetheart. That's just the wind. I heard it too. We'll get used to it. Maybe we can get some earplugs. But I want you to promise me that Lily will not come around anymore. If you really want to see Julia's horses and maybe take riding lessons on one of her ponies, all that will be for you, not for Lily. She is not good for you or for us, so you have to send her away."

Lexi thrust out her lower lip and snatched up the stuffed animal to hug it hard. "How is she going to get off this island? On that ferry? And then how will she get home?"

So much, Claire thought, for behavior modification or rationality. But it hadn't worked for her to use the approach that Lily wasn't real when she was real to a frightened, uprooted little girl.

"We'll get her help to get home. Where does she live?" Claire asked.

Lexi sighed in exasperation. "In our old house in Naples, where we should be. The big boat a friend gave us for a while wasn't really our home."

Claire sighed. While they had lived on the borrowed yacht while solving the Mangrove Murder case, Lexi had not mentioned Lily, but had she been haunted by her alter ego then? Claire pulled Lexi, stuffed whale and all, onto her lap and held her tight. "I'll be sure Lily gets back to Florida. But as for us, we will have a home someday, with real friends—just like Cousin Jilly is to you. But right now, we are kind of playing hide-and-seek."

"More like tag, and we're not it. Someone else is it, like that bad Mr. Ames people whisper about."

Claire was shocked anew. The child was so perceptive, so easily damaged. "Yes, kind of like that. But we will all be safe and happy here," she promised, kissing the top of her head and wishing so hard that she might, just possibly—*please, God*—be telling her the truth.

After promising Lexi they could visit Julia's stables tomorrow, Claire left her in Nita's care, learning more Spanish words. Gina went with Claire for a walk, leaving Heck, Nick and Julia in a planning meeting while Bronco kept an eye on things. Claire had learned yesterday at their hotel lunch where Liz Collister's shop was, and they were going to drop in, though neither she nor Gina wanted to buy a corset, evidently the new rage for some women and a fashion statement for others. Who knew?

The men had been as much avid listeners as the women when Liz had shown off the one she was wearing and had talked about her hopes to "move off this island to the bigger island of Manhattan" to set herself up in a shop. Claire had noted well that Julia had been eager to praise Liz's Island Corset Shoppe but was cold to the idea of one in New York City. It had also seemed to Claire, who had long made her career listening to and evaluating what people said and didn't say, that there was tension on more than that between mother and daughter. Maybe about Liz's beau, Wade?

Claire and Gina found the small shop wedged in between two larger ones on French Street not far from the ferry dock.

"Pretty close to the Market Street shops, yes, but you'd have to be looking for it," Gina observed.

"In Northern Michigan, don't you think you'd need to be looking for a corset shop to find it anywhere?"

Gina almost smiled. Claire had spent some time with her this morning too, privately in the parlor, just listening to the young woman talk about her misgivings at what she'd got herself into. Heck adored her and she cared for him, but once out of Cuba, she felt she was, as she put it, "still at sea." And she kept worrying about her mother.

"Not one more hair on her head can turn white over me," she'd said. "Losing Alfredito nearly killed her—and now this."

"Despite your parents' grief at your leaving, they want what is best for you. Once we get through this, we can get you into med school, hopefully, in Florida. If the US reconciles with Cuba, things will open up, and you can more easily visit."

"And my father, he yelled at me and Berto, to marry right away, and he wants to, but I say not yet, not now."

"You're doing the right thing. I married much too fast—twice."

Claire had reached out to grasp Gina's hands. "I'm happy with Jack, but nothing's been normal for us. And certainly it isn't now."

They'd sat like that in the parlor, silent for a few moments, but somehow that had been a huge building block for their friendship.

"Oh, her shop is upstairs!" Gina said now. "That Liz's Island Corset Shoppe sign says stairs around the back. I hope we find her there."

They did. Bent over a laptop screen on a worktable littered with beautiful things like leather and satin swatches in various colors, lace, crystal beads and gold cord trim.

"Oh, you came!" Liz cried, bouncing up to greet them. "Let me show you around, though it's only this workroom, since I've been saving every dime for a couple of years. Manhattan rent is out of sight! But before Mother came back to the island, I had to work out of our house, listening to Granddad's Western music and movie soundtracks over and over. Manhattan's my dream, to move into a little shop there where the Kardashians can easily come for a fitting and not send things back and forth."

"The Kardashians?" Claire gasped.

"Who are they?" Gina asked, and Claire tried to explain.

"And others they sent my way," Liz interrupted in her exuberance. "The latest for them was an eight-hundred-dollar corset absolutely ablaze with hand-beaded Swarovski crystals! And another couple for undergarments you wouldn't believe, though the way they are, they may show up in one of their selfies online or in *People* or *Us* magazines. Onward and upward, because, like I said, they've told others about my designs. Don't think when you see gorgeous personalities on a red carpet for some movie or the Oscars that they have natural waists that small. Ten to one, it's a corset."

"Amazing," Claire said as Liz showed them her designs and samples.

"It's all online if you want to check, and I don't do all the finishing work myself, though I do for my A-listers. I have three island women who sew for me too and usually take their work home."

Liz stopped her stream of talk and stared off into space for a moment as if she was having a petit mal. Claire recalled Julia had done that too, so maybe it ran in the family.

"Well," Liz said, as if snapping back to reality, "now that Mother's back here to watch Granddad and I've built a business, I need to get out of this attic and off the island. My father wants me to come to Baltimore, but Manhattan would be better. Mother's dead set against my plan, and we've had words about it."

"I picked up on that," Claire said. "So your father's in Baltimore?"

"Right. Where he thinks not only I but Mother should be too. They're divorced, but he still carries a torch for her. He comes here once in a while to see me—and her, but they're hardly simpatico."

Shades of Jace and me? Claire wondered, but she said, "So your mother came back not only to take care of your grandfather, but so you could have your dream and leave?"

"More like to convince me to stay here and just sell online, but she doesn't understand about fittings, sometimes several for one garment. I love the island, but I've got to go. She loved it here, but she left for a career. So," she said, as if snapping out of another place with a faraway look, "you let me know if you'd like a custom-made corset at a very good price. Men love them too for their women, the newest thing in bedroom lingerie!"

Bedroom lingerie. Claire had asked Julia this morning in private if she could recommend an ob-gyn on the mainland, and she had a name. If she was pregnant, it was no time for a corset.

"So no childhood sweethearts to keep you here?" Gina asked the question that Claire had decided not to. She'd really like to ask about Wade.

"Would you believe I've been proposed to twice by islanders and turned them down both times?"

When Liz walked them downstairs to say goodbye, a handsome young man was just heading up the steps. He had slicked-back raven-dark hair and the touch of beard stubble that was supposed to be so sexy these days.

"Oh, Wade," she said. "You promised to at least wait til Saturday."

Perhaps realizing she had said too much, Liz told them. "This is a friend, Wade Buxton. I'm referring to a huge convention this weekend of that old romantic movie *Somewhere in Time* at Grand Hotel, and Wade has promised to help me hand out ads for corsets—the perfect captive audience for Victorian-era fans.

"So," she rushed on before he could speak, "these ladies are Gina and Jenna, renters in Granddad's Widow's Watch house, and they're just leaving."

Liz practically dragged Wade past them up the stairs and called down another goodbye. So was this man one of Liz's suitors she'd turned down and Julia didn't like him? What Claire had overheard at the hotel had made her think he might actually be another WITSEC refugee. Julia had introduced Liz to them, but if Wade was also a witness in hiding and had got too close to Liz, Julia could be panicked over that.

Claire almost missed the bottom step when Wade called down to them, "Just thought of something, ladies. That old Widow's Watch place is the one with the ghost that walks upstairs near the roof."

"Really?" Claire said, turning back and looking up. Her pulse began to pound.

"Yeah, looking for her man lost at sea." Wade had some sort of Eastern accent—Brooklyn?—but Claire stayed riveted on his words. "I guess she keeps crying. Some say they've seen her too."

"Wade, never mind," Liz scolded. "All superstitions."

"Caramba!" Gina whispered.

"That's all we need," Claire muttered, but, with a wave back at Liz, steering Gina away, she kept on going.

CHAPTER FIFTEEN

Claire waited in Dr. Manning's examination room, staring at a chart on the wall of a baby in utero. The test had been simple. Just a urine sample, then wait for the results to test for a particular hormone, which they did on-site. But why was it taking them so long to get Nick from the waiting room so he could hear the news with her? The nurse had gone out to bring him in, and the doctor had said he'd be right back with the results.

And could this really be happening? A baby when her marriage to Nick had just begun? So many things had happened to get them off to a difficult and dangerous start.

They'd taken a taxi to get from the ferry to this St. Ignace doctor Julia had recommended. All the islanders went to him, she'd said, and had their babies off island. At least, Claire thought, it was great to have someone people trusted. She'd been through so much trauma and upheaval, so maybe that was the cause of her missed period, her exhaustion, her strange stomachache.

The door opened and Nick entered.

"The nurse says he'll be right in."

"I heard him go into the next room. He's very kind, says he's delivered island babies for years."

"Would you mind?" he asked, sitting in the chair next to her and leaning toward her to take her hands in his.

"You mean, being pregnant right now? With everything we still have to face?"

"And when we haven't been married—or together—that long?"

"Is that what you're thinking?"

"I'm thinking how much I love you, that I did hope we'd have a family someday and that I'm excited about the idea of a child, even when we're hiding out and probably being hunted."

She leaned closer to him and they kissed, quickly, then slowly, then parted when they heard the doctor's voice in the hall. "Despite the distractions," she told him, "I'm starting to feel safe on the island. It will be even better when the water ices over, though Jace said they still fly into the airport in the winter, weather willing."

A quick rap sounded on the door and the doctor came in. He had a clipboard in his hands.

"Congratulations!" he told them with a smile lighting his weathered face. "It's early, so not much more to say because this hormone test will be positive even ten days after conception. But you said your prediction is probably less than a month along, Mrs. Randal? I'd have to say you two know more than I do about that right now."

Nick squeezed her hands, and she pressed his back. A baby, a brother or sister for Lexi! But also, someone else precious to fear for and protect.

Claire and Nick ate that night at the nearby Island House restaurant, telling the others they just needed to get away for a bit. Walking with a cane, Nick managed the distance by himself.

They had decided not to tell anyone about the pregnancy for now. Over dinner, they made plans, happy ones about safety and a future home. They talked of the day that Ames would be indicted and judged guilty and rot in some American prison that had no luxury suites, flesh-eating goldfish or poison garden flowers, and no kingdom of spies at his beck and call.

"One other thing," Claire said as they went out and strolled slowly home along Main Street. "Something else I don't want to share with everyone, at least yet. I told you we met that Wade guy—Wade Buxton—that Julia wants to steer clear of Liz. Well, when Liz mentioned where we were living, he said something like, 'Oh, the place with the ghost, the woman who lost her husband.'"

"Ghost! Oh, great, just great, not that I believe in ghosts, only in human hauntings. But I can see why that superstition got started since the wind shrieks up there. Claire, you're not letting that get to you, are you? You don't believe there's a ghost up there wailing, right?"

"I never believed in ghosts until that time I nearly drowned. And then—I know it sounds insane—but I saw something. Two people helping to save me then, two dead people from the past."

"You were delusional. Lack of oxygen, and the brain can do weird things in that circumstance. Plus you'd been off your meds."

She gripped his arm and they stopped walking. "Nick, Wade Buxton said some people have seen our ghost widow."

"Baloney! But Julia should have mentioned it. Hope there's nothing else she didn't tell us."

When they got back to Widow's Watch, Claire decided to wait for Nick downstairs in the parlor while he huddled with Heck in the dining room. Happy to have a laptop, he had been writing up statements Nick had made about Ames's past, including Nick's insistence that Ames, once a family friend, had actually killed his father and staged it to look like a suicide.

That shattering event was what had inspired Nick to form South Shores years later. Through it, often privately and without fees, he helped families whose loved one had suffered an apparent suicide to prove it actually had been murder or even an accident. Insurance companies often had clauses that refused payment of life insurance death benefits if the person killed himself or herself, so a lot of money could be involved. Nick's support could be legal once he'd disproved suicide, and that was why he'd first hired Claire. Interviewing the family, friends—and psyching out the dead person's state of mind—was the realm of a forensic psychologist.

To Claire's surprise as she entered the dim, silent parlor and snapped on a lamp, Jace unwound his tall frame from being slumped on the sofa.

"Oh, sorry if you were sleeping," she said. "Something wrong with your bed upstairs?"

"Should I say something lovelorn, like I'm lonely, especially there? Everybody else is more or less paired off."

"How did your first day at the airport go?" she asked, taking the coward's way out by not pursuing that. She instantly felt guilty for not saying she understood. After all, she'd reached out to Gina and the others, but this was different—delicate.

"The airport was all right," he said with a shrug. "Boring but better than hanging around here. I hear Julia was here for a while today, so it's a good thing I was elsewhere, right?"

"I didn't say that."

"Maybe I made a Freudian slip, Ms. Psychologist."

"Jace, that's not a Freudian slip but you've obviously realized it's bad judgment to flirt with her."

"Flirt? Sounds like we're back in middle school. She's an interesting, important woman to us."

"Interesting and important, all right. So cozying up to her is against policy and not a good idea. If someone's onto her, they could find us. That's why she wants to keep that Wade Buxton character away from her daughter, I think. What if he's a WIT-SEC refugee here too?"

He shrugged again and shook his head, frowning. "I've seen you're very friendly with Julia, so why not me?"

"That's different, and you know it."

"Mrs. Jack Randal, what I know is that you're sounding as if you're jealous of my finding her very attractive."

"Disaster on the horizon, brother-in-law Seth Randal."

"Hey, no man's an island, even on an island. I resent your thinking I'd do something to risk our safety. Julia's obviously safe, whereas who knows about someone else I might meet here? Now, I'm going upstairs to read Meggie a story tonight instead of you. Or better yet, since we haven't seen any kids' books here, I'll make up a story about a family who lived safely on an island. No divorce, no lies, no jealousy—no hard times."

He walked past her so fast she felt a breeze. Or actually, a cold wind blowing between her and the man she'd once loved and had a child with. The one who had kindly, courageously saved her husband just last week. The one she still cared for more than she ever wanted him—or anyone—to know.

Once they got down from the carriage Julia had sent for them the next morning, Lexi skipped along at Claire's side, so excited to be going to see horses and ponies. Bronco had come along with the two of them, planning to meet Julia's father, Hunter Logan, with whom he'd spend some time to free up Julia and Liz from keeping an eye on the old man. Liz had said he was sinking deeper into the dark pit of dementia, living in the past, obsessed with his Western collection, but not unhappy.

The stable was across a treed lawn from the large home, on a back road above the harbor and the fort. Julia had been reared here, evidently soaking up good guy vs. bad guy Western movies that, in a way, had sent her toward a career in law enforcement in the FBI. Claire's mother always used to say, "What goes around comes around," and maybe that was true. Now Liz wanted to leave just as her mother had.

It was a brisk but sunny day, and Julia was washing down a pinto pony with a hose and brush, just inside the stable door while soapy water from her hose spun into a floor drain.

"Oh, good, you're here!" she greeted them. "Meggie, I'd like you to meet Scout."

"That's a funny name," Lexi said, barely able to stand still in her excitement. "What does it mean?"

"It's named for a horse that used to be on a TV Western, but not the Gene Autry show like you'd guess, once you step inside the house. It was the name of a faithful Indian companion's horse on a show called *The Lone Ranger*.

"Here," she went on, "I'm almost done and I'll show you around the stable, if your mom and Cody want to go inside. Dad's physical therapist that visits from the med center is just about to leave, so he could use some company."

"We'll go right in," Claire said.

"Just introduce yourselves, though he won't remember later," she said, sluicing the soap off the pony. "If you'd just let him talk and show you around his part of the house—upstairs—I'd really appreciate the time. Meggie and I will be right in after I show her around. Then we can talk about Cody spending some time with Dad for a salary. Meanwhile, just pretend you've stepped into some old Western movie."

"You do everything Julia says, now, Meggie," Claire said, giving her a swift side hug. But the child was so wrapped up in the horse, she paid about as much attention to Claire as the horse did. Good, she thought. Something to occupy her mind other than Lily, who was supposedly on her way to Florida, just like they all would love to be.

Claire glanced back at Lexi as Julia gave her the hose to wash the pony. What a blessing, a positive reinforcement, something to look forward to. Claire decided to go to the island's public library and get some girl-and-horse books they could share.

Strange, but of all the people Claire had not only counseled but tried to psych out, she realized Lexi was the hardest to deal with because she loved her so much. And now there would be a second child.

As they went in the back door Julia had indicated, strains of a man singing greeted them. A mellow tenor voice with tinny musical background crooning, "Back in the saddle again."

"Gotta be Gene Autry," Bronco said. "I was too young and missed his heyday."

"Me too, but I bet we're about to make up for that right now. I'm impressed Julia had befriended us the way she has, trusting us to meet her family."

As soon as they walked in through the kitchen, they saw a sign with an arrow, HUNTER LOGAN'S WILD WEST UP-STAIRS. They followed the arrow and the music. When they entered a large room on the second floor, a young man, evidently the physical therapist, jumped up, greeted them and made for the door. Claire realized he must have had orders to stay with Mr. Logan until someone else came.

They introduced themselves, but there was no chatter after. "This is really Gene's theme song, you know," Mr. Logan told them, humming, then singing along with the words. "It's the essence of him—love of the West, closeness to his horse, friend-ship. But, of course, unlike the so-called heroes of today, that man knew right from wrong. You know, the good guys vs. the bad guys and the good guys win."

"Sure," Bronco said. "I like that too. It's the gray guys, the ones that hide the truth and are phonies, I can't stand."

"Let me show you my things," Mr. Logan said, gesturing. He was dressed in jeans, a turquoise-studded silver belt, a fringed plaid shirt and Western boots. A tall, handsome man, he looked tan and fit, though he walked with a limp. He gestured toward the wall behind them on which at least twenty still photos of scenes from Western movies hung.

"That one's from *Rim of the Canyon*, my favorite," he told them, pointing. "That frame shows an old prospector warning Gene that killers are in the area."

Claire's gaze snagged with Bronco's. They'd seen enough of something like that, she thought.

"There's a spooky building in that movie, too, see," Mr. Logan said, tapping the black frame of the next photo. "And this third one's from *Goldtown Ghost Riders*. You won't believe it, but at the end of that film, ghosts might have been the ones to knock off the villains and save the day."

"Oh, look at all this!" Claire cried as she got a glimpse into the next room where six-shooters and old rifles were mounted on the wall in labeled glass cases, then lower, in glassed-in shelves with a guitar, boots, ten-gallon hats and autographed copies of letters, contracts and pictures of the singing cowboy. The old man was so knowledgeable, so sharp about every little detail—and he had dementia?

"This here's my favorite gun on display," he said, pointing to one in the glass-and-wood case mounted on the wall. "It's one Gene actually owned for a while, the old, trusty six-shooter. When he sings 'Back in the Saddle Again,' you just listen for that line about 'my old .44,' 'cause that may be this very gun," he said with a sigh.

Julia soon joined them with Lexi in tow. "Mom, I fed Scout an apple! And—oh, look at these pictures of a real big horse!"

"That's Champion, little girl, but I won't let Julia name any other horses that, because there is only one."

"One favorite horse?"

"No, one favorite cowboy. But did you say your name was Cody, young man?" Mr. Logan said, turning to Bronco. "Julia and I don't see eye to eye on horses, that's for sure. She fusses if I want to go off riding on my own—back in the saddle again," he said with a frown in his daughter's direction.

Well, he remembered Cody's name and that was good, Claire

thought. People with dementia often didn't recall what happened a few minutes ago. But still she'd picked up on bad vibes from Mr. Logan toward Julia.

"Yes, sir, I'm Cody Carson," Bronco said. "I hope we can be friends."

"You'll have to explain which you are, of course, and get back to looking like you should," Mr. Logan said, going now into lecture mode with a bobbing, pointed index finger, but at least not glaring at Julia anymore. "And you cannot be two people at once, even if I am. So are you Buffalo Bill Cody or Kit Carson? You look more like Kit. There is no room for your photos or guns here, but I'd like to ride out to visit wherever you keep all that."

For a second, silence reigned. Bronco looked, to use the best word, buffaloed. Claire, psych major that she was, was taken aback that the old man could slide from apparent rationality to these delusions. Julia looked more than embarrassed—dismayed. And Lexi was quiet for once.

"Well, Cody Carson," Julia said, "I'll just let you explain that—and don't worry whichever way you go. Just your being here is so much appreciated. Jenna," she said to Claire, "how about you and Meggie come with me while I fix some coffee and we talk pony lessons and decide when you'll get the back-of-the-island tour before the weather turns bad."

"Sure," Claire said and tugged Lexi away. She saw Julia wipe a tear from the corner of one eye. Here, dealing with her father she obviously loved and wanted to protect, with her daughter, who wanted to leave island security for the big city—well, maybe the coming bad weather and even hiding WITSEC fugitives were the least of Julia's worries.

CHAPTER SIXTEEN

When Nick and Claire finally headed up for bed, he noted Bronco standing on one foot then the other at the bottom of the staircase.

"Something come up?" Nick asked him.

"Didn't get a chance to tell neither of you what Julia said to me today. You know, after I stayed with her dad for a while, watched a movie with him."

"Tell us," Nick said with a quick glance around, a habit he hadn't been able to shake, even here.

"She told me a guy named Wade Buxton—looks like some kinda movie star, she said—and a Vern Kirkpatrick from Las Vegas not allowed to come in her house or get near her dad. Just to tell them no if they called or showed up."

"Claire's told me about Buxton, so what did she tell you about the Las Vegas guy?" Nick asked. "I'll bet he's the one she mentioned who's trying to buy her father's Western collection. From what Claire told me, it sounds like Hunter Logan would go off the deep end of dementia without all that to keep him occupied."

A voice from above. Jace leaned over the banister at the top of the stairs. "I can tell you about Kirkpatrick. Sorry to say, I met him at the airport," he said, coming down the steps. "He's arrogant and obnoxious without even trying, so he reminded me of someone we all love to hate."

Nick saw Jace's gaze hold Claire's for a moment before she looked away. "First of all," Nick said, "Bronco, did Julia say why she wanted you to keep Kirkpatrick away from her dad?"

"Yeah. You're right about him. He is the one tryin' to buy her dad's entire Gene Autry collection. But he doesn't run what you'd think of as a Wild West show in Vegas, she said. It's got half-naked girl shows, lap dancing, drinks, and it would kill the old guy to lose his stuff to a place like that—or anyplace. I swear, he thinks he *is* Gene Autry, and he calls me Kit Carson, not Cody Carson."

"I bet that's exactly right about the Vegas place," Jace put in. "I saw the guy's business card because he wanted me to keep an eye on the rented plane he has here—even said he'd need help transporting a lot of stuff to it soon. He grabbed the card back when I said no thanks, but I saw his place is called Las Vegas Wild West Museum and Show. Some show, huh, and not steer roping. Who knows it's not a front for something worse?"

"I'll have Heck check all that out online tomorrow," Nick said. "Anything else about the Wade Buxton guy, Bronco?"

Bronco shook his head, but Claire put in, "He's obviously pursuing Liz, and Julia doesn't trust him. Or else Julia knows something about him that means he should steer clear of Liz. I told Nick, so I might as well tell both of you too. When Gina and I met Wade, he said some people think that sound we hear at night is from a ghost up on the widow's walk. He said some people claim to have actually seen the grieving, shrieking widow's ghost. I was tempted to go up there the other day, but with Nick's leg…"

"I can check that out with you," Jace said.

"I don't believe in them—we'll see," she said.

Jace shrugged and turned toward Nick. "So, Jack Randal,

all this is starting to sound like something we should steer clear of, since I give credit to Julia for handling things. I think she's sure-footed in more ways than one."

Actually, Nick agreed with Jace's warning to ignore Wade and Kirkpatrick, but he had to admit he was starting to miss this sort of give-and-take evidence gathering with his law team. But there was no crime, so he had to let it all go.

"Claire and I are going with Lexi, Gina and Nita on a tour of the island with Julia tomorrow," Nick said, "so we'll pass on what you said about Kirkpatrick to her so you won't have to."

"I hear you, counselor," Jace said with a mock salute. "But, maybe since I have to miss that backwoods island tour, Julia will give me a private one."

Jace was starting to think Julia had been a genius to get him a job at the airport. Without being around many people, he learned who came and went and he'd really floored Nick last night with all he knew about Kirkpatrick. The Vegas guy needed watching all right, but no way Jace believed he was actually tied to Ames.

Here it was only his second morning on the job—he got off early at 3:00 p.m. today—and he'd also seen the local mayor and the doctor Nick was planning to visit to keep an eye on his healing bullet wound. Actually, with a couple of other people, several local bigwigs were here for a meeting about something that had to do with the airport.

But the big bonanza of the day so far was the chat with a guy whose name he overheard was Michael Collister. He'd been one of four passengers off the regular Great Lakes morning flight. He was a good-looking, slender, physically fit guy, maybe fifty, casually dressed, who seemed to know his way around in the terminal where Jace had gone for his break. Collister had greeted the two reservation desk workers by name and they'd called out his.

"Did I overhear your last name is Collister?" Jace asked as

he held the door for the man when he headed outside. He had a suitcase in one hand and two huge bouquets of roses in clear plastic in the other. "There's a Collister family here—one I've heard of, at least."

"Collister Stables?" he asked. "That's it. I'm Mike Collister. My ex-wife runs that, and my daughter has a shop here, though I won't mention what she sells. See you around. Thanks for playing doorman."

Jace watched while he went out and chatted with a driver holding the reins of a carriage. Then motioning for him not to bother to get down to help, Collister hefted his bag up and climbed in.

Jace went back inside, wanting to not like the guy, but first impressions—he did. The opposite of Kirkpatrick. Julia may have said she had no husband, but then, they were divorced. At least one of those bouquets had to be for her. Scratch off the idea of taking her a thank-you gift like that tonight and asking her to give him a private island tour later, at least for now. Didn't that big suitcase mean the guy was here to stay for a while? On the other hand, maybe she'd prefer to take a new guy called Seth on an island jaunt instead of her ex.

"I appreciate the heads-up on Vern Kirkpatrick," Julia told Claire and Nick as she harnessed two of her horses to one of the stable's wagons just after lunch that afternoon, so they could see what she called the "back side" of the island in broad daylight. "I know he's still lurking, even though I've told him to steer clear. I appreciate Bronco's spending some time with Dad again today, especially since Liz is set on leaving, no matter how I try to fight that. I had hired Jeremy Archer, the sheriff's son, to help watch Dad before. He's got school and his pizza delivery job, but at least that kept the sheriff up on Kirkpatrick's attempts to hound and con Dad. That man's determined. But I don't want to ruin this trip with talk about him, believe me."

"The sheriff knows you do something else besides the stable, right?" Claire asked.

"It's the law—WITSEC law—that the local authorities always know, so even though they ride bikes here, they are real law enforcement, if you ever need any help, or I'm not available. Okay, let's go, right, Meggie? How about your mom and dad sit back in the wagon and you sit up here on the seat with me?"

"Can I, Mommy and Daddy Jack too? I'm glad we're not taking that rented carriage we came in, and we're going with Julia's horses now."

"If you're going to be taking riding lessons," Claire told her, "you need to learn to do what Julia says, so you be careful up there."

"Too bad Cody can't go too," Lexi said. "And why can't your daddy go, Julia?"

"He used to love to ride where we're going, but he always wants to get out of the wagon and I'm afraid to let him ride a horse anymore. His mind isn't quite right, Meggie. He used to be an excellent rider. Lately he's taken a horse from time to time before I could stop him. Once in the interior of the island, he rides off into the woods and is hard to find or, worse yet, sometimes stands at the edge of a cliff, and I worry he might slip."

"That's something, isn't it?" Lexi asked. "I mean that a dad doesn't do what the daughter says 'stead of the other way round."

Claire had to smile at that, and Nick grinned and rolled his eyes. Surely, this place and these people—especially Julia—were going to help Lexi get over her past traumas and, Claire hoped, losing Lily.

All smiles, Lexi scrambled up to sit proudly next to Julia, and she flapped the reins. They headed past the house and down the drive, but it was blocked by a carriage.

A man bounded down from it, holding a huge bouquet of red roses in a plastic wrap.

"Oh, Michael," Julia cried and halted her horses. "I had no idea. I— We… Some friends and I are just heading out."

"Mind if I take the guest room? I'm sure Dad can use the company."

"He has someone with him now and too much change upsets him." She turned around and told them, "This is my former husband, Michael Collister, from Baltimore, obviously here for a surprise visit."

She briefly introduced them all as renters of one of her father's properties, then individually. As flustered as she appeared, she didn't miss a beat on their fake names or cover story. After brief hellos, Julia ended with, "I hope those roses are for Liz, Michael, because they'll go perfectly with the reds in her shop. She works this far ahead for Christmas and even Valentine's Day, you know."

"Yeah, well, she needs some parental guidance not to be working on that kind of thing at all, and since she's not getting advice here, I came in person. But to see you too."

Claire's stomach clenched. Shades—actually dark shadows—of herself and Jace, tensions just below the surface, the tug and pull of past dilemmas and disasters as well as the good times.

When Julia just stared at him, he said, "Yes, I have some roses for her too. I'll go see her first, then. Is she home or at the shop?"

"At the shop, but as busy as ever."

"I'll be back. Meet you at our old spot later, if I can borrow a horse."

"A restaurant will do. Are you staying at the Island House again?"

Ironic, Claire thought, since that was where she and Nick had eaten dinner. Like Nick, she sat riveted to this little domestic drama.

Michael only nodded, as if he'd run out of civil words, though he was well-spoken with a calm demeanor and managing to hold his anger in, especially under the circumstances of being publicly shafted by his ex-wife. But, crashing in like this, what did he expect?

Julia sat like a statue until he motioned for his carriage driver to pull up so their wagon could get out into the street.

As crazy as her life had been lately, Claire couldn't help thinking Julia's no doubt tough FBI training would pull her through the stress of a former husband hanging on. But then, had her own psychology and forensic training helped her handle Jace?

CHAPTER SEVENTEEN

As Julia drove the wagon away from her house, Claire noticed Bronco, who was staying with Hunter Logan, peering from an upstairs window. Maybe he was wondering if Michael Collister was Wade Buxton or Vern Kirkpatrick. Poor guy: he might now have another persona non grata to watch out for.

"We're heading through the heart of the island to get to the north shore," Julia told them as she turned the team right to start up the hill on Fort Street. As they passed Fort Mackinac, Claire stared at the statue of Father Marquette standing alone in the middle of a grassy yard. Even in the sun and in this wider setting, her brain flashed back to that statue of the dead woman in the cemetery with the baby in her stony arms.

She shook her head to clear it. They were turning onto Huron Street, going more uphill into a heavily forested area, then onto Arch Rock Road. Wasn't Arch Rock the site Julia had said she especially wanted them to see today?

As if Julia could read her thoughts, she said, "Wait until you see Arch Rock and the amazing staircase that climbs up the side of the cliff near it."

"Maybe great for looking at," Nick said. "But with my leg

and Meggie being small, it sounds like the staircase should be saved for later."

"The Arch Rock view is worth the trip," Julia insisted. "I'll just show the stairs to Jenna, and she can take you back there when you're ready. There was an older staircase there for years, just log steps, dangerous and rotting with erosion under it. But it's all been rebuilt, widened, and the view is breathtaking, my favorite place anywhere on Earth."

"Are there flowers to pick around here?" Lexi asked. "You're not 'sposed to pick them in the Everglades, only in gardens."

"Let me put it this way," Julia said, gesturing at the magnificent orange, gold and scarlet hues of the October trees on both sides of the narrow road. "Mackinac State Park, which we're in now, is 80 percent of our island and includes all these big trees with their beautiful, colored leaves, so you can pick those off the ground. We're proud of its being the second created of all the national parks, after the more famous Yellowstone out west. And, Meggie," she said, looking down at her seat partner, who kept watching the two-horse team over everything else, "though the woodland flowers are gone right now, the park rangers can make you pay a fifty-dollar fine *per flower* if you're caught with them. They are protected and how!"

"I think that's real good," Lexi said. "I'd like to be protected or somebody has to pay."

At that, Claire's eyes filled with tears she blinked back before Nick could see them. Out of the mouths of children…her child and yet, a ways off yet, another to come.

"Ta-da!" Julia sang out and pointed ahead after a twenty-minute drive through what became mostly dark green spruce, pine and cedar. Their lofty limbs seemed to lord it over the dense, shadowed forest floor with its thick carpet of leaves and needles. "Arch Rock ahead, but we'll tie up here and just enjoy the view. Usually, this place is crawling with people, but not this time of year. Great—no one else in sight!"

The view of Arch Rock, framed by the autumn trees, was stunning. They climbed down from the wagon and walked slowly closer to the edge of the cliff from which to view it. They stopped and stared. Rising from supporting stone below, with the azure Lake Huron beyond, rose a huge, rough rock arch of stone with a hollowed-out center, like a massive, open gate.

"Can you believe people used to be allowed to climb all over that?" Julia asked. "Way back to Native American times when the tribes believed this was the entry door to Earth for their Great Spirit, people have been in awe. They thought Gitche Manitou would then climb the giant staircase, which has since tumbled into the sea, so they believed mankind built a staircase from this height down to the shore level. It's a bike trail and picnic place below now, on Lake Shore Drive if you ever want to ride your bikes or even snowmobiles there—when Jack's leg heals. This place has meant many things to many people over the centuries, including me."

Claire noted that even Lexi was quiet at the sight.

"It's amazing," Nick said.

"Thanks for sharing it with us," Claire added.

"I'll be right back," Julia said, suddenly sounding stuffed up. "Just give me a moment."

Claire and Nick looked at each other as Julia walked away. Nick shrugged. Claire wondered if she was heading for the public restrooms she'd seen nearby. But no, she wasn't going that direction.

"Hold Meggie's hand," Claire whispered. "I think Julia needs someone to hold hers."

"She more or less said she wants to be alone."

"I know. I'll just see if she's okay. It's everything at once for her, being kind to us, her ex showing up, Liz leaving, her father's situation, then Buxton and Kirkpatrick."

"And getting ready to give me riding lessons," Lexi put in.

Claire gave Nick the take-care-of-Lexi look and hurried after

Julia. Though at first she thought she'd disappeared, she saw she had sat just a few board steps down on what must be the new staircase she'd talked about. Yes, a sign read SPRING STAIR-CASE TO LAKE SHORE DRIVE.

Claire hesitated a moment as she looked down at Julia and below. The staircase was ingeniously constructed with a bolted concrete base to cling to the side of a very steep hill, really a cliff, though trees, rocks and exposed roots clung too. And yes, in spots were remnants of the much older staircase Julia had mentioned, one much cruder and narrower.

Holding on to the sturdy railing, Claire went down a few steps and halted. "I don't want to bother you, Julia, but just want to know you're all right."

She didn't look up but nodded. "Well, not really. I'm try-ing." She dug into her jacket pocket, produced a tissue and blew her nose.

Claire went down a few more steps and sat three up from Julia. "You don't have to say anything," she added.

"Your dossier said you have a psych degree," Julia said and blew her nose again. "Even if my life was on an even keel right now, I'd probably cry at this place. It moves me deeply, the beauty and timelessness of it, even with this fairly new stair-case. I love it here when it's not swamped with tourists, though I'm glad they come. These winding, steep steps and my life—intertwined."

Claire avoided filling the silences with her own words or questions, a tough task, always her weakness as she wanted to reach out and help, to comfort and advise.

Arch Rock seemed so close, as if they could touch it, despite its distance. It felt to Claire as if the forest hovered behind them, both views soothing and somehow threatening. The road far below and the distant crashing waves on the edge of the lake wove a strange spell.

Julia suddenly spoke again. "Just a bit farther down, I accepted a proposal of marriage and several years later told my husband there we were going to have a child. Sadly, my mother died right here on these older steps you can see below this spot. Heart attack when she was hiking. She loved it here too."

"I'm sorry about your mother, but the other two things— happy events, at least then, no doubt."

"Which didn't stay that way. Lost Michael and I'm losing Liz if I stay here, but I need to stay here. Not only because of my father or my career, but because I want to live and die here. Michael could do his consulting work from here, but he refuses. Other things—even another woman—keep him in Baltimore." She heaved a huge sigh. "Yet I could stay here forever."

"But he brought you roses."

"He wants Liz in Baltimore, so needs me to help convince her to go there and not New York."

Claire wanted to argue that she sensed it was not just Liz that had brought him, but she had no right to intrude more than she had. Still, Julia had been so kind and gracious that she'd love to give back to her. But wouldn't that be stepping over the WIT-SEC line that Jace had been warned against?

"So," Julia said, suddenly standing and leaning stiff-armed on the railing, bending slightly over to look down. Then, still without turning to face Claire, she wiped her cheeks with both hands and turned to come up the steps.

Claire stood too and went up the few stairs to the top ahead of Julia. "So," she echoed Julia's single word when she joined her, "you said there was one more place you wanted to show us on the way back, but you can't top this view."

"Nothing can, at least for me," she repeated as they walked to where Nick and Lexi were waiting. "And maybe, as morose as I've been just now—and I apologize for that—we shouldn't even make that other stop today or it might give Meggie nightmares. There's a place called Skull Cave on the route I was going to take back, called that because a white man hiding out there from the Native Americans one night thought he felt rocks and stones of all shapes around him in the dark. When he woke in the morning, he was hiding in a cave where the Native Americans buried their dead, and those were bones and skulls."

"Ugh. Yes, maybe Skull Cave for another day. Jack and I would love to see Meggie get up on Scout's back if there's time for that."

"Great idea," Julia said with a sniff. "Something happy. Something good."

"I hope I'll be riding a bike soon, but this darn leg may just have to wait for a snowmobile to get me around," Nick told Claire after they'd covered Lexi up where she'd fallen asleep on the couch in the family room. She'd been so excited and used muscles gripping Scout's sides so hard that she was exhausted. "And to think," Nick went on with a sigh, "we're all going to learn how to drive again—snowmobiles."

"Bronco should be back by now, shouldn't he?" Claire asked Nick as they sat like old folks in wicker rockers on the front porch of Widow's Watch. "Nita's been wearing out that stretch of sidewalk waiting for him. Maybe I should walk down with her to meet him or get him."

"It's crazy not having a cell phone or landline, but Julia warned against using either, even though we have them. The fewer trails we leave, the better off we are, even here."

"She scared me today, Nick. I glimpsed not only a chink in her armor, but a huge hole. It's wrong for us to think law enforcement or FBI like her are always strong and steady with no problems, like they are just here to take care of us."

"I know. I've seen desperate people look at me as if I can save them from prison or bring back someone who was murdered. My mother used to look at me that way after Dad died. I was so young then and I was all she had left. But, hey, you don't need another client begging for your psychological services today, and a nonpaying client at that. Sure, take a turn helping Nita so she quits worrying about why Bronco isn't back. Heck's researching info about Vern Kirkpatrick, Gina's gone to interview at the medical center, so I'll just be Mr. Mom with Lexi, in practice for when we'll have two to tend."

She leaned over the arm of her rocker and kissed him soundly, then, without even going for her purse or sunglasses, went out to Nita so they could walk up the hill to Julia's.

Julia wasn't in the stables. And things just didn't seem right to Claire. Someone—Julia, of course—must have reharnessed the two horses to the wagon they took this morning. They stood stomping and snorting, impatient to be driven. Scout looked fine in his stall, but two other horses were missing because there were only six here. For one moment, Claire imagined— hoped—that Michael had come back, Julia had talked Bronco into staying awhile longer, and they'd gone for a ride. Maybe they were going to take the wagon at first, then decided to take the horses. Claire had to admit she wanted things to go well for her. Maybe they went back to that romantic spot where Julia had said he'd proposed and where she'd told him a child was on the way.

But everything that had happened today told Claire that was mere wishing. Her instincts, her intuition, her training told her something was wrong.

The house door was open and no one answered when Claire called in.

"I suppose Bronco and Hunter Logan—that's Julia's father's name—could have gone for a walk," Claire told the nervous Nita.

She had been driving Claire crazy, saying all the way she thought something was wrong. But after all they'd been through since they'd hired Nita back in Naples, no wonder she'd learned to be on edge.

"Cody! Mr. Logan!" Claire called into the kitchen and then from the bottom of the stairs. "I know the upstairs layout. Julia won't mind. Let's go check on them."

Her stomach cramped with foreboding, Claire hurried upstairs, still calling for "Cody" and Mr. Logan. Strange, but she was sure she smelled cigar smoke. Julia's father could smoke, but she hadn't smelled that before, and the odor usually clung.

Maybe they were watching another Gene Autry movie or TV show and couldn't hear, but all she heard was that same "Back in the Saddle Again" song playing over and over again.

Nothing amiss in the main room, but in the next with all the glass display cases, Claire saw one was open and the gun was gone, the old man's favorite silver six-shooter he had proudly shown them.

Claire put her hand on Nita's arm to hold her back; they both froze for a moment, listening. Cigar smoke again. Or could something be on fire? They stepped in farther.

Beyond the case with the array of cowboy boots and hats, Claire gasped and Nita screamed.

Unmoving, with videocassettes and CDs strewed around, Bronco was sprawled facedown on the floor with a puddle of blood under his head.

CHAPTER EIGHTEEN

Heck carried his laptop out to where Nick was sitting on the front porch, waiting for Claire and Nita to come back with Bronco. "I see our new horse rider's out like a light."

Nick nodded. "You know, Heck, Lexi's a light in my life, despite the darkness we've all been through."

"I can say I know what you mean now, boss. Gina's something, isn't she? I do want to marry her, but not here. Soon as we get back home, if she'll have me. I hope you can help to get her legal, if Patterson's magic goes away when we're out of here. I'll pay for her education, whatever it takes to make her happy."

"I'd say she's a great investment in more ways than one."

"Right. *Caramba*, like she says. I better get used to her earning a lot more money than me someday. You'll just have to raise my salary again, right? But here—look at this stuff on Vern Kirkpatrick. Wanting the old man's Gene Autry collection must be to fit the theme in his casino and show. Yeah," he said as he lifted the laptop onto Nick's lap, "he's a rich one. Jace was right about him. Thanks to Julia again, Jace is in a good spot at the airport to keep an eye on things, maybe including this guy, make sure he doesn't run off with her father's cowboy collection."

"If Jace can keep his cool and not hijack a plane just to get back in the cockpit." Nick looked at the laptop screen. It listed Kirkpatrick's top investment deals in Q2—the second quarter—as millions of dollars. Megadeals in technology and luxury real estate, but, of course, no names of clients. It was a long shot, but he could know or work with Ames.

"Then here," Heck said, leaning over to hit a few keys to bring up another page. "The interior of his Las Vegas Wild West Museum and Show, which must be a hobby to amuse him, or even some kind of tax shelter."

Nick whistled low as a page with a topless chorus line filled the screen. Well, not topless, since the six women were wearing tiny fringed vests and minuscule skirts that hid very little. "A hobby," Nick said, "or a way to get access to the—ah, workers he pays."

"Yeah, he's done that too, evidently even married a couple of them." Heck brought up another page of a large display room with cowboy posters, shelves of memorabilia—and slot machines. "See," Heck said, "he's got decent Roy Rogers and Lone Ranger memorabilia collections, but it says here the Gene Autry display will be open soon. There's an official Gene Autry Museum in California."

"What's this Kirkpatrick's background?"

"Born and raised in Vegas, twice divorced from former showgirls, no children, not sure how he made his fortune before his appearing on the financial stage, yada yada."

"Shades of Ames in the way he goes after what he wants and maybe flies under the legal radar. And, no doubt, his wealth. Julia said he'd offered her dad a fortune. But she also made clear that, even if her father passed away and Liz didn't want one cowboy boot of the collection, Julia would never sell to this guy. I have the feeling—actually, Claire's convinced me—that Julia doesn't like Wade Buxton either. Claire thinks he might be a WITSEC witness. If he is, he's using an alias, so your trying to research him might be a dead end. Julia partly judges people by who she likes and trusts, and neither of those guys make that cut."

"Not my place to say this maybe, boss, but does she like Jace? He likes her. He said the forbidden fruit is best."

Nick swore under his breath. "I'd trust her to keep her head, but I don't know about him." And, he thought, *He'd better quit looking at Claire like she's forbidden fruit too.*

Claire tried to beat back her panic. Bronco's head looked split open on the back right side, like he'd been hit from behind. The blood still looked sticky and had that fresh copper smell. This had happened recently. Where were Julia and Mr. Logan?

Nita was whispering a prayer in Spanish.

Claire knew better than to move Bronco. Trembling, she touched the side of his neck. He was warm and had a pulse.

"He's alive," she told Nita. "Stop crying. Put your jacket carefully against his head wound to stop the bleeding. Some of it is starting to crust over. We've got to call for help. Stay with him, and I'll look for a phone. I don't care what Julia says—we need phones even here in paradise."

She was angry Julia had talked them out of the ones the FBI had given them. She got to her feet and tore through the upstairs. No landline phones, at least not up here, and Julia and Liz would have their cell phones with them. So where was Julia?

"Stay there!" she shouted to Nita as she passed the room again to go downstairs.

Her forensic training instincts kicked in. She should not be leaving fingerprints everywhere like this, on the banister, doorknobs.

No phone she could see in the living room. She burst into the first room at the front of the house. What was once a parlor and dining room must have been converted into bedrooms for Julia and Liz with a bathroom between.

She could tell whose room was whose. Liz's in mauve and pink was a mess, including a worktable with sketches of corset styles strewed across it. Julia's bedroom in blues and greens had photos of Liz and a middle-aged couple that were Mr. Logan and no doubt her mother. The woman had been beautiful. Liz looked like her. And, despite the fact she'd seen Julia had a cell phone, here was a mobile phone on the bedside table!

Using the hem of her jacket to preserve any previous prints, Claire snatched the phone from its cradle and hit 9-1-1.

Considering that everyone showed up on bicycles, Claire thought the sheriff and medical help had arrived quickly. The two EMTs soon had Bronco conscious but woozy. Claire told Sheriff Archer and his deputy, Officer Stan McCallum, that Bronco's name was Cody Carson. When the sheriff just nodded, Claire blessed the WITSEC rule that local law enforcement knew about Julia and the rest of them.

At first, Bronco just stared at Claire and the tearful Nita as if he didn't know them. But he'd responded to his alias and then reached out to hold hands with Nita, so he might not have a concussion. His eyes seemed dilated, and he talked even slower than usual.

"Do you know who hit you?" Sheriff Archer was asking.

He looked the part of a rural sheriff, Claire thought, calm, steady, even laid-back. His gray hair was cut marine-short, and his eyes were steely blue. He was probably late forties or early fifties. His son, the pizza boy, resembled him, but why was she thinking of such things now?

"Yeah," Bronco muttered, even as one medic worked on cleaning and patching up his head wound. "He musta hit me. The old man wanted to be called Gene but I said he was Hunter Logan."

The sheriff said, "He thinks he's Gene Autry sometimes. So

he hit you for that? It looks like the display box labeled 'Gene Autry's six-shooter' is empty."

"Yeah," Bronco said again, followed by a long pause. "Musta been that. I told him he couldn't go out on the range again, like he kept saying—singing."

"Do you know where the gun is?" the sheriff asked. "It doesn't seem to be anywhere we can see."

"No idea. Hope he didn't have bullets too."

"You got that right. We'll have to ask that of Julia or even Liz."

"Cody," Claire said, unable to contain herself, "where's Julia? Was she here?"

He started to shake his head, then just groaned.

"I'll ask the questions here, Mrs. Randal," the sheriff said. "But go ahead, if you know, Cody."

"Don't know. Did I see her? Didn't see him when he hit me..."

Claire said to the two medical men, "I hope you'll check him for a concussion. Sheriff, will Lorena be able to go with him to the medical center?"

"Sure. I'll need statements from both of you, but that can be later." He rose from his stooped position and motioned Claire out of the room in the hall by the staircase.

"I'd like you and your friend to make private statements later so you don't attract attention in front of others. She can go with him, but you should probably get back to Widow's Watch."

"But don't you see? Not only might Mr. Logan have hit him, but he's missing. And Julia might be too. Two horses from the stables are gone."

"He did wander sometimes and liked to ride, but she put an end to that."

"Or thought she did. Maybe wished she could."

"He used to hightail it into the forest over by Arch Rock. She'd usually find him, but twice he was out all night, and she refused to lock him up. Once he was found peering in windows of one of his rental properties on the island, the one you're in, I think. Finally, she had to take to locking him in."

"So he might have gone off again. Maybe she went after him on the second horse."

"Horses are better than bikes back in the forest to look for someone, especially if they get off the trail."

"Julia advised us not to use phones, so I can't call my husband to help look for her. Could you send someone to tell him what happened? Cody's his employee."

"So I read in the dossier. I'm gonna make this house off-limits until we find who hit Cody for sure and contact Julia. I'll call her on my cell right now, but there's lots of places deep in the woods where they don't work. Can you keep an eye on the stables out back til I get a few more men here? Didn't have many on duty. Stan!" he called over his shoulder. "You got an extra phone on you?"

"In my saddlebag on the bike."

"Get it for Mrs. Randal, will you? So, Jenna," he said with a hard but, she thought, trusting look at her, "you punch the star on it, direct line to me, but like I said, it won't work everywhere."

Claire went back and told Nita she'd be in the stables. Still looking shaken, Nita nodded as she followed the two medics outside, where a wagon had appeared to take Bronco to the med center. When the cell phone was pressed into Claire's hand, she was so grateful she almost cried.

She waited while the sheriff called Julia. She didn't answer, so he left a voice message, then called Liz, who said she was still at her shop, and told her it looked like her grandfather had not only "flown the coop" again but might have committed assault and battery.

The sheriff put Officer McCallum in charge of the house and, before he left, made another call to his office to get a search party to "help Julia find Hunter Logan again. Just tell them to shout for Gene Autry!" After that, Claire went back out to the stable and leaned exhausted against the door.

So everyone knew everything about everyone else here on the island, she thought, as the wagon with Bronco and Nita pulled away. Except, of course, those stashed here as WITSEC witnesses and visitors like Vern Kirkpatrick.

The sheriff had ordered her to go home, but that would waste time. That heavily forested park they'd seen today was the best place to begin looking. Clear to Arch Rock? Strange how Julia had shared so much with her today about her past, her sadness, how she loved the view of that massive stone gate from the steps where she said she could stay forever. She'd been so honest. Yet the strong woman in her had seemed broken.

Claire gasped. She didn't really know where Hunter Logan might be, but she knew one place Julia would check for him. Or what if Julia had ridden off before she knew her father was missing? Maybe she had second thoughts about Michael and had arranged to meet him at their "old spot." Perhaps her father had been desperate to go after her—maybe because, whatever his mental state, he knew that she was depressed, maybe even desperate?

Darned if Claire was going to ride a horse to help him or Julia, but the horses were harnessed again to that wagon. It was as if Julia had intentionally left them that way, then, in haste maybe, had taken a horse to catch her dad or just because she had to be alone again—on that steep stairway.

Claire ran to the front of the house, where Officer McCallum sat with a roll of DO NOT CROSS police tape he hadn't yet unwound.

"I think I know where Julia would go to look for her father or vice versa," she told him. "I'm going to take her wagon and check at Arch Rock and keep my eyes out on the way for them."

"Others will be searching soon. You know how to get there, ma'am?"

"Yes, Julia took us there just today. I'll be all right. Please tell the sheriff and my husband, Jack Randal, if you see him…that… that I'll be fine and I'll be back before dark."

She ran to the stables and climbed onto the wagon seat. She unwrapped the reins, holding them the way she'd seen Julia do. Surely, these horses knew the way too. They seemed eager to stop just standing here.

Whatever had happened, Claire thought, their WITSEC handler and friend needed help, and Mr. Logan did too. She'd just check the familiar way they'd gone today, look at Arch Rock and head back before the search team the sheriff would send got started.

Wishing Nick, or even Jace, was with her, she flapped the reins and the wagon lurched ahead.

CHAPTER NINETEEN

"I'll go look for the old guy and Julia, boss," Heck insisted after the officer with a message from the sheriff left. "You can't pedal a bike."

"Jace took one, but there are more in the carriage house—and that bike for two. I can hang on and use one leg while you pedal. Let's go. I can't believe this, but, thank God, Bronco's all right."

"We going to Julia's house? We can call a horse taxi for that."

"No, we're going back where Julia took us today, since Claire phoned the sheriff to say that's where she's going. He's gathering others there for a search, and the officer said that's where Julia's dad has gone before. Thing is, Claire has a head start on anyone, but at least she has a cell phone with a direct line to the sheriff. And, thank heavens, Officer McCallum said he saw her take the wagon and not a horse. I'll bet she's never driven a horse team in her life. She always gets too damned involved in people's lives and gets into trouble."

"That's her all right, boss, but it's you too."

"Never mind that. Let's go."

Claire tried to tell herself she was not afraid. She finally had a cell phone, one that, with a simple touch, would get Sheriff

Archer on the line, though he'd warned there could be dead spots out here. And she was doing the right thing. She had to help Julia, partly to make up for missing something.

A trained forensic psych, she'd still overlooked signs earlier today that Julia was barely clinging to her inner strength the way that old staircase had clung to the cliff. Why hadn't she picked up on the cues earlier? Oh, sure, she'd known Julia was upset and had reached out to her. But she'd let her initial reading of Julia—confident, in control, sure-footed—cloud reality. Beset by family problems with her father, her daughter, even her ex, Julia was shaky.

Besides that, both Vern Kirkpatrick and Wade Buxton had put pressure on her. Now here Julia was, in charge of seven— no, with Gina, eight—more WITSEC refugees, trying to play tour guide for them, get them settled and keep them safe.

On the cliffside staircase, Julia had said she wanted to live and die "here." But by that did she mean die someday on the island or right there on those steps the way her mother had? She'd said she could stay there forever, and Claire should have picked up on that too. People who were thinking of leaving—of death— sometimes wanted to pick the place for...

No, surely, that strong woman would not consider suicide.

She urged the horses faster though. For steering them, she was going strictly on watching Julia today and movies. She'd only seen a few Westerns, not the hundreds that Hunter Logan seemed to lose himself in. Maybe he saw Julia as his jailer and wanted to escape to "Back in the Saddle Again," that song that was playing over and over in their house.

But other thoughts haunted her about Julia: If she had found Bronco on the floor, wouldn't she have called for help first before chasing after her father? Or could she have seen her dad riding away without knowing Bronco was hurt? Worse, could she have decided to ride out alone, maybe even head back to

Arch Rock, and her father had then hit Bronco so he could go after her?

Parents! Her and Darcy's father had deserted them, and then their mother had become almost a recluse with her voracious, constant book-reading mania. Even now, as Claire turned the wagon into the depths of the shadowy conifer forest, she thought of a line from the long poem *Evangeline* by Longfellow their mother had read them amid countless other things. It was something about the forest looking primeval and the whispering of pine trees. Those words were the beginning to the tragic story of separated lovers who didn't find each other until, in old age, they were reunited only in time for one to die in the other's arms.

Suddenly, the trees seemed so much thicker than earlier today, but then, she'd had her attention on the people she was with, not so much the forest primeval and the looming tragedy at the end of the story she and Darcy dreaded. She shuddered and shook her head to clear it of her agonizing. Surely, not far behind her were the island police and others to look for the old man—and Julia.

Finally, yes, there in the familiar opening up ahead, Arch Rock. If only it was the busy season, Julia had said many would be here. But if Mr. Logan had a loaded gun, perhaps fewer people was best.

She almost cried in relief when she saw two horses tethered to the big beige-and-green Arch Rock sign. They were here, together. Julia knew how to handle her father, didn't she, even if he'd turned violent today?

Not wanting to take the wagon too near the edge, Claire pulled back on the reins and headed the team toward a place to tie up. An errant thought in her panic: Wouldn't Lexi be proud of her for driving a horse-drawn wagon for the first time?

She scrambled down in the shadow of tall white pines, limbless for the first ten feet or so of their trunks before their delicate needles began. It made her feel she walked among giant posts guarding the site.

She couldn't decide whether to call for Julia or her father or just look. Would it be wise or not to sneak up on the old man if he had a loaded gun? What she'd love to see is both of them sitting near the top of the steps as she and Julia had earlier today, just talking.

A chill wind picked up, rustling the branches overhead and tugging at her hair. By glancing west, she tried to gauge how much daylight was left, but the sun was shrouded by hulking cumulus clouds. Darkness came early in late autumn. She stood still at first, looking out toward Arch Rock, not getting too near the edge, then walked toward the stairs. The two tied horses snorted and stamped, looking nervously her way, the whites of their eyes showing.

Claire nearly jumped into them in alarm when she heard a man's voice behind her.

She spun. It was as if Hunter Logan had emerged from a tree. He was wearing a ten-gallon hat and was dressed the same way she'd seen him yesterday but also wore a fringed beige suede jacket. And he was wearing a side holster with a pistol in it.

"This is cattleman's land, young lady. A friend of mine owns it."

Claire just stared for a moment. He had suddenly developed a Western drawl. This was like walking into fantasy island. And she had next to no experience dealing with a person with dementia.

"It's lovely land," she said, deciding it would be wiser and safer to play along. "I didn't mean to trespass and mean no harm."

"That's one of Gene's cowboy rules, you know, number three, so it's pretty danged important. A cowboy must always tell the truth."

"Yes, I admire that. Actually, I'm here looking for a friend of mine."

"Not the rancher?"

"Ah, no. Maybe his daughter. Her name is Julia."

"I just run off that man who owns the saloon with dancing girls. I don't want to run you off, but Julia's not here, just her horse."

"Maybe she was talking to the man with the saloon. Do you remember his name?"

"Vern. He's a cattle rustler in several of Gene's movies."

"Really? Would it be all right with you and your friend who owns this land—"

"It's a spread. And don't get pushy with me, ma'am, 'cause I know how to push back."

"Oh, no, I'm not. Being polite to ladies is probably a cowboy rule too."

He just nodded but moved his right hand to the pistol.

"Would it be all right," she said, "if I walk over to the stairs to look at more of the view? I thought my friend might be there. She likes to sit there."

"You'd need to be real careful. A woman I once knew died there."

"I'm sorry to hear that."

He must be referring to his wife, but she said only, "Was that the lady who had the heart attack?"

"It might have been an Indian attack. They can still be seen here'bouts, you know. No, I reckon someone shot her, someone escaping from a posse," he said, frowning.

Claire's pulse pounded harder as Mr. Logan drew his pistol from his holster in one smooth move and spun it once, then again, around his index finger.

"I wasn't here in time to help her," he said and sniffed hard. He blinked back tears. "The sixth rule is that a cowboy must always help people in distress, but I couldn't help her. Not the one who died there or her ghost who rode that horse in," he added, pointing at one of the horses from Julia's stables.

"Please put your six-shooter away," she said, trying to sound calm when she wanted to run and scream.

"Now, don't you be afraid I'd hurt a lady. Cowboys respect women and this nation's law, rule number nine, so you can tell there's nothing wrong with my thinking. I just needed to get out, especially to ward off thieves and rustlers like that Vern fella."

He turned toward a sound Claire heard too. Several horses, yes, but at least four men on bicycles. Two were on the same bike, a tandem. Oh, thank heavens, Heck and even Nick!

But Mr. Logan raised his pistol and aimed their way. Claire leaped forward, hit his arm. He swatted at her but his shot went down, awry. A woman screamed. Oh, Liz. Liz was here too, on a bike barely visible through the scrim of trees.

Two police officers jumped off their bikes and wrestled the old man's gun away. Claire didn't even wait for Nick but sprinted to the staircase.

Julia was not there. Maybe she was sitting farther down. With all the ruckus, why didn't she climb back up? But the wind was whining so loud that she just didn't hear their voices, that was all. Claire had expected to see her—wanted to see her, sitting here, maybe crying.

As she heard Nick's voice calling "Jenna! Jenna!" above, she didn't see Julia.

Then she did. *Dear God, help us all.* She was sprawled on a rock, facedown, far below.

CHAPTER TWENTY

Claire was still trembling when she collapsed into a chair between Nick and Jace at the dining room table late that night. She glanced at her watch: nearly eleven. She hadn't been to bed yet, but she felt as if she'd just had a narcoleptic nightmare. Even Nick's presence, his holding her, had not helped. Horror clung to her like a cold, wet sheet.

Julia dead. Liz hysterical. Officer McCallum had to handcuff Hunter Logan to take him away, for now back to a friend's house where Liz had managed to arrange for someone to stay with him. Mr. Logan had shouted at Sheriff Archer that he was not really "the law" and the posse was coming "to hang him high."

When they had all finally got back to Widow's Watch and told Jace, he'd been stunned and furious.

Though at first, Nick had wanted to make this a strategy meeting with just the three of them, he'd also asked Heck to sit in. Bronco was upstairs, back from the medical center, trying to sleep with a raging headache from his concussion. Nita kept running between tending the ice pack on his head and making sure that Lexi, whom they hadn't told about Julia's death yet, was asleep.

Gina, who was the one really overseeing Bronco's concussion, came into the dining room with a pot of cocoa and four cups.

"Anything else I can do?" she asked. She didn't go across the table to Heck but put her hands on Claire's shoulders. "I know you're still in shock, all of you, yes?" she asked, kneading Claire's tense muscles.

"Yes, but you've been great," Claire told her. "Sorry I was too upset to eat the quesadillas you fixed when we got back."

"Even though I had to use ketchup for salsa, yes?"

"Meggie said she loved them, called them 'Cuban grilled cheese sandwiches.'"

"You plan to tell her tomorrow? She knew everyone was upset about something."

"She will be too, big-time. But I needed her at least to get a good night's sleep before we try to explain it to her. I'm scared it's going to set her back—set all of us back."

"So," Gina said, still hovering, "like I said, I brought you cocoa, but you just remember, it has some caffeine, so you should eat something too. You need to sleep."

"Yes, Dr. Hermez," Claire said, reaching back to clasp her hand. "But after today, I don't think I could sleep anyway."

"Any of us," Nick put in with a sigh. Claire saw he'd been twisting his watch around his wrist, again and again.

Jace sat stoic and stone-faced but still seething. And fidgeting, as if something else was eating at him and he wanted to say something but was holding back—so unlike him.

When Gina went out, sliding the pocket door to the kitchen closed behind her, Nick said, "I know we're all distraught and exhausted, but we need to decide how to handle this, since Julia was our contact and handler."

"Damn FBI job of hers," Jace muttered. "Who knows who she had to deal with before us. Like Claire said, maybe that Buxton character. What if someone held a grudge against her for how she dealt with things? Claire said Julia had navigated

those stairs for years—the old ones, the new ones. Her job endangered her. Someone knew and hurt her so—"

Nick interrupted, "We can't assume that it was an FBI connection, even if Wade Buxton is a WITSEC refugee and was
upset Julia wanted him to steer clear of Liz. Most WITSECs,
present company excepted, are criminals trading testimonies
for protection."

"My point exactly," Jace put in.

Claire said, "Julia also had problems with Vern Kirkpatrick,
but there were family tensions too. Her father was acting weird,
which I guess is par for the course for him. He was angry she
didn't let him ride the range anymore. And then," she added,
her voice shakier than ever, "her ex was back in town and that
could be—well—touchy."

"Tell me about it," Jace said. "And didn't she have words with
her daughter about her decamping for New York City?"

Nick hit his fist on the table. "Let's not try a murder case
right here, okay? Both of you, back off with all the theories.
We don't know what the offshore coroner will rule after the au-
topsy. What I want us to get clear right now is that—if there was
foul play—other than statements any of us have to give Sheriff
Archer, we stay out of an investigation, out of the limelight, to
stay safe. We have to wait for Rob Patterson or another contact
to reach out to us, tell us what's happening next. Ordinarily, I'd
be looking over my shoulder for Ames and his goons, thinking they'd hurt Julia, but I really think we've found a sanctu-
ary here. I just hope this doesn't somehow screw it up. And yes,
I'm mourning her too."

"I agree we should stay out of it," Claire said, "but we know
who could have wanted her hurt—dead—if there is an investigation."

"You know what I hate too?" Jace blurted. "It's the idea of
that strong, beautiful woman being autopsied. After a nearly

one-hundred-foot fall, she's got to be really—really hurt," he finished lamely with a loud sniff.

Claire covered her face with her hands so she wouldn't burst into tears in front of the three men. She was so tired of being strong, of running, hiding, fearing. She took her hands away, swiping at her tears, then blew her nose. "Julia's beyond our help but maybe we can help Liz or even Hunter Logan," she said, her voice cracking. "That, and helping whoever does the investigation—if they think it might be murder—is one way to honor Julia."

Nick said, "Claire, did you hear me? As my wife and my forensic psychologist, don't go there!"

Jace swung around to face her. "You've always been a bleeding heart, but he's right. I say steer clear too," he insisted, pointing a thumb at his own chest.

"Boss, you got a way to contact Patterson?" Heck asked as if to break the tension.

"Did have. Julia. But he'll surely hear about this and will contact us. Soon, I hope."

"If he flies in while I'm at the airport," Jace said, "I'll brief him, get him here—as long as no one's followed him in."

"Yeah," Nick said, still twisting his watch as if he'd rip it off his wrist. "Who knows that Ames and his lackeys don't have a tail on Rob, even if he's FBI."

"Rob's not stupid," Jace insisted. "And Julia wasn't either, so what the hell happened? Maybe, considering what Claire said about her father, they argued and he pushed her. The guy's obviously delusional and dangerous to hit Bronco like that."

"*If* he hit Bronco like that," Nick said. "I repeat, we can't make assumptions."

"Got that, counselor," Jace muttered. "So why does it seem you're controlling a court scene and Claire's testifying?"

"Come to think of it," Claire put in, as a thought she'd buried hit her, "and this is a fact, not an assumption—there had to be someone else there at the house. If only Bronco could remember, even if he told the sheriff it was all a blank until the rescue squad came. I smelled smoke in the room where we found him. Nita can back me up on that."

"A distant fire?" Nick asked, still in lawyer mode despite his denials. "Their fireplace downstairs?"

"More like a cigar. Upstairs."

"Bingo," Jace said, smacking his palm on the table. "I'm sure there's more than one cigar smoker around here, but Kirkpatrick smokes stogies that must be real expensive. He puts them out if they're partly smoked and saves them in a fancy-dancy tooled leather case that matches his Western boots."

"Unless he keeps the butts because he doesn't want his DNA around, but duly noted," Nick said. "Still, I repeat, we can't jump to conclusions, and we can't get involved."

"Easier said than done in this case," Claire insisted. "Well, it's not a case yet. I've got to go upstairs and take my meds and check on Lexi," she said, standing and pushing her chair back. "Thank heavens, Sheriff Archer said he's coming to take Nita's and my statements first thing in the morning instead of tonight, because I hardly know what I'm saying."

Fearing she'd break into tears again, she hurried from the room.

The bedside clock read 2:00 a.m. in bright red numerals, and Claire still couldn't sleep. Nick had finally quit thrashing and sighing and slept the sleep of the dead—no, that was a terrible way to think of that.

Carefully, Claire slid out of bed and felt for her slippers on the cold floor. She grabbed her flannel robe, one perhaps Julia herself had picked out for her to face the coming cold winter here. She had to comfort herself by just peeking in to see that Lexi was all right. She'd be careful not to wake Nita and Gina, who slept in bunk beds across the room from Lexi's bed.

The dim hall was lit only by night-lights from the two open bathroom doors down the way. She tiptoed across the short space from their room, but the floorboards of the old house creaked as if two people walked here. She was grateful there was not much wind for once so the shrieking from above was a mere moan—or was that sound coming from this room?

Carefully, she turned the doorknob, then pushed the door open. Her eyes were well adjusted to the dark. A dim night-light in the room illuminated Lexi's little bed with its carved maple headboard.

Empty!

Claire gasped and her stomach went into free fall. Not again! First Ames took her, then the search for her in the Havana hotel when...

She got hold of herself. The child could have crawled in with Nita or even Gina up above since there was a bunk-bed ladder. But she usually came to Claire if she woke up. Holding her breath, she bent to look in Nita's bed, where she slept alone, one arm flung out. On her tiptoes, Claire peered at Gina, curled into a ball alone.

Though tempted to wake them to help her search, she backed from the room and quietly closed their door. When she found Lexi, she was going to be much firmer with her. However disturbed she was—and rightly so with all that she'd been through—she had to stop just wandering off.

All right, Claire told herself, *search the house, then wake up the others. Keep calm.* Julia was dead, and they were refugees from their loved ones and all they knew, but she had to keep calm. Perhaps Lexi had even gone downstairs to the den, was watching TV or getting something to eat.

She froze partway down the hall. Low voices. Jace's? Could Lexi have gone to him?

She hurried toward the front left bedroom. A sliver of light shone under Jace's door, so at least he could help her search.

But—yes, Lexi's voice! Oh, thank God, she'd just gone to her father.

She knocked quietly on the door, and Jace called low, "It's open."

Claire pushed it inward. Jace sat in bed with Lexi in his lap, her face glazed with tears. He'd put one of his big sweatshirts over her nightgown, and she wore his huge socks on her little feet. He wore a T-shirt and plaid Jockey shorts with only his feet stuck under the ruffled sheet and quilt.

"Don't scold her," he said. "She knew something was wrong and wanted to know, so I told her there had been a bad and sad accident."

"Mommy, Julia fell and got killed!"

Leaving the door ajar, Claire went in and sat on the side of the mussed bed where she could reach Lexi but avoid Jace's long legs. She leaned closer to pat her shoulder, then hold her hand.

"Yes, sweetheart, and we are all so sorry because she was our friend. I was going to tell you in the morning because I wanted you to sleep first."

"Looks like you haven't," Jace observed. "Did you take your precious midnight meds?"

She just narrowed her eyes at him. One reason their marriage had blown up was because she'd tried to keep her narcolepsy a secret, even hiding and sneaking doses when he was home. It hurt her too that Lexi had run to Jace instead of her.

"Mommy, what about Scout?"

"I don't know, honey. I'll bet we can visit him, but without Julia to be your riding teacher, I just don't know. I do promise, though, we'll get you riding lessons someday, somewhere."

"But I want them now. If I can't have Scout and Julia for new friends, you have to get Lily back from where you sent her."

Claire's wide-eyed stare slammed into Jace's gaze. She opened her mouth, then shut it. She didn't want to upset Lexi even more.

"No psych words of wisdom?" Jace asked. "Don't get involved with all this, Claire, like Nick warned. Just take care of our girl."

A voice made them all jump. "At least, I heard my name in here."

Nick swung the door wider. Shadows silhouetted his big form. "Is she all right? Meggie, I mean. Bedside family reunion?"

Claire stood and turned to face him, still holding Lexi's hand. She felt caught between the two men in her life. Nick looked distressed, and she could feel Jace's stare boring into her back. "She woke and came here, and he told her about Julia," she said.

"I'm sorry, sweetheart," Nick told Lexi, coming a few steps in and peering around Claire. "I know you liked Julia and her horses. We all liked her."

"I'll bet she didn't fall," the child said. "I'll bet somebody bad hurt her like they try to hurt us!"

"A sad worldview," Jace muttered, with a glare at Nick. "Here, better take her back with you so I don't have to go in Nita and Gina's room later."

He kicked back the covers and stood, handing Lexi to Claire. Their foreheads, faces, lips almost met as he passed the child to her.

"Mommy, can I sleep with Daddy? I mean, with Uncle Seth?"

"Not tonight, sweetheart. Besides, remember how much he moves around and might bump you?"

"Oh, yeah. Did he use to bump you too?"

At that, Claire clung to Lexi, went past Nick and hurried out and down the hall. She heard nothing else between the two men but a closed door.

"We'll all miss Julia," Claire whispered to Lexi as Nick caught up to them. He was walking better than before. She saw he had no robe or slippers on and had left his cane behind, perhaps panicked at first when both she and Lexi were gone. And then, when he'd found them with Jace...

"I'll miss Scout if I can't see him lots," Lexi said, with her arms clasped even tighter around Claire's neck. "I know Julia's daughter, Liz, will miss her too, 'cause I sure would miss you if you got dead."

"Don't you worry about that," Claire told her. "We'll all be fine and we'll take good care of you."

Strange then, but as Nick opened their bedroom door for them, the shrill sound on the cupola overhead started in again, as if the widow's ghost was mourning Julia too or warning of dangers yet to come.

CHAPTER TWENTY-ONE

Sheriff Archer arrived just after Claire and Nick shared a solemn, almost silent breakfast. Archer said he wanted to talk to Nita in the parlor first. Jace had seemed only too happy to head for the airport for once, promising to keep an eye out there for anyone they knew—or didn't really know.

"I mean like Kirkpatrick coming or going again," Jace had told Nick. "I know you said lay off, but we can certainly pass intel on if we get it."

Nick had nodded. The two men had been on even tenser terms than ever this morning, Claire thought. Heavy frost had blanketed the grass this morning, and that was the way it felt in here.

"Nita's really nervous," Heck said, hovering in the hall after she went into the parlor with the sheriff. "But she'll do just fine. Poor girl. She didn't ask for any of this. At least Bronco's splitting headache is better, even if he still doesn't remember one thing from the time the old man wanted to show him that six-shooter."

"Did you ask him if he smelled cigar smoke?" Claire asked.

"He doesn't remember."

"Cigar smoke—inadmissible, right, counselor?" she asked

Nick, trying to cajole him a bit. Lexi had slept in the middle of their bed last night, but Claire felt there was more between them than that. Surely, he didn't think she'd been the one to seek Jace out so they could tell Lexi about Julia's death together—or for any other reason. She wanted to clear the air on that, but so much else was going on.

After about fifteen minutes, Nita came back into the dining room, looking shaky with watery eyes, though she wasn't crying. "He said you can come now, Jenna," she said. "Berto," she said to Heck, "you promised you'd let Meggie play a game on your laptop, so can you do it now while I keep an eye on Cody?"

"Sure. Fine. That'll keep her busy for a while. Come on up with me."

"I don't know what I'd do without you," Claire called to Nita as she left the room with Heck.

Claire stood and took a few steps toward the parlor door. "And the same to you, Jack-Nick," she whispered.

"Good to hear," he said, but he didn't even look at her as she left to talk to Sheriff Archer.

Trying to buck herself up, Claire went into the parlor and slid the pocket door closed behind her.

"Hope you don't mind a voice recorder," the sheriff said. "Full disclosure. I'm lousy at taking notes and listening too."

"I sympathize with that," she said, sitting down in the upholstered chair facing his. "When I interview witnesses, I'm the same way."

"Yeah, I read you're a forensic psych," he told her and hesitated with his hand hovering over the on button on his recorder that looked like one she'd left in Florida. "So let me get right to the nitty-gritty here, and I know you'll understand."

He clicked the recorder on and went through the protocols of identifying the two who would be speaking, the time and date and place—and the investigation of the death of Julia Collister, age forty-eight, a resident of Mackinac Island in Mackinac County, Michigan.

Gripping her hands in her lap, then telling herself to relax as she had tried to calm many a witness, Claire sat waiting to hear what he considered the nitty-gritty.

"Of course," he said, "the four possibilities for any apparently unobserved death like this are natural, accident, suicide or homicide. Jenna, in the time you spent with Julia Collister on the day she died, and as a trained psychologist who has worked with people under pressure before, did you pick up on anything that might indicate Julia was suicidal?"

Claire's insides cartwheeled. This man might be sheriff on a far-flung island, but he knew how to go for the jugular. She didn't want to overemphasize that aspect of Julia's personal sharing time with her, in case it was an accident or someone had murdered her.

"Let me note first," she said, trying to keep her voice steady and calm when she felt just the opposite, "that I did spend a few minutes with her privately, earlier that day—early afternoon—on those Spring Trail stairs, which might have been the spot from which she—maybe fell later. She said the view from there was her favorite and she could spend a lot of time there. And she did mention that her mother had a heart attack there, evidently years ago, and died there."

"Actually, ten years ago, yesterday," the sheriff put in. "I wasn't in office then, but I looked it up in the records of the island newspaper, *The Town Crier*."

Claire nodded. She'd known suicides could be triggered by anniversaries, especially tragic ones. And she really hadn't answered his question about suicide yet.

"She didn't mention the date of her mother's death," she said. "She did tell me she was having a hard day."

"Did she say anything to indicate why it was a hard day, if she didn't reference her mother's death? I'm already aware of her father's dementia, which made him hostile at times, and her distress that her daughter was planning to leave the island for 'the big city,' as Julia put it to me once. Those things could lead to depression."

"They surely could. And I think it unnerved her that her former husband was back on the island not only to advise Liz but to see Julia."

The sheriff sat bolt upright. "She told you that? I didn't know Michael Collister was here again."

"Actually, I—we—met him. Julia introduced us when he showed up at her house as we were setting out in the wagon for Arch Rock earlier in the day. He wanted to stay at her father's house but she said no. She asked him if he'd be staying at the Island House again. Technically hearsay, I know, but it's my testimony."

"So things seemed tense between them?"

"They both seemed under control, but yes. He'd brought her roses she didn't take and she said to give to Liz, but he said he'd brought some for their daughter too."

To her surprise, the sheriff snapped off the recorder. "Sorry," he said, "but we'll have to continue this later today. I've known Michael Collister for a long time from his visits. Mr. Charm, but a guy who manages to get his own way. I've got to go find him. I used to have his cell number, but he changes it a lot. The way word travels around here, he has to have heard of her death, so maybe he's with Liz. The Collisters had a custody battle over her when they divorced, but she stayed with her mother. I hope we can keep this interview open-ended, so I can pick up on this later. I wanted to explore the smell of cigar smoke where you found Cody Carson, which your nanny, Lorena, mentioned."

He rose and gathered his things, still talking.

"Each of you have given me a valuable person of interest, because she said your brother-in-law Seth had a little run-in at the airport with that guy Kirkpatrick from Las Vegas. Julia told me he wouldn't take no for an answer about getting his hands on Hunter Logan's Western collection. Cigars sprout from Kirkpatrick's mouth along with ordering everyone around, including me. I'm telling you this so you all steer clear of him. Sorry to run, but I know you understand.

"And," he said, turning back at the door, "I'll try to keep this all low-key, even if I can't keep it hush-hush. This may turn into a situation where you have to testify in an inquest or worse. Maybe you can do it in absentia, but we'll see, as I know you all have to fly under the radar. I've contacted Julia's one-step-up colleague in the FBI. He seemed very, very upset and said he'll contact me soon and send someone to settle things with you."

Settle things with you sounded ominous. "Thank you. We need that," she managed.

He touched his hat brim and headed out the front door. Only after he was gone did Claire see Nick hovering in the hall.

She walked toward him and explained, "He didn't know Julia's ex, Michael Collister, was here, and he's going to find him."

"Gotta watch those ex-husbands who still carry torches, because those can burn," Nick said and went back into the TV room.

Jace pedaled his bike hard through the cold morning wind toward the airport. Snow was imminent, even before Halloween here, and he'd have to drive a snowmobile then. All of them had to learn how. They'd managed to get a third used one from a neighborhood garage sale.

But his thoughts were on more than that. He was scared to death to tell Claire or Nick—anyone—that when he'd got off his shift early about three yesterday afternoon, he'd gone to Julia's house to talk to her, kid her about showing him the sights at Arch Rock since he'd missed the tour there. He'd found her in the stable. He was amazed when she'd said she was going back to Arch Rock, but that she wanted to be alone. Actually, she'd seemed strange and abrupt, put him off and gave him the cold shoulder. Still, he'd really wanted to see it, and like an idiot, he'd followed her at a distance.

"Damn," he said aloud as he pedaled onto the airport grounds and headed toward the terminal to begin his day shift. "I shouldn't have. But everyone else had seen the site. I should've just gone home."

And Julia wasn't the only one in a bad mood. He'd love to have Claire back, Lexi too, of course. But with an investigation, he'd have to tread carefully, work on that lead to Vern Kirkpatrick being guilty, stinking cigar and all. Not that he'd seen what happened to Julia once she went down the stairs. He'd looked at the rock and left, but would the sheriff believe that? If Nick and Claire, even Heck and the others, had to testify, they'd say he was coming on to Julia and she'd snubbed him. At least he didn't think anyone had seen him at her house. Who knew if her father was already gone then and poor Bronco was already lying out cold on the floor.

He blinked back tears and cursed again, wishing he could just fly off into the wild blue yonder. Poor Julia had evidently done that.

About an hour after the sheriff left in a rush, Nick answered the knock on the front door. His wounded leg was feeling better but his heart wasn't. Jeremy Archer, the sheriff's son, stood there. No pizza this time, but an envelope in his hand. The kid's bike was leaning against a front porch pillar.

"Your dad was here but he left," Nick told him. "Do you need to see him?"

"A message came for him, but it's to be passed on to you too, Officer McCallum said," the boy explained, fidgeting as he stepped inside. "That's the kind I have to deliver if the deputies are busy like they are today with Mrs. Collister's death and all. I guess I'm like one of those old-time delivery boys on a bike, like in *The Sound of Music*, which my mom makes us watch every year, but the kid delivering in the movie ended up being a Nazi spy."

"Well, I hope you're not a Nazi or a spy," Nick said. "Thanks for the message. Wait a sec, and I'll get you a tip."

"No, that's okay. Not for police business. I asked Dad once what the messages were for, 'cause I used to take them to Mrs. Collister too, but he said it was enough to know it's not to pick up something from the grocery store and it's not the latest of his fantasy-football bets on the Detroit Lions."

Nick really liked this kid—had liked the island before yesterday—but he was nervous about what was in this envelope. If things like this had come for Julia, it must be WITSEC news.

After Jeremy left, he saw Claire had come downstairs and was standing on the lowest step, just watching him. He knew he'd been acting like a jerk when she needed his strength and understanding, but it had really rocked him to see her with Jace and Lexi, all on Jace's bed, so—so cozy and close.

"Aren't you going to open it?" she asked as she came closer.

"Sure. I just don't want any more bad news."

She put her hand on his shoulder. He craned around and kissed that hand. As they stepped into the den together, he opened the envelope with his finger. They didn't sit but stood, both leaning a shoulder against the wall while he unfolded the single piece of paper.

"You okay?" she asked.

"Not really. Are you?"

"Nick, I'm sorry about last night, but I was glad to find Lexi with her 'uncle Seth.' Before you came in, she mentioned that she wanted Lily back. Then in our bed when we went to sleep, I had another of those narcoleptic dreams I dread, that Lily was the one screaming from the rooftop and she looked just like Lexi. In the nightmare, I went up to stop her and—and I fell."

He tugged her to him, held her hard, and her arms went tight around him. "Sorry," he whispered. "Guess we don't need Freud for that interpretation. But we need to go up there when it's windy and see if we can stop that, buffer it or something. No ghost for sure, but it leads to bad thinking. And I know, despite how Jace and I don't get along sometimes, we can trust him. Not that I really trust his feelings for you."

"Nick, that's over. Only Lexi holds us together. At least last night you didn't lose sleep over it. I might have been awake instead of conking out for once, but you slept like a rock."

"I'd like to be a rock in all this—for you, for everyone. But I—"

He set her back gently, turned toward the window and opened the paper to read it in good light. In a hushed voice he told her, "It's from Rob Patterson but in FBI-speak. He's flying in day after tomorrow."

Claire came closer. Without a sound, she mouthed the words *You mean it doesn't use his name?*

"The person we'll meet with is Pat Robart, my supposed literary agent from New York City. So not only am I writing the great American novel but I now have an agent."

Nick scanned more of the page. "He'll let us know where we can have a meeting with him about the deadline for my novel. He says he hopes our mutual friend rests in peace. Rob Patterson, aka Pat Robart, has always known what to do."

"I don't want to leave here. I can't bear to move again right now. And despite what happened to Julia, I—I like it here, at least until we can go home free and clear."

"Yeah. And if Pat Robart knows what to do, that puts him way ahead of me right now," he said and his voice broke. "Like you, my gut instinct is to jump into this investigation of Julia's death with both feet. It's a classic example of what I founded South Shores to do—and it brings back my father's supposed suicide when I know Ames killed him."

They stood there, not speaking again, but holding each other tight.

CHAPTER TWENTY-TWO

Jace knew one thing he could do to help work his way out of a potentially explosive situation over Julia's death. Vern Kirkpatrick had given him the perfect way to keep an eye on his plans to either pay for or pirate away her father's extensive and, no doubt, expensive Gene Autry collection.

With Julia out of the way, Kirkpatrick's door to ownership of all that was much more wide open. The guy had to be an obvious person of interest in her death. It was, of course, still possible the coroner would rule accidental death or even suicide.

So two days after Julia's death, Jace zoned in on Vern Kirkpatrick. He put his bike in the rack near the Grand Hotel ice cream shop, then walked around to the lobby entrance. He talked his way past the woman collecting money for self-guided tours and asked the man at the hotel desk to call Vern Kirkpatrick's room and tell him a man was here to see him in the lobby about a job offer he'd made.

"Your name, sir?"

"Seth Randal. Tell him the airport worker."

Jace paced, then realized he looked too nervous, so he sat on a floral-patterned sofa with his ankle crossed over his other knee.

The best defense was a good offense, he thought. Absolutely, this guy would be one of the top picks to have harmed Julia to get her out of his way. The other, sadly, would be her ex-husband.

That made him think of Claire again. However revved up he got over her and Nick in bed together right down the hall from him at night, however much it irked him to be cast as Lexi's uncle, he'd never hurt Claire. Too many good memories among the bad, though he'd been a jerk to not think of that before he went nuts and demanded a divorce. He'd never quite learned to control his impulses, at least when it came to women.

He had thought the hotel would look emptier, more ready to shut down soon, right after Halloween. But it seemed busy, mostly women but some men too. People were all over, and he'd seen more than one of those handsome, dark maroon Grand Hotel carriages letting people out in front.

Oh, that's right. He'd heard at the airport that there would be a big shindig the last weekend in October. He'd just passed a poster about it on the way in and had hardly paid attention to it. People were flocking in by ferry and a few by air, so he'd probably bring in some private planes when he went to work this afternoon. The convention was all about that old romantic flick, *Somewhere in Time,* that starred Christopher Reeve, the guy who used to play Superman. A tragedy that he'd fallen off a horse, been paralyzed and died young and then his wife had died soon after of some disease, leaving behind their loved ones.

He shuddered at that thought and tried to focus his mind back on Kirkpatrick looking guilty of Julia's death. The only other plan the guy might have had was to get rid of Hunter Logan himself, so had he gone to their house to argue or cajole the old guy and left his cigar smoke behind in the air? Maybe he'd knocked Bronco out and left him for dead, wanting to make it look like old man Logan did it. Bronco was a big guy, so that took some nerve. What would happen if Bronco got his memory back about all that?

Jace smelled Kirkpatrick's smoky approach before he saw or heard him. He hadn't come from the elevator but from down the hall. Jace stood to greet him but they didn't shake hands. And, yes, Kirkpatrick had a cigar cupped in his hand. It looked as if he'd been hiding it. Surely, there were "no smoking" rules around here, but this guy had already told him he didn't play by the rules.

"Good to hear you changed your mind, Randal," the man said.

"Please use my first name in case you ever try to contact me, because I'm living right now with my brother, Jack Randal."

"Point is, you changed your mind."

"I don't usually moonlight, but they don't pay me much at the airport, and two of us split the duties, so I'm part-time."

"Bet there aren't a lot of job options on this little island, especially with winter coming. Let's sit over here," he said and moved toward two high-backed chairs facing each other over a small table in the corner. Once they were seated, Kirkpatrick added, "So, I assume you heard about the death of Hunter Logan's daughter."

"Word travels fast here. But I didn't put things together until someone mentioned his great Western collection."

"And, gotta admit, word's out around here I want to buy that. But tragic, his daughter's death. Now I'll have to deal with Julia Collister's daughter because the old man has dementia."

Jace disliked this guy more than ever but he had to pretend to be slime, to cozy up to him for cash. Did he imply the tragedy was having to deal with Liz now or did he think that was a break?

"So you still want me available in case you do get that stuff and need it packed quickly and quietly to fly it out of here? I'll bet more than just his family would be upset to see that stuff go to Vegas. You still have that business card you showed me and took back?"

He put his cigar in a china dish on the end table and dug into his inside coat pocket to produce a card. As Jace skimmed it, Kirkpatrick retrieved the unsmoked half of his cigar butt and placed it in the tooled leather case again.

"Those babies are precious, huh?" Jace asked. He'd been trying to tone down the way he usually talked to sound rough.

"The best. I always go for the best, so I'm glad you're working for me, my man. Here, on the back of this other card, write down your phone number. How's fifty bucks an hour and some perks I'll mention later—like a trip to a really great place to meet some really friendly girls?"

Jace had the urge to hit the guy, but he managed to nod and smile, before looking down to write his phone number on the card. He hoped any call this bastard made to him would be when others weren't around. He was damn lucky they even had phones and wouldn't have if Julia hadn't died and Rob Patterson wasn't in charge now. He didn't intend to tell him or anyone that he was spying on a suspect for Julia's murder, not until the time was ripe. Kirkpatrick was quite a talker, so maybe he'd make a misstep and hang himself by then.

"Yeah," the man said, "these aren't just stogies or any cigars. Cuban. Cohibas, sell for around sixty bucks apiece if you don't have connections. It's the private brand rolled for Fidel Castro, they say."

Jace felt a chill slide up his spine as he handed the card with his phone number back. His earlier suspicion that this guy had Cuban ties, however circumstantial so far, would freak out Gina—and Nick.

Kirkpatrick went on, "They say they have a grassy taste with touches of cocoa and coffee. Old man Logan was citing some cowboy rule to me that a cowboy must keep himself clean in personal habits, so I told him I would give up cigars, but no way."

"So you've met him and not just his daughter?"

"With difficulty. Well, enough chitchat for now. If I call you at night, no problem?"

"That's fine. It's going to snow soon, you know, but I'll have access to a snowmobile," Jace said, realizing he still hadn't gone over with the others how to drive one of those. But, hell, he could control a 747, so how hard would a snowmobile be? Things were falling together here already. Kirkpatrick had no doubt been at Julia's house and had words with her. He could have followed her to Arch Rock somehow.

"Good man," Kirkpatrick said and bounced a fist off Jace's shoulder. "This place closes in a couple of days, you know. It's crawling with movie buffs right now and more on the way. I was lucky to get a room. Can't wait to get out of here and back to the desert. You know, play your cards right and maybe I can take you along for the ride out of here."

Jace almost cringed when he shook the man's hand. Actually, he was planning to take this man for a ride, one way or the other.

Two days after Julia's death, Nick, Claire and Lexi hired a carriage and took a large potted plant, brownies and pecan rolls to Liz at her house—and some apples for Scout. Last night the sheriff had returned to finish taking Claire's statement and left them with a warning not to get involved further than they were. But neither of them considered taking gifts to someone who was bereaved getting involved the way he meant.

"I wish the sheriff would have told us what he got out of Michael Collister, since he finally found him," Claire told Nick as they got down from the carriage. Lexi ran ahead, straight for the stable, and they followed, toting their gifts.

"Sorry to say this, but hands off this case, remember," Nick warned.

"Right. Like you aren't thinking about it day and ni— Well, we both finally slept from exhaustion last night."

"I gather from what Sheriff Archer didn't say that Julia's ex had an alibi for when Julia fell. Maybe Rob—I mean, Pat Robart—will know. Damn, everyone who really knows who we are has phony names. We're living double lives, but at least, after escaping Cuba and Clayton Ames, we have our lives."

"As if Rob will tell us anything. If he thinks ignorance is bliss, he's crazy. I don't care what WITSEC rules are. I'd rather go with those cowboy rules Mr. Logan goes by. Rob will probably be on the sheriff's side for us to steer clear when this is something I could help with and you too. It's exactly what you founded South Shores for."

"Oh, hi, Miss Liz!" Lexi called out when she reached the stable's open door. "Can I help you? They said so!" the child went on, pointing at Claire and Nick as Liz, in jeans and a muddy-looking flannel shirt and with straw in her hair, came to the stable door to greet them.

"I'm trying to fill in for my mother—here at least," Liz said. "But, of course, I can't." She burst into tears.

Claire hardly knew this young woman but she quickly put the planter she carried down, stepped closer and put an arm around Liz's shaking shoulders. She had covered her face with her muddy hands.

"Everyone's so nice, but she's gone." Her words came out muffled. "I have to hire a live-in caregiver to get Granddad back from a friend's house where they're keeping him more or less under house arrest, my dad's a wreck, and I am too…"

Claire steered her to sit on a bale of hay while Nick put the food packages he carried down, then took Lexi to Scout's stall.

"Of course, you're grieving," Claire said in her best soothing voice when she felt like dissolving in sobs too. "Your mother's loss is a terrible tragedy, but she would want you to go on, for yourself and for her. She went on when her mother died, and you will too."

Liz lowered her hands from her smeared, dirty face. "But now I have all Granddad's rental property as well as him to oversee.

And my hopes to move my shop… Sorry to have a meltdown in front of you, but I've been trying to hold myself together with the police and all. I swear they think I have a motive, but I'd never, ever hurt her, however much we argued sometimes. Oh, I don't mean to be dumping this on you."

"It's fine. It's why we came today, to comfort and support you. Flowers and food are one thing, but—though I realize we don't know each other well—I lost my mother fairly young too and had mixed feelings about her."

"Like, misery loves company?"

"Like to have a friend, be a friend."

Liz nodded, and when she tried to wipe her eyes on her dirty shirttail, Claire dug a tissue out of her purse and offered it.

"Your little girl—was it Megan?" When Liz talked, she sounded stuffed up now, like she was in a barrel.

"Meggie, yes."

"I'm sure she's upset too—about riding lessons and all. I'll have to get someone to help out here with the horses. It's just not my thing—I can't be my mother. And we can't get her body back from the mainland for a few days, though I'll plan the funeral with Dad's help—maybe with his money too since Mom's bank account is frozen right now. I've got corset orders to fill, even for Halloween, and that's soon, and what am I going to do about publicity at the *Somewhere in Time* conference this weekend?"

"You're part of that? What publicity?"

"I paid a lot for postcards advertising my corset creations to be handed out to attenders before their evening meal Saturday. A lot of them love costumes from the corset eras. They'll be all dressed up and in a great mood. Wade Buxton—you met him at my shop—was going to help me pass them out. But Mother's last wish—I mean, the last thing she said to me the morning she died… I didn't know it was her last—was to stay away from him. So I'll honor that. I already told him when he came here to please just stay away, though he wasn't too happy about that."

"I'd be glad to help you pass those postcards out, though I don't have a costume if that's involved. I could bring Meggie, maybe her nanny, Lorena, and our friend Gina too so we can cover the crowd."

Liz's red and swollen eyes seemed to light at that. "Well, all right. I have some local friends I could call, but with your red hair, you'd be great. If the other two could put their hair up, I've got extra costumes, bonnets, gloves and corsets galore. It would just be for an hour or so this coming Saturday. And thank you for these thoughtful gifts," she said, stooping to pick up the potted plant with blooming dahlias and camellias interspersed among the greenery.

"Mommy and Miss Liz, Scout liked the apple!" Lexi called to them. "Can I give him another one?"

Liz turned to her. "Since he's just a pony, how about you save that for later. But I'll put his saddle on so you can ride him in a circle around the yard, if that's okay with your mom and dad. One of us can hold the rope that goes to his bridle while you ride."

"Oh, thank you! I know you're really sad about your mommy and I am too—about her, not my mommy, I mean. I know I'd be crying too if anything happened to mine."

Tears blurred Claire's vision of Lexi and Nick. From the mouths of children. She had to be so careful to protect herself for Lexi's sake.

"I'll saddle Scout, then," Liz promised, putting the planter down. "And thank you all for the gifts. We'll have to be careful the horses don't eat those plants, won't we, Meggie?" she said. She turned back to Claire. "If you and Jack can stay after Meggie's ride, I'll give you a box of costume pieces you can mix and match for Saturday for yourself and the others. Just a little early for Halloween, right?"

"We'll take all this into the house and put it in the kitchen for you," Claire told her as Liz took Lexi's hand and led her back toward Scout's stall.

"And," Nick whispered to Claire, "we'd better come right back out to be sure she's okay with Lexi."

"She will be," Claire assured him. "She's Julia's daughter at heart—a good heart. But it upset me to hear her describe her mother's 'last words' and some other things she tried to cover for. She sounded so shaky on that, but I suppose that's understandable. Accidents do happen and can be construed as intentional. She's guilt-ridden over their arguing and she's trying to atone by dumping Wade Buxton. But how deep is her guilt and exactly for what?"

"That sort of thinking is precisely what we can't do," he said as they went in the side door of the house into the kitchen. "We are not going to track down and interview possible suspects or we endanger more than a murderer."

They both jumped when a male voice nearby said, "That's enough about suspects and a murderer!"

Michael Collister stood in the kitchen with a raised butcher knife in his hands.

CHAPTER TWENTY-THREE

When she saw the knife, Claire gasped and jumped behind Nick.

"Hey, Collister, put that down," Nick said in a strong voice, though he backed up a step too, bumping into her. He raised the sacks he held like a shield. "We just brought these things to Liz, and she's out in the stable with our little girl."

"Oh, sorry," he said, but instead of putting the knife down, he stabbed it into a ham he'd evidently been carving. He put both hands on the Formica counter and leaned stiff-armed there, head down. Then he snatched a dish towel and started to wipe his hands, over and over while he turned around to lean against the counter, not quite meeting their eyes.

"Nerves," he said. "Loss. Then to hear you saying something about suspects and murder. I— She must have just slipped. But so near the place her mother died. Liz wanted to be out there alone in the stable for a while. Is she all right?"

"Better now," Claire put in.

He nodded and looked them in the eye for the first time, still wiping his hands. Crazy how things came back to Claire that her mother had read to them and both she and Darcy had hated at the time. But now from the recesses of memory came Lady Macbeth's guilt-ridden words after she'd committed a murder and was trying to wash the blood away from her hands: *Out, damned spot!...*

"We're sorry for your loss and Liz's too," Claire told him and stepped forward to put the planter on the table. She saw Michael had been slicing not only ham but a loaf of bread on the counter. Perhaps the food had been a gift from a neighbor, and they were expecting more condolence calls.

"Even for an ex-husband, it's a great loss," he said. "You're welcome to sit down. We've—Liz, that is—has been given a lot of food and support, but of course, she's devastated. I'm just glad I happened to be here when it happened, though it's not helping my position with our illustrious sheriff. Look, I know you are new renters, and Julia was showing you around. How did she seem to you that day?"

Claire could sense that Nick didn't want to answer that or get into a discussion with this man, even though she did. She disagreed with Nick that they shouldn't find out what they could, even if only to pass it on to the sheriff or Rob Patterson and not get openly involved.

"Are you staying here now?" Nick countered instead of answering. "I guess we overheard you might go to the Island House."

"I did at first. But with my former father-in-law staying at a friend's until we can get someone to live here with him, all that's fallen on Liz now, and she asked me to move in. You know, without Julia or him here, the place seems haunted. So you're in the big Victorian rental that supposedly does have a ghost, aren't you?"

Before Nick could put him off again, Claire put in, "We learned that after we moved in. So sad, the thought of death hovering, haunting those left behind."

"Yeah," he said in a whisper, staring wide-eyed beyond her now as if someone else stood there. "And the Widow's Watch house—some say she threw herself off the cupola walk when she lost her husband. Well, at this moment, I can almost understand."

Claire noted he had gained control again. At first, his emotions had seemed so raw—and revealing. But of what? Now Michael sniffed, blew his nose, then washed his hands and dried them thoroughly again.

Before Nick could drag her out the door, Claire asked, "So will you still try to get Liz to move to Baltimore or will her grandfather and other obligations keep her here?"

"Did Liz or Julia share that with you?" he said, finally tossing the towel on the counter. Claire also noted that he never really turned fully toward them but stood sideways, the typical body language to indicate subconscious, wishful flight.

"Sorry to cut this short," Nick said, "and please accept our condolences again, but we've got to get back out where Liz is letting our daughter ride a pony. Jenna," he said and took her elbow none too gently.

"Sure," Michael said. "Okay. Maybe I'll come out too. This silent place is getting to me. No more tinny Gene Autry songs, at least right now, no footsteps with those cowboy boots upstairs—and no Julia."

"Do you ride the horses if it snows?" Nick asked before Claire could get in another word about Julia. "Or use a snowmobile?"

"Depends on how deep it is," Michael called after them.

"See you outside," Nick said and hustled Claire out the door. She shook his grip off her arm and muttered, "Chats about the weather when we might have got something from him?"

"Look, Jenna Randal. It's not easy for me either, but I repeat one more time. We have to steer clear of interrogation and investigation here and you know why. Now let's get our Meggie and head home until we hear from my agent about the supposed book deadline."

"Yes, well, there may be other deadlines, ones we don't even know about, and we'd better get ready for those."

Jace was really nervous as he signaled the Great Lakes Air prop plane into its gate. This was Wednesday, the day Rob Patterson was coming to the island, and he hadn't been on any earlier flights. Did he change his mind to charter his own plane or had something happened to him? Since their Key West plane, which Rob had arranged for, went down in the Straits of Florida near Cuba, crashes obsessed Jace. The airport closed at 5:30, so this had to be his plane or else.

But as he watched the four passengers deplane, he was disappointed. Still, back at Widow's Watch, it was interesting to see Claire and Nick at each other's throats over something for once instead of lovey-dovey, and how would they be if Patterson didn't show?

He saw no one coming across the tarmac in the biting wind who looked like Rob. Only one was a man, and he was gray-haired and walked with a slight limp. Had a mustache too, while Patterson had always been clean shaven and—

Wait. Could he be here in disguise? The man was his height and had his build. He could tell that even in that bulky parka he wore with the hood up. Hell, maybe they should all be disguised in addition to their fake names. This guy must be a master at this.

"Can I get you a carriage, sir?" Jace asked. Yeah, this close up, he could tell it was Rob Patterson.

"No, and don't want to be seen talking to you out in the open. I'll phone your brother, Jack, later. Meeting with you, him and Jenna tonight."

Rob Patterson/Pat Robart went brusquely on, still limping, pretty much like Nick the days after he was shot. Well, Jace thought, meet the master of working undercover and keeping one's mouth shut until it was time to make a move. He'd try to learn from that.

Claire hovered near Nick while he paced in the parlor, on the phone with Rob Patterson. She was so relieved he was here, advising Nick, planning to meet with them. Jace had phoned to say their former acquaintance had got off the last plane from St.

Ignace and didn't look like himself or talk much. But none of that mattered. Without Julia here as their WITSEC handler—and their friend—Claire had been scared about what was coming next. And if Julia had been murdered, was someone onto them hiding here? Though neither she nor Nick had brought it up, it went unspoken that an attack on Julia could mean trouble for them, if the murder wasn't related to Julia's own problems.

"Right. Got it. Can do," Nick was saying even as Jace knocked on the parlor door and peeked in. It was at least a couple of hours after he'd called them to say Rob was on the island.

Is it him? Jace mouthed.

Claire nodded and gestured for him to leave. Frowning, Jace ducked back out and closed the door.

"Just the three of us?" Nick was saying. "But in a public place? Okay, okay. Thanks. We're really shocked about all this. Glad you're here."

He punched off his cell and heaved a deep sigh.

"He's meeting us in a public place?" Claire asked.

"He says he likes to do the unexpected."

"It's dark outside with flakes of snow. Lexi's going to want to go out in it, and for her first time seeing snow, I wanted to—"

"Claire, for heaven's sake! Let the others show her snow. We'll be seeing plenty of it, probably get sick of it, if we're staying here."

Pouting, she folded her arms over her breasts and bit her lower lip. "So, you think we're remaining on the island?"

"To be decided, I suppose. He hardly wanted to chat, the way you did with Michael Collister today. And he really sounded upset about Julia's loss. So, here's the deal. We're meeting my agent in a half hour uptown—walkable—at the Draught House, also called Mary's Bistro, next to the Star Line Ferry dock."

"But still, more or less out in the open? Is he crazy?"

"Like a fox. I'll be happy to have him tell you to quit playing detective too. I'll go tell Jace, and you get ready. Tomorrow,

God and Rob willing, we'll go back to an undercover life with a new handler. We'll mourn Julia, but we'll also play with Lexi in the snow and be grateful our enemy doesn't know where we are—and doesn't realize that, I swear, with the FBI's help, I'm going to nail Clayton Ames yet."

"See there?" she asked, gripping his arm with both hands. "I know how passionate you are about stopping him. If I feel even a tiny bit of that about getting whoever hurt Julia—"

"If someone hurt her, besides herself... Yeah, I understand. But you have to balance that desire with the danger, like I've done for years."

"Right. I'll be careful. But now I know you understand."

Like most of the uptown establishments on Main Street, the Draught House combined with Mary's Bistro had real ambience, Nick thought. It exuded a rustic character with its wooden bar, dark wood tables and captain's chairs. Its long list of ales, lagers and beers dwarfed the good-sized menu posted as they went in. A children's menu too, a couple of things Lexi liked. Man, he had changed if he even paid attention to that under these dire circumstances.

But he felt better already when he saw the man Jace had described sitting at a table in the far corner with his back to the wall, evidently watching for them. No doubt, he was watching for anyone who looked too interested. Nick supposed he could learn a lot from dealing with Rob—Pat. If Jace hadn't described how he looked, he wasn't sure he could have picked him out even from the few patrons here already, several locals at the bar, three tables of diners. He assumed this place was packed in season, but he realized now that Rob had probably chosen it to avoid coming to their house.

The four of them shook hands like old friends, and Rob gave Claire a one-armed hug before they sat. Jace quickly maneuvered to sit with his back to the wall, too, next to Rob.

Rob motioned they shouldn't say anything until they ordered. The TV hung high over the bar had a Vikings–Packers pro football game on and, wherever it was being played, there were snowflakes in the air and dusting the playing field. The volume was on low and blended with the blur of other voices. Now and then, the guys at the bar cheered or groaned.

"They say something called a polar vortex is headed this way," Rob said when the waiter approached, "and that it can be brutal. Bundle up, right?"

The waiter took their order. It annoyed Nick that Jace actually perused the drink list and ordered something called a Lake Erie Monster. Claire ordered a ginger ale, and Nick got the same as Rob, a foreign lager.

"So, so damn sorry," Rob said when they were alone with their menus. He spoke partway behind his hand, despite the noise in the large room. "Sorry for Julia, her family and all of you too. She was special, as an agent and as a person." He actually blinked back tears.

"And without her here?" Nick asked, keeping his voice low too but ignoring his menu.

"Remains to be seen if we can find another handler/liaison, at least for the several of you. The logical person would be someone in the sheriff's office, but I prefer separation of church and state, if you know what I mean."

"So," Claire put in, "you plan for us to stay here?"

"For the immediate future. It's proved to be an excellent location."

"Which means," she said, "along with your mention of 'the several of you,' there could be other WITSEC witnesses here, or at least some have been here in the past."

"Copy that," Rob said, finally putting his menu down. Nick noted he hadn't clearly answered Claire's question. He'd go after him for that in court, but not here. Rob took a long drag of his lager while Nick tried to warn Claire to cool it by pressing his leg against hers.

"I forget," Rob went on, looking at Claire, "that I'm dealing with a forensic psych, who reads between all the lines. But here's the thing. The hallmark of WITSEC is deception. A necessity, of course. Sadly, only about 6 percent of people in the program have no criminal record, so we're not usually dealing with good, solid citizens like you."

Claire expected Nick or even Jace to say something, but they didn't, so she kept quiet too. But Rob was still in lecture mode. "Without Julia to keep warning you of the need for deception and urging you to keep your spirits up, you're going to feel more isolated, more desperate, than ever." He looked from one to the other of them. "After all, you're forced to live a lie. It can destroy your sense of self. At least you're not alone, totally separated from family, like most. You're going to have to rely on each other even more than ever."

Jace shifted in his chair so hard it creaked. He took a swallow of his "monster" drink.

"Any word," Nick said, "of the coroner's ruling about Julia's death?"

"Not yet, and I realize from things she's told me recently that she had problems—pressure. But she'd been in tough personal situations before, was well trained, so I find the possibility she slipped on the cliff or jumped is moot. You're nodding, Claire."

"Despite her problems and some things she said that revealed classic depression, although she mostly hid it, you just voiced what I believe."

"But," Nick said, kneeing her again, "we'll let things work out through the proper channels."

"Unless you happen to stumble over something—even if it's technically hearsay—that's a good idea," Rob agreed. "If she was harmed, I want to know whodunit and whydunit."

Jace cleared his throat and finally spoke. "Besides family pressures, you're aware there are three outsiders who were giving her grief, a Vern Kirkpatrick, who wants to get his hands on her father's Western collection, and a pushy guy, Wade Buxton, who was evidently after her daughter."

Nick noticed even the master of deception and disguise drew in a sharp breath when Wade's name flew by.

"And the third?" Rob asked.

"Her ex-husband, who still wants their daughter near him, not here," Jace told him.

"I'll check that out," Rob said, frowning. "Oh, one thing I do have to pass on to all of you. Our common acquaintance who has lived in Grand Cayman and, more recently, Cuba was not at his home in Havana. Let's just say, we checked. Vacated—even took his flesh-eating fish—and whereabouts unknown. Ah, let's order our food. I've got a room for tonight and, after stopping to see Sheriff Archer tomorrow, will be on the first plane out, weather willing."

He signaled for the waiter, and the men ordered two large pizzas to share and Claire a soup and salad.

"I like your courage and smarts, Jenna," Rob said when the waiter was gone again. "I know it's very hard not to follow your instincts and desires—like how Seth here wants to fly and Jack not only to defend someone in court but nail his nemesis as badly as I do. And you, Jenna, want to jump in with both feet and testify in that court, after you drag someone in."

"True," she said, "but you, of all people, know what I'm trained to do is not like what you see on the TV shows, with risks and arrests. Good forensics is really about asking the right questions of the right—or wrong—people. If I'm very careful, that's not dangerous. Truly, crime is all about character."

Rob pursed his lips and nodded. He knocked twice on the table. "So is life. I'll keep in touch. Come back if I have to. I'm not asking you to hang out in your house. Go ahead and attend the memorial service, do what you can to act normal—whatever that means when you're in WITSEC. If any of you pick up on something or someone else who could have hurt Julia, let me as well as the authorities here know but don't get deeply involved. Got that?"

"Sure, sure," Jace said, looking uncomfortable again.

"That's what I've been telling Jenna," Nick said.

"Jenna?" Rob said, staring her down.

"Family first," she said. "Our extended family here. Their safety trumps everything else."

"Fair enough," Rob said. "Fair enough for now."

CHAPTER TWENTY-FOUR

"Mommy, this snow is so beautiful, better than in movies!" Lexi cried and ran in crazy circles in the backyard the next morning after breakfast. "The snowflakes taste good too! Like cold water!"

Despite her sorrow, Claire forced a smile. "There's only about an inch of it right now, but we'll build a snowman if more falls."

If more falls echoed in her mind. The off-island coroner had ruled that the cause of Julia's fall and death was *undetermined*, that was, he was unable to rule whether it was an accident, suicide or homicide. The fact that it was not a *natural* death was all he could state at this time. He had also said that her body was so injured that pre-fall battery or assault could not be specified.

The sheriff had called to say the coroner confirmed there was no alcohol in her blood, no drugs, no toxins. Officially he had to close the case, and he'd advised them to do the same in their minds, for their own sakes. But it mattered. It really mattered to Claire.

She knew Julia's death would haunt her. She frowned up at the snow-etched cupola on the roof, glad to see no sign of anything amiss, but no wind was blowing.

She hated to admit it, but this Victorian house she liked so much reminded her of the first murder/suicide case she'd worked with Nick at a historic Florida mansion. There, years before, a woman had thrown herself off a balcony to her death and was said to be a ghost seen by some. But Claire was certain sure-footed Julia had not thrown herself off the cliff. The sad thoughts she had shared did not necessarily indicate suicide. She would not have abandoned her father, her daughter or her FBI duties. But how Claire wished she'd followed up on what Julia had said that day to determine whether she needed counseling instead of just support and sympathy.

"Mommy, I said, can we sneak up on Berto and Gina and hit them real hard with snowballs? They're right down the hill, see?"

"Lexi, that would be mean," Claire said, shaken by the frown on Lexi's face. She pointed her finger at her daughter. "You like them. I'm sure you don't mean that." As far as Claire knew, it was her only Lily-like comment since Lexi had said her imaginary friend should come back. "Besides, honey, this snow is so soft I don't think it will pack together well, but we'll see plenty of bigger snows this winter and have fun, including with Berto and Gina."

"Lots of snow is why we have to go for snowmobile lessons, right?"

"Yes. Cody's even going to work in the store that rents them since he won't be spending time with Mr. Logan anymore."

"'Cause got his head hurt and he fell?"

"Kind of. Mr. Logan's going to come back to his house, but have someone with him all the time. Now you'd better run in and say goodbye to your uncle Seth before he heads to work at the airport today."

"Oh, yeah. But it's not airplane work like he wants to do." Lexi zoomed her mittened hand around like an airplane. "Maybe he'll help us build a snowman later too."

She ran into the house. The back door slammed behind her.

Claire had no clue what she would do without her. She desperately wanted to keep her spirits up for Lexi, Nick and the others. And for this child she carried, but the weight of grief kept pulling her down. Even the house and cupola seemed to loom over her, watching, staring. At night, her meds didn't seem to be mellowing her out as much. Last night again, she'd dreamed a statue of a woman came to life and held a dead stone baby in her arms.

The hill that slanted down behind the yard toward the harbor was not steep, and she leaned against a tree there. The ferry was still running, no doubt bringing in *Somewhere in Time* fans for the convention this weekend. Maybe it would cheer her up to dig into those costume boxes Liz had given her and try on costumes with Gina and Nita. Nick had been iffy at first about their going to an event with so many outsiders, but she'd convinced him since they'd look so different costumed, wearing big hats with their hair swept up under them. Besides, would bad guys like the ones Ames usually had working for him truly hide at a romance-movie convention?

She shuddered as the extra push of chill wind buffeted her face, making her eyes water. Amazing to think that the snowmobiles they were going to learn to operate would be able to travel over an ice bridge to St. Ignace this winter. And Rob had said the freeze would come sooner than usual if the polar vortex hit here with a vengeance.

The shift in wind lifted Heck's voice to her. "Gina, *mi chica*, you know what Christopher Columbus said when he first saw Cuba?"

Gina said something in return, and Claire saw her cuddle closer to him about twelve feet below, where they stood, gazing over the harbor. Claire turned away so she wouldn't be eavesdropping, but his words floated to her again. "He said it was the most beautiful sight he'd ever seen. And that's what I thought the first time I saw you and I still…"

Claire hurried back toward the house. Julia had said something similar about the view of the lake and Arch Rock the day she died, her favorite view... And, come hell or high water—Nick or snow or danger—Claire was going to prove the woman did not kill herself.

Nick was glad the snow had let up by the time they all—except Jace, who was at the airport—trekked to the snowmobile rental place on Bogan Street late that afternoon. Before the real snowstorms hit, they needed to learn how to drive the three machines sitting in their carriage house. Two were doubles, one a single, and that one had chains to connect it to a box mounted on a sled for transporting groceries or other goods. Hard to believe that the horse/bicycle culture here morphed to snowmobiles soon.

Nick and Claire brought up the rear of the group. Lexi, who would only be riding not driving a snowmobile, was skipping along at Nita's side, kicking up snow where it had caught or made a small drift. Heck and Gina held hands, which Nick thought was great since they'd seemed so uptight lately. But weren't they all? He wasn't sure how they'd get through the memorial service for Julia on Friday.

"Our friend Pat did a lot in the short time he was here," Nick told Claire. "But he still didn't say if we're going to have another handler."

"He said there would be more information soon."

"Man, I wish they'd at least nailed down where Ames is right now. But he's obviously not a cold-weather guy—and neither am I."

"I'm just grateful Pat Robart didn't move us again. I almost feel safe here—or did before what happened to Julia."

"Yeah," Nick said only. He was aching to keep after the sheriff for details about Julia's death. Ruled undetermined, but maybe, considering things Claire told him Julia had said, a suicide. Yet

there were motives for murder. Every fiber of his being yearned
to jump in with both feet—lawyer and South Shores feet. He'd
felt that way ever since that shattering boyhood moment he'd
found his father dead of a bullet to his head with the gun in his
hand and knew damn well he hadn't killed himself.

Despite the official ruling, Nick didn't think Julia fell or
jumped. Yet he couldn't risk everyone's safety by pursuing it and
possible perps, or even by drawing attention to himself. But as
they passed a store with books in the window, an idea hit him:
maybe he could let word out he was writing a mystery novel
about a murder that could be an accident, and he was just curious about anything like that.

The sign over their destination read AA SNOWMOBILE
PURCHASE AND REPAIR.

"Good thing we have three in the carriage house," Nick said,
"because you can't rent them on the island. Our visitor said they
don't want a bunch of daredevils here messing up their extensive
natural trails in the winter. I hear they have lanterns on some
trails at night, and that must be beautiful."

Claire didn't say so, but she still was leery of riding these machines, and at night, lanterns or not.

The owner was Andrew Archer, the sheriff's younger brother.
Rob had asked the sheriff to set this up before he left, making
Nick realize he had been shortsighted not to arrange it himself.
But living in the North still felt like a foreign country to him,
even with Claire and the others here.

"Hi, guys. I'm Andy Archer," the lanky man said as they
streamed into his shop. He had freckles, blond-red hair and a
big grin with a slight gap between his two front teeth. "Yep, I'm
Sheriff Archer's little brother, but I'm taller and smarter, proved
by my not running for office and chasing bad guys," he greeted
them with what was, no doubt, an often-used line.

Nick introduced everyone and said that Cody, who was going
to be working here, could make sure Seth, who was not here

today, learned how to run a snowmobile. Bronco/Cody just grinned and nodded. The back of his head was still bandaged. Nick was glad to see the big guy in a place where he didn't have to deal with an old man who wasn't in his right mind. Nick was also grateful that, besides the fact that Bronco's short-term memory loss might be permanent, he was pretty much back to normal.

Andy promised to come to the house with Bronco and be sure their three machines were "good to go." As Andy began with a short safety lecture, Nick was amazed there was so much to learn. And safety—for sure, they all needed that.

"A lot more to know than flying across the water on a Jet Ski," he told Andy.

"You're used to warmer weather, right?"

"Right," Nick said, suddenly realizing even little things that slipped out could lead to too much information. The next question would be *So where are you from?* As a man who lived on his words in a courtroom, Nick knew he needed to watch it with other people, even the sheriff's kin. So he said, "We're ready to hear the basics of this machine."

Andy ran through the layout of the typical snowmobile: pull cord, brake lever on the left, throttle on the right, headlights, brake lights. It was, Nick thought, a unique-looking contraption with its water skis–like front and circular tread on the rear that propelled it.

"These babies can be dangerous," Andy was saying, "so all riders should always wear a helmet with shatterproof goggles or face shield. And it's a whole new bag if you ride one over the ice instead of the snow, but you'll have to learn that too in case you need to go to the mainland this winter and don't want to pay the fee to fly. I think it's about forty-some bucks one way in the plane, so these are most folks' winter vehicle of choice."

"So what would you say is the hardest thing to manage?" Heck asked.

"Body-weight maneuvers. Shifting your body to get what you want, especially on hills or turns," Andy told them. "Comes with experience, comes with the territory. Hate to say it, but knowing that can mean life or death, so as much fun as this is, what I'm telling you is serious stuff."

Which, Nick thought, fit the way things had to be for them here. Yeah, without letting Claire know, he might just keep close contact with the sheriff or his deputy, using the excuse of research for his novel, but really researching who might have hurt Julia Collister.

Jace had decided not to try his bike even in shallow snow, and to his surprise, just when he was about to walk home from the airport, Vern Kirkpatrick pulled up in a small wagon he was driving.

"Don't look so damned surprised," the older man said, looking down at him. "You can rent these here, you know. I think your sister-in-law proved anybody can drive one."

The hair on the back of Jace's neck prickled. "You mean Jenna, the day Julia Collister died?" Did that imply this guy was around the murder site and saw her? No, news spread fast here about anything, but he still asked, "How did you learn that?"

"Word gets around, that's all. It'll probably be in that little local paper that's out weekly in season but has gone to once a month now." He gave a loud snort. "Jeez, like living in the boondocks for sure here. Get in. I've got something I need your help with."

Jace's gut clenched. Maybe he'd got in over his head with this guy. He probably wasn't to be trusted, but that was why Jace had cozied up to him.

"Well, you with me or not? I've got a hundred-dollar bill for you here, says you are. So, look, I've got a plastic tub of stuff I want to stash out here, not keep in my hotel room or even on my charter plane yet. I need help to bury it in the Crack in the Island."

Jace's first instinct was to ask what the hell the Crack in the Island was, but that would for sure give away he was an outsider.

"It's just off the airport grounds over yonder," Vern said, sounding even more impatient.

"Right. Okay," Jace agreed, hoping he'd be able to see inside the plastic tub to whatever the stuff was the guy was hiding.

"You drive horses?" Vern asked as Jace climbed up beside him and they pulled away, skirting the airport property just past the runway. They turned left down a dirt road, which told Jace this guy had been here before.

"Drive horses? Not really," Jace said. "About my sister-in-law, Jenna... I suppose word's all over town she found Julia Collister. Which reminds me—that dead woman owned a stable in town. I wonder who will take that over now? You didn't hire these horses there, did you?" Jace knew he was stumbling through this but he'd been jolted by Vern's earlier mention of Claire. He wasn't very good at this pretend stuff, and he was in deep now.

"Naw, not at Collister's. Maybe Julia's daughter will take it over. Her grandfather owns it and real estate around the island, but he's got Alzheimer's or something, which is one reason I thought they might want to sell his memorabilia to someone who would take good care of it, honor it. They're probably land-poor. You think they'd be eager to unload stuff the old man can't so much as inventory anymore."

"So, you've spent some time there?"

"They let me see it once before they heard I want to buy it."

Jace listened intently. He wished he had Claire, even Nick, to help separate the truth from the lies here. He'd need more, something to prove Vern Kirkpatrick was at the Collister house that day so the link to hitting Bronco and letting the old guy loose could be checked out—and the possibility he'd followed Julia or the old guy, argued with her and pushed her to her death.

"I learned to ride horses and drive a team out west." Vern kept up chatter. "But limos and private planes are my transport of choice. Stick with me, buddy boy, and we'll see where this C-note and loyalty takes you."

Vern fished a crisp hundred-dollar bill out of the inside of his coat pocket and thrust it at him. Jace hesitated a moment. If he took money from the man, that elevated—or sank—this clumsy charade to a whole new level. Maybe he'd better clue Nick or Claire in on this, even the sheriff. But would they then home in on the fact he had seen Julia the day she died? Damn it, he'd managed to trap himself in more ways than one.

Just off the runway, on the other side of a white fence, Vern reined in the two-horse team and wrapped the reins around the brake. Jace finally twisted around to look at what was in the wagon, but the large, hard plastic under-the-bed type storage chest was wrapped in an old sheet.

"Help me get that down," Vern ordered, and they hefted it up and over the side. Jace scanned the area—scrub brush, saplings and a rocky outcrop—looking for what could possibly be called the Crack in the Island. At first he saw nothing but a path that quickly sank into the earth with rough, gray limestone outcrop-pings on both sides. The so-called crack was a little over a body width wide and full of leaf litter, so their feet rustled dead, dry autumn leaves as they went in knee-deep.

Vern was panting, so the guy wasn't in good shape, though the plastic box was heavy. Jace heard a single prop plane approach, then land. He pictured the other guy he took turns with sig-naling it into the gate.

"Heard at the hotel this crack used to be deeper," Vern said, stopping for a breath. "Pioneers used it for a garbage dump. Just here. Stop. Put it down."

At least, Jace thought, Vern hadn't brought a lit cigar in here where he'd do one of his rub-it-out half-smoked and possibly start a fire. Vern kicked some leaves away at the level of their knees. A low, flat hollow appeared, like a dark shelf.

"Shove it in there," he ordered. "I got one more under there, lot smaller'n this one."

Still keeping an eye on the man—damned if he was going to turn his back on him the way Bronco might have—Jace bent to slide the box through the pile of leaves. Maybe he'd come back later, with Nick, Bronco or Heck, to see what was in there. He figured he could take this guy in a fight, but who needed that, and what if he had a gun or knife? Maybe he was trying too hard to check him out, risking his own neck.

But nothing happened except for the fact that, right before they slid the box clear under the rock outcrop and shoved leaves back over the site, Vern pulled off the old, ratty sheet. And through the thick, milky-hued polyethylene, Jace glimpsed a ten-gallon hat, a lot of loose CDs and a pair of really nice tooled Western boots. And the initials on the side of the boots were G.A.

CHAPTER TWENTY-FIVE

"Ooh," Nita said. "This fancy hat, it is so big and heavy. I don't know if I can balance it."

"You'll get used to it," Liz told her, adjusting the big-brimmed bonnet. "Stand straighter. Don't look down. But we'll put it on with hatpins—into your hair, not your head, so don't worry."

Claire knew she had meant that as a joke, but it came out flat and no one laughed. Liz had asked them to come to her house Thursday morning for a dress rehearsal, so they were trying on the costumes for the Saturday convention at Grand Hotel. Claire sensed Liz was desperate to keep busy before facing her mother's funeral service and burial tomorrow. She hoped no one would criticize the young woman for attending the convention the very next day to promote her business. Keeping busy was one way to cope. People mourned in different ways.

Claire had brought Lexi too, and Liz had quickly hemmed up a gown for her. The hats were all too big for a child, so she would just have ribbons in her hair, but she was ecstatic to be included and had a basket to carry the postcard handouts—and no corset for her. She was across the room, preening in front of a mirror. Of course, they had already visited Scout out in the stables. Claire had been looking for ways to keep Lexi's alter ego, nasty Lily, away and this seemed to be helping.

The adults were all going to wear fancy corsets outside of their dresses, so they were really models for Liz's creations too. But, without saying why, Claire had insisted her corset not be laced too tight. Of course, she wouldn't be showing for a long time, but she was starting to feel queasy in the mornings, just as she had when she was pregnant with Lexi.

"So when is your grandfather coming home?" Claire asked quietly as Liz fussed over pinning up her hair. She needed it a certain way to balance her hat laden with silk flowers and butterflies.

"Sunday. I take it the sheriff got nowhere trying to question him about what happened. How I wish I could risk taking him to the funeral service tomorrow, but I have no idea what he'd do and say. Maybe invite everyone to a saloon, maybe try to rope the pastor or raise a posse."

"You're holding up well."

"Not really. Since Granddad is so unpredictable—well, you saw that in the cliffside chat you had with him before you—you found her. It's scary to have him back, even with his new live-in companion Dad hired. Listen, I'm sorry if he hit Cody. It had to be him since he went riding out either ahead of or after Mother, and Cody obviously stood in his way of that."

"Wouldn't you like to know what really happened?" Claire whispered as Gina laced Nita into a lace corset across the room, and they kept giggling.

"You mean, what happened that sprang him from his Gene Autry prison upstairs?" Liz countered with her own question. Claire was reminded again that her forensic psych training had stressed that asking a question was one way to avoid answering one.

Liz seemed really jumpy now, trying to fill the private moments between them with talk. "Granddad seemed happy there, except for wanting to get 'Back in the Saddle Again' on one of our horses. I may try to sell them in the spring, so if you want to buy Scout, let me know. I must admit Granddad got furious with Mother and me when we wouldn't let him go out and ride anymore—that on top of Mother and me having words about my leaving. I suppose—you said Cody hasn't got that piece of memory back from when he was hit."

Claire also noted Liz kept changing subjects with each sentence. Was it because she'd admitted her grandfather was angry at Julia and that might implicate him in her death, or because she'd blurted out that she and her mother had argued?

"No, and he might never recall," Claire said. "But short-term memory loss does return sometimes, especially if something or someone gives it a little boost."

"Are you thinking we should try to ask Granddad what happened? Look, I don't need a lawsuit from Cody on top of everything else, if Granddad did hit him. That cigar smoke you mentioned tends to cling, so that doesn't mean that leech Vern Kirkpatrick was here recently. Is that what you were thinking?"

"Believe me, Cody would not sue. As for Kirkpatrick, I don't know, but I'm sure the sheriff will check on his whereabouts on that day. I just thought you might want more answers, and maybe what happened might be good for your grandfather's new companion to know, so he can be watchful."

Liz narrowed her eyes, swollen and red from crying. "Are you a shrink?"

"Not exactly. Just someone who cares—really."

"A lawyer?"

Claire shook her head. She supposed she'd gone too far here, hoping to re-create what led up to Julia's death so she could probe if there was foul play involved and by whom. Nick would lower the boom on her head in place of this big hat.

"I plead guilty to neither of those careers," she assured Liz.

After all, Claire thought, a psychologist was not a psychiatrist and she'd leave the lawyering up to Nick.

When Gina sucked in a huge breath as Nita tried to lace her up, Liz rushed over to help. She told them, "Just think of all the ways women used to suffer for fashion's sake, and we run around today in next to nothing. So little structure in what we wear, even in our lives, but my corsets bring a bit of structure back, a good compromise of old and new...because are we any happier?"

She gave a little hiccup and stopped talking. They all stood like statues, dressed and laced and balancing big hats, just staring at Liz. Even Lexi quit looking at her dress in the mirror.

"So free and happy unless things go all wrong..." Liz choked out and collapsed onto the window seat.

Silence hung heavy in the air. Nita was wide-eyed, and Gina narrowed her eyes, then stepped forward to feel Liz's forehead and take her pulse.

"I'm all right," Liz said. "As all right as I can be. I just don't think she killed herself and I can't believe someone would hurt her—that she'd let someone shove her. I really don't, so, Jenna, it's okay if we question my granddad on Sunday when he gets back."

Claire sat on the window seat next to her and took her other hand. Lexi came over and leaned against her mother's shoulder. Nita hovered behind Lexi as they made a protective wall around Liz. Whatever women wore, Claire thought, the styles of female friendship hadn't really changed.

The next snowmobile class, which would include some hands-on riding, was held behind Andy's store, where twelve people had gathered. Claire was shocked to see Wade Buxton. Could it be that he was in WITSEC too and their friend "Pat Robart" had also arranged for him to take these classes? Rob had not responded when Jace had brought up Wade's name, but she was certain she'd seen him react. She supposed it was some WITSEC rule not to fraternize with other witnesses. If a pursuer found one, he'd find them all.

"That young man over there in the black jacket—" she whispered to Nick as the group moved closer around the demo snowmobile "—no, don't look yet and don't stare—is Wade Buxton."

"The one who looks like he stepped off a *GQ* cover?" Nick whispered. "If he's here, not a coincidence."

"Pat could have arranged it for him too. Or else, if he's just new to the area, he needs to learn snowmobiling."

When Wade caught Claire's eyes, he smiled and waved at her. She nodded back and looked away. He obviously remembered her from their brief meeting at Liz's shop. But if he was in WITSEC protection, wouldn't he be more careful? Julia had not liked or trusted him. Was that just because he was hitting on Liz, or did Julia know what sort of man he really was? At the Draught House, Rob had mentioned that only about 6 percent of people in the WITSEC program didn't have criminal backgrounds. This guy could be doubly dangerous. To Liz. To them. He'd argued with Julia, so could he have decided she had to go, or in the passion of the moment in an argument or anger on the cliffside stairs, had he struck out at her?

"I give him credit for recognizing a pretty face," Nick muttered. "He keeps watching you out of the corner of his eye. Look out if he's on the make after Liz told him to forget it. Avoid him at all costs."

Everyone quieted as Andy went over the dashboard instruments and explained about how the shock absorbers worked when the skis hit bumps. Claire's mind wandered. She felt like that right now, shocked to see Wade here. For sure, she took Nick's warning about Wade to heart. But if there was any chance he had hurt Julia, she'd like to keep an eye on him too.

"This front bumper is good crash protection," Andy was explaining. "Remember, you're sitting on an engine that's similar to a medium-to-large motorcycle, so safety, safety, safety!"

Glancing through her lashes, she saw Wade watching her again. She decided right then not to drive the snowmobile herself even in the daylight unless she absolutely had to. And, despite her curiosity, to steer clear of Wade Buxton too.

Julia's early-afternoon funeral service on Friday was held at the old Mission Church. The sign in front said it was on the Register of Historic Places and was the oldest standing church in Michigan. It was a sturdy-looking colonial with steep stairs leading up to the front entry and, above it, a square tower and octagonal belfry. Looking up at that as they waited outside in the crowd for the horse-drawn hearse to arrive with the coffin, Claire reminded herself that she wanted to go up on their roof to look at the widow's walk. She'd taken to wearing earplugs to mute the wail of the wind that sounded so human at times.

When the Victorian-era wood-and-glass hearse arrived, six men stepped forward to carry the polished oak coffin up the stairs. Claire saw that Sheriff Archer and Officer McCallum were here, both in civilian dress and serving as pallbearers. Liz and her father followed close behind, and then the rest of them filed in, but not before Claire noted that Liz refused to take her father's proffered arm. Claire saw neither Wade Buxton nor Vern Kirkpatrick in the crowd of locals, thank heavens. She knew cases where some murderers were drawn to attend funerals or burials of their victims.

Their contingent filed into a dark wood pew about three-fourths of the way back in the small church that was soon packed. Julia and her family obviously meant a lot to this community. Heck and Gina sat together at the outer end of their pew, then Bronco next to Nita. Lexi had plopped herself down between Claire and Jace. Nick sat on the aisle on Claire's other side.

Claire quit looking around and stared straight ahead. She saw that Michael Collister, just as he had wiped his hands repeatedly with a dish towel, wiped under his eyes with a twisted white handkerchief while Liz sat stoically, staring straight ahead at the coffin. An unusually wide space loomed between them. Wouldn't you think they needed each other right now? It seemed Liz was trying to ignore him.

She also wondered if Michael's reactions were indicative of too much mourning for an ex-wife. Of course, he felt bad for Liz and had once loved Julia, evidently still had feelings for her. She'd sensed that the one tense time she'd seen them together. Maybe he blamed himself for their divorce. But he seemed to be exhibiting more grief and guilt than even all that deserved—or he could be distressed by his daughter's icy attitude? Claire made a mental note to delve into that with Liz.

Jace had his arm across the back of the pew behind Lexi, but his fingers brushed Claire's shoulder. He kept shifting positions. He was especially nervous lately, as if her own ex was holding something back. He might also feel guilty, just regretting he'd tried to move in on Julia.

Claire was glad the coffin was closed. She wanted to remember Julia as she was in the brief time she had known her. Capable, caring, bright Julia but, like everyone, hiding frustrations and fears. How touched Claire was that Julia had let her glimpse all that, and how she wished she could have helped her.

"Dearly beloved," the silver-haired minister began, "we are gathered here today to bid farewell to this mother, friend and cherished citizen of our island. Though many off-islanders know this church as a place for special weddings, today we call it hallowed ground and honor an entire life lived well, despite a tragic ending. But Julia Grace Logan Collister now has a new and wonderful beginning in her heavenly home, where no doubt, she will find something purposeful to do, just as she did in her days among all of us."

A few sighs and sniffles. Someone behind them began coughing, and someone else blew a nose too hard. Lexi was trying to see over the people in the rows ahead, so Claire pulled her onto her lap, despite the frown Jace shot her.

Claire soon saw that the family and the minister had decided on a theme of "Christ as the rock" since Julia had loved the Arch Rock site and died near there. A woman played the organ while they sang *"Rock of ages, cleft for me, let me hide myself in Thee..."*

Again, Claire agonized, was someone hiding in plain sight who had killed Julia, or was it truly a sudden stumble that sent her to her death on the rocks below?

The minister read from two Psalms, verses he said that Julia's daughter, Liz, had chosen. *"The Lord is my rock and my fortress and my deliverer"* and *"For in the time of trouble... He shall set me high upon a rock."*

Hugging Lexi, Claire listened intently while the minister spoke about Julia's life, mentioning she'd once served her country by working for the FBI, but, of course, there was not even a hint of her WITSEC duties. Claire did learn that Julia still was on the off-season security staff for Grand Hotel, when she'd got the impression that Julia had only done that when she'd first returned to the island after her divorce.

So if Julia had faced some sort of terrible trouble she could not find a way to get through, Claire didn't learn about it here. Enemies? Evidently no one who was an islander. Still, someone could have forced trouble on her—and maybe death.

Everyone stood while the casket was carried out to the hearse, and then they followed, row by row, starting with the front pews. Outside, the wind was bitter cold, but it was not snowing. A row of carriages and several wagons were lined up to take people to the Protestant Cemetery for the burial if they wanted to go. Nick and Claire climbed in the fourth one, while the others headed back to Widow's Watch.

There was little talking in the wagon, though one woman welcomed them to the island and another said she'd heard he—

Jack Randal—was writing a book. "A history of Mackinac?" she whispered as if they were still in church. "A lot of history here!"

"That's pretty well covered," Nick told her. "Actually, I'm writing a murder mystery set on an island."

Claire sat up straighter. He hadn't discussed that with her.

"Set here?" the woman asked.

"Not here, but I thought the winter solitude would be just what I needed to get it written. The victim, however, is a man who was beloved by the islanders but he was living a double life which came—well, came back to haunt him."

"Oh, my," she said and moved farther away from them when everyone climbed out at the cemetery.

"Oh, my, indeed," Claire said. "What a story—really."

To Claire, he spoke quietly. "I'm hoping it will be an excuse to keep me close to anything the sheriff turns up about Julia. He said case closed but that he was keeping it open in his mind. Not that I'm going to consult with him, but I plan to pick his brain."

"The plot thickens."

"Sweetheart, look," he said, tugging her off the path a ways where they were bringing up the rear of the mourners. "I can see the wheels turning in your mind. You're not letting this go, are you?"

"No. It haunts me. It's like fear of the Castros still haunts Gina. Like not flying hurts Jace. Like Clayton Ames obsesses you."

"Okay, I'm with you, then, but we have to be very careful. You're getting close to Liz, but watch your step and keep clear of Wade and Vern Kirkpatrick, at least if I'm not there. I'll try to get Heck to check both of them out more. I'll befriend the sheriff. It's a start."

"I'm going to talk to Julia's father on Sunday, see what he might come up with—"

"I believe you failed to mention that, so don't lecture me about dropping a surprise."

"I was going to tell you later. I'm also going to take Bronco with me to see if being back there can jog his memory."

"Then I'm going too to ride shotgun, pard'ner."

They held hands as they walked quickly through the tombstones to catch up with the others now standing under a canvas awning above the open grave. Some headstones were old, worn ones with praying hands and long-past death dates; some new ones of polished marble had the person's picture etched or mounted on them.

Nick said, "The last time we were in a cemetery…"

"I know. I about lost it when I saw the statue of that Cuban saint holding the dead child. It still gets to me."

He squeezed her hand. At least she and Nick were working together again, no secrets, except their identities here.

As they stopped at the edge of the group of mourners, Claire turned her head to survey the sweep of gravestones clear to the iron fence and jolted.

"What?" Nick whispered.

She turned toward him and nodded toward the iron gate. Almost hidden by the parked wagons, she'd seen Wade Buxton, leaning there against the bulky, short stone wall.

"Wade Buxton, watching from afar," she whispered.

"Where?"

When she looked again, Wade was gone.

CHAPTER TWENTY-SIX

The *Somewhere in Time* convention was like stepping back in time. As Claire, Liz, Gina, Nita and Lexi mingled with guests who were waiting to go in for their Saturday evening cocktails and dinner, it seemed everyone was dressed in costumes from the so-called Gilded Age.

"Except for the corsets, we blend in pretty well," Liz told Claire as they meandered through the buzzing crowd, passing out publicity postcards and chatting. They had Lexi in tow, while Nita and Gina were nearby looking every bit like Edwardian ladies they were not. They had to avoid stepping on long skirts and toes. Several women carried parasols, and, though they'd closed them, their tips and spikes needed watching. Several gentlemen had tall hats. One man's fell off when he turned fast to ogle Liz in her corset. She was putting on a good show with smiles and chatter, but Claire could see she was still hurting.

"How are you and your father getting on together after everything?" Claire had slipped in the question earlier.

"You might know, when he could be so helpful, he told me his wife is coming. I said, 'Please, no. Not now.' We had a few words about his moving out. All I need is her underfoot in my mother's house, near her things, her horses. I swear, he never did get over Mother, and they could have put things back together, but then he found that woman and—"

It was all she could say—but it was a lot—before the next cluster of people came along and they began handing out postcards again. Claire overheard a thin woman say, "Did you see that TV tabloid type show *Inside Edition* sent a camera crew here? That just shows how important this wonderful movie still is. Deborah Norville's not here though. I think she looks amazing for her age, in her upper fifties if she's a day. You know Jane Seymour actually attended one of these conventions recently, and wouldn't it be awesome if she came in person and..."

Gently herding Lexi ahead of them, Claire and Liz moved on to another group. But for swollen eyelids, Liz was amazing as she began smiling and chatting again.

But when the three of them approached the next group of women, Wade Buxton stood in their way.

"Oh, Wade!" Liz said. "I didn't know you'd be here."

"You'd wanted me to help, remember?" he asked, tipping his bowler hat to Claire and winking at Lexi. "I still had these duds you loaned me."

"But that was before—before... I assumed you'd know better now."

"But *knowing* involves the brain and not the heart. I'm doing this from the heart."

Claire was tempted to roll her eyes, but she just stood there like a chaperone—like Julia might have done if she was here.

"Well, thank you for the effort," Liz said, "and you do look handsome as usual, but—"

"I've had more than one woman tonight stop me to say I looked like Christopher Reeve in the movie. I get noticed."

"You do, indeed," Claire cut in. "Guarding the cemetery gate but not coming in."

"Again, Jenna—that was your name, I think—it was a matter

of the heart. I knew Liz was suffering but that I'd best stay away right then."

"Like now," Claire countered. She had promised Nick she'd steer clear of this man, but he'd put himself in her path and he annoyed her. He was as slick as oil, the kind of man who liked to live off his looks. He didn't need to circle back to Liz like a vulture the moment her mother was gone. And if he was in WITSEC, that didn't make her feel any better. She recalled again that Rob had said a huge percentage of the hidden witnesses were criminals—if this man was a WITSEC refugee.

Wade turned his shoulder to cut Claire off from Liz. "Liz, look. You're of age," he said quietly, but his words carried to Claire. "We have that special something between us. I'm sorry your mother is gone," he went on, his voice almost swallowed by the crowd noise, "but you don't need another protector to stand between us, so why don't we get rid of her."

Claire knew she was being overly sensitive, but somehow that sounded like a threat. She shuddered, despite how warm it was in this costume. Maybe she should not have come.

"Please, Wade," Liz said, "it was my decision too. I just—"

"Excuse me," another man's voice cut in. A third man lifted a video camera and turned on very bright lights in their faces.

"You all look perfect," the first man said. "*Inside Edition* here and we are shooting a segment that will run on Monday. Oh, a child too. How darling. Go ahead, Greg. Shoot."

Instinctively, Claire ducked her head to cover her face with her bonnet brim as the camera rolled. She pulled Lexi to her and lowered her basket of postcards in front of the child's face.

"Mommy!" she said. "Don't. They're taking my picture!"

Claire was grateful when Liz stepped forward to give a short interview, modeling her costume, talking about her corset shop, giving her name, mentioning the Kardashians had bought her specially designed, hand-finished products. Claire was happy for her. What a break for Liz. And again, after doffing his bowler and smiling for the video camera, Wade seemed to suddenly have disappeared.

Just before dusk that evening, the wind was up and there was no precipitation, so Claire talked Nick into going into the attic to access the widow's walk. She had mixed feelings about it when, the moment they started up the stairs, Jace joined them. It had already been a hard day. She'd dreaded telling Nick about both Wade Buxton and a TV film crew materializing from the crowd at Grand Hotel, but, when she'd explained, he'd said none of that was her fault.

Still tugging on his outdoor jacket as they climbed, Nick said, "Jace, I told Bronco and Heck not to come up with us, because we don't know how much weight that old structure will hold. You're not as big as Bronco but you weigh more than Heck."

"Your leg isn't completely healed yet," Jace countered, keeping right behind them up the stairs and zipping up his own jacket. Claire wondered how he overheard they were going to do this because he wasn't downstairs when Nick discussed it.

Jace went on, "After all, if it's at all iffy up there, I'll go out on the walk and you and Claire can enjoy the view from inside. I think that howling is louder back by your room, but it drives me nuts too. Like a cry for help."

"In that case, it might have been me," Claire said. "I could use some help, because I'm going crazy waiting for Pat Robart to contact us again about whether we're staying."

Jace said, "Odds are good since he signed everyone up for snowmobile lessons to get us through the winter."

"I looked at the door to the walkway earlier," Nick said, as if to stop the chitchat. "Let's do this while we still have daylight."

Claire held the flashlight they'd brought to navigate the dark attic, and Nick tried to turn the rusty-looking metal bolt. "It turns hard," he said as he twisted it, then the knob. "Maybe that's a sign. We should have had Julia show us this when she mentioned it and not waited this long."

"Need help?" Jace asked.

"Nope. Got it."

"Here, let me go out first," Jace said as Nick opened the door. "Damn highest I've been since our plane went down, so I just might take off from here."

"Don't joke about that," Claire insisted. "It's high, and we don't need anyone to fall in this coming darkness."

"Darkness Falling," Nick said. "I'll use that for the working title for the murder mystery I'm not writing."

"Falling Darkness makes more sense," Jace said as he leaned out to reach one hand to the railing and just one foot down on the walk at first. Then he stood, carefully, slowly, on both feet.

"Fabulous view of the harbor," he called back in to them, "but I guess that's why the widow kept watching from here."

"The point is," Claire said, stepping out carefully beside him, while Nick fussed with the door to be sure the wind wouldn't close it on them, "I don't believe she still watches from here and moans when the wind's up. Let's look for whatever it is that makes that sound. I don't hear it right now."

"The wind direction shifted," Jace said. "Be careful up here. You go around that way, and I'll meet you at the back."

"It looks sturdy enough," Nick said and stepped out on the three-foot-wide walkway as Jace and Claire walked slowly away in opposite directions.

"Watch your leg," Jace called back to him. "We'll look around the corners."

Claire didn't see anything amiss and met Jace, waiting for her on the other side. "I think I see where it is—the spot," he told her as they faced each other on the narrow walkway. "See that northeast corner back there? Its flashing is broken. Go back around. It's too narrow for both of us at once."

Jace called to Nick, "I think I see the culprit, and with a ham-

mer, nails and something curved to nail down, maybe we can
get a good night's sleep again. Can you yell down to Heck or
Bronco to find something like that?"

Nick looked at Claire as she came back around from her side.
"Sure," he said and stepped inside again.

Awkwardly, Jace and Claire stood side by side, looking out
over the backyard, the slant of grass below where she'd heard
Heck courting Gina, then the harbor, breakwall, lighthouse
and lake beyond.

"Don't get sick up here," Jace said.

"What? You know heights don't bother me."

"Not even on a day when you've had morning sickness?"

"What?"

"Claire, Jenna, whatever I'm supposed to call you, you're
not eating breakfast well and you look green in the gills in the
a.m. I've seen it all before, remember? I think you're pregnant
and telling no one. Wow, fast work for starting a family since
you two never really had a honeymoon—unless you count the
weeks you've been here and there running from Clayton Ames.
Hey, maybe my brother, Jack, can put that in his mystery novel."

She was stunned. It seemed Jace knew a lot of things, as if
he'd been spying on them.

"My pregnancy is no one else's business right now," she insisted, holding on to the railing and not looking at him. "Well,
I didn't mean that as harsh as it sounded. I'll tell Lexi later, when
some of these challenges have passed. I'd really appreciate it if
you'd keep that a secret."

"Sure."

"I know you told Lexi about Julia's death before I could, so
I hope you mean that."

"No one else will notice for a while. Can't say you have a
glow—more like you look too pale." His voice was husky and
intimate even in the sweep of wind as it shifted again and the

very place he'd pointed out began to moan. "Besides," he added, "I'm a dedicated Claire watcher."

"You and someone else, I'm afraid."

"What's that supposed to mean? Nick lurking?" he asked and turned around to the attic door, which still stood empty.

"Wade Buxton keeps turning up, then disappearing, and he's no ghost. I'm just wondering if he did that to Julia."

"You need a bodyguard, let me know."

"Very funny."

"It wasn't meant to be. Claire, you and I may have had tough times, but Nick Markwood has had you in trouble from the first day you met him, so watch your step—up here, everywhere."

"Hey," Bronco called from just inside the door where he'd suddenly appeared with Nick behind him, "I found an old bathtub mat that should work. I cut it in half. Want me to do it?"

Claire spun around, worried they'd overheard, but evidently not.

"Just hand it out since I know right where it is," Jace said. Claire took a last look at the bird's-eye view of the area while Bronco handed the hammer and nails out to Jace and handed her the rubber mat and some duct tape.

She sidled along where Jace knelt and handed him the tape and mat.

"What's that?" she asked, pointing at the corner where he was going to work.

"What's what? This corner edging just came loose and traps the wind. Now that it's shifted again, hear it?"

"No, I mean that little piece of material caught there," she said and leaned carefully over to pluck the small square of dirty, torn and windblown cloth and lace from where it had snagged.

"Beats me," Jace said and started to fit the mat to the corner.

Claire held the remnant of fabric close to her eyes in the fading daylight. A puckered piece of white cotton someone had shirred with tiny hand stitches and attached to a strip of antique-looking lace, which was now ripped. It was as if someone walking here had caught and torn the hem of an old-fashioned slip or fancy dress, even like the ones they'd worn at the *Somewhere in Time* conference earlier today.

CHAPTER TWENTY-SEVEN

Sunday morning, Nick took Claire and Lexi back to the church where Julia's funeral had been held. He'd liked the place and the minister, but—God forgive him—that wasn't why he came today. He'd learned Sheriff Archer was a member and was hoping to corner him informally after the service. Which he managed, sending Claire and Lexi to wait for him in the entryway. It was snowing outside, and Lexi was antsy to play snow games, whatever those were.

Luckily, Nick thought, the sheriff opened the topic he wanted.

"Hi, Jack. So how's your wife holding up after finding Julia like that? I saw you both at the funeral."

"She's been trying to support Liz. And, of course, wondering if any of the three men who look like they might have had motives for harm—I know the coroner ruled the cause undecided—look like persons of interest. They're all in the clear, of course, but that worries Jenna. So they are of interest to us."

"Everybody knows cop talk from TV and movies these days, don't they? I mean like, *persons of interest.*"

Nick nodded. If this guy only realized that he knew cop talk, attorney talk, prosecution talk, even constitution talk. It hurt his pride to have to play dumb, but he kept his mouth shut on all that and said only, "Julia was kind to us the few days we knew her, and Jenna feels sorry for Liz."

The sheriff looked around before he said, "She was a compassionate contact. Helpful and kind to me too. Actually, each of the three persons you refer to have alibis, though hardly ironclad. Fuzzy time frames. Each elsewhere but alone at that time. I'm not letting it go, no matter what the ruling, but you should. I can tell you the coroner found no signs of trauma such as gunshot or stab wounds. Leave it to the professionals, Jack. Tell Jenna that, and I thank her for her clear and complete testimony. Have a good day." Instinctively, he reached up to touch the brim of a hat he didn't wear and headed back into the crowd.

"Well?" Claire asked as they started walking home and Lexi ran ahead, kicking up snow from the grass and sidewalk.

"Well what? We'd better step up our snowmobile driving if it's going to keep falling like this."

"You know that's not what I mean."

"Michael, Kirkpatrick, pretty boy Wade—all have alibis, but hardly ironclad, as the sheriff put it, so we'll see what unfolds. Carefully. Quietly. That's our deal, right?"

"One of them," she said, linking her arm through his.

"If we have other, more intimate deals," he said, his voice husky, "I'd like to see what unfolds there too. Now that we've quieted the woman on the roof, I can give more attention to the one in my bed, if you're comfortable with that."

"Very. Just because I'm with child doesn't mean we have to be strangers."

"I know you haven't felt well in the mornings."

"Jack Randal, I haven't felt well about Julia, but it makes me feel a lot better we're working together on this. Are you sure you want to go to Liz's this afternoon with Bronco and me to see if we can jog his—or Hunter Logan's—memory?"

"Wouldn't miss it for the world."

Lexi turned back. "If you go there, I want to go to see Scout too."

"Not this time," Claire said. Nick could tell she was startled Lexi had overheard them. "Remember our deal? We play snow games, and you go to see Scout later this week, not today. Sunday is the day of rest for horses too."

For one second, Nick thought Lexi was going to flip back into what Claire called the "bad Lily" routine. Her pretty little face crumpled into a scowl. "Just so long as no one else feeds him apples," she said.

He told Lexi, "I'll make sure of that. So what's this snow game we're going to play?"

"We're going to play fox and geese, right, Mommy?"

"For sure."

"How do you play that?" Nick asked as they neared their house.

Hands on her hips, Lexi stopped and turned to face them. "You have a person who is 'it,' like a bad guy. He chases everybody else. If he hits them—"

"Tags them," Claire put in.

"Right, then they are dead and fall down like Julia did."

Claire gave a little gasp. "No, the it who is the fox just pens the geese up until all are caught, and everyone has to stay on the paths drawn in the snow—like following the rules which parents give to children."

Lexi pouted and shook her head. "Maybe that's what happened to Julia," Lexi said, looking and sounding every bit like Lily again. "The fox caught her and threw her off the rock and she couldn't fly. Now, if she was like Daddy—I mean, Uncle Seth—he'd fly and catch her, but then be sorry he hurt her."

Claire's wide gaze collided with Nick's as Lexi ran up the steps ahead of them and pounded on the front door that Nita opened to let her in. Nick motioned that they'd be in soon.

"Lily strikes again," Nick said. "Where did she get all that?

Her uncle Seth is the one who told her about Julia's death, so how did he explain it to her?"

"I don't know," Claire told him, looking shaken. "She obviously has a wild imagination and is still troubled by all she's been through. She jumbles things up sometimes." She shook her head as she went into the house too.

Talk about alibis of those three other guys, Nick thought as he followed. How about a fourth man? Jace had got off work midafternoon the day Julia died but hadn't come home for hours and said he was uptown having a beer. Another excuse, hardly ironclad? And motive—Jace had been hitting on Julia just the way Wade had been after Liz and with a lot less success. Maybe he'd either wanted another chance with her or wanted to apologize. He'd mentioned he'd been to Arch Rock, but had said it was after Julia's death, just to see the place she'd died. Surely it wasn't the afternoon she died—or even the moment she died.

Claire made sure she, Nick and Bronco arrived at Liz's house a couple of hours after Hunter Logan had been brought back with his new companion, a widower hired from St. Ignace named Doug Fremont. Liz had said Fremont was around seventy-five and seemed younger, strong too, so she thought he'd do quite well. He was evidently willing to go along with the cowboy theme since he wore a plaid shirt with a string tie, Liz had told them.

"Doug knows all the background here, so he'll be watchful," she assured them. "Mother's orders still go, to make sure Kirkpatrick and Wade stay away. And," she said, lowering her voice even more, "Dad and I did have to sell a few Gene Autry items online to get money to hire Doug since our insurance won't cover it all, things that were still boxed up I think Granddad won't miss. While Doug unpacks in the guest room Dad's vacated upstairs, if you want to try—well, you know. Now's a good time to jog memories. I'll go get Granddad. Dad's here, packing to leave for the Island House again, then back to Baltimore in a few days. I talked him out of having his wife join him here. But how are you feeling, Cody?" she asked, turning to Bronco.

"Good, 'less I touch the back of my head, Miss Liz. Haven't figured out what happened though, so maybe today."

It soon became apparent that Mr. Logan didn't remember any of them, even Bronco, who'd spent hours with him. Claire hesitated to bring up his taking a horse from the stables to go after Julia. She didn't want to get him upset again, after all he'd been through. Maybe she'd overstepped to try to set this up. She'd rehearsed several opening questions, but now it all seemed so futile.

"Where's Gene's boots?" Mr. Logan asked suddenly, staring at the glass cases across the room and getting to his feet.

"Granddad," Liz said, "they're on your feet. Your favorite ones so you don't worry about—"

"No, the ones he wore in *Rim of the Canyon*. I know I got three pairs but those are gone. In that movie, his horse Champion got stolen, just like my boots! I'll show you," he said, getting more agitated as he opened a drawer and clawed through some CDs stored there. "Well, dagnabbit, *Rim of the Canyon*'s gone too and some of the others!"

Claire marveled at how the old man knew his extensive collection so well but not much else. He must have realized the things Liz and Michael sold were gone.

"Now, just relax, Granddad," Liz said. "I'll bet they're just misplaced. Cody, would you please go get Doug?"

Claire was glad she hadn't started this. She'd never worked with dementia patients, only studied the disease. She caught Nick's warning gaze and shook her head. So much for this idea, she thought.

When Bronco came back in with Doug, the old man shouted, "Rustlers been here and taken more than cattle! I tried to stop their leader, but he hit my right-hand man over the head from behind and stole them anyway!"

"Hey, Hunter," Doug said in a calm voice, "we'll find them and get them back."

"And when we do, I'll shoot them but I'd never hit them on the head or shove them off a bluff. Only thieving cowards do that, I tell you!"

While Doug calmed Mr. Logan down, Liz's wide, teary gaze snagged Claire's. "Those are not items we sold," she whispered. "I swear they're not."

Claire kept quiet. But she'd learned some things anyway.

After Mr. Logan calmed down and seemed to forget the "rustled" items, Liz said she'd be right back and ran from the room, wiping her eyes. Claire knew where her bedroom was and thought she'd see if she could help before they left. She told Nick and Bronco she'd be right back and went down the hall where she'd desperately looked for a phone the day she and Nita found Bronco unconscious on the floor. If Liz's door was closed, perhaps she'd give her more time, but she had the excuse that Liz had said she'd put their coats on her bed.

Both Julia's and Liz's bedroom doors were open, though, and Liz's shrill voice came suddenly from her mother's bedroom. "Dad, what are you doing in here? You said you'd be packing upstairs!"

"Let's just say I'm looking for a memento."

"In her dresser drawers? And you've been in her closet? What are you doing?" she repeated. "You gave up your rights to this—to her—years ago. Just go back to your second wife!"

Claire froze, her back pressed to the wall. She needed to retreat, maybe grab their coats and go. But as she turned away to do so, Michael said, "All right, I should have told you. I'm looking for your mother's diary because I need to protect myself and that second wife."

"What?"

"Sweetheart, please, just sit down a minute. Let me explain. Are your guests all gone?"

"Not yet, but don't change the subject. If she had a diary, I never saw it. And why would you have any right to it?"

"It's one she kept just before we were divorced. Sit down, please. It will just take a minute to explain and maybe you can think where it might be. Susan's interior-design business is having some financial problems, and one of her designers is claiming she falsified tax records and I helped her."

"And—and that's one of the things Mother claimed you'd helped Susan do—when the two of you got involved? You think that's in the diary? Then Mother found out and divorced you?"

"Yes, well—right. More or less. I'm glad you're an adult now and can understand that even parents make mistakes."

"Susan was a mistake for you."

"Don't go there. Listen, sweetheart, I suppose your mother could have destroyed the diary, but if it's around, I need to see it—get rid of it before this new mess gets sticky."

"Dad, she's dead. She's not going to turn up with some old diary. I just can't believe it," Liz said in a choked voice. Claire heard her give a big gasp. "Oh, damn. That's the real reason you wanted to go with me to see what was in Mother's safe-deposit box."

"The woman used to work for the FBI, for heaven's sake, Liz, and believe me, she's a master at hiding things, including people. You think I didn't know she was being interviewed by the WITSEC program about the time we divorced? Grow up. Even from the grave, she can hurt me again if that diary's out there somewhere!"

"Is that why you went through Granddad's things when he was away for a few days? Not to help me decide what we could sell to pay for hiring him a full-time companion, but to see if she'd hidden it in there?"

"Liz, please."

"Dad, I really needed you right now. I really trusted you. You— Did you discuss demanding that diary with her? Did you argue with her about it? I know you came in here all charming and friendly, but is that the real reason you came this time?"

"This is out of control. Forget it!" he shouted and a drawer slammed in the room, then a door.

Claire almost vaulted into Liz's bedroom. He was no doubt coming out into the hall. But what if he hurt Liz?

Instead, when she heard fast footsteps, she darted through Liz's open bedroom door and began to pick up their coats from the bed, praying he wouldn't come in.

But he did.

She held the four coats in front of her like a shield.

"Oh," she said, hoping she looked surprised. "Mr. Collister, I didn't know you were here. Liz said you were upstairs. Just came to get our coats as we're leaving."

He narrowed his eyes and frowned at her, no doubt analyzing if she could have heard. He was sputtering mad but made an obvious effort to calm himself. "Actually, I'm leaving too," he said. "Said goodbye to Liz. I've done what I could here."

"And I know Liz appreciates it," Claire lied, hoping to bolster the impression that she had not heard their argument. This man might actually be a threat to her if he realized that. But worse, he could have well been a threat to Julia if, as Liz said, he'd argued with her about the diary and then, accidentally or intentionally, struck out. Maybe came here, hit Bronco first, searched for the diary while Mr. Logan rode away, then followed Julia to the cliffside stairs and confronted her there.

And killed her?

CHAPTER TWENTY-EIGHT

Nick's lovemaking seemed possessive and almost desperate that night. Yet it somehow comforted Claire to be mastered, to let Nick make the moves and decisions.

"I love you, Claire, and always will," he vowed as he rolled them over and fit her naked back and bottom to his chest and thighs. He nibbled kisses down the nape of her neck as if they would begin all over again. "I'm so sorry we got off to such a rough and dangerous start—with our marriage, I mean."

"Mmm," she said, stretching luxuriously. "You are worth it. Know what I thought about you after the first couple of times I met you?"

"That if you got too close to me we'd be fleeing for our lives and hiding out with fake names?"

"Very funny," she said and poked him gently in the ribs with an elbow, "but not far from the truth that you were probably mad, bad and dangerous to know."

"The forensic psych/expert witness is right again. I plead guilty to all three of those charges, my love. But I want to tell you this. Once we get Ames in court and both of us—probably Jace too—testify against him, he's going away for a long, long time. And then you and I will also, maybe on a cruise ship or to a desert island or back here in the winter to hide out again."

"With two children in tow? Batten down the hatches, believe me."

He hugged her closer again. His warm breath stirred her hair, and he moved even closer under the cozy covers they'd thrashed to waves. He whispered, "I was relieved to see how happy Lexi was when we were all out back playing fox and geese in the snow tonight. I'll bet Jace didn't like it though, that she kept wanting him to be the fox and called him a bad guy."

"He understood it was a game. But I do think she somehow caught on to the fact he was not nice to Julia at times. Actually, he tried to be too nice."

"Lexi's too young to pick up on how he was trying to move in on Julia."

"I thought so too. Maybe it's something he said to her, like the night he told her Julia was dead and had fallen off the cliff. I wish he wouldn't have done that without me there. Who knows how he said it and what she picked up under the surface. For a young child, she's really good at reading people."

"Then it's in the genes," he said with a little squeeze.

"And her insistence on doing things a certain way is inherited, I know that," she said and yawned.

"She was a little tyrant if anyone so much as stepped off the circle and crossed paths in the snow we'd cleared. No way was anybody going to cut across the clean areas of snow." As he spoke, his voice became less lazy and more raspy. He lowered his head to lick the skin along her shoulder, a move she always felt through her belly and clear down to her toes. But she felt so exhausted, so floaty. She'd taken her first dose of night meds, but when Nick had started to caress and kiss her, forget nodding off. Now, darn it, but what a time to have to go to the bathroom.

"Nick?"

"Mmm? Your wish is my command."

"Bathroom call. Be right back."

She turned and kissed him, then got up quickly as the chilly air hit her. She padded barefoot and naked, not pausing to grab her slippers or a robe. She made quick work of it, then headed back to bed. As she passed their bedroom window overlooking the backyard, she noted strong moonlight flooding in on the floor. Such a romantic night in so many ways. No howling from above. Bright moonlight on the pattern they had all created by running across the new snow.

She glanced out through the break in the curtain.

"Nick."

"You okay?"

"The backyard. Someone came in and messed it up, added something to the fox and geese pattern. Lexi will have a fit."

He threw the covers off and got up, dragging the top comforter with him and wrapping it around them both as they leaned over to peer through the lightly frost-etched glass.

"You're right," he said. "What is it? It's too exact for a dog to have run through. It looks like some kind of cartoon drawing."

"I can't tell. Let's put on robes and go quietly downstairs to turn on the back door light. What if someone's still out there? And what's the message?"

They jammed their feet into slippers, pulled on flannel pajamas and sweatshirts, grabbed a flashlight and went downstairs in the dark. In the kitchen, they hovered over the window above the sink as Nick clicked on the back door light.

At the top right corner of the fox and geese square that enclosed the four cross paths within, someone had drawn a stick figure of a man with both arms straight out.

"On his feet," Nick whispered. "Are those supposed to be cowboy boots?"

"I guess. But look, tumbling over the side of the square, as if he'd pushed her—that other stick figure. It's a woman falling as if over the edge of a cliff."

Nick hugged her close in a hard grip.

"But what's that sticking out of his mouth?" Claire asked.

They heard footsteps and rough breathing behind them and turned as a dark form came in the kitchen. Nick thrust Claire behind him. It was just Jace, but they both jumped anyway.

"I saw it earlier when I was in here to get a sandwich," he told them. "If you ask me, the thing in the man's mouth is supposed to be a damned expensive cigar, probably the same kind Kirkpatrick smokes."

After closing the curtains, the three of them sat at the kitchen table, drinking hot cider. Nick hoped Claire's tousled look didn't set Jace off on one of his jealous snits again, but they needed this quick conference.

"It's 3:00 a.m. I can't believe you were still up," Nick told him.

"I couldn't sleep and went out in front to watch the stars and moon and clear my head in the cold air. Honestly, I used to think I could navigate by those heavenly signs if the Airbus systems failed. But I saw no one go by and didn't hear a thing when I was out there."

Nick had no choice but to believe him, but Jace had seemed out of breath when he first came into the kitchen. And he was still fully dressed with melted snow on his boots.

"So," Claire said in the awkward silence, "someone is telling us Vern Kirkpatrick shoved Julia off the cliff, right?"

"He sure had a motive," Jace said.

"And Sheriff Archer said his alibi was not ironclad," she said, when Nick kept quiet. "But neither were whatever Julia's ex-husband, Michael, and Liz's would-be suitor Wade Buxton came up with."

"Okay, counselor and expert witness," Jace said, turning to Nick, "I've got to level with you."

For one crazy moment, Nick thought he was going to say that he'd been outside to add the telltale stick figures, because surely not more of a confession than that was coming. It had really been gnawing at him that Jace could have tried to see Julia the afternoon she died.

"Go ahead," Nick urged when he hesitated.

"The first time I met Kirkpatrick at the airport, he offered me a grunt job to help him load some purchases he planned to have in his possession soon. I blew him off, but after Julia died, decided to tell him I'd help—just to keep an eye on him, maybe get the goods on him to tell the sheriff. He's full of himself, won't take no for an answer. He thinks he can do no wrong."

"The way you described him before," Claire said, "he sounded to me like he is a classic case of a mask narcissist, and all those things fit. Insecure inside, so if people don't adore him and go along with his every whim, he attacks them one way or the other."

"But that's not the end of it. He drove a wagon to the airport when I was leaving. He had some Gene Autry stuff he didn't explain or want seen but I recognized. I helped him stash the plastic container with those items near the airport at the site the locals call the Crack in the Island."

Claire sucked in a big breath. "Jace, you should have told us."

"Yeah, maybe so. With this artwork in the backyard tonight, I'm starting to think I had a crack in the head to try to get involved with him."

"Just great," Nick put in. "You may be aiding and abetting a murderer."

"It was a way to keep an eye on him, maybe make it up to Julia—hell, you know what I mean—if I could help find her killer. I don't think she'd slip. She knew the area, her mother had died there, Claire said, and we all saw how sure-footed she was in more ways than one on that rocking ferry that brought us to the island the first time we met her."

"And you fell for her," Claire put in after that rush of words and emotion. Then she added, "I didn't mean it that way—fell for her."

"Yeah, I did," Jace said, turning his mug of hot cider in his hands as if to keep warm when Nick saw sweat already beading his upper lip. "I was odd man out in our new little family and didn't know how I was going to make it through the winter here. I still don't."

Nick said, "I see why you tried to get close to Kirkpatrick, but you can be known by the company you keep. He's leaving soon, isn't he? Grand Hotel, where he's evidently hanging out, is closing the day after Halloween."

"And great timing for that," Jace muttered. "Ghosts and goblins and witches—maybe some pre-Halloween prankster did that drawing outside, and—"

"The point is," Nick interrupted, "someone has made a move, as if he or she knows we're working on who killed Julia. I think Jace and I should take turns keeping an eye on the backyard for the rest of the night—front yard too, maybe—and I'll call Sheriff Archer at eight in the morning to come look at this. And, Seth, take it from your older brother, Jack, and tell Archer what you've told us tonight."

"He'll blow my undercover work if he goes to recover the stuff or interviews Kirkpatrick again."

"Nick," Claire said, "remember how Mr. Logan was sure he was missing things, and Liz said they weren't the things she and her dad took to sell? Despite the fact that Mr. Logan makes next to no sense, he did insist he'd never hit someone over the head or shove them off a cliff. But as I told you, people with dementia sometimes project what they've done onto someone else. And that smell of cigar smoke in the room—Kirkpatrick must have just been there."

"Is Julia's father really a suspect?" Jace asked, looking strangely hopeful, Nick thought.

"I'd say he's in the second tier of the sheriff's persons of interest," Nick said. "Archer is no more accepting of the coroner's undetermined or accidental-death verdict than we are. After all, the medical examiner didn't know Julia and only had a battered body to make his ruling. But when we get the sheriff here tomorrow, I'll try to find out more about who he's targeting. It sure muddies the waters that Julia's dealt with criminals for years, even WITSEC witnesses. Like a criminal lawyer who's made a lot of enemies, she could have too, and some came back to—to haunt her."

"In short," Jace said, getting up to slosh the rest of his cider in the sink, "Ames aside, you could have other enemies out there somewhere who would like to settle a score with you. I'll take the first watch and you come on down around five. I probably couldn't sleep anyway—and looks to me like you two should give it a try after all you've been through."

Nick saw Claire blush. For a woman who was usually so aware of body language, she'd been frequently brushing back her tousled hair.

"Of course," Jace went on as he cracked open the kitchen curtain over the sink to peer out again, "now that we've got ghost woman on the roof silenced, maybe she got angry and came down to mess things up at ground level."

Nick didn't like his words or his tone, but at least he was helping. He pulled out Claire's chair for her and ushered her upstairs.

"Who did that, Mommy? They are so bad. I would like to stomp on them! They aren't very good drawers either! If Daddy—I mean, Uncle Seth—was watching, why didn't he stop them?"

"No, I said, both your daddy Jack and your uncle Seth were watching it after it happened. They didn't see who did it, but the sheriff will be here in a few minutes and he will want to find out who did it."

"Oh," she said, looking crestfallen. "So Uncle Seth feels bad about it too, just like he did when Julia got dead?"

"Yes, we all felt very bad about that, didn't we?"

"I could tell he really did. 'Cause when he told me she was gone—then I had to ask, 'Gone where?'—that he was almost crying and mad at himself. I could tell."

Claire's insides flip-flopped. "Did he say anything else about it?"

"He said he was very, very sorry and that people make mistakes. I should remember that, but here I almost forgot. Know what, Mommy?"

"What?" she said, pulling Lexi to her for a hug.

"I know you don't like my bad friend Lily, but I think Da— Uncle Seth, I mean—might have a pretend friend that does bad things too."

Claire held her close. She'd resented Nick's thinking Jace could have hurt Julia, even accidentally. There was so much tension among the three of them, and this whole role-play situation was a powder keg, but could Jace know more than he was saying about Julia's death too?

She had to admit that she'd much rather believe the possible murderer was Julia's ex-husband than her own.

CHAPTER TWENTY-NINE

Jace kept shifting his weight from one foot to the other. His footprints were out there in the snow, just down the hill too, and he figured the sheriff had seen them.

"The thing is," Sheriff Archer told him, Claire and Nick as he came back onto their small back porch and stomped the snow off his feet, "that crude drawing is so obviously accusing Vern Kirkpatrick that it makes me think someone else is setting him up. Actually, if he did this sketch of himself—which I doubt—I'd say he's doing it to cast doubt or blame on the other two. Besides, there's a second set of footprints down there aside from whoever added that crude murder scene," he said, pointing to the slant of hill that went down from their backyard and led toward the shoreline far below.

"Mine," Jace told him, realizing he had to come clean on that. "When I saw it last night, I looked around, walked around. I only realized I shouldn't have later."

"So Jack here says Kirkpatrick told you his cigars are Cuban imports. That's illegal, but not enough to snag him on. And he told you what about Castro?"

Jace's gaze snagged Nick's. He was grateful Nick had only

told the sheriff that much, or he'd be all over him about working for Kirkpatrick. Nick had said that it was up to him if he
wanted to explain about their relationship. If he was going to
tell the truth, at least about that, now was the time.

"Yeah," Jace said, trying to keep his voice steady. "I told Jack
and Jenna that, according to Kirkpatrick, he smokes the brand
made 'specially for Fidel Castro. Of course, he was bragging
they were as expensive, but I don't know how he gets them. I
first met Kirkpatrick at the airport, and he offered me a kind of
gofer job, which I turned down. But after I'd heard how Julia
was standing in the way of his buying her father's big Western
collection—and after she was found dead—I decided to take
him up on that job to see if he'd say anything incriminating I
could pass on to you."

"A noble cause but dangerous and maybe even destructive,"
Sheriff Archer said when Jace hesitated. Jace knew he had to
watch what he said here. It was one thing to implicate Kirkpatrick, but he had to keep quiet about the fact he'd talked to Julia
and she'd told him to leave her house the afternoon she'd died.

Folding his arms across his chest, Jace decided he'd better go
for broke—at least about Kirkpatrick, so he said, "He's either
bought or taken some of the Gene Autry items and stashed them
near the airport. If you tell him I said so, he'll be gunning for
me too, one way or the other like he maybe did for Julia, so I
hope you don't tell him that, at least right now."

"You followed him there? Saw where he stashed the items?"

"Playing along, I helped him do it."

"Damn it, man. I figured it would be your two comrades-in-
arms here who would jump in with both feet when all of you
should steer clear and you know why. I'm the pro tem contact
for all of you until WITSEC gets someone else here, so you're
going by my rules, got it?"

"I figured we owed it to Julia," Jace insisted with a frown at
Claire and Nick. Why didn't they speak up? They usually did.

It was like they were letting him hang in the wind. They were in this in their own ways with both feet. Finally, Nick spoke.

"Sheriff, is there any way you could question Kirkpatrick again without tipping him off to the fact that Seth is keeping an eye on him for you? Why don't you step inside and have some coffee while we figure this out?"

"Thanks, but I need to push on. Yeah, I'll try that with Mr. Las Vegas, because, like any FBI refugees here, you need to keep a low profile, a lot lower than at least one of you has been keeping. Seth, you're in deep right now, but the rest of you steer clear, unless you have anything else to divulge. So do you?"

Jace could tell Claire wanted to say something. He'd like to think she'd somehow come to his rescue, since even Nick had tried.

She said, "Sheriff, Jack and I were at the Collister house yesterday, and there seemed to be some tension between Liz and her father. Did Michael just happen to be here when Julia died, or has he been here often?"

"Not often. Off and on. I thought he and Liz were supporting each other pretty well through all this."

"Does he ever bring his wife here? I thought some of it might be over that, which would certainly be understandable."

"She hardly ever comes. I think she's a high-up exec at an interior-design type store, maybe an East Coast chain of them. But it was a contentious divorce for some reason, not that many aren't. Look, all of you, I know it's tough losing your contact and handler Julia like this, since you also saw her as a friend, but just enjoy the beauty of this place and the people and avoid the outsiders, even if you're outsiders yourselves, okay?"

"Sure," Jace said, figuring he'd got off easy. "No doubt good advice, and thanks for all your help."

"I may ask you to show me where Mr. Las Vegas stashes his stuff—once I'm sure where he is. He told me he's staying for a few more days, and is furious he has to vacate his room at Grand

Hotel when they mothball the place soon. Of course, he thinks he should be the exception to all kinds of rules."

"That's exactly what he told me," Jace said. "I think his exact words were 'The rules are for those who need them. The rest of us rise above.' He wasn't real happy when I turned down working for him at first. Like I said, I only agreed after I heard he had it out for Julia and then she—she fell."

"Got that loud and clear. Thanks to all of you and sit tight."

He touched his index finger to his cap and walked off the back porch and around to the front of the house. The three of them went inside. From the front parlor windows, Jace watched the sheriff drive away on his snowmobile. At least those things were so loud you could hear them coming. The four men here had mastered driving them but the women had all said they'd rather not. Still, one of these evenings, they were going out on them in a group, taking a lantern-lit path through the state park, evidently a popular thing to do around here.

Everybody else had a sweetheart, but he'd be odd man out again. Still, if Lexi could ride with him, that would be fun. He just hoped the trail Nick and Heck had said was good for beginners didn't go anywhere near the steps facing Arch Rock.

For once Claire couldn't sleep, and it annoyed her that Nick had conked out so fast tonight when she wanted to bounce ideas off him. Why didn't her usual sleepy-time med kick in? However much she coped with life, sometimes memories of her terrible narcoleptic and cataplexic days haunted her: dropping off to sleep in the wrong place; feeling temporarily paralyzed at times when she woke up; suffering from terrible nightmares, usually that she was being chased and couldn't move. Sometimes, especially when she felt alone, all of that haunted her worse than the memory of the wind on the roof that sounded like the shrieking soul she used to be...

No, she had Nick and Lexi and a new child on the way. She

couldn't let those dark days get to her. She had to think logically, to reason things out, but that scared her too.

Her frenzied thoughts kept bouncing back and forth between her latest two obsessions and fears. One, that Wade Buxton was WITSEC and that he might therefore know, or guess, that they were too. He could have a criminal past. He kept popping up in her life, just as he, no doubt, had in Liz's. Yes, Wade Buxton reeked of smugness and danger. He reminded her of a cat toying with a mouse it meant to kill—like the master of terror, Clayton Ames.

Two things the sheriff had said today made her think Buxton might be WITSEC. He'd said *I'm the pro tem contact for all of you*. Of course, *all of you* could mean all of them living here at Widow's Watch, but she felt sure he would just have said *you* then. He meant he was a temporary contact for at least someone else here.

Second, the sheriff had said they were *like any other FBI refugees here* and that they should *avoid outsiders*. Was that a cloaked comment to avoid Wade Buxton? Didn't that mean there was at least another WITSEC refugee here, or did he mean avoid Vern Kirkpatrick or even Michael Collister? But worse than all her worry about Wade was her fear for Jace.

Because she'd realized today that Jace might be lying, and to the sheriff, no less. Yes, he'd admitted some things. But she knew Jace almost better than she knew anyone, his strengths and his weaknesses. She'd loved him once, his bravado and self-confidence that actually hid his insecurities. He was lucky he'd emotionally survived his brutal father, who had loved the young marines he was in charge of more than he loved his son. Much of Jace's early career and quest for excellence had been to either please or defy his father.

When the four of them had stood on the back porch today in the cold, Jace, who never really felt the cold or let on if he did, was shaking, however confident he'd seemed. He'd folded his arms over his chest as if to protect himself, and he'd stood on one foot, then the other. His voice had been a bit too loud when he told Sheriff Archer about his dealing with Vern Kirkpatrick, as if he was trying to convince himself of something as well as the sheriff. She understood some of that, of course, but there was something Jace was still holding back. She sensed it and she feared Nick knew it. Even Lexi had picked up on it.

Oh, please, dear Lord, she prayed, *don't let Jace have had anything to do with Julia's death.*

"The checkout girl at Doud's Market joked that we'd brought the polar vortex with us this year," Claire told everyone at dinner before they planned a group ride on their three snowmobiles. "She said because the ice is forming early, the winter boat with the double hull, I think it's called the *Huron,* usually runs from about November fifteenth until the lake freezes. But it's so cold now, it's already running and may not be able to for long."

She tried to sound lighthearted, but she'd felt as if she was being watched today and followed as she'd walked back from the store. No one was in sight, but she'd been alone, and the sensation was strong. Of course, there had been others on the streets or on snowmobiles. Half expecting to see Wade Buxton appear only to disappear again, she'd hurried home out of breath, glancing back. She felt foolish and didn't even mention it to Nick.

Heck said, "Yeah, it's cold so early that the lake's starting to freeze solid already. The entire US and Canada are supposed to have a rough winter, according to what I've read online."

Jace said, "I heard they send out some daring souls to try the so-called four-mile-long ice bridge between here and St. Ignace. Then, in the New Year, everyone donates their Christmas trees to line the safest, strongest path over the ice. I also heard the ice is often crystal clear, so you can see water swirling below."

"*Caramba!* Did anyone ever break through it?" Gina asked.

"I heard so," Jace told her. "One guy even put down snag

lines and resurrected his snowmobile, though how he hauled up all that weight, I don't know."

"Well," Claire said, "we're not going over any ice bridge on those heavy snowmobiles across one of the Great Lakes. No way."

"But it will be fun tonight, Mommy," Lexi coaxed, for once, seeming like the adult. "Don't be afraid."

They finished up and went outside into the vast, cold night, studded with stars. Their breath made puffy white clouds when they spoke or even breathed. All bundled up, even with scarves across their faces under their helmets and goggles that made them look like a group of bandits—Mr. Logan would have had a posse after them—they mounted their snowmobiles. Bronco steered the first one with Nita sitting behind him. Jace drove the second alone but towing Heck and Gina, who rode in the large sled box, which would ordinarily carry groceries or supplies. Bringing up the rear to keep an eye on the others, Nick drove the largest one, and Claire held on behind him with Lexi warmly wedged in between them. Jace had planned to ride with Lexi, but the stubborn child had wanted to stick with Claire. Poor Jace—again, she thought.

They took what Andy Archer had told them was the shortest and tamest of the two-lane, two-way trails through the snow-laden trees. Battery-powered lanterns were hung along the path at regular intervals, though their headlights also lit the way and others had left tracks to follow. Claire felt good that people were on this dark path, as they headed into the dense forest of firs. The tree limbs had snagged snow, making a beautiful sight, as if the dark green branches were etched in white. Claire thought the only problem with the frosty beauty of the night was the noise their machines made. It would be so perfectly lovely if it was silent here. People increased on the trail, both ahead and behind them, and occasionally coming at them, shining headlights, or sometimes even helmet light, in their eyes.

She held on to Nick's waist and that kept Lexi firmly in place. The child had squealed in delight at first but was quiet now, peering around Nick at oncoming snowmobiles. Some drivers waved, some nodded, some just plunged on. No way to know who was who, of course, since they all wore helmets and visors, which seemed to isolate each of them.

She heard Nick shout, however muffled it came out, "Ahead! Look ahead!"

She leaned a bit around him and gasped. A flash from the past flew through her mind. The approaching driver was not wearing a helmet but a black-and-white distorted fright mask that reminded her of that dreadful painting *The Scream*. She and Nick had seen it before—on someone in Florida, someone they'd decided must have been sent to torment them by Clayton Ames.

In the darkness between two lanterns, that solo rider plunged not past them but right at her and Nick's vehicle.

She heard a scream and knew it was her own.

CHAPTER THIRTY

The masked driver of the vehicle hit into their snowmobile near the front and veered away, gunning his engine. Claire hung on hard to Nick and Lexi as their vehicle spun madly off the path and slammed its back bumper into a tree trunk. The impact sent them all flying sideways into the snow.

For a moment, they lay stunned. Nick must have killed the engine. The fir branches on the tree they hit quivered, shaking snow onto them like a wake-up call.

"Are you all right?" Nick asked, getting up and hovering over where Claire still held Lexi. "Anything broken? Hurting?"

"I'm just—just shocked," Claire said, her voice not her own.

"Lexi?" Nick asked again, helping them to sit up in the snow.

"He didn't know how to drive," she choked out and burst into tears. "And he can't see with that mask!"

Nick hugged Claire with Lexi between them.

"I say he did know," Claire insisted. "Remember driving from Naples to St. Augustine that day we saw the man with that mask?"

"But are you all right?" Nick demanded. "Not shaken up—inside."

He meant the baby. She felt all right, at least that way. Her big down coat and the cushioning snow had helped. But there had been a big jolt.

"I think I'm okay, just shook in general," she told him. "Our helmets helped too." She took hers off and shook her hair free, then gasped. "But, look, there's a ravine just beyond. Maybe he knew that and wanted us to fall…" She said no more because of Lexi.

A sudden confusion of people exploded around them. It had surely been just a few minutes since they were hit.

Heck's voice: "It took us a minute to see you weren't behind us and turn around to come back, boss."

Nita hugged and held Lexi; Gina helped Claire up while Heck and Bronco hovered near Nick. Jace, dedicated pilot that he was, after he hugged Lexi and saw that everyone was all right, walked around the snowmobile to assess the damage.

Kind strangers stopped on the trail to help, and it seemed everyone spoke at once. Several people had flashlights, so sharp beams of light zigzagged about as some asked questions, some tried to comfort them and some just stared and murmured.

Jace announced, "The front bumper and fiberglass hood have deep dents, but the tree took the worst of it."

Claire muttered to herself, "No, my courage did."

Jace, whom they had never told about the man with a fright mask in Florida, was obviously trying to buck them up. "Andy Archer can get it back in shape in no time at his shop. And you'll have to call the sheriff." Then he whispered, "Again."

As other people slowly scattered, driving away on their own machines, a bearded man said, "After all, Halloween's tomorrow. Some idiot probably got juiced up, put on a mask to freak folks out and lost control. If the sheriff finds him, he'll pay a fine, 'cause driving drunk on these machines is against the law. Thank God you didn't spin out more and flip out into the ravine right here."

And, Claire thought, if they didn't go straight home, that was exactly what she was going to do: freak out and lose control.

One of the last of the sympathizers, a tall woman, said, "Listen, didn't want to say this in front of everyone, but I seen a man carrying around that mask earlier, before he'd put it on. Real scary, ugly-looking man."

"Thanks for the tip," Nick told her, but Claire thought that description might be the result of Halloween and darkness. Besides, the man who had tried to run them off the road in Florida months ago could not be this man. She was certain this had been Wade Buxton, following her again, even though he'd come from the other direction so he could make a quick escape. As fast a glance as she got before she'd instinctively closed her eyes just before he hit them, she'd seen their attacker was his approximate size and build.

Although everyone but their group had gone, Claire again scanned the area for Wade Buxton. She wouldn't put it past him to appear, then disappear, with or without the mask. He must have meant murder with that ravine so close and all these trees. Perhaps he was Julia's killer and feared they'd find out or knew something about him that could give him away. Or, the way Claire had stood up to him at the movie convention, maybe she'd now become to him the woman trying to keep him from Liz. His cheery, smiling nature was a false face.

So she was going to unmask him no matter what the sheriff said.

The sheriff was back again the next morning to take their statements for the snowmobile incident. After talking to the others, he sat in the parlor with Claire and Nick.

Nick told him, "Sorry this is getting to be routine when you told us to keep a low profile, Sheriff."

"Guess I didn't give you good advice to enjoy the place and the people. Sorry you were hurt doing exactly that."

Claire said, "I love the island, but someone here is getting pretty hard to enjoy. I hope we can stay the winter though. If we have to leave, I'd want to be sure Liz is okay first, and our daughter can't take being moved again right now. That pony in Julia's stables means the world to her."

"It sounds like you were targeted, but the driver could have been drunk, and the mask— Yeah, it's Halloween today. I'll have my brother keep an eye out for a dented snowmobile brought in for repairs and get him to fix yours up. Outsiders aren't allowed to bring them onto the island, but there's a lot of them here, so that driver's dented one won't necessarily stand out. So now to the nitty-gritty. I have a message for you from the friend you had dinner with the other night."

At first they both froze, sitting on the sofa side by side. Then Nick leaned farther forward. "Let's hear it."

"He thinks this is still the best place for you, at least until spring, when the Lilac Festival brings thousands of outsiders back here again."

Claire sighed. "I could use spring and some lilacs right now. That is good news, if we can only stop whoever's trying to scare and harm us."

"But," Nick said, "there's more from my book editor, isn't there?"

"Two more things. You will soon have a new WITSEC contact here, so I won't keep getting in the middle of things and can concentrate on finding who's out to scare you off or—or worse with Julia. The new handler/contact is a visiting doctor, who will be working at the Mackinac Island Medical Center for the winter. So, sorry for putting it this way, but he'll oversee diseases and you. That will mean your med student, Gina, who works part-time there, will be the liaison with information. Hope that works. I assume you can trust her."

"Yes, we can trust her," Nick said.

"Good. Gotta tell you, we haven't had anything or anyone

Cuban here, and now we have Kirkpatrick's imported Cuban cigars and your friend Gina."

"And the second thing you have to mention from our friend?" Nick prodded.

"Can't say I understand this part of it, but he said your so-called 'uncle'—he said you'd know what he meant, Jack—may have fled to Mexico, and they're trying to trace him with hopes to extradite him for trial. So you're to keep gathering research for your book. That's the last of the messages. Oh, yeah, and to be careful."

"Did you tell him about the almost-accident last night?"

"I did. Anything else?"

"Sheriff," Claire put in, "I swear Wade Buxton has been following me—or us. The man who hit us was built like him."

"If he has, why?"

"Who is he really? Is he a WITSEC witness too?"

"I can't say."

"Can't or won't? Could he think that I know something about Julia's death that implicates him? I did try to keep him from harassing Liz at the movie conference Saturday evening."

"Let me know if you or Liz want to file harassment charges against him, but my advice to you is to stay wary and stay safe. Just leave him alone, and I'll talk to him. Like I told Jack at church last Sunday, Wade's definitely in the mix for having a motive to harm Julia. Liz has explained all that to me—and I guess he used to dog her steps too, a guy who's used to getting his way on his looks and charisma."

"Used to getting his way, like Kirkpatrick," Nick put in. "They're a pair."

"Funny you say that," the sheriff said as he stood, "but I can't find anything to link them to each other. As for Julia's death, I plan to speak to Michael again before he leaves the island. My job on Mackinac may even be more remote than a county sheriff's, but it's common practice to look at the family members—especially ex-mates—first."

Jace's nervous revelations weighed heavy on Claire's heart again. They'd never mentioned to the sheriff how her own ex had tried to hit on Julia.

After Nick saw the sheriff out and came back in, Claire said, "I swear he's protecting Wade because he's WITSEC."

"Yeah, but so are we WITSEC, so take his advice. If you go out, and I can't go—or Jace—take Bronco, not just Nita or Gina. And not Lexi unless we're together."

"So what does this mean for trick-or-treating tonight? We promised her days ago we'd at least visit a few houses, and she still has her *Somewhere in Time* costume she's dying to wear again. I don't think she'd go for us having a party here. I told her we could go out in the snowmobile, though that was before that fiend hit us."

"Then we'll take one of the good snowmobiles and just go to Liz's, if we call ahead and arrange it with her. We'll take an apple for Scout, maybe a whole bushel of them. If Lexi gets to spend time with the pony, I'll bet nothing else will matter."

"You're a genius," she told him and looped her arms up around his neck to press a kiss on his cheek.

"Well, you've got to be to write this huge murder mystery I'm working on," he said, hugging her to him. "You know, if I really were doing that instead of preparing court documents and testimony to use against 'my uncle,' I'd sure have a cast of characters. But these are real guys, Claire, possibly very, very bad guys."

Considering how upset Liz had been last time Claire was at her house, she seemed in a mellow mood on Halloween evening. They had called her to set up a visit, so she'd turned on all the lights in the stable. She let Lexi feed and curry Scout, so other thoughts of trick-or-treating seemed to fly out of the child's head. Miracle of miracles, all seemed fine, at least with Lexi.

The three adults leaned against Scout's waist-high stall door, watching Lexi comb the pony's mane for the third time. Jace had gone uptown to a gym to work out, then planned to, as he'd put it, "undo all that good work by hoisting a few brews back at the Draught House." Bronco and Nita were in the stable, looking at the other horses. Heck and Gina were at Widow's Watch, handing out candy. They'd figured their house might be a popular stop for kids because of the legend of the ghost they had now quieted.

Claire hadn't shared with anyone the scrap of cotton and lace she'd found up there. It seemed like her secret, and she didn't want someone to think she was foolish enough to think it was left by a woman decades ago—or a ghost. In the weather here, it could have blown up mere years ago and still be that tattered. She liked to think it was a reminder that the widow had not thrown herself off the walkway in despair, and she was sure Julia had not done that either.

"Has your father left the island yet?" Claire asked Liz, hoping that sounded merely conversational.

"Soon, he says. He thinks I need support, but—well, I'm better."

"Grieving the loss of a loved one can take a long time, go through stages. Everyone has regrets too, things they wished they'd done differently or wished they could do over or again."

"I still say you're a shrink. Isn't she, Jack?" Liz asked.

"Just acts and talks like one."

"I'll tell you who's the psychiatrist here," Claire interrupted their banter. "Scout. It calms Meggie to be near him. Would you mind if I bring her back tomorrow? I'm going to make a deal with her about homeschooling this winter. I'll teach her how to write and read better—horse stories, no doubt—and Lorena and Gina are going to teach her some Spanish. If she agrees and the snow's not too deep, I'll tell her she can come visit Scout on a regular basis, if it's okay with you. If we can help with the upkeep of the stables, we'd be glad to."

"Sounds good. Bring her back as often as you want, tomorrow, even. I'll teach you how to saddle the pony, and she can ride him up and down the aisle in here. He could use the exercise. I don't think I told you but, for now, I'm going to move my shop home to save money."

"A great idea," Claire said, but she was thinking that, at least, would keep Wade from cornering her alone since Mr. Logan and Doug would be here.

"Any new corset orders from the publicity we passed out at Grand Hotel?" Claire asked.

"A few. I'm thinking, though, since that crowd was mostly visitors, it would take a few days for them to get home and then contact me. Fingers crossed," she said and lifted two crossed fingers.

Claire crossed hers too, and they touched fingers. Claire thought it was their own version of two friends clinking glasses or bumping fists. She felt better than she had in a while. They would stay here this winter. Lexi was happy. The attack by the man in the mask hadn't really hurt any of them beyond a few sore spots and black-and-blue bruises. They knew to be extra vigilant and careful. Surely, things had to be better now.

That night, a strange noise dragged Claire from heavy sleep. In bright red numerals, her bedside clock read 3:13 a.m. Once she cleared her head, she realized that Nick was awake too, propped up on one elbow next to her, listening.

There it was again, a hollow, erratic *rat, tat, tat.*

"What?" she whispered.

"Not sure. Maybe a shingle loose, but it sounds like a knocking at the window. I've heard creaking from the attic, but this is definitely the window glass. Maybe a branch blew against it or something. The wind's up off the harbor."

Now it sounded to Claire like something scratching to get in. A bird or squirrel? And was the sound really against their backyard window or even up on the roof, where the shrieking sound had been? Perhaps the repair Jace had done had come loose somehow and slipped down.

"Stay put," Nick ordered and threw the covers off. Keeping low, he tiptoed to the window. He hunkered down beside it, then slowly drew the drapes apart.

At first, Claire had a better view than he did. Floating in the night, white, skeletal in the familiar, silent scream, that horrid face from the forest was staring in their bedroom window.

CHAPTER THIRTY-ONE

"What in the world?" Nick sputtered and swore.

Ignoring his order to stay in bed, Claire leaped out and, hugging the wall, edged around to the window. "Could it be someone on a ladder?" she asked, craning her neck to peer out.

"It's floating—flying. I've got to go down."

"No," she said, grabbing his arm as he got to his feet. "It's not just some Halloween night prank. Someone could be waiting down there, trying to flush us out to hurt us. Should we call the sheriff?"

"No. Whoever it is would be gone the minute he heard a snowmobile. Go wake up Bronco, Heck and Jace. I'm going down, just to look out. Someone's out there for sure."

Just then the face rotated away and darkness reigned. Had it disappeared into thin air? And then in the moonlight outside, Claire saw what it was. A kite. A black kite with that mask on one side of it.

"It's a kite," she told Nick as he headed for their bedroom door in his pajamas and bare feet. "Someone's down there flying a kite."

"And I'm going to find out who. Tell the guys no lights," he said and ran from the room.

She shoved her feet in her slippers, grabbed a robe and knocked on Bronco and Heck's door. "Someone's outside and Nick needs you downstairs!" she called to them. "Don't turn on any lights."

Jace appeared instantly, opening his own door, wearing shorts and a T-shirt. "He's doing what?" he asked.

"Someone's outside, and—"

He grabbed a sweatshirt from his inside doorknob and started down the stairs barefoot.

"Flying a kite with that screaming face mask on it," she called after him.

She started downstairs too as Bronco and Heck thudded after her, then passed her. They found Nick in the kitchen, going from window to window, peering out, like a caged beast.

"I didn't hit the outside lights," he told them as they came huffing in behind him. "Thought he might still be out there, but I don't see anyone. I'm going to get dressed, get a light and go out. There will be footprints at least."

"Somebody wants us to leave the island, boss," Heck said. "Or just scare us to death."

The next morning, Nick and Jace went outside again and carefully looked closer at the footprints they didn't want to get near to disturb last night. As they trooped back in for breakfast, Nick told her, "Whoever it was either intentionally smeared his footprints or dragged both feet. No sign of the kite either. But how in the heck does someone know that's our bedroom?"

"Maybe they don't," Jace said. "Maybe any window would have done to shake us up, get us to pull up stakes here. Or the bastard just picked the window closest to the ghost shrieks that we finally shut up."

"It *was* Halloween," Claire said. "The house is known to be haunted on the widow's walk. It could be someone's idea of a prank, even by the same idiot who hit our snowmobile, though that could have been deadly. Let's just be sure Lexi doesn't hear about it."

The three of them sat down to a very healthful breakfast of sliced fruit and grain cereals Gina had arranged on the table next to the juice and milk pitchers and coffeepot. Heck sat there as if guarding the food, not eating. He'd already taken Gina to the medical center for her early shift today.

"You're looking better, Mrs. Randal," Jace said to Claire. "Color in your cheeks, pink, not white."

Claire glared at him. She hadn't told Nick that Jace had guessed about her pregnancy, and Heck didn't know, but he looked as if the world was on his shoulders too.

"It worries me bad," Heck said, "that Gina's supposed to be the go-between for us and the new handler. A doctor, no less, and FBI. I hope he's ugly, looks like that fright mask or worse. And what's that you said the sheriff called her? A lying down?"

"A liaison," Nick said. "It's a French word and means a go-between."

"Well, you know how the French are about women," Heck muttered.

Nick told him, "Don't worry about Gina. She cares for you."

"Oh, yeah, cares. But she's ambitious and bright and—"

"Mommy! Someone took some of my Halloween candy left over from trick-or-treaters. It was on the upstairs hall table. And I have a bad stomachache!" Lexi cried and came into the room, rubbing her belly through her flannel nightie and robe.

"Sweetheart, if you have a stomachache, are you sure you didn't eat too much of the candy Berto and Gina had left over when we got home?"

"No, it's gone. Did you guys eat it?"

Jace said, "Don't look at me, honey. Are you sure it's not hidden in your tummy?"

"Maybe Lily ate it, since she finally got back here on a snowmobile," the child insisted. "But she's not going to take the apples I have for Scout."

Pulling her next to her chair, Claire said, "Lily is not here. Where would she live? All the rooms and beds are taken."

Her lower lip thrust out, still rubbing her stomach, Lexi blinked back tears and said, "She's living in the attic. I heard her up there."

"No," Nick said. "Your uncle Seth fixed the broken piece of flashing that made the wind sounds. Last night it was just a kite that got away from someone and hit against our window. You know, eating too much candy can give you bad dreams."

"I didn't eat that candy!" Lexi insisted. "But I think I am going to get sick."

Claire barely got a napkin up to her mouth before she did.

After sitting with Lexi until she fell asleep, Claire left her in Nita's care and went, as promised, to give Scout his apple without Lexi—just for today. Bronco took Claire in a snowmobile, acting as both driver and guard. Nick and Heck were working hard on a list of people to depose if Ames could be arrested and brought to trial.

"It's amazing about the snowmobiles here," Claire told Bronco as they got off the machine in Liz's driveway, where another almost identical one sat. "The sheriff assured us that none were ever stolen until lately. He said most people leave the keys right in theirs, and they're always in the same place unless one of the winter repairmen move it just a little ways."

"Yeah, well, the way things been goin' for us lately, I'm not leavin' the keys in this one or leavin' it unguarded so someone can smash into it, like the other one. That one's already been in the shop for two days. I'm guardin' you but this snowmobile too. Hope I do a better job'n I did watching Mr. Logan."

"I'm sure that wasn't your fault."

"Yeah, well, not that I can remember, but I'm startin' to

think he mighta been the one hit me, so hope his new watch-dog does better."

"I'll be right back. I'm just going to give Scout this apple like I promised Lexi. We're about ten minutes earlier than I told Liz we'd be. She wants to show me the clip from that TV show that was shot at the *Somewhere in Time* party."

"I'd ask for your autograph for being famous, but not sure which name you'd sign."

She had to laugh. For Bronco, that was a pretty clever remark.

She hurried into the barn through the side door so she wouldn't have to wrestle with the big double ones where the horses came in and out. There was another door around the back too, near the bales of hay and sacks of feed stacked for the winter.

"Scout," she called out, "your favorite fan sent me with your apple."

She walked past the other horses' stalls. Scout must know his name, for he was whinnying and shuffling through the straw, evidently eager for the treat. She didn't like to get her hand licked the way Lexi did, so she put the apple in the feed tray and stepped back.

Right into a big, hard body.

She gasped. Bronco? No, he hadn't followed her in. No one had.

She tried to shift away, but the stall door was there. She spun around, expecting to have to run from Wade Buxton. It was Michael.

"Oh! You!"

"Yeah, me. The truth is, I feel closer to Julia here. She loved horses, this stable and her little start-up of a riding school."

Claire tried to step past him, but he didn't budge, blocking her into the corner made by the wall and the stall door. She felt fear and beat it down. "Does Liz know you're out here?" she demanded.

"No more than you did. I'm just looking around, getting

ready to say goodbye, maybe for good. You're pretty close to her, I see. Liz, I mean, but I guess you were to Julia too, considering you've been here such a short time."

This man knew too much. Was she being followed and targeted by someone who feared she knew a lot about Julia? It hit Claire hard that Michael could be out here looking for the diary again. She needed to get away from him. He wasn't to be trusted and maybe he suspected she'd overheard him and Liz, or even knew he had a motive to hurt Julia.

"I've got to get back to my friend, and Liz is expecting me, so excuse me," she said in her strongest voice. She narrowed her eyes and tried to stare him down. Did Julia face him like this on the cliffside stairs and then—

"Sure. No problem. I'm glad you and Liz are friends. She may live here now, but she doesn't seem tight with many locals since she left for a while. I think she can't wait to take her sexy undies east and conquer the world. I usually tell my friends she designs for a lingerie line and leave it at that."

Claire stepped sideways again, put her shoulder against his outstretched arm and walked around and away from him. Thank God, he didn't follow. Perhaps he'd seen she had someone outside waiting for her. She had the strangest feeling he meant her harm.

"Don't tell her I'm trying to keep an eye on her," he called. "She thinks she's too big to need that, but I worry about her. Julia told me that Buxton guy was a real bad choice, so I'm tempted to tell him to keep away from Liz before I go."

Claire decided not to answer any of that. But she was thinking that the discussion between Michael and Julia about Wade—and the missing diary—might have been on those steep stairs by Arch Rock.

Claire didn't tell Liz that her father was in the stable. She didn't want her to be more upset about his possibly looking for the diary so she would run out there to confront him like the other day. She would mention him before she left and hope that he had cleared out by then. The way she'd felt penned in by him, she feared Liz wouldn't necessarily come out the winner.

She decided not to mention Michael to Bronco either so he wouldn't endanger himself. He sat by the window where he could keep an eye on the snowmobile—the other one must have been Liz's, not Michael's. That meant Michael was sneaking around on foot in the snow.

Today, like yesterday, Liz seemed in a calm, even pleasant mood. She dragged Claire toward the TV in her bedroom, which had become a corset workroom too.

"Okay, here's the recording of our national TV debut," Liz told her and started punching buttons on her remote. "Those infomercials have nothing on me. And see that box over there on the worktable? Nearly seventy customer inquiries and orders, some by snail mail, most from phone or online orders from my website. Handing out that publicity really helped, but not as much as this one-minute-and-fifty-seven-second interview I did for *Inside Edition!*"

Claire watched with bated breath. At least keeping busy would stop Liz from sitting around, grieving for her mother's loss. Yes, there they were on the screen, looking good in their costumes. Thank heavens she'd managed to hide behind her bonnet brim, though there was a clear flash of her face first. She looked both surprised and annoyed by the sudden lights and camera. And though Claire had tried to hide Lexi's face too, there she was in full view for a moment, crying in frustration, "Mommy, don't! They're taking my picture!"

Claire watched the following well-done spiel Liz gave about her business with name-dropping, her clever, quick mention of her website that must have reached thousands and brought this early deluge of orders.

"Liz, congrats on this!" Claire cried when the screen went blank. "You were poised and great, really smooth."

"I get why you tried to hide. Sorry about that. I—I've guessed why you're all really here, considering Mom's second occupation."

"Don't answer this if you can't or don't want to, but was that the Wade connection at first? I mean, your mother extended to him the same help and hospitality that she did to us and then he found you and figured you should be extra helpful too?"

Liz sucked in her lips and nodded. She was about to say something, when her cell rang. Obviously glad for the intrusion, she dug it out of her jeans pocket to stare at the screen. "My father's been calling," she said, "but I don't want to talk to him, I mean right now. Oh, no, it's not him. I don't know this number. It's local, maybe another order."

She took the call. Claire could hear a woman's voice, maybe something about someone being locked up.

"Yes. Okay and thank you," Liz said. "I'll come soon, maybe right away. Wow," Liz told Claire when she punched off. "I had no idea that Mother left some stuff in a locker at Grand Hotel. It's where the security staff keeps their uniforms, I guess, but who knows what's in it. They'd like me to come empty it out. I swear, it's like a ghost town when it's all locked up. I'd like to do it now. I thought—well, I thought I had everything of hers, but each thing's important to me."

Claire did not have to wonder what Liz was thinking. The diary might be there. It sounded like such a little thing, but in the first case she had worked for Nick, a diary had given them some key answers.

"Can Cody and I go with you?" Claire asked. "Who knows how much you'll have to bring back? I guess I'm just paranoid since that snowmobile accident I told you about Halloween Eve. Safety in numbers."

"Okay, sure."

As they got their coats on and headed out to the snowmobiles with Bronco, Claire called Nick to tell him where they were going and that Bronco was going too. She could tell by Nick's tone of voice—and what he didn't say—that he realized what she was thinking. "Hope there's something worthwhile there," he said. "Take care."

With the fresh inches of snow, Grand Hotel looked every bit the grand lady of the lake, Claire thought. So much white, like the place wore a cloak of ermine. Even the overcast late afternoon and the shuttered windows and rolled-up awnings could not dim the vast sweep of the exterior. But the lady of the lake did look alone and deserted, no people, no carriages, no flowers. The familiar rows of white rocking chairs had been taken from the now-naked porch.

Liz, on her own snowmobile, led them around to a back entrance not visible from the front. Only two snowmobiles were parked there.

"Claire and I won't be long, Cody," she called to him. "If I recall right, that locker room is just inside. I'm sure, since I just got that call, others will be there. But you can come in too, if you want, because it's cold out here. It would be okay to leave the keys. I do in mine."

"No, Miss Liz, I'll just keep an eye on both of them out here. I'll be fine."

After all she'd been through, Claire would ordinarily have asked Bronco to come with them, but since Liz seemed to know her way and others would be inside, she followed Liz into the building. The first room was evidently a storage area for supplies delivered at the receiving dock in back, but few boxes sat upon the wooden pallets now.

"I was only in this area a couple of times before, and not for a while," Liz said as they walked through, then down a dimly lit hall. A door at one end was labeled WOMEN'S RESTROOM AND SHOWER and the MEN'S at the other. They entered the room that was obviously their goal. Claire was surprised to find it deserted. It reminded her of a high school locker room with wooden benches facing two walls of gray metal lockers. Almost none had combination locks on them.

Liz found the one with Julia's name. "The woman on the phone told me that, if I didn't have the combination, which I don't, I could get a pair of bolt cutters from the custodian's room down the hall, even though he's left for the day. Be right back."

Claire felt she was guarding the locker just the way Bronco was the snowmobile. Sad to have to live that way, to be so wary and—yes, afraid. But she had the feeling things were opening up now. Perhaps the diary was in this locker. If Julia had tried to be extra cautious and maybe had WITSEC information in it, smart of her to keep it off her property. Maybe info on Wade was there. Claire would love to know his past, but without his real name, she had no way to research that. And Michael wanted the diary for a different reason. As for Vern Kirkpatrick, wasn't he just after the Gene Autry items at any cost? And had that cost included Julia's life?

Claire heard footsteps in the hall. It must be Liz coming back with the cutters, but the footsteps seemed heavier than hers. Then she heard a loud bang-click from the hall that seemed to echo even here.

The room and hall—maybe the whole vast building—plunged into total darkness.

CHAPTER THIRTY-TWO

Claire gasped as the world closed in, black and blank. She could not see her hand before her face. Nothing.

Her first instinct was to flee for the door to the hall—at least where she thought the door was. But she'd heard footsteps there. Nothing. Nothing now. Maybe a distant thudding. Footsteps? Her own heart? Should she call out for Liz to be sure she was safe? But then someone would know where she was. She had learned to be afraid.

Of course, this could be something normal, if plunging the basement level of Grand Hotel into darkness was normal right now when they were closing up the place. Perhaps they thought no one was here. Did the island suffer common blackouts?

But where was Liz? Why wasn't she calling out? Maybe there was an emergency generator that had kicked on in the custodian's office where she'd gone. She had to find Liz. But after how silently Michael had come up behind her earlier, he could have followed them here. He was hell-bent on getting his hands on that diary. Or Wade might have followed Liz again, followed both of them, then got inside past Bronco somehow. Still, Vern Kirkpatrick was the one who had been staying here and knew this building. Maybe, when it was time to leave, he'd hidden and stayed behind.

Claire tried to calm her breathing, but her pulse pounded so loud it was like the *thud, thud* of a hollow drum. The footsteps in the hall had halted. She felt for the row of lockers nearest her and fumbled along until she came to the end of them. Her phone! Her phone would have a light and she could call Bronco for help.

She fumbled for the phone in her purse and found it. Leaning against a locker, she felt for the on button, pushed it, hoping her voice would not draw whoever had been in the hall.

The little rectangle of light exploded at her, nearly blinding her. She could use her flashlight app to get out of here, but she'd call Bronco first, get help.

Before she could punch the phone icon, something came at her. She tried to turn the lit phone toward him—the silhouette of a man—then tried to turn it off as she dodged. He yanked her arm, her purse. Her phone fell to the floor and went out. The man tried to haul her to him by her purse.

She pulled back, but he was stronger. She kicked and scratched at flesh, caught a face, a forehead or a cheek. Did she smell smoke? Cigarette or cigar smoke? What if this place was on fire? She let her purse go and heard it hit a locker, then the floor. "Liz! Liz! Run!" she screamed and pulled free of him and ran.

She bounced off the doorframe, then threw herself through it. She'd been lucky not to be hurt before, not in the sea or the snow. She was just as scared now. Lexi at least was safe at home. But the beginnings of a baby she carried...

The man chasing her grunted, but it wasn't enough to place his voice. Should she run toward where Liz had gone or back the way to the door near Bronco? Would she be able to find her way to either?

A stairway with a dim Exit sign at the top loomed above her, one she hadn't noticed on the way in. That must be on a generator. It would be lighter upstairs, and there might be people. She headed up.

She stumbled twice on the stairs, banged her knee, climbed with feet and hands. The man was still behind her. She had to get help. Help for Liz. Had someone hurt her just like they had her mother?

The stairs seemed endless, and the door at the top so heavy. At least it opened. Wishing she had time to slam it and hold it closed, she knew better. The nightmare of fleeing through the hotel in Cuba rushed at her. But then, she'd had the others with her. Now, alone, she ran on.

It was still dark up here but not as bad. More like twilight. All the lights were off, but remnants of daylight seeped through the closed window draperies, and some of those were even covered over. Was that call Liz got about her mother's locker a setup? If so, who had that woman made the call for?

Claire wished she had time to rip a dustcover from a window to get light in here, but she still heard her pursuer behind her, breathing hard. If she stopped and turned around, she'd surely get a glimpse of him, but that could be more dangerous if she could ID him. Unless he didn't intend to let her go anyway.

She tore down the dim, carpeted hall, past the entry to the main dining room she recognized even in the gray fog of shuttered windows. She passed the room where they'd had a private luncheon with Julia, where they had first met Liz—and Wade. So Wade knew this place, but, of course, Kirkpatrick and maybe Michael did too.

Gasping for breath, with a stitch in her side, Claire tried to reckon how to get to Bronco from here. If only she could circle back to Liz. Surely, she had not led Claire into this trap. No, she knew Liz. She trusted Liz as she had Julia.

When she turned another corner into a hallway with side rooms and furniture, she tried to decide whether to keep going or to hide. But she could be cornered if she stopped, though she felt that way already. Was it worth the risk of being caught to see who her pursuer was? She could pick up one of these heavy-looking lamps for a weapon. The tables looked bare of smaller things, but maybe the lamps had been unplugged for the winter.

Around the turn of a hallway, Claire saw another flight of stairs—two of them, one down, one up. She'd be insane to try to navigate the maze of halls lined with bedrooms above.

But as she started down the stairs, she heard him, panting, closer. Grabbing the banister, she nearly leaped downward, trying not to fall. At the turn in the stairs, she saw a dust cloth over closed curtains covering a window. She yanked it down and heaved it behind her on the stairs as he thudded after her.

She'd see him now, know who he was, maybe be able to use her skills to calm him, talk him down. She'd done that with Bronco once. Expecting to see Wade, she glanced up and screamed.

The man vaulting down the stairs had been tripped up by the curtain she'd thrown and the daylight filtered in here to reveal that—

He wore a wig and that horrible mask again. Was this a narcoleptic nightmare? No. No! Run!

She tore down one more flight. What if the door at the bottom didn't open? What did Vern Kirkpatrick look like? This man was well built and surely must be athletic. He was about Jace's size.

The door opened, but it led only to more darkness. She felt her way along a wall, praying she was heading in the right direction toward Liz. Suddenly, she realized she didn't hear her pursuer, nor his footsteps or that awful breathing.

More panicked thoughts slammed into her. Did someone want to stop her from befriending Liz? Or were she and Nick too close to learning who hurt—surely, killed—Julia?

Claire's head nearly exploded when the hall lights suddenly came back on, blinked once, then held. She also blinked in the brightness. Should she run outside to find Bronco, or look for Liz? Surely, that man had turned them off, but had he or someone else turned them back on?

She ran into the locker room and grabbed her purse and phone from the floor. The screen was cracked but maybe it still worked. As she dialed Bronco, looking around, listening intently, she rushed down the hall in the direction Liz had disappeared.

Bronco answered instantly. Claire cried, "There's a man chasing me in here. If the door's not locked come in and turn left!" She left the phone on, but jammed it back in her purse as she ran into the custodian's room. Good light in here too. She saw an array of tools and what might be a closet door. She heard muffled pounding and Liz's voice.

"Liz? Liz?"

"I'm locked in here. Someone locked me in and the lights went out!"

Claire almost laughed through her tears. "No kidding," she whispered to herself.

She tried to open the closet door, but it didn't budge. Liz pounded harder on the door, screaming, "Jenna! Jenna!" In her stunned state, the use of her WITSEC name shocked Claire. She twisted the bolt lock, and Liz lunged out of the small area crammed with boxes of supplies. She held the bolt cutters in her hands like a weapon.

"The lights went out and someone locked me in there!" she said again. "I left my phone back in the locker room."

"I broke mine fighting with someone who chased me, but let's get outside."

"What? Did you see him?"

"Yes, but when I got upstairs where it was gray instead of black, he wore a mask, then disappeared."

"Let's call the sheriff."

"I should have him on speed dial lately. I called Cody, but maybe he can't get in. I hope we're not locked in here."

"Yeah, how much does it cost to break a Grand Hotel window with these cutters? But, you mean, you've had trouble where you needed the sheriff before this?"

"Never mind. You have enough to worry about. Let's get out of here."

"You go get Cody, then, but I've got to open that locker. I'm thinking, like—maybe when they close this place up, they just turn the lights out sometimes. What kind of mask?"

"Later. Let's go!"

"It will only take a second on our way out. Maybe someone just wanted to scare us."

"That's for sure. How about now-you-see-him, now-you-don't Wade?" Claire asked as they hurried down the hall. "And, sorry, but I overheard some of what you and your father argued about the other day."

"But—but he'd never hurt me or my mother—at least not on purpose. It's that Vern Las Vegas guy who knows his way around this hotel!"

In a way Claire was glad Liz still insisted on getting into Julia's locker. Claire had to admit she knew that kind of stubbornness, even admired it.

She stood nervously at the door of the locker room, punching in Nick's phone number as Liz struggled with the unwieldy cutters and got the lock off. Claire moved closer. Inside the small, dark space hung a security uniform, and, on the floor in a clear plastic sack, a flat, black book. And taped to the back of the locker was a picture of a smiling Julia in a bathing suit with Rob Patterson!

Claire gasped. They had their arms around each other. They looked very happy, and it hadn't been taken too long ago. And not here. A palm tree swayed behind them and waves smashed onto a south shore.

"Who the heck is he?" Liz muttered as she grabbed the book and the photo.

"Never mind now. Let's get out of here!" Claire said for the tenth time, and they fled only to find Cody trying to get in the door someone had evidently locked from inside.

"I swear, I'm not sure who it was," Claire told Nick and Jace, as the three of them huddled in the parlor after she got home and explained what had happened. "I expected it to be Wade. I haven't seen Kirkpatrick. I did think I smelled smoke on the guy, but maybe not that cigar smoke that hung in the room the day Bronco was hit over the head—and maybe the smell of smoke just hangs in my head. Michael could have followed us. Who else, I'm not sure," she said, with a glance at Jace.

It was an absolutely insane thought, of course, but the man had reminded her of Jace. But how much of what she recalled was from raw panic and not reality? With the lights out, it had all seemed a dreadful nightmare. What would that man have done to her if he'd caught her? Had she left a scratch on his face? And since he'd only locked Liz up—in case he meant to come back for her after he'd caught and hurt Claire first—what did he want?

"And," Nick said, "all this on top of that loose cannon Michael Collister cornering you in the stable. It makes me think it's not even safe for Lexi to visit Scout until he leaves the island. Sad to say, Claire, but I'm putting you under house arrest. Wait until the sheriff hears about all this. I thought since Bronco was with you, that would keep you safe."

She hated being scolded. "I was with Liz inside. Bronco was right outside keeping an eye on the snowmobile after what happened to the other one."

"I get it, but one or the other—or both of us—" he said with a nod at Jace, which surprised her "—should go out with you, if it's absolutely necessary you even leave the house. At least until we stop the attacks or nail who killed Julia."

"I wonder if Wade smokes cigarettes. I haven't smelled it on him. I should have asked Liz."

"Are you even listening?" Nick demanded, leaning toward her on the couch to seize her shoulders and turn her toward him. "You're evidently being targeted for being close to Julia, Liz or both. You have a child to worry about—"

"Two," Jace put in.

Nick's head snapped around. "She told you?"

"Not until I guessed."

Nick swore under his breath, then visibly calmed himself before he went on, a tactic—a talent—she'd seen him use in court. "The point is," he went on in a calmer voice, "you need to stay safe, stay in until we or the sheriff get a handle on this."

"I'll go stark crazy staying in this winter, especially when Liz needs help. I need a look at that diary we found in the locker before Michael gets his hands on it. You know I'm trained in hand-writing analysis. That reminds me of something huge I forgot to tell you. Besides some work clothes and the diary, which Liz is now guarding with her life, there was a crush picture taped in the back of Julia's locker, just like in high school."

"A crush picture?" Jace asked. "Julia with some guy, not Michael?"

"Fasten your seat belts, both of you. The photo was taken in some tropical place, some south shore with waves behind them and a palm tree frond hanging over them—Julia with Rob Patterson."

For once, both men were speechless. Finally, Jace said, "So—no wonder he didn't put the total skids on our looking into her death. I tend to think of him as all business, and I'll bet the FBI doesn't really condone fraternizing, but—hell, Julia had a lot going for her, and a woman too often falls for her boss."

Claire glared at Jace, if he was implying that was the case for her with Nick, but Jace wasn't looking at her. He was frowning and seemed so suddenly inward. She'd seen it before when she'd been interviewing potential perps and didn't like to see it here. Grief? Guilt?

"Later on that," Nick put into the awkward silence. "Rob's human. Who knows when the photo was taken, maybe recently, after her divorce."

Claire said, "If it was before, that's another motive for Michael to have harbored hatred for her."

"Let's just focus on us right now. That diary is legally Liz's, unless it's all FBI information. If so, she has to show it to the sheriff until the new WITSEC handler gets here. I'm sure Liz has enough sense that, if there are any threats against Julia in it, she'll share it with the sheriff."

"Nick, Liz's life may be in danger," Claire insisted. "I think I should stay close to her, not just suddenly shut myself off."

"Fine—invite her here."

"Yeah," Jace suddenly exploded in a loud voice so unlike him, "your life's obviously in danger too. I'd like to think—and I'm sure Nick and Lexi do too—that you'll be around to write in your own diary someday and not be thrown down some flight of stairs or out the window or off that porch at the Grand Hotel or anywhere else!"

Claire turned to stare at Jace. His eyes shifted away for a moment before he met her gaze. She had to talk to him alone. He was hiding something, being overly defensive. It seemed he was almost picturing where she'd been chased. He had been off work just as he had the afternoon Julia died.

She vowed then that, somehow, she must question and face down Jace alone without telling Nick.

CHAPTER THIRTY-THREE

"See you in a little while," Nick told Claire when he finally calmed down after hearing what had happened in Julia's stable and at Grand Hotel. "I'm tempted to tie you to my waist or to our bed," he muttered as he finally got up from nearly pinning her onto the couch. "I need to head back to working with Heck for an hour or so. We've got a lot of the lock-Ames-up-for-life work done but we need to finish this section today so we can get it to Rob. And then," he added, his voice bitter, "if they can ever get their hands on him in Mexico or on whatever south shore where he's hiding out now, the government can prosecute."

For once, he seemed content to leave her alone with Jace. Anything to keep someone's eye on her, she supposed. But she couldn't let this go any more than Nick could stop his obsession with stopping Clayton Ames.

Claire was going to try to bring up the day of Julia's death, because something about that was bothering him, and she hoped it wasn't that he'd been with her at Arch Rock. He'd wanted to see it, since Julia had taken the rest of them there. But before she could speak, Jace glanced out the window and blurted, "Who the heck is that?"

She turned around to look out. "Where? Oh, that man with the camera? I've seen others taking pictures of this house and others along here. It is so picturesque, even with the snow. No way to stop that, I guess, unless they really trespass, and he's in the street."

"But he's got one of those big telephoto lenses," he said, standing and squinting out the window. "And the face behind it is really ugly, poor guy."

"Jace! I know we're all on edge, but do you need to say that?" She didn't mean to scold but she was very nervous about questioning him, and this was not a good beginning. She sighed and turned back around on the couch. "So, do you have the whole day off?" she asked, hoping to just sound conversational. Always start with something seemingly innocuous, then circle in, she told herself.

"Just working the twilight shift," he said, sitting back down. He propped his elbows on his spread knees and stared at the floor instead of out the window or at her. "The ill guy I replaced is getting better, so I hope they don't cut my hours. If so, you and I will suffer from cabin fever together this winter."

"I'm going to homeschool Lexi in reading and writing. Since you've been all over the world, you could work with her about foreign places, kind of prekindergarten-age history or geography."

"Yeah. Yeah, I'd like that. Poor little girl with two daddies."

"Jace, I know that's been hard, but that aside—"

"I can't put it aside."

"Just listen, please. Speaking of your getting erratic time off from the airport job, you also had the afternoon off the day Julia died."

She tried not to sound and look as tense as she was. His head snapped up. His eyes narrowed before he looked away again. When he didn't respond at first, Claire swallowed hard because she saw sweat break out on his upper lip in this cool house. Even

under duress as a wartime pilot, the word she'd heard from his
buddies was "Jace never sweats."

"So?"

"I know you well, Jace. Something's been really bothering
you about Julia's death, besides the death itself."

"Yeah. It's why I risked a lot to try to see if Kirkpatrick hurt
her."

"I don't mean to pry, but maybe you felt guilty you came on
to her? I thought maybe that day she died you tried to apologize to her."

"What are you, some sort of damned psychic now?" He
heaved a huge sigh, and his shoulders slumped. "But I did regret I came on to her like I did. She was attractive and impres-
sive and seemed unattached. And like I said, I felt like the odd
man out in our group. In a way, I'd even lost Lexi."

"No, you didn't and never will," she insisted, sitting forward
on the couch to touch his arm. "And you and I are still friends,
aren't we?"

He gave a loud snort. "Oh, yeah, right. That will work out
just great, especially when we get out of here and go home, if
Naples is even home to me now."

"Of course it is. Rob Patterson offered you that spy-fly airplane job. You can live in South Florida and still fly, do something for your country."

"You sound like the marine recruiters, but that's what you're
good at. Getting people to open up, to opt in, to tell you things
so you can psych them out. Swear you won't run to Nick or the
sheriff with this?"

"With what? My suspicion you might have seen Julia the day
she died?"

"Well, you are good, forensic psych! Thanks for all the hand-
holding before you hit me with that suspicion!"

He pulled his chair so close to the couch he blocked her in.
Again, her heartbeat kicked up. Michael today, then that man

who had grabbed at her and chased her. Thank God there was no scratch on Jace's face, but, in the dark, she wasn't really sure where she had scratched that man. And now Jace was going to admit something dreadful, she was sure of it.

"Well?" she said, her voice sounding choked as she blinked back tears.

"Claire, you know I didn't harm her, don't you?"

"I do, but why did you really agree to work for that Vern Kirkpatrick and—did you see him with her that day? I think he was in her house, maybe was the one who hit Bronco."

"No, I didn't see him—just her. Damn, I wish I could have kept her there, talking, so she wouldn't have left and ended up dead. Truth is, I went to her house, maybe to apologize, maybe to tell her I wanted to be friends, I don't know. She hardly gave me the time of day and was on her way out, and that was that. I didn't follow her, I didn't see her again. You want me to swear on a Bible, Your Honor?"

"You should have told Nick and the sher—"

"No way! Someone like Wade what's-his-name might need protection from past crimes, but I don't need the sheriff—or you or Nick—thinking I was there when she fell. God's truth, I swear I didn't hurt her. She was fine when I left her, well, maybe a little upset about something. I need you to believe that, Nick too, if you tell him."

"Jace, I'll say it again. You should have told him, told the sheriff. Your evidence goes to her state of mind, that she would—or would not—have killed herself. Don't blame yourself that you might have upset her, because she had plenty else to be upset about. But she knew those stairs and would not have just slipped, even though 'accidents do happen.' You commented from that day on the rocking ferry when we first met her how sure-footed she was."

He seized her hands and she squeezed his back. She thought he would pull her into his arms, but they stayed like that, fro-

zen somehow. Yet all her forensic psych training told her he'd
hit several of the keys for telling someone was lying or guilty:
he'd offered a lot of detail; he'd invoked God's name and swore
he was telling the truth; he'd been more emotional than usual.
He'd even tried to set someone else up as the guilty party by
getting close to Kirkpatrick. But—but it just couldn't be he was
guilty. Not Jace. He was surely telling her the truth.

Her voice shaky, she said, "I've kept my fears to myself because I wanted to protect you, but you have to tell the authorities exactly what happened. Sheriff Archer is helping us, and we
have to help him. Please. Otherwise, it's obstruction of justice."

Claire blinked back tears and went on, "It's up to you. Otherwise, things only get worse. Someone's out not only to scare
us, but stop us too, any way he can, maybe the same person
who killed Julia. Of course, it wasn't you, but we have to find
out who."

Jace squirmed in his chair when the sheriff phoned Nick a
short time later while some of them ate a late dinner. Nick ex-
cused himself from the table and took the call in the hall. Claire
was the only woman at the table. Nita was upstairs giving Lexi
a bath, and Gina was trying to convince the child that just because her tummy ache was gone, that didn't mean she should
have the rest of the leftover Halloween candy.

At this point, Jace had to admit to himself that Claire was
right. He had to talk to Nick and the sheriff about what he'd
been hiding. He surprised himself by wishing Nick could be
his lawyer and represent him in case the sheriff actually wanted
to press charges of some kind—like Claire said, obstruction of
justice, or something worse. At the least, he'd have to swear he
saw nothing suspicious at her house, no one hanging around.
If only he'd lingered longer, he might have seen who came to
hit Bronco and let the old man loose. It had to be Kirkpatrick

shortly after he left, because of the cigar smell mentioned—which he had not caught a whiff of.

Smiling for once, Nick came back in and sat down at the table again. Jace clenched his fork tighter. Some good news, for once?

"One suspect down, and you're in the clear on it," Nick told Jace.

His insides plummeted. Had Claire had time to tell Nick he'd been with Julia?

Nick went on, "So that you wouldn't be implicated or have to testify that Kirkpatrick was stealing from Hunter Logan, the sheriff had his deputy tail Kirkpatrick, who led him to the stash of things you mentioned. The sheriff gave Kirkpatrick the choice of leaving the island for good—and a cease and desist order about never contacting Hunter Logan again—or being charged with a felony, namely grand theft. Kirkpatrick said he'd fight him on that, said the old man had agreed to let him have those items."

"In Hunter Logan's condition?" Claire said. "Unless he thought Gene Autry came back from the grave to ask for them, no way. But good for Sheriff Archer!"

"I'll drink to that," Jace said and raised his wineglass, trying to keep his hand from shaking. "I regret I was a party to hiding that contraband."

"It's just lucky you were on the record for telling him about that before he found it out some other way," Nick said, lifting his glass as the others followed. "A toast to a small island sheriff who is a big man in my eyes. And to my brother, Seth, here for coming clean about it before he was implicated for aiding and abetting."

They reached across the table to clink glasses and drank. Jace could feel Claire's steady gaze on him, burning into his forehead and his brain, but damned if he was going to make some kind of mea culpa speech right now about being with Julia shortly before she died.

He drank, but the wine tasted bitter.

★ ★ ★

Claire went up to tuck Lexi into bed with a happier heart. The FBI did indeed try to shield its WITSEC witnesses, though she still had to talk with Jace again. Maybe, now that he'd been cleared from helping hide stolen items by telling the truth, he'd tell the sheriff his brief background with Julia.

If he didn't, she hated to think how she'd keep silent about that, how she'd avoid telling Nick. It was so hard to be caught between the two of them. Once they got back home and weren't all together so often in such a hothouse—in a cold house—situation, surely tensions would ease up.

"Mommy, I'm glad you're here!" Lexi said as Nita left the bedroom and Claire sat down on the bed beside her. "Lorena says Lily isn't real, but you talked to me about her, so I know she is."

Claire unwrapped the child's arms from over her chest and pulled her a bit upright so she could hold her. Dealing with a desperately needed imaginary friend was delicate. There was a fine line to walk between the child's needs and the truth. She'd try reality first but tread carefully. Then, depending on Lexi's reaction, maybe backtrack some.

"I know I've talked to you about her," Claire said in her best soothing voice, "but only to try to say she isn't real. I can see you wanting a friend and I know you miss your cousin. I think it's okay to have an imaginary friend when you are lonely, but not one like Lily who acts bad and is mean."

"She is only mean to others, not me, because she's my friend."

"You know Lorena is your friend too, so she would tell you the truth. All of us here at the house on the island for the winter are friends. Uncle Seth and your daddy and I—"

"They're not real either—their names, I mean. I'm not Meggie either. I'm Lexi, and Lily knows the truth. Meggie is pretend, not Lily. She is back from Florida, where you sent her, and she's living in the attic. I heard her up there, and she goes up and down the back steps. I bet she's up there now."

"It's cold in the attic. I've been up there. So have several others, and we haven't seen her or any sign or her living there."

"Maybe that was before she came back. I want to go up to see her."

"Tell you what," Claire said, deciding to change tactics so that Lexi wouldn't be sneaking up in that cold, dark attic. "I'll go up now. I'll take that lantern from downstairs and check all around. I sure hope she went back to Florida again, where it's warmer, but I'll be sure, then come back down to tell you. Meanwhile, you just cover up here," she said, edging her down under the covers, "and wait here until I report in."

"All right," she said with a yawn. "I'm sleepy but I'll wait til you find her. If it's cold up there where that lady was screaming before Daddy—I mean, Uncle Seth—fixed the roof, tell Lily to come down here, where it's warm."

Claire kissed her cheek and went out and down to get the battery-operated lantern. The door to the parlor was open; Nita, Bronco and Gina were talking inside. She could hear Nick and Heck working at the kitchen table. Nick was dictating to Heck about how Ames had used Lexi to force her and Nick to fly to Grand Cayman. No wonder Lexi was so unstable, she thought. As Jace had accused once, there had been nothing but trouble and trauma since she'd known Nick Markwood. Yet he was worth it, every bit of it.

She took the lantern from where it hung near the china umbrella stand in the front hall and went upstairs. She peeked in at Lexi again. Wide-eyed and still awake, she said, "Did you do it yet?"

"No, but I have the lantern. Going up now."

A blast of cold air hit her when she opened the door to the attic stairs. Why hadn't someone put a ceiling light up here years ago? She was tempted to just go up a few steps and say she'd checked the place, but she wanted to be able to tell the truth to

Lexi, even though they'd hidden so much from her about Julia's death and the aftermath.

Holding the lantern aloft, she climbed the creaky stairs, sneezing twice from the dust. She'd been up here so briefly before, so intent on the widow's walk outside, that she barely recalled the structure of the vast attic. Since this was a Victorian-era house, the servants must have slept here.

In the attic, she saw the dark hollow where the back stairs came clear up here. After her horrid experience at Grand Hotel today, this dim place was nothing to scare her. At the edge of the vast room and in the corners, the eaves slanted down in darkness. Occasional support pillars made of wooden two-by-fours threw strange, shifting shadows. She recalled the humpbacked chest and some other items stored here. Florida homes seldom had attics and no basements either, and she was glad for that despite the lack of extra storage space.

Her teeth began to chatter from the cold and nerves. Just swing the lantern around once or twice, look behind the chest and the boxes so she could describe that to Lexi. In broad daylight, maybe she'd bring her up here to prove it all, but she had to get downstairs, back to warmth, back to reality, safety and sanity.

She shuddered when she thought she heard a mouse—or worse—skitter away in the dim corner. Had they made a nest over there in what looked like a pile of blankets and someone's old, deserted sleeping bag?

Did she smell not only dust and old wood but the hint of smoke here or was that her imagination, her memories? The scent was light, lacing the air, not heavy cigar smoke. Maybe it was just the smell of old buildings.

A board creaked behind her. Definitely a footstep. "Lexi, I told you not to come up here now," she said and swung around.

As if her earlier horror had never ended, a man leaped at her, knocked her down. The back of her head hit the floor hard. She actually saw falling stars in spinning darkness.

Her lantern fell to the floor, but the man had a big flashlight he turned on. Its beam blinded her as his hard hand covered her mouth and his body pressed her down on the floor. He wore no mask. She saw who it was.

CHAPTER THIRTY-FOUR

"We have to stop meeting like this," he whispered with a low chuckle. His breath, laced with the tinge of cigarette smoke, heated her face. She was so stunned from hitting her head that his words sank in slowly.

"Sadly," he went on, "you and I are now going to break up, because, like Julia, you are in my way. This is going to be one damn long, boring winter, and I'm spending it with Liz at her house. Then I'll take her to New York with me when I testify. It's where she wants to go. And you—you're going off the edge of that widow's walk."

Wade. It was Wade. A maniac hiding in their attic, one being protected by WITSEC. He'd murdered Julia. And he'd just said he meant to kill her. If only she could talk to him—better yet, cry out, but would they hear her all the way downstairs?

She could not let him shove or throw her off the way he must have Julia. And not for one minute did she believe Liz was in on this. She had to save not only Liz but herself too.

When she saw he wasn't going to move his hand from her mouth, she did what she had to, not fighting but lying still, moaning to make him think she was even more dizzy or injured than she was. She let her eyelids flutter, moved her eyes erratically. She began to shiver from shock, but she felt hot.

"Sad too," he whispered, "'cause I like redheads even more than blondes. But time's a wastin', baby. Let's go. I've had a ball visiting up here, took the key to your back stairs out of Julia's bedroom when I was waiting for Liz once and Julia was out somewheres. Now, don't fight me, 'cause lots of people made that mistake. Luckily, I got the goods on some higher-ups than me, so I'll testify, change my name again, get outta Dodge. And, man, if I can get my hands on Liz, she comes with a real nice inheritance, if you like old cowboy stuff, when the old man dies—real soon, I think. I hit that guy of yours hard enough to do him in, but he must have a skull of concrete."

Claire murmured against the press of his palm over her mouth. He had to let her talk. Michael might want to get Julia's diary from Liz, but this madman wanted Liz.

"You trying to kiss my hand, baby?" he asked, pushing harder into her mouth when she struggled to speak. "I'd like that, more than that, but, like I said, time's a wastin'. No talking, no screaming, no way." He lifted his hand only long enough to push some sort of cloth into her mouth.

She instantly began to gag, but she overdid how bad it was, pretending to choke, desperate to do anything to distract him from his intent, to stall for time. Once before, when she was trapped, she'd faked going limp to save her energy for one last strike. At least, if he intended to make it look like she jumped or fell, he wasn't going to try to rape her and leave evidence. He'd just take his sleeping bag and stroll down the back stairs as easily as he'd disappeared after shoving Julia to her death. It made her want to throw up that he'd been staying here, sleeping so close to all of them, especially Lexi. What if she'd come up to find Lily herself and found Wade instead?

Claire was desperate for someone to find her, but prayed

it would not be Lexi. And this new life she carried, her and
Nick's... He was pressing her down so hard.

"Damn," he said and shifted slightly off her, "but we're crush-
ing the cigarettes I got in my pocket under this down jacket.
Down jacket, for a mastermind who pushes people down, get it?"

She hardly heard all that. She was gagging, fighting for air
through her nose. She almost lost track of what he was saying.

"I'm always a hit with the ladies," he was saying with
a chuckle, as if he had to keep entertaining and explaining.
"Maybe that's why I've been a professional hit man, huh? But I
don't even have a gun here on the island. Part of the deal. So I
have this," he said and, with a smile, produced a long knife he
flashed before her face.

Again, she fought to calm her panic. He wouldn't use that if
he wanted it to look like she jumped or fell. How many victims
had he terrorized and murdered? Horrible that WITSEC had
to protect such people to get to the more horrible ones on top.

As if he was bored with talking, he hauled her to her feet and
shoved her toward the locked door to the widow's walk. She
managed to snag the wire handle of her overturned, lit lantern
with one foot and drag it the few steps to the door. But it was
no good to her since he held her arms brutally behind her as he
fumbled with the bolt on the door.

She concentrated on breathing through her nose, trying to
calm herself, but her brain rattled on. When they found her
body, would they be able to tell he'd bruised her wrists, that
she'd been gagged? Wade had drawn the message in the snow to
blame Kirkpatrick. He must have flown the kite, maybe sneaked
down at night and ate Lexi's candy, but why the mask sometimes and not others? She still felt he wasn't the one who had
chased her at the hotel earlier today. That man was built like
Jace. But Wade was probably working with someone, had hired
someone to scare her, even a woman to phone Liz to come get
things out of the locker.

As he opened the door to the walkway under the cupola, an icy blast of air smacked them. No one would believe she fell or jumped, not those who loved her, knew her. Nick and Jace would see a pattern, a terrible pattern.

When he tried to pull her gag out, she writhed in his grasp and bit down to keep it in so whoever found her dead below would know…would know…

He cursed and shook her hard. Her head bobbed like a rag doll's. She remembered she had the lantern handle around her ankle, but what good was that? She was sweating, freezing. It was so cold out here that her limbs went numb. Like Julia, she was going to fly and die.

She let her knees buckle, went completely limp. As he tried to grab her, she pulled him off balance. With one hand free, she ripped the gag out and screamed, but her voice was muted, ragged in the wind and the dark, cold night.

But then, from below, somewhere on the ground outside, a man's voice shouted, "Leave her the hell alone, you bastard!"

But the voice—not one she knew. Not Nick, not Jace, not even Bronco or Heck. Someone had heard them or the lantern had drawn attention. Just someone passing by the house? But they were facing the harbor, the backyard.

"Let her go, or you're a dead man!" sounded from below.

Did that voice have a Southern accent?

Wade swore again and threw her, facedown, on the narrow floor of the widow's walk. She tried to scramble away, but he blocked her attempt to get back inside. On hands and knees, she realized she was still dragging the lantern.

She yanked it off her foot and swung it upward at him. It caught him on the chin. In that split second his face was lit, she saw no scratch on his skin. Thank God, his knife flew away and several pieces of what looked like Halloween candy—Lexi's!—spilled onto the floor.

Wade scrambled inside on all fours, and then she heard a voice she knew.

Nick! Nick, calling her name from the attic.

"Nick, stop him!" she cried, but her voice was not her own and lost in the rush of cold wind. "It's Wade. Stop him!"

She saw an erratic light beam inside. Despite the wind, she heard both men's voices raised. A scuffle. Grunts and blows.

Dear God, Wade was younger and stronger. Nick nursed his bullet wound sometimes and still limped a bit. She had to help him.

She staggered to her feet, picked up the lantern again. Dizzy, she stumbled back inside, nearly slipped on a flashlight on the floor. Then she coldcocked Wade Buxton with the lantern so hard its light went out and glass shattered all over the floor.

Nick held Claire hard to him as she sobbed in his arms in the reflected light of his flashlight beam. They had rushed together and then sank to the floor in relief. Though Nick had closed the door to the walkway with his foot, they were both shaking. Wade Buxton lay sprawled facedown next to them.

"I went to find you in Lexi's room," he told her, his lips in her wild hair. "She said you went upstairs to find Lily."

"And found him instead," she choked out, holding tight to him. "Who knows how long he's gone in and out of here on the back stairs. Is he dead?"

"No, he's breathing. While I watch him, can you make it downstairs to get someone to call the sheriff and ask Gina to bring that medical kit of hers up here to tend to us?"

"He hurt you too. Yes, yes, I can do it," she said, but didn't budge at first.

"He must have been stalking you, been the man in the hotel in the dark today."

"I—I don't think so. That man was built differently. I'll bet when Wade's questioned, he'll admit he had hired someone else.

Hopefully, all that will come out when the sheriff—or Rob—questions him. And Wade doesn't have a mark on his face, where I'm sure I scratched the man in the dark. Nick," she said, lifting her head from his shoulder, "he killed Julia but—but when I was struggling on the walkway with him, someone from outside yelled at him to stop hurting me."

"From outside? On the ground? Are you sure?" he asked as she got to her knees and then her feet. "Who? You were under great strain and you said you hit your head. Are you sure it wasn't me, calling for you as I came up the stairs?"

"I'm sure. I'll have someone call the sheriff. I'll get Gina and be right back."

"Claire, sweetheart," he said and reached out to grasp her ankle before she could move away, "Julia's death is solved. If the terrorist in the hotel wasn't Wade, it must have been, like you said, someone he hired or knew. You can testify all that privately to the sheriff, even to Rob, but they'll want to keep us—and what Wade did—hidden so he doesn't spill everything about WITSEC. We'll be safe here now, even if WITSEC might have just lost one of their witnesses. Thank God, not you."

"You don't think they'll trust him to testify, do you? After all this? I mean, he said he was a hit man, I guess based in New York, but since he killed Julia and meant to kill me—"

"I don't know if they'll still use him, but maybe that picture of Rob with Julia will come into play here. If he cared for her more than as a coworker, ten to one he gives Buxton a one-way ride to incarceration. Maybe they could just reduce the bastard's sentence of life without parole instead of lethal injection for his hired-gun testimony. Go on now and be careful on the stairs."

"That's what the man below called him, a bastard," she said as she moved away. "Whoever he was, he was a guardian angel. One with a Southern accent, here in Northern Michigan, no less."

"Lots of things have been strange around here," he whispered, almost to himself.

As she went downstairs, Wade started to stir and moan, so Nick tied his hands behind his back with the guy's belt and sat against a support pillar with his feet on Wade's rump like a footstool.

Nick heaved a huge sigh. He knew Claire was not the kind of woman to ever stay barefoot and pregnant in the house as people liked to say, but she had to stop solving their cases this way. Man, it was cold in here, and he could hear the waves crashing into the harbor seawall below. But somehow, he felt a warm glow that this island of refuge would give them smooth sailing from now on.

CHAPTER THIRTY-FIVE

Relief and a sense of immense triumph filled the Widow's Watch that night. After the sheriff had left with Wade under arrest, Officer McCallum had taken Claire's and Nick's statements. Even as Wade departed in handcuffs, bruised and battered, he was boasting he'd be released because he could send several very rich Manhattan movers and shakers away for life as well as a New York congressman.

After that tirade, Claire had taken time to call Liz with the news.

"Answers, at last, but how horrible!" Liz had said. Claire could tell she was crying. "It's my fault that he thought Mother stood in his way to dating me. I should never have encouraged him at first, but he—he was such a handsome diversion."

"You're not to blame. He was obviously a sick, evil man. I'll just bet if we looked into his childhood, he had some female figure he hated or who abused him. But you were blessed with a wonderful mother to remember always."

"See—you are a shrink to psychoanalyze Wade that way. And a good friend to comfort me. Want to figure out my father? He was hell-bent on getting his hands on Mother's diary.

Jenna, I don't know if the sheriff told you, but that book from the locker must have been a WITSEC business book, because it's all in some sort of code she made up. I called the sheriff and turned it over, so he's been a busy man tonight. I—I still can't believe it was murder...and that Wade did it. Thank God he didn't kill you too."

Claire heard her dissolve in tears. She let her cry a minute, praying she didn't just hang up. Then she tried again. "Liz, listen, I'll be there late tomorrow morning, so we can talk more. But this is really going to upset your father too, so better let the sheriff tell him—if you tell him."

They had talked a little longer while Nick waited nearby. Strange how good she felt to have exposed all that evil. She was grateful to the stranger, her guardian angel, who had called up to Wade from the backyard below. Sometimes in dreadful situations, people were saved by unexplained, heavenly help—but with a Southern accent?

Jace hugged her in front of Nick before he went upstairs to bed. She hugged him back, so relieved he had not been the one who had hurt Julia and that there was no need for him to explain everything about going to see her on her last day. She felt so much better. Nick actually made her laugh about something that had looked so dire and dangerous. "Sweetheart," he said, "you're simply going to have to stop fleeing for your life through historical hotels. There has to be a better way to visit them."

"You should talk," she said, lightly punching him in his hard midriff. "But I did like it better when we were running together and it wasn't pitch-dark."

"Then from now on, let's just run after Lexi playing tag and run on the beach once we get home and have our baby. Let's keep Nita on as a nanny for now so we can work together sometimes too."

"That will keep Bronco nearby—if not in the house. Nick,

we're going to have to look for a bigger house once we get home."

Finally, they went up to bed together. He held her close, and when she slept, she did not dream of running for her life through sugarcane fields, or of a snowmobile accident, desperate darkness, or of a widow walking high up above, grieving her husband's loss. No nightmares, though near morning she had a crazy dream that her and Nick's baby was born in the dark attic with a scar on her forehead, and everyone insisted they name her Lily.

Jace went to work at the airport the next morning. Despite the fact they'd got rid of Vern Kirkpatrick and Wade Buxton, he was still uptight over everything that had happened. And a freezing fog suddenly settling in from Lake Huron to turn the air an icy gray didn't help. At least the plane with Sheriff Archer taking Buxton to jail on the mainland had taken off before this all set in.

Jace had one more plane to get to its gate despite this soupy atmosphere, one where the pilot, when directed to land at St. Ignace instead, had radioed that was even more socked in and he was coming here.

It was so cold out on the tarmac that Jace waited just inside the glass doors, listening to the continued control-tower chatter in his headphones. The pilot would only see the runway lights about two minutes before he landed, but the guys in the tower had said he sounded professional. The plane had come from somewhere points south, so he hoped the pilot was used to ice on the wings and the runway, even though it had been plowed clear of snow.

He glanced down at a discarded copy of the island *The Town Crier* newspaper, which had predicted an early, brutal winter. "No kidding," Jace whispered to himself. For the first time in years, the polar vortex had frozen the so-called ice bridge over Lake Huron to St. Ignace solid already. Several daredevils on

snowmobiles had tested it and marked it with pine branches for
the day and lanterns at night, but some people were using it
already. When they'd picked up their repaired snowmobile at
Andy Archer's shop, he'd advised waiting a week, because spots
could be soft, especially if you got just a little off the marked
trail.

"Seth," sounded in his headphones from the tower, "plane
approach. It's all yours."

He yanked his gloves on, pulled up his hood and grabbed his
two batons, hitting their lights on. He strode out, straining to
listen in the wind, squinting to see the headlights. Yes, there it
was, on track. The guy was good if he could do an instrument
landing at an airport he'd never seen, one with a short runway
in the fog. There must be something or someone important on
board.

It landed with just one bump and braked beautifully, turned
in, and Jace took over, signaling the small jet to the gate. It was
a new one, really nice and worth big bucks. Its engines pow-
ered down, and Jace turned off the lights on his signals. In the
lit cockpit, through wisps of floating fog, he could see the pilot
turning off his instruments. How he longed to be at the controls again.

The stairs popped out, and two men descended, met by another man Jace hadn't noticed. They were all bundled up against
the cold. Only one of the passengers carried a small suitcase. The
greeter gestured broadly, talking away, as he led them into the
terminal. Their faces were hidden by their parka hoods.

Jace was tempted to hang out and try to speak to the pilot, but
he went in the side door while the three men entered the airport
by the nearby passenger door. The greeter was showing them
what looked like a small map and maybe some photographs.

Once inside, they threw their hoods back. The guy closest
to Jace had a really craggy face, one that looked like he'd been
in an accident or been scratched. Oh, yeah, it was that ugly guy

who had taken photos of their historic house. He didn't know the guy on the far side, but the man in the middle, looking at the pictures—damn, it was Clayton Ames!

"So how was Liz?" Nick asked Claire after she came back in with Bronco, who had taken her and Lexi in a snowmobile to see Liz.

"Holding up better than I expected. Michael's going home, though he's still trying to get her to move Mr. Logan and herself to Baltimore. But she's not going. I suggested moving to Naples—new and old money, I told her, and a real sense of fashion. Needless to say, I didn't mention places like Goodland and roughing it in the Glades, not in a corset, anyway."

He laughed, and they hugged with Lexi pressed between them. "I hope you two got to see Scout," he told the child.

"Of course we did," Lexi said with a smile. "When Mommy said Naples to Miss Liz, I told her, bring Scout! We're going to go home there, aren't we, and real soon?"

"If winter comes, can spring—or home—be far behind?" Claire mused, almost to herself. "Not right now, sweetheart, but soon."

Lexi said, "Remember what Dorothy said in *The Wizard of Oz*? 'There's no place like home, there's no place like home.' So all we need is red shoes to click together—and Scout," she added as she headed upstairs to tell Nita they were back.

Claire sighed with relief. Lexi had accepted that Scout would be her friend this winter instead of Lily. Things were definitely looking up.

"I'm going to call Liz again because I told her I'd check in when we got home. She's still scared something will go wrong."

"You two remind me of you and Darcy," he said and patted her bottom. "I'm going to phone that number the sheriff gave us to see if he knows what all they're going to charge Wade with."

"Always the lawyer," she teased.

"Always the forensic psychologist," he countered. "Stick with me, my love, and together, we'll conquer the world—and Clayton Ames."

Jace pushed his snowmobile to top speed. Clayton Ames here! However that happened, no time to analyze or agonize. There was only one reason he would be here, and that was to stop Nick—all of them—before they could stop him. He had to warn everyone, but the monster had a head start on a large snowmobile the ugly guy was driving, and the greeter was with them. All three men were on it, and they had a good lead. Jace had tried to phone both Claire and Nick, but their cell numbers were busy and he didn't have the others' numbers on him, so he'd left a desperate voice mail.

He tried to plan ahead. He had one advantage, and that was that Ames hadn't seen him. You might know the sheriff wasn't on the island. If he didn't have to steer this thing with both hands, he'd call his office anyway, find out where Officer Stan McCallum was, get him to Widow's Watch to guard the place. He had no doubt that was where they were headed, if not directly, soon. No wonder Ames's lackey had taken pictures of the house. Not just to ID it, but to make a plan to access it. But how had they located them here on a Northern island, with new names?

He had to catch up but he had to be careful in these turns. The branches of the fir trees hung heavy. In the fog, his headlights didn't go far, but at least, in these conditions, no other vehicles were coming at him.

Once on Main Street, he pushed the snowmobile as fast as it would go. At least there were some lights here, but he didn't see Ames's machine ahead. He'd go directly into the carriage house, then rush in to warn everyone.

Even in late afternoon, this area was nearly deserted with the snow, cold and fog. He was almost tempted to cry out for help to the few strangers abroad, get a posse like in the old days. He thought of Mr. Logan, whom he hadn't met but had heard about, lost in his imaginary world of good guys vs. bad guys. Trouble was, with Ames here, that was the real world too.

"I heard Jace's snowmobile in the carriage house," Claire told Nick, "so I'd better put that other pizza in the oven. He can split that one with Gina and Heck when they get back. I wasn't expecting him yet, but I should have known there'd be no planes with this freezing fog socking everything in."

"Sure. Fine," he said, hardly paying attention as he watched a Detroit Lions football game on the muted TV set mounted on the kitchen wall.

"My pizza is pretty hot, Mommy. I'm blowing on it," Lexi said. "Oh, I think I heard Gina outside yelling, so they're back too."

"Maybe they forgot their key," Claire said, "but that isn't like Heck. And Jace would have a key, but maybe that wasn't his snowmobile we heard."

Claire went to the side door. Gina stood there, wide-eyed and gagged, with a gun to her head. The man who had taken photos of the house—and who had a livid scratch on his forehead—was the one holding the barrel of a handgun to her temple.

Worse—was she hallucinating?—another man holding a gun to Heck's head stood behind him, and behind him... Clayton Ames. Her knees almost buckled. Her first instinct was to slam the door, but they could shoot Gina and Heck. And where was Jace? Her mind went into overdrive.

"Ah, I've found you, my dear," Clayton said. "Claire Markwood, formerly Mrs. Jason Britten, I presume? Oh, and everyone's favorite hotshot pilot, your previous husband, is unconscious from a rap on his hard head and tied up in the carriage house here, so don't be expecting him for dinner. He appeared to be in such a rush he didn't even know what hit him. Now may we come in?"

Claire gasped and stumbled backward as the man shoved Gina in the door with Heck behind her. Both had their hands tied, and Heck was gagged too. After everything—this was impossible, the ultimate nightmare. Surely, Wade had not been working for Ames and had tipped him off—no, that could not be.

Ames himself had a gun, which he now pressed into Claire's back as he pushed her ahead of him, leading the others in. He whispered, "Shall we not tell Nick you and little Lexi are the ones to blame for this impromptu, final visit? One of my Acapulco maids watches American TV and had *Inside Edition* on when I was passing through the room, and there you were. What a surprise! Everything is luck and timing, isn't it?"

Claire felt sick to her soul. This was her fault. She had blown it, trying to help Liz.

In the kitchen, Nita saw them first and screamed. Nick had a piece of pizza partway to his mouth. Her fault. Her fault, sounded in her head.

"Nicky," Ames said in his most taunting tone, "you're together again with Uncle Clay, but you can consider this a farewell visit. I thought my plan to send you all down in that FBI plane would work. My, but that cost me a lot of money in bribes to have you followed to Key West and have the plane tampered with. I was hoping an accidental, watery crash would end your conspiracy against me, but then you turn up nearly on my doorstep in Havana!"

"How did you find us there?" Claire demanded when Nick looked, for once, too stunned to speak. She could only hope that he was thinking of a way out of this, planning something. If she could somehow keep Ames talking, maybe that would help. At least he seemed in a boastful, almost jovial mood—and more dangerous than ever.

Ames went on, ignoring her, still talking to Nick, "One of my men spotted you at the Hotel Nacional, where I sometimes do business. I put a tail on you, but it was your friends who found my hacienda," he said with a nod at Heck and Gina. "We almost snagged you that day but you disappeared from the hotel and then Havana. Learning things from your uncle Clay, aren't you? Like a cat, you seem to have nine lives. Sadly, you're all out of them now."

The color drained from Nick's face. He blinked, shook his head as if he could erase it all.

"You've betrayed me, Nicky, and now everyone will have to pay. You and your lovely bride have made my Grand Cayman home off-limits to me, watched by the US feds, and you've even screwed up my Cuban retreat by tipping them off—the FBI, no less. So let's just end this all now and be done with it."

To Claire's amazement, Nick merely dropped the piece of pizza on his plate, shrugged and said, "The FBI has so much on you that you'd have to get a mansion on Mars to escape them. Trying to stop me won't stop them." He looked shocked and shaken, but his voice was lawyer-steady.

"Well, aren't they clever to stash you here in a Northern never-never land? Hello, little Lexi," he said and dared to smile at the child as she clung to Nita. "Your uncle Clay is here."

"My name is Meggie, but you are not my uncle. And Lily's upstairs calling the police because we are friends with them."

Ames jerked his head to the side. "You said from who was here they are all accounted for," he barked at the ugly man. No doubt he was the one with the mask who hit them on the snowy trail. Claire recalled a woman who stopped after their accident had said she'd seen an ugly man before he put on that mask.

As if Nick was thinking the same thing—or wanted to get Ames's focus off Lexi—he said, "That always was your philosophy, wasn't it? Torment not only the person in your crosshairs but someone closest to them? Kidnap Lexi? Terrify Claire?"

"Shut up," Ames said, dropping the fake friendly tone. "Tom, go check the rooms upstairs for this Lily. The child must have told the truth, and now Nick's trying to get us off track."

"Sure, boss. I'll check right now."

Claire was shocked again. This Tom had a Southern accent. He had yelled at Wade to let her go. But he must have only done that to save her so that they could torment her and Nick. As Nick had said, it was always Ames's MO to attack those his real target loved.

But what terrified her now was that he'd said *final* and *farewell*. He was here not only to terrify them but to end it all.

The man he'd called Tom took the pistol away from Heck's head and ducked out. They heard him take the stairs up two at a time. For once, Claire thought, Lily might serve some purpose. One fewer man with a gun in the room. If she could only get Ames's gun off her back, that left only one gun here.

For the first time, her eyes met Bronco's. He looked shocked, but he was furious too. He'd slowly inched sideways to stand between Nita, Lexi and the third gun. The big man looked coiled to strike. And with a sudden shout—"Hide up there, Lily! Hide!"—Bronco leaped into action.

In one quick move, he threw Nita down with Lexi under her and rolled low into the third man's legs to send him flying. That gun flew across the floor and skidded way under the old-fashioned chest freezer.

In the chaos, Claire jumped aside, elbowed Ames, caught him in the stomach and tried to grab his gun but couldn't. Nick leaped up from behind the table and slammed a fist into his face. Ames went down to the floor but still had the gun. Nick stepped on it and his hand, and ripped the gun away, then pulled the tablecloth off the table, sending everything flying, and rolled Ames up in it.

"I have others coming," he gritted out. "They're already here on the island. I called them before we came in. You're all dead. The game is over, and I win."

Claire grabbed a dish towel and gagged Ames, then untied Gina's and Heck's hands. Bronco stopped beating the third man's head against the floor to stuff one of his own gloves in his mouth, then bound his wrists behind his back with his belt. But the guy upstairs still had a gun—and a lot of rooms and an attic to search to give them some time.

"We've got to run," Nick said. "Snowmobiles. Grab coats on the way to the carriage house."

"Jace is tied there," Claire said. "The sheriff's off island but are we calling Officer McCallum or taking these guys to him?"

Nick ignored all that. "Out! Out!" he ordered and swung Lexi up into his arms. "Bronco, drag Ames. We can't take a chance on staying here, even on the island, since he said others may be coming."

Those who weren't in their coats ripped them off the pegs by the side door and tore into the carriage house, where Nick turned on the light. Jace was conscious but woozy, gagged, tied hand and foot, lying beside one of their three snowmobiles. Nick grabbed the hedge clippers off the wall and cut Jace's wrist and ankle bonds.

"Bronco, dump Ames in the sled box," Nick ordered. "Then help Jace in with him. Glad we learned to leave the keys and hope we have enough gas. Everybody on now. We're going toward Lake Shore Drive and over the ice bridge to safety, and we'll get law enforcement there."

His gaze snagged Claire's. He sounded strong but he was still shocked and scared. And so was she.

CHAPTER THIRTY-SIX

Their three snowmobiles roared out of the carriage house. They heard shots—at least the two men left behind didn't hit anyone. Nick feared pursuit, but they kept going away from their lit house that was to have been their refuge. If they got enough of a head start, pursuit might be futile.

Without a look back, he led them along the curving shoreside road into the teeth of the wind. They had to go slower than he wanted because of the fog, though, thank God, it seemed to be lifting.

Nick and Claire rode on the first snowmobile with Lexi between them. Bronco and Nita came second, pulling the supply sled with Jace and Ames. Heck and Gina brought up the rear.

They found the entrance to the ice bridge, the only nonflight exit from the island now. It was clearly marked. Nick's heart pounded so loud he wasn't sure what was the engine and what was him. Claire held to him hard. Was this attempted escape over the ice insane? But, especially if Ames had others coming to kidnap or kill them, this was saving lives, not hazarding them. If it was the last thing he ever did, he was handing Ames over to Rob for trial.

He braced his feet on the running boards. He'd been told riding on ice was different, more risky. Hell, he was risking all their lives, but escape was the best way for now. With the airport closed for the night, what else could they do?

He knew to stick to the marked trail to avoid spots of thin ice. Electric lanterns and fir branches marked the way. He could only hope the wind had not shifted some of them. At least, out here, the fog was blowing away. He saw in the fading winter light that it was true what they said about the ice. It was glass-like, so clear he could see through it to the water. Beautiful, but scary. It seemed deserted out here, but in this weather, normal, sane people were home.

"We've stopped Ames and we've got him now!" Claire shouted over the roar of the engine. "Nick, this is my fault! He saw Lexi and me on TV in Mexico and traced us that way, sent that Tom guy here to watch us and scare us!"

"None of this is your fault," he shouted back. "It's mine, and we're going to begin to live the way we should as soon as…"

He stopped in midthought when he heard shouts from behind—Bronco, Heck—a woman's scream. Fearing they were being followed, he leaned out to look back.

Bronco must have steered or slid off the path. He'd either made or hit a hole in the ice, which Heck had bypassed. But the second snowmobile pulling Jace and Ames was tilted hood up with its red tail brake lights sinking into the jagged, widening hole.

Nita had scrambled away, but Bronco was trying to reach the wooden supply box sled they'd towed. It was not floating but was being sucked into the lake by its heavy metal runners. Beside it, in the water, Jace floundered in the frigid water, trying to hold Ames's head up.

Nick killed the motor of his machine. "Get off and stay away!" he shouted at Claire. "Move Lexi back."

"Bronco, you're too heavy!" he yelled at the big man. "Back off! Heck, see if your cell works out here to call for help."

Nick crawled toward the hole, then slid closer on his belly, using the toes of his shoes to propel himself along. If Ames's men were trailing them, they were sitting ducks now, but Ames usually lied. Nick had always known that he had killed his father and staged his suicide.

Jace was trying to hold Ames's head above water, since he was still wrapped in the tablecloth. Both were gasping for air and kept going under in their heavy, soaked winter coats. If Jace was lost here, Claire would be his alone, because he knew she still cared for Jace. Lexi would really need a new dad then. But he meant to save Jace over Ames, if it came to that. He owed Jace, and his girls loved him.

"Jace, take my hand to keep your head up!" he yelled.

"He's too heavy," Jace gasped out. "We're going under. I know you want him to stand trial—all that work…"

"Shut up and take my hand before you go numb. If you have to, let him go, and we'll fish him out later. Do it, Jace!"

Jace's hand was slippery, so cold. They locked wrists.

"I can't hold him! I can't boost him up," Jace cried as the snowmobile shifted lower.

"He doomed himself years ago. If we can get him out, we will. You first. Heck!" Nick shouted when he realized he had no traction to haul Jace out. "Lie down and hold my legs! Pull my legs! Bronco's too heavy!"

Heck did, and Gina held his legs. Slowly, they pulled Jace out, head, shoulders, onto his stomach. The ice began to crack around him again.

"Pull now!" Nick yelled and they did, dragging Jace out where Heck could get to him and tug him back.

Nick, on his belly on the ice, inched closer to the hole, wondering if Ames might surface again. But he only stared at empty, choppy water where the snowmobile and Ames had been. He'd slipped under and—God help them all—was staring wide-eyed and very dead with his mouth and eyes open, gazing up at Nick through the glassy ice.

Nick saw again his father's dead gaze when he'd found him so many years ago. Finally, justice. Salvation. It was over, and a new, safe life for him, his little family and their friends had just begun.

CHAPTER THIRTY-SEVEN

Three months later in Naples, Florida

With Ames dead and the henchmen who had been with him under arrest, there was no need for a trial, or for Nick and Claire to testify more than they already had privately to Rob Patterson and an FBI panel. Dangerous WITSEC and lovely Mackinac Island were in the past, although Claire still grieved Julia's death. If this baby she carried was a girl, she and Nick had decided that Julia would be her middle name.

So much had happened since they'd left the island. Nick sometimes had nightmares of Clayton Ames climbing out of that hole in the ice of Lake Huron, shaking off the frozen tablecloth and coming after them. Wade Buxton had been set to go on trial for Julia's murder, though no doubt, he was responsible for others. Rob had assured them Wade would get a life sentence without the possibility of parole.

But months before his trial, it appeared that Wade had hanged himself in his jail cell with a window blind cord someone must have smuggled to him. Nick figured whoever was afraid Wade might name them in the trial—from petty hoods to powerful politicians—just might have arranged that murder/suicide too. "And that is one," he'd vowed to Claire, "you and I are not going to investigate."

So at last, they felt safe and free. They were living in Nick's house, but they were looking for a newer, larger home, one not too far from Claire's sister, Darcy. Nita was living in a nearby rented condo with Bronco, who was job hunting, and they were planning a wedding. Nick was helping Heck pay for Gina's medical school in Miami, and Heck was burning up his tires visiting her whenever she had a few hours off.

Best of all, Lexi was once again best friends with her cousin Jilly, and there was no hint of Lily.

"But if Lily ever does appear again," Nick whispered to Claire as they sat on the back patio overlooking the canal, "I'm giving her a pass to live with us since she hid out from Ames's hit man upstairs at Widow's Watch to give us time to escape."

Claire had to laugh at that. Now she too lowered her voice since Lexi and Jilly were playing nearby with their Barbie dolls and plastic Saddle 'N Ride Horses. "I hated to praise Lexi for invoking Lily, but she probably saved us from him. Rob got a good laugh out of that when we told him. Have you heard anything else from him lately?"

"No, but I take it Jace has and will start on those South Florida spy-fly missions soon to track cell phones of criminals from the air. He's like a fish out of water without flying. I don't even think he'll mind being away from that friends-of-the-animals, friend-of-your-sister he's been dating."

"I'm glad to think he might have found someone, even if she does have to play second fiddle to an airplane. Speaking of Rob getting Jace that job, I still can't figure out why, when Rob debriefed us on Mackinac before he sent us home, he was so emotional about Julia's coded WITSEC diary."

"Claire, sweetheart," he said, leaning sideways and taking her hand, "I didn't tell you before because I thought it would upset you to know another sad thing about Julia."

"Tell me what? Wasn't she allowed to keep a WITSEC diary, even in code?"

"It wasn't about that. There was info in there on Michael and his wife embezzling from her business. But a couple years before, she and Rob had an intense but short affair, and she'd written her feelings in that book, including love letters she never sent him. In short, she never got over him, even when he went back to his wife."

"Oh. Oh, my," she said, blinking back tears. "Her loss was doubly sad for him, then. He held all that in when he met us on the island after her death because he was mourning for more than her being a good agent and WITSEC handler. I wonder what happened to that picture of them together that was in the back of her locker. Liz had no idea who it was, and—and I didn't tell her. But I suppose I should."

"I'm sure he has pictures of his own—if only in his head and heart. So you'll tell Liz about Rob when she gets here?"

"I don't think so. Obviously, Julia didn't want her to know, and I should honor that. Secrets—family secrets, especially— can be bad."

"Did you say Liz's name?" Lexi said, coming over with the horse and cowgirl Barbie in her hand. "Only two more weeks, and she'll be here with Scout."

Although Liz had wanted to move to New York City, three things had changed her mind. She'd become good friends with Claire, she finally admitted Manhattan rents were too high and Wade's passion for New York had turned her off it. She was already advertising Naples as a great place for her wealthy and celebrity clients to visit while she did their corset fittings.

"Yes, and your dad is going to fly Gina up there so she can drive back with Liz, pulling that trailer with all her house goods and clothes—and Scout for you. Then Mr. Logan's friend Doug is going to fly with him to a new kind of retirement place here where he can have his cowboy things and we'll all go visit him with Liz someday."

"I hope Liz and Gina bring those pretty clothes we wore on TV," Lexi said, bouncing her horse across Claire's knees.

"Well, they have an awful lot to bring, but maybe those will be in the boxes Liz is mailing us."

Claire's mind skipped to Gina's confession last week that she'd torn one of the dresses when she'd had Heck take her picture up on the walkway the day they'd dressed up in grand style. Her hem had snagged and she'd torn a piece off the gown. So another fear and ghost for Claire was laid to rest. Oh, well, with Ames gone now, things would be so calm and tame.

"Wish we could keep Scout in the garage," Lexi said for the fifteen hundredth time.

"No," Claire said, "Scout needs to be at a stable where you and Jilly can visit him."

"Now listen," Nick put in, raising his voice. "Stop asking your mother that over and over. Scout will be happier with other horses, just like you are happier to be back with Jilly, okay?"

Lexi's eyes widened at his stern tone. "Okay," she said. "Jilly, it's just like those Florida panthers your mommy tries to help. They need other panthers with them, but they are hard to find. And in danger."

"It's called endangered," Jilly said as Lexi went back to her. "Because they might get extinct, which means all gone. And we're all going to visit that place soon where they keep them, a wildlife ranch, but there are still ones hiding and sneaking around at night if they didn't get killed by a car."

"Our environmental lesson for the day," Nick whispered as he began to stroke the soft inside of Claire's wrist with his thumb. She smiled at him as he moved both their hands to rest on her growing belly.

It felt so great, she thought, to resolve issues, to be content, not tense. To be home with the family and extended family of friends who had been with them through so much. Yes, it was wonderful to know the only wildlife facing them was a visit to a Florida wilderness animal rescue ranch tomorrow with Darcy and these little girls.

Claire leaned closer to Nick, and they kissed. Surely, after all that they'd been through, nothing else could harm them now.

★ ★ ★ ★ ★

AUTHOR'S NOTE

I hope you have enjoyed these first three books in the South Shores series—*Chasing Shadows*, *Drowning Tides* and *Falling Darkness*. Most of the books in this series will be set in Southern climates; however, I could not resist using Mackinac Island in *Falling Darkness* since I visited there last summer and fell in love with the unique place and its ambience of "somewhere in time." I have been to all the places in these first three books—except for Cuba. I did interview people who had been there before the new US-Cuba relationship and read several books about life there under the Castros.

I would like to thank our friend Jim Parsons for sharing his expertise about and affection for Gene Autry, which helped me create the character of Hunter Logan. Jim, however, is of sound mind, and the Parsons home has many Autry pictures on the walls as well as collections of movies, TV shows and other Autry memorabilia. Thanks to Dr. Roy Manning for his information in these current, past and future books about pregnancy and delivery.

I am grateful to my literary agent, Annelise Robey, and my excellent MIRA editors who worked on these books with me,

Nicole Brebner and Emily Ohanjanians, for their feedback and especially for help with titles for the novels.

Also to our friends Roy and Mary Anne Manning, for enjoying beautiful Mackinac Island with us. And ever and always, thanks to my husband, Don, for being proofreader, travel companion, business manager and for coping with an author who spends part of her time with fictional people.

I hope you will be looking for future stories starring Claire, Nick, Jace and their growing and extended family and friends, not to mention enemies.

Please drop by my website, www.KarenHarperAuthor.com, and my Facebook page, www.facebook.com/KarenHarper Author, and say hello.

Karen Harper